D1140983

THE
GOOD
KILLER

THE
GOOD
KILLER

HARRY
DOLAN

HEAD
of ZEUS

First published in the UK in 2020 by Head of Zeus Ltd
First published in the US by Mysterious Press, an imprint
of Grove/Atlantic

London Borough of Richmond Upon Thames		
RTR		
90710 000 427 125		
Askews & Holts		
AF THR	£18.99	
	9781838933746	

9 7 5 3 1 2 4 6 0

A catalogue record for this book is available from
the British Library.

ISBN (HB):9781838933746
ISBN (XTPB): 9781838933753
ISBN (E): 9781838933739

Printed and bound in Great Britain by
CPI Group (UK) Ltd, Croydon CRO 4YY

Head of Zeus Ltd
First Floor East
5–8 Hardwick Street
London ECIR 4RG

WWW.HEADOFZEUS.COM

This one is for Lesa

THE
GOOD
KILLER

1

Henry Keen

It's like a caterpillar in a jar, this idea he's got in his head.

Sometimes Henry imagines he's watching it through the glass: It's alive in there. It's growing. If you gave it long enough, he thinks, you could watch it evolve. If you left it for a while and came back, you'd have a butterfly.

It starts out as this thing he needs to do, and he wants to do it without leaving a mess behind. Because he'd like to believe he's not the kind of person who leaves a mess behind.

So he won't do it at home. He'll drive out, someplace far, where it's green. He can picture the spot. There's a field and an unpaved road, and he can see himself pulling over to the side and getting out of the car.

There's a hill with grass, and a tree at the top. He walks up until he's in the shade of the tree. He looks around at the grass and the blue sky.

He's in a high place and it's windy, and he's wearing a black wool coat. There's a gun in the right-hand pocket. A pistol with fifteen bullets, even though he'll only need one.

He'll go out on his feet, standing in the shade. He'll hold the gun to his temple. He has practiced at home in a mirror. He'll pull the trigger and his body will crumple to the ground. His blood will end up on the grass.

That's the idea.

But the idea evolves.

2

Sean Tennant

Morning. The windows in the bedroom face south. There's sunlight falling on the white sheets and on the pale-gray blanket that's been thrown aside.

Sean is half-tangled in the top sheet. His eyes are closed, but he's awake. He hears Molly come in from the kitchen. She has coffee. He can smell it.

She sets a glass on the bedside table. Orange juice. For him. He never developed a taste for coffee.

"I know how this goes," she says.

Sean opens his eyes. Molly is perched on the edge of the bed now, holding her mug. She's wearing one of his shirts. Her legs are bare.

"How does this go?" Sean asks.

She takes a drink of coffee before she answers.

"I'm gonna take a shower now and wash my hair. Then I'll dry it and put on makeup. And you'll be in here, all lazy. But eventually you'll remember you're not gonna see me for five days. And then . . . we both know what will happen then."

"What will happen?"

"You'll make a move. I'll resist at first, but then I'll give in. Because I'm a good sport."

Sean smiles. "That's true."

"Afterward I'll have to shower again and redo my makeup," Molly says. "And we'll be late getting to the airport. I don't mind being late, but I know it makes you nervous, even if you're not the one catching a flight."

"That's true too."

"So if you're gonna make a move, you need to do it now."

Sean sits up and reaches for the orange juice. He takes a sip and puts on a face as if he's thinking.

"All right," he says. "If that's the way it's got to be."

After: Sean is lying in bed, one leg dangling from under the sheet. Molly is in the shower. The bathroom door is open, and he can hear her in there, singing.

He's keeping track of the time. It's a forty-minute drive to the airport from their house outside Houston. He wants to get her there at least ninety minutes before her flight is scheduled to depart. She's flying to Bozeman, Montana.

She's been planning the trip for months. It's a retreat on a ranch: yoga and meditation and riding horses. It's designed just for women, so there was never any thought of Sean going along.

The first time she mentioned the trip, it made him uneasy.

"It's a long way," he said.

Molly nodded. "Sure."

"There must be yoga retreats in Texas."

"There must be."

"But you don't want one of those."

"I want this one," she said. "Montana's not against the rules."

"I know."

"You worry too much."

He couldn't argue with that, so he said nothing.

"You think about it," she said. "If you don't want me to go, I won't go."

She didn't bring it up again. He's sure she would have let it drop. But later that week, one night before they went to bed, he told her: "You should go. It's not against the rules."

She takes a while getting ready. Long enough for Sean to shower and dress and fry two eggs and make toast. He eats his breakfast standing in the kitchen. She's already had hers: fruit and yogurt. She left him a bowl of grapes. He eats some of those, too, carrying the bowl into the bedroom.

He lingers there, leaning against the oak dresser at the foot of the bed. It's long and low: six drawers in two rows of three. It's the first thing he made when he and Molly moved into this house.

Molly is in the bathroom fixing her hair. Sean watches her in profile through the open door. She's dressed casually for her flight: jeans and a sky-blue sweater.

She's taking a final look at herself in the mirror, and the palm of her right hand comes to rest on her stomach, just above the buckle of her belt.

It only stays there for a moment, but Sean sees it. It's a gesture he remembers. Two years ago she got pregnant, and sometimes he would catch her in front of the mirror, her hand coming up to rest there. As if to remind herself that it was real.

She never had the baby. She lost it after three months. She cried for a week, in bed with the curtains closed. He didn't know what to do, so he brought her meals she didn't eat and stroked her hair and said things he thought would be soothing. Eventually the crying passed.

Now he wonders if she's pregnant again. They haven't been trying, but they haven't been *not* trying. And if she is, he wonders if she'll tell him or if she'll want to wait.

She turns her head and catches him watching her. Her lips part as if she might say something, but she doesn't.

She's quiet on the drive to the airport. The traffic is mild. He pulls up in front of the terminal and gets out to lift her suitcase from the trunk. Kisses her and holds on to her. She draws back to look into his eyes, and he can see that she knows what he's thinking.

"Let's not get ahead of ourselves," she says softly.

He keeps hold of her a little longer.

"Okay."

He watches her walk in, the suitcase trailing behind her. The glass doors slide open to admit her and close again when she's gone through.

When Sean arrives back home, he leaves the car in the driveway and raises the garage door. The garage is designed to hold two vehicles, but half of it is given over to his workshop. A long bench holds the pieces of his latest project: an armoire he's building for a dentist in Houston.

He puts on some music—the Strokes, *Is This It*—and gets to work. The armoire is based on an eighteenth-century design, but he's modernized it, made the lines cleaner. There's trim on either side of the doors that's meant to resemble tall, stylized pillars. There are two drawers at the bottom, each with a diamond-shaped ornament on its face.

Today he's working on the feet for the piece. They're broad and rounded at the bottom and narrow at the top. He turns them on the lathe, starting with blocks of cherry and cutting away everything that doesn't belong. It takes patience to make them match.

He works until the early afternoon. When he stops it's because he's feeling restless, and he realizes he missed his usual morning walk. He closes the garage and drives out to Bear Creek Park.

6

The park covers twenty-one hundred acres, fifteen miles west of Houston. It has pavilions and tennis courts, fields for soccer and soft-ball. There's even a small zoo with buffalo and emus. The visitors now are mostly mothers with small children, but when the schools let out, the fields will fill up with young athletes. Sean finds a space in the park-ing lot at a distance from the other cars.

His hiking boots are in the trunk. He puts them on and locks the car. He sets out for one of the hiking trails, but after only a few paces he turns back.

There's a Glock nine-millimeter in his glove compartment with a shoulder rig to hold it. He sits in the passenger seat and straps it on. He reaches into the back seat for his gray windbreaker. He puts it on to cover the gun.

Locking the car again, he heads out. He walks south on the trail that rambles along roughly parallel with Bear Creek, moving away from the busy part of the park and into the woods.

It's October and the sun is obscured by clouds. The trail is well main-tained, covered with mulch in the low-lying spots that would otherwise turn muddy. Sean encounters a few people—joggers and dog walkers—but as he pushes south, he feels more and more alone. Which is what he wants.

He listens to birdsong and the lilt of the wind through the trees. The trail curves toward the creek and veers away again. Sean treks along, thinking about Molly and the child they're going to have—and the one they almost had. The one they lost. He remembers how he felt then, during those days that Molly spent crying. He was afraid that he would lose her too, that she would drift away from him. He thought he would wake up one morning and find her side of the bed empty.

The time seemed to crawl by, especially in the long afternoons when he sat with her in the dim of the bedroom, with only a sliver of light coming through the curtains. He started to long for the times when she would fall asleep, so he could slip out and get away from that dimness.

On the seventh day of it, he left to pick up some groceries, and when he returned he found Molly sitting up, hugging the blanket over her knees, her hair in tangles.

"What time is it?" she asked him.

He looked at his watch. "Four thirty."

"I'm tired," she said.

"It's okay," he told her.

"No. It's not." She rubbed her face, looked around the room. "I thought you were gone."

"I went to the store."

"*Gone* gone," she said. "Not coming back."

He went to the side of the bed and laid his palm between her shoulder blades.

"Well, you were mistaken," he said.

She shrank away from him. "You shouldn't touch me. I'm all sweaty."

"I don't care."

"I need a bath."

"I don't care about that either."

"You could go, if you wanted to."

"I don't want to."

"Find a woman who's not going to have a breakdown every time some little thing goes wrong."

A big statement there. A lot packed into it. Sean stood by the bed with his hand pressed against her back, trying to decide how to respond. The air felt thick in the room. She spoke before he did, in a small voice, hunched over, her face turned away from him.

"I thought you were *gone*."

He bent to kiss the top of her head. "I wasn't," he said. "I wouldn't."

He felt her shoulders tremble and he breathed the words into her hair: "I will never leave you. Never. Not ever."

The words were true then, and they're true now as Sean walks in the woods of Bear Creek Park, his thoughts shifting to the future. To the baby Molly's going to have. He's not worried that they might lose this one the way they lost the other. He's not exactly an optimist, but he believes that when things go wrong, they go wrong in ways you're not expecting. So he takes it for granted that the child is coming and that plans need to be made.

Raising children requires money. Sean expects to make three thousand dollars for the armoire he's building, but most of the projects he takes on don't pay quite so well. He and Molly keep their expenses low, but having a child will alter the equation. Sean plays with some numbers in his head, trying to guess how much more he'll need to earn. He slows down without meaning to, from a brisk walk to a stroll.

He thinks he hears footsteps behind him.

He stops and turns to look. There's no one there.

He scans the woods to find the source of the sound. A few yards back along the trail, a small gray bird swoops down from the canopy of the trees. It peels off in the direction of the creek.

Sean starts walking again, waiting for the sound he heard to repeat itself. He knows it didn't come from a bird. He goes along for half a mile before he hears it again.

He doesn't turn this time. He knows what it is now.

It's Cole Harper.

Sean spent long stretches of his childhood walking with Cole, on sidewalks and through the halls of schools. When they were older they spent fifteen months in Iraq. They walked together on the streets of East Baghdad, sweating in the heat under body armor, surrounded by the smell of dust and burning trash. Sean knows the sound of Cole's footsteps.

He listens to them now as the trail bends toward the creek again. He stops by the bank and catches sight of a family of ducks floating in the current.

No sound of footsteps now. Only the rush of the water.

Sean watches the ducks as they glide away downstream, but his thoughts are elsewhere. He's wondering if he'll see Cole. It hasn't happened in a while. Cole is hard to see these days. Sometimes you can glimpse him out of the corner of your eye, but if you turn and look directly he won't be there. Because Cole doesn't exist. He died years ago.

All that's left of him are the things Sean carries around in his head. Like Cole's voice.

"What are you doing out here?" it says.

The tone is calm and steady. Sean doesn't answer. He gets back on the trail. It moves away from the creek, and the sound of the water grows distant. A post from some forgotten fence leans crooked by the trailside, and when Sean sees it he leaves the path and makes his way deeper into the woods. He's guided by a few familiar landmarks. There's a tall elm that cracked from rot near the base of its trunk and keeled over. There's a clearing with a hickory tree on its eastern edge.

Sean skirts past that hickory and finds another beyond it. Some of the bark has been peeled off, but the tree is still alive. He kicks away some fallen leaves and exposes two of its larger roots. There's a shallow depression between them, and in the middle of it rests a flat rock nearly a foot wide.

Sean sets his back against the tree and looks down at the rock.

"It's still here," Cole's voice says. It's coming from a remove, as if Cole is lurking on the other side of the tree.

"Yeah," Sean says.

"Well, go ahead," says Cole. "You came all this way."

There's a dead branch on the ground. Sean uses the sharper end of it to pry up the rock and move it aside. He takes a folding knife from his pocket, crouches down, and uses the blade to begin to loosen the earth.

He pauses, looks around to be sure there's no one watching.

"Paranoid," Cole says.

Sean digs with the knife and the branch. Soon he's sweating, but he doesn't need to go very deep. Less than a foot.

It's there, as he knew it would be: a small bundle wrapped in a white plastic trash bag. He opens it, and inside there's a cigar box with an image of a stag on the lid.

The weight of it feels right. Sean lifts the lid and sees the ziplock freezer bag, just the way he left it. Within the bag are fourteen white cotton handkerchiefs rolled up like napkins.

He draws one out and unwraps it. At the center is a cylindrical stone about the size of his thumb.

The stone is amethyst and there's an intricate image carved into its surface: a hunting scene. If you rolled it over a clay tablet, the image would be pressed into the clay. You'd see men with spears tracking wild goats.

It's more than four thousand years old, and there are thirteen others in the bag. Each one carved with a different scene. There are fourteen more buried near the shore of a lake in Kentucky and sixteen in upstate New York.

They're called cylinder seals, and if Sean had a clear legal title to them they might sell at auction for six million dollars. They might go as high as twelve.

Even without legal title, he might be able to get a million for them, if he could find the right buyer.

"You could pay for a kid with that," Cole says.

It's true. A million dollars would make things easier. Sean wouldn't need to worry as much about finding rich people who want to buy custom-made furniture.

Standing in the woods with the cigar box at his feet, he considers it. It's tempting: to gather them up and try to sell them. But he knows it's only a fantasy. It's too dangerous.

Sean used to be reckless, but he lives differently now. Because something happened that divided his life in two. It divided both their lives, his and Molly's. They follow new rules now.

They joke about the rules sometimes, but the rules are necessary.

One: They've left the people they used to know behind. They don't see them or talk to them, ever.

Two: They stay clear of where they used to live. The state of Michigan is off-limits. Living in Texas puts them at a nice safe distance. But they're allowed to travel—which is why it's all right for Molly to take her trip to Montana.

Those are the two main rules, and they've kept Sean and Molly safe for years. The third rule is one they rarely talk about, but it's still important: They leave the cylinder seals hidden. They don't try to sell them.

Sean takes a final look at the seal he's holding, then wraps it in the handkerchief and returns it to the bag. The bag goes into the cigar box, and the box gets swaddled in plastic again and goes into the ground. Covering it over with dirt takes only a few seconds. Sean puts the flat rock back in place and sweeps the leaves over it with his feet, and everything looks the way it did before.

The walk back to his car takes less than an hour, and in that time he doesn't hear Cole's voice or any footsteps but his own. As he catches sight of the trailhead he feels a prick of pain in his right foot, as if a pebble has gotten into his boot. On a bench near the trailhead, he sits and takes the boot off. Turns it over and shakes it. Nothing comes out.

When Sean looks closer at the sole, he finds a split running between two of the treads. There's a small stone wedged in there, something he must have picked up on the trail. He pries it out with his pocketknife and drops it on the ground. Then slips his foot back into the boot.

Later on, he'll think about chance and fate, about what might have happened if not for that stone. But right now, he ties his laces and makes up his mind. If his boots were in better shape, he might have them resoled. But they're old and worn out. He needs to replace them.

There are plenty of places to shop for boots in Houston. He considers his options as he walks to his car, then starts it up and drives to the Galleria.

3

Henry Keen

He's been living with the idea for weeks.

He tried to snuff it out. He pictured it very clearly, the caterpillar in the jar. But he imagined the jar with a lid this time. A metal lid that you could twist into place. No air holes. No way for the thing to breathe.

It didn't work. The thing kept squirming in there. It wouldn't die.

He decided he would give in to it.

He drove out to the spot he had in mind and climbed the hill. He took the gun from the pocket of his black wool coat and held it to his head. It was a hot day, too hot for the coat, and there was barely any wind. And he couldn't go through with it.

Not because of the heat or the wind. Let's not be silly.

He wrote a note, and he had it with him up there beneath the tree. He made the mistake of unfolding it and reading it over. It sounded awful. Poor pitiful Henry. A lot of talk about how he never got a fair chance.

Which is debatable.

He had a good job once, and he lost it. The job that came after paid half as well, but he could still get by. His mother died and then his father. His sister is still around. She has a family of her own. She invites him to visit on holidays. She worries that he's alone.

And that's the thing, being alone.

It doesn't seem right.

He hasn't always been alone. There have been women over the years. There was one, when he was young, who wanted to have children. But he wasn't ready.

Katy. That was her name.

She was sweet. But she's not the one he was thinking of that day up on the hill.

He was thinking of the last one: Rose Dillon.

Early thirties. Auburn hair. Pretty smile. Tall but not too tall.

Henry met her seven weeks ago when he was shopping. She sold him the black wool coat. She said it looked good on him.

He asked for her number, thinking she would turn him down. She didn't. She met him for coffee on a Saturday afternoon. He spent two hours with her, and he found things to say. A week later they went out to dinner, and afterward he kissed her impulsively on the street.

She returned the kiss. She was happy with the kiss. He's almost certain of that.

Another week and they made plans to go to a concert. A few hours before they were supposed to meet, she sent him a text saying she wasn't feeling well. Nothing serious, but she wouldn't be able to make it. He went to the concert on his own. Since then, nothing. She doesn't answer his calls or his texts.

He would like to understand what happened. He would like the world to make sense.

He's not naive. He's not surprised that Rose doesn't want to talk to him. The puzzling thing is why she agreed to go out with him at all.

He's too old for her. His hair is too thin. It's been too long since he saw the inside of a gym.

She should never have given him her number. But she did.

He would like to understand her, and he would like to be understood. He would like her to know that she meant something to him.

Which is why he couldn't do it on the hill. Why he tore the note in half and put the gun back in his pocket.

That was when his idea started to evolve. He wanted Rose to be there. He wanted her to see. He didn't want to blame her for anything. He just wanted her to know: *This is what I've come to.*

He would like to see her face when it happens. This is the new idea.

The plan will have to change. He can't expect her to go with him to the hill. He'll have to go to her. But he knows where to find her. He knows where she works.

At the mall. At Brooks Brothers.

4

Sean Tennant and Henry Keen

The Houston Galleria is the biggest shopping mall in Texas. It has an ice-skating rink and two hotels and close to four hundred stores and restaurants.

Sean finds what he's looking for at Macy's: a pair of waterproof Timberlands that fit him well. He pays for them in cash and wears them out of the store, leaving the box behind and dropping his old boots in the first trash can he comes to.

He eats a Cuban sandwich at the Kona Grill and then wanders along the concourse. The shops don't tempt him, but there's something compelling about the place. It's the bright light and the sound. The mall is full of people on a Friday evening. Sean finds a cluster of armchairs—put there for shoppers who want a break. It's not far from the lobby of the Westin Galleria hotel. He sinks into one of the chairs and lets the mix of sounds wash over him:

Voices young and old. Footsteps clipping over the hard floor. Occasional laughter.

The whirr of a plastic propeller: a twentysomething guy at a kiosk, demonstrating a toy helicopter.

The mechanical tread of an escalator rising.

Henry Keen is listening to the same sounds. He's sitting in another armchair, less than a dozen feet away.

He has already walked past Brooks Brothers and confirmed that Rose Dillon is there. He's taking a few minutes to work up his nerve.

Sean sees him sitting there: a man in a black wool coat. But Sean's attention is elsewhere. He's sifting through the noise around him and picking out bits of conversation:

A mother and son coming out of the Gap. The boy says, "I want pizza."

"You're not hungry," his mother says.

"Yes I am."

"We're not getting pizza."

"You said we could."

"When?"

"Yesterday."

"I didn't see you yesterday. Your father had you yesterday."

"The day before."

"You should get your story straight."

They move off together, and Sean shifts his attention to the guy selling toy helicopters. He's trying to flirt with a girl.

"You want one. I can tell," he says to her.

"I don't know."

"At least one. Maybe more. One for each of your boyfriends."

She laughs. "Just one then, I guess."

"Oh, I don't believe that. I don't believe that for a second."

There's a little more back-and-forth but no sale. The girl walks away, carrying a bag from Abercrombie and Fitch. She passes Sean. Her bag almost brushes his knee.

Sean takes out his phone. He's expecting to hear from Molly. Her plane should have landed by now.

As he's looking at the screen, a feeling passes through him like a flush of heat. There's a smell of cement and smoke. And Cole Harper's voice, right beside him: "Why are you here?"

Sean doesn't turn. He can see Cole out of the corner of his eye. Sprawled in the next chair, dressed in camouflage and heavy boots, a clean white bandage taped to his throat.

The bandage is always there. It shimmers at the edges.

Cole asks his question again: "Why are you here?"

Sean puts his phone away and says, "Where should I be?"

"Anywhere you like," says Cole. "But not at the *mall*."

People are walking by. They're paying no attention.

"I needed boots," Sean says.

"Sure you did. And you had to get them here. There's nowhere else to buy a pair of boots."

Sean lets some time tick by. He doesn't respond.

"I know why you're here," Cole says. "Practice."

Sean sighs. "I don't need practice."

"Yes you do. Being around all these people. It would be enough to put anyone on edge. You have to remind yourself what it's like. What are you carrying?"

"Why do you assume I'm carrying?"

"Christ, what a question. Is it the Beretta?"

"No."

"You always liked the Beretta."

"I don't have it anymore," Sean says. "I've got a Glock."

He almost forgot about it, but it's still there. In the shoulder rig, under his gray windbreaker.

"That's good," says Cole. "What else?"

"Nothing else."

"No helmet. I can see that. No gloves?"

"No gloves."

"No gear?"

"Nothing."

"Not even a tourniquet?"

Everyone carried a tourniquet back then, over there. In Baghdad. Sean carried two. Even after he came back home, he felt safer if he kept one in his pocket.

"I don't do that anymore," he says.

Cole nods. "You'll probably be all right. These people, look at them. They're sheep anyway."

Sean looks around. There's another mom with another son, not the ones from before. The mom is digging for something in her purse. The boy grins and makes a gun with his thumb and index finger. Points it at Sean. Sean makes his own, and the two of them have a standoff.

Across the way, the man in the black coat is leaning forward in his chair with his face in his hands.

"Watch out for that one," Cole says. "He doesn't look right. He's been talking to himself."

Down along the concourse, at the Starbucks, someone knocks over a stool. It hits the floor with a metal clang. The man in the black coat jumps in his seat at the sound. Sean does too.

Cole chuckles beside him. "It's like a damn war zone."

Just then, Sean's phone rings in his pocket. He's slow to answer. He's still scanning the concourse to be sure that a falling stool is just a stool.

"Relax," Cole says. "Talk to her."

Sean brings the phone out and raises it to his ear.

"You got there," he says.

"I got here," Molly agrees. "I'm on the road now. Driving from Bozeman to Clyde Park. Should take another twenty minutes, if I don't stop to look at the mountains."

"Have you been stopping to look at the mountains?"

"Possibly."

"I bet they're something."

"They are," Molly says. "I'll send you a picture. But I'm trying not to take too many pictures. I want to *see* things, you know—"

"I know."

"With my eyes, not through a camera. I'm turning my phone off as soon as you and I are done talking. They'll take it anyway when I get there. Did I tell you?"

"You told me." Sean says.

"They take everybody's phone. I think they tie them in a sack and throw them down a well. These people are serious. The whole point is to unplug."

"I know."

"And look at the mountains. And ride horses."

"And breathe," Sean says.

"Yes! You're making fun of me. But that's the point. To breathe."

"I'm not making fun of you."

Molly is quiet on the line. Skeptical.

"All right," she says. "It's five days. Nothing's gonna happen in five days."

"No."

"Except I'll miss you."

"Except that."

"So tell me you're wild about me and hang up the phone."

Sean pictures her cruising along in a rental car on a highway in Montana. Windows down. Dark hair loose in the wind.

"I'm wild about you," he says.

"Same here."

He slips the phone back in his pocket and waits for Cole to make some sly comment. But the chair beside him is empty. Cole is gone.

The man in the black coat is gone too.

Sean thinks about getting up, going home. He watches as the guy at the kiosk puts the toy helicopter through some basic maneuvers:

vertical climbs and descents, straight-and-level flight. The chopper comes in low and skims across the floor, then zooms up, up to the mall's second level. It banks left, and the propeller clips a railing and stalls out. The chopper crashes down, breaking apart into plastic pieces.

The guy at the kiosk says, "Shit."

Sean gives him a sympathetic look. Rises from the chair.

That's when he hears the shot.

5

Rose Dillon

In the men's apparel section of Brooks Brothers, Rose is helping a customer in his fifties who wants to buy a suit. He's trying on a jacket: 44 regular in navy blue. He's not happy. He asks her to find him a 44 long.

She's looking—and then there's Henry Keen, walking toward her. His face is strange. Rose can read sadness in it but eagerness too. She believes she knows why he's here. She should have resolved things with him instead of going silent. She thinks she's in for an awkward conversation.

The man she's helping clears his throat impatiently. She turns to him, and there's a crazy loud noise that she can feel in her bones. The man's head snaps back and his left eye isn't there anymore. There's just a void. His knees give and he drops over sideways. There's blood running over the bridge of his nose.

Rose looks at Henry and sees the gun—a black shape in his hand—and she's slow to put things together. When she does, there's only shock. She doesn't scream. She can't even speak.

Henry Keen

The expression on her face is everything he wanted.

He was worried, but he knows now that he got it right.

His old idea was wrong. The truth came to him earlier today, as he played the scenario out in his mind. He saw himself putting the gun to his temple and pulling the trigger. In front of Rose, so they could see each other in that moment. And he realized his mistake.

He realized that when he pulled the trigger, that would be the end. He wouldn't see anything. He wouldn't see her reaction.

He almost decided to forget the whole thing. But then the idea evolved.

To this.

He watches her mouth drop open. Her eyes are big, and they're riveted on him. She can see him, finally, and he can see her, and what he sees is awe.

This is just the beginning. She doesn't know yet, but she will. The pockets of Henry's coat are filled with extra clips for his gun. He's glad he brought them. Because the feeling he's having right now, looking at Rose's face, is good. He wants more of it.

He grabs her by the wrist and goes looking for more.

Sean Tennant

There's a delay after the first shot, and Sean has time to doubt that he heard what he thought he heard. Then come three more shots in quick succession and there's no mistake.

He expects chaos, but the people around him are calm at first. They're confused. Some of them stop and listen. They can't see where the noise is coming from. They don't want to overreact.

The kiosk guy looks puzzled, kneeling by the pieces of the toy helicopter. Sean grabs his arm and pulls him up.

"Did you hear that?" the guy says.

"I heard."

"Could have been balloons. You know. Popping."

There's another shot. The fifth. And a scream.

"It's not balloons," Sean says.

"You sure?"

"Call nine-one-one," Sean says. "Tell them shots fired."

The kiosk guy squints at him.

"Gunshots," Sean says. "Are you listening to me?"

"Yeah."

Sean gives him a push, away from the sound of the gunfire. Toward the entrance of the Westin Galleria hotel.

"Go. Get out of here. And make the call."

He goes. Sean moves in the direction of the gunfire. It's coming from somewhere on the other side of the Starbucks.

There are three more shots: six, seven, eight. There's shouting.

People are starting to catch on. There's a rush of them along the concourse. Sean weaves through them.

Shot number nine. Number ten.

A pair of teenagers are standing still. Trying to gawk. A short one and a tall one. The tall one is holding up his cell phone, shooting video.

Sean grabs the phone and throws it as far as he can.

"Run away, you idiots," he says.

On the other side of Starbucks there's a gray-haired man dressed in white linen sitting on the floor. A barista kneels beside him. She's patting at his pockets. Sean looks for a wound, for blood. But there's nothing.

"He's having an asthma attack," the barista says.

She finds the man's inhaler. There's another shot. Louder than the others. A pair of older ladies run out of the Brooks Brothers store in their stocking feet. One of them is holding her shoes.

There's a whip-crack sound and the woman with the shoes pitches forward. Her companion cries out and drops to the floor with her.

Then two more people tumble out of Brooks Brothers. One is the gunman—the man in the black coat. The other is a thirtysomething woman with auburn hair. She's weeping. The gunman holds her tight by the wrist.

He raises his pistol in the air and squeezes off three shots. At first Sean thinks the gunman is firing at nothing, but there are people up there, gathered at the railing on the second level, looking down.

Three shots and the pistol locks in the open position. The clip is empty.

The gunman works a button on the pistol with his thumb. The empty clip falls to the floor. He lets loose the woman's wrist, pushes her down. His hand dips into a pocket of his black coat and comes out with a fresh clip.

The woman is retreating from him, scrambling with her head down, locks of hair obscuring her face.

"Don't do that," the gunman says to her. "Don't look away from me."

He jams the clip into the pistol and works the slide to put a round in the chamber.

His attention is on the woman. He never looks up. He never sees Sean coming.

Sean listens to his own footsteps. Counts them off: one, two, three . . . His breathing is relaxed. His pulse doesn't race. He reaches inside his coat. Feels the Glock slip free of the holster.

Sean's arm extends, and the sights line up along the barrel. The first shot goes into the gunman's chest and stops his heart. The second goes through his temple and into his brain.

6

Sean Tennant

It was quiet when he fired the shots. That's how he remembers it in the car driving away. Then the sound rushed back in. People screaming.

He comes to the on-ramp for the 610 and accelerates, heading south. He's alone in the car. And then he's not.

"That was brave," Cole says.

Sean keeps his eyes on the road. "I don't need you right now."

"It's like Hemingway said: Courage is grace under pressure. Or grace is courage under pressure. Or something. Of course, he was kind of a blowhard. But still."

"Don't need you."

"You did good. That's all I'm saying. But it's starting to hit you now, starting to sink in. So settle down. Watch your speed."

Sean glances at the needle. It's edging toward ninety. He eases up on the pedal.

"That's better," Cole says. "There's blood on your knuckles. I'm not criticizing. You'll want to think about wiping it off."

* * *

After the gunman was down, Sean went to the pair of women—the ones who ran out of Brooks Brothers in their stocking feet. One of them wore glasses with cat's-eye frames. She was yelling for help. Her friend was lying prone on the floor, shot in the back.

Sean crouched down beside them.

"Is she breathing?" he asked the woman with the glasses.

"I think so . . . Yes."

"Good. Don't try to move her."

He heard a gasp. Not from the wounded woman. From the other. She stared at his right hand, which still held the Glock.

He slipped it back into the holster. Showed her his palms.

"It's okay," he said.

Her eyes stayed wide. The wounded woman had a green silk scarf around her neck. Sean drew it off carefully and folded it into a small square. He laid it on the wound and put the other woman's hand over it.

"Press down," he said. "And keep pressing. All right?"

She nodded. Sean lifted his head and took things in. The barista had the asthma man on his feet. The woman with auburn hair was sitting cross-legged, wiping tears from her face. She had put some distance between herself and the dead gunman.

A boy stood near the gunman's feet. He had vacant eyes. Slumped shoulders. Red hands. Sean walked toward him. He recognized him. He was the kid who wanted pizza.

"Where's your mom?" Sean said.

The boy's mouth opened but nothing came out.

"Where is she? Show me."

She was inside Brooks Brothers, lying on the floor between two racks of women's jackets. Pale. Unconscious. Barely breathing. Blood darkened the carpet between her legs. She wore a black skirt and black leggings, so it took Sean a moment to find the wound: it was on her right thigh, midway between hip and knee.

He wanted to believe that the bullet had missed the femoral artery. He couldn't quite convince himself.

The woman's handbag was lying by her elbow. Sean drew his knife from his pocket and sliced through the leather strap.

The boy was standing over him, watching. The woman with auburn hair had come in too. She spoke to the boy softly, tried to lead him away.

"Wait," Sean said. "I need you."

He tied the strap around the wounded woman's thigh. Dumped the contents of the handbag and sifted through them. Found a hairbrush.

He tucked the handle of the brush underneath the leather strap and used it as a lever to twist the strap tight.

"You need to hold this," he said to the woman with auburn hair.

She knelt down but didn't reach for the brush.

"You should do it," she said.

"I can't stay," he said. "It's got to be you."

She frowned, but her hands took the place of his. One gripping the head of the brush, the other the handle.

"Twist it tight," he said. "It has to be tight to close off the artery. Or she'll bleed out."

She bit her lip. Twisted the brush.

"More," he said. "That's good. You're gonna save her life."

In the car, Cole Harper has one booted foot braced against the dash.

"That was inspirational," he says.

"Fuck you," says Sean.

"That line: *You're gonna save her life.* You know how to rally the troops. How much blood do you think that woman lost?"

"I don't know."

"Never rains but it pours. You think the EMTs are there yet?"

"Yes."

"Yeah, they probably are. Maybe they'll save her. Maybe you got that tourniquet on in time. Maybe her brain didn't get too fried."

Sean says nothing.

"Maybe that kid still has a mom. Maybe it'll turn out all right for him. He looked a little iffy though, don't you think? Like he checked out."

Sean watches the taillights of the car ahead of him.

"Reminded me of someone," Cole says. "Another kid who lost his mom."

"Go fuck yourself."

Cole laughs. "There you are. I thought you'd left me." His boot comes down from the dash. "What's the plan here?"

"I'm not sure."

"Because you're a hero now. Have you thought about that?"

Sean's grip tightens on the steering wheel.

"A mass shooting at a mall, that'll make the news," Cole says. "The guy who stopped it, people will wonder about him. 'Why didn't he stick around?' they'll say. They'll want to know his name. They'll want to hear his story."

"Maybe they won't get what they want," Sean says.

"They'll get it. Your picture will be on television. And when that happens—"

"Maybe it won't."

Cole's voice turns impatient. "All those people, you think none of them were taking pictures?"

Sean focuses on the road. A dot of rain appears on the windshield. Then another.

"Your face will be on television," Cole says. "And on the internet. Everyone will see it. *Everyone.*"

The dots of rain come faster.

"Which means *he'll* see it," Cole says. "That's bad. Unless he's forgotten you. Do you suppose he's forgotten you?"

The question isn't real. Sean doesn't answer.

"No," Cole says. "He hasn't. How long has it been?"

Sean turns a switch and the wipers clear away the rain.

"Five years," he says. "Almost six."

"It's not long enough," Cole says. "You know him. He's still the same. He hasn't mellowed. He doesn't forgive. He'll see your face, and that'll be enough. If he hasn't been looking for you, it's because he hasn't had a place to look. Now he will. You know what he'll do. He'll come for you."

Sean listens to the rhythm of the wipers.

"I know," he says.

"Good. So what's the plan?"

7

Nick Ensen

Jimmy Harper told him to sit and wait, so Nick Ensen sits and waits.

He's in the customer lounge at Jimmy's repair shop on Michigan Avenue in Detroit. There's a stale coffee smell in the air and a big flat-screen TV on the wall, tuned to one of those syndicated talk shows. Not the bright, upbeat kind where they chat with celebrities—this is one of the dark ones, where they bring on lowlifes and hope that a fight breaks out. *So you got drunk and slept with your best friend's wife and now she's pregnant. Well, the results of the paternity test are in . . .*

Perfect, really, because it's a show about people screwing up. It's about mistakes. And right now, Nick is thinking about all his mistakes.

It's hard to know how far back he should go. Nick is pretty sure it was a mistake when he was born, but that one's not on him. It's on his mother. So let it go. Jump ahead to high school, to smoking too much weed, to crashing and burning when he tried to take the SATs. Then laughing at the guidance counselor who said he should enroll in community college and learn a trade. Then painting houses for a summer, and tearing off roofs, and ending up at one of those quick oil change places: sweating under cars all day and making no money.

Then getting mixed up with Kelly Harper—Kelly who has a chip on his shoulder because he stands about five foot four and has a girl's name.

Kelly's the one who convinced Nick to quit the oil change place and come work here, at Harper Auto Repair. Kelly is Jimmy Harper's cousin.

At first it seemed like a good move. The pay was better, and Nick was learning things: how to replace shocks and brake pads and mufflers, how to swap out a carburetor.

But there's more to the job than meets the eye. That's what Nick has discovered.

It's not as if he had no warning. He heard things about Jimmy Harper long before he took the job. Rumors.

Like this:

If you stole a car—if you stole just about anything—you could go to Jimmy and unload it.

If someone owed you money and wouldn't pay, Jimmy could help you collect.

If some asshole was giving you trouble, Jimmy could have a talk with him and set things straight. If talking didn't work, Jimmy had other ways of sending a message.

All these things Nick knew. But what he discovered was: If you took a job from Jimmy fixing cars, it might not end there. He might find other work for you to do.

He might send you to have a conversation with a guy who was running an illegal poker game—a guy who bragged that he was under Jimmy Harper's protection to keep the players in line when they lost, but never paid Jimmy a dime.

That was Nick's first non-car-related assignment: going to see this guy, last night. Not alone. Kelly Harper went with him.

The two of them on a mission. It didn't go as planned.

Now, Friday evening, Nick sits and waits. There's one other person in the lounge, an old lady waiting for her car. Her attention is fixed on the TV, eager for the results of the paternity test. The smarmy host builds things up, teases the audience, then cuts to a commercial. The old lady frowns and goes looking for the remote.

She finds it and flips through channels: AMC, USA, HGTV, ESPN, CNN.

She stops there. Split screen: There's the anchor in the studio on one side, a reporter in the field on the other. There's a banner at the bottom that says: BREAKING NEWS. The anchor looks stiff in his suit. His voice drones, but you can tell he's excited. There's been a series of shootings at a shopping mall in Houston. Details are still coming in. The number of victims is unknown. Police are on the scene.

The old lady nudges up the volume. She has forgotten about the paternity test. This is a much better show. Nick watches it half-heartedly. It feels familiar, like he's seen it before.

His mind is elsewhere. There's another scene he's watching.

Jimmy's office is adjacent to the lounge. The door is closed, but the walls are mostly glass and the blinds are up. Nick can see in: Jimmy behind his desk, Kelly in a chair with his bruised face. His nose is twice as big as it should be.

Nick can't hear what they're saying. But he can guess.

Ten minutes drag by, and Jimmy stands up and comes around the desk. He puts a hand on Kelly's shoulder, a fatherly gesture, and ushers him toward the door. Sees him out through the lounge—Kelly gives Nick a dark look as he passes—and along the hall to the front of the shop.

Nick is on his feet when Jimmy returns. He expects to be ordered into the office, but Jimmy ignores him and goes to the coffeemaker instead. Pours a mug and doses it with sugar and cream. Finally turns and notices Nick.

Stares at him with eyes that Nick can't begin to read.

Jimmy steps into the office and waits. Nick passes in and moves toward the chair where Kelly was sitting. He hears the office door close and has the wild thought that Jimmy Harper is going to kill him.

It could happen. Jimmy is older by twenty years, but he's also three inches taller and twenty pounds heavier, and those twenty pounds are muscle. Jimmy could close the blinds on the windows and slip an arm around Nick's throat and slowly choke him to death, and the old lady in the lounge would be none the wiser.

Nick feels a pressure on his neck, but it's a phantom. The blinds are open. Jimmy is watching him from behind the desk, feet up on the blotter.

"Sit," Jimmy says.

It should be easy, sitting, but Nick takes it slow, like he might mess it up. The chair has wheels. It threatens to roll away beneath him. He plants his feet to steady it.

"Tell me about Metzger," Jimmy says.

His tone is flat and his eyes look lifeless. Nick hears the name, but it doesn't register. He's wondering who the hell Metzger is. But there's another part of him that knows. *Get a grip,* he tells himself. Alvin Metzger is the guy with the card game. The one he and Kelly went to see last night.

"We went around two in the morning, to his place on Grand River Ave. We parked a block away and watched. The game broke up a little before three. People started coming out."

Nick's voice is sluggish, and he hates the sound of it. Still, there's nothing to do but keep going.

"Metzger came out last and locked up. We approached him, cut him off before he could get to his car. I think he knew what it was about when he saw us. He recognized Kelly."

"What did you say to him?" Jimmy asks.

"We gave him your message. No more free ride. If he wants protection, he'll have to start paying."

"What did he say?"

"He tried to get slick about it, like you said he would. He would pay, but he didn't have the money right now. He'd have it next week."

Jimmy breathes out through his nose. "What happened then?"

Nick hesitates. He'd like to get a sense of Jimmy's mood, but the man's eyes are still unreadable. There's a hint of impatience in his questions, but this whole interrogation strikes Nick as an empty exercise.

"I'm sure Kelly told you what happened," he says.

"I want to hear your version," says Jimmy.

There's a silence that stretches out for a few seconds. Maybe it's a battle of wills. If it is, Nick surrenders.

"Metzger tried to get in his car," he says. "Kelly grabbed his arm. Spun him around. Punched him."

It was more a slap than a punch. Didn't do any damage.

In fact, it made Metzger laugh. "Jesus, Kelly," he said. "You hit like a girl."

Nick decides to leave that detail out.

He shrugs and looks across the desk at Jimmy. "Then there was a fight," he says.

Jimmy sips his coffee. Sets the mug aside.

"This fight," he says. "This brawl. That's what I'm interested in. Did Alvin Metzger break my cousin's nose?"

"No," says Nick. "I broke it."

"How'd that happen? Was it an accident?"

Nick shakes his head. "It wasn't an accident."

You hit like a girl. The words set Kelly off. Wrestling with Metzger, trying to knee him in the groin. But it was Nick who put Metzger on the ground, sweeping his legs out from under him. Once he was down, Kelly went crazy: kicking Metzger in the ribs, in the spine, in the head. Not letting him up.

"I thought he might kill him," Nick says.

Jimmy seems unmoved. "And what if he did?"

"You told us to talk to the guy. To give him a beating if we had to. You didn't tell us to kill him."

Jimmy tips his head to one side. "The way I remember it, I told you to follow Kelly's lead."

That's true, and it's exactly what Nick was thinking as he watched Alvin Metzger squirm on the ground. Watched him try to shield himself, try to curl up into nothing.

"I had to make a decision," Nick says to Jimmy. "I got between them. Pushed Kelly away. He didn't like it. He took a swing at me. And I reacted. It was a charged situation."

Jimmy brings his feet down off the desk. "So you broke his nose."

"Yeah."

"Because it was a charged situation." Jimmy braces his hands on the arms of his chair. The hands are broad, with thick tendons and rounded knuckles. But the nails are clean. Hard to tell if they're the hands of a businessman or a brute.

"I did what I thought was right," Nick says.

Jimmy rises and steps around the desk to the glass wall that separates the office from the lounge.

"I guess you did," he says. He's facing the wall, not Nick. "Let me ask you: Do you think Metzger got the message?"

Nick pictures the man crying and shaking on the ground.

"Yes."

There's a moment when Jimmy seems to reach for the cord of the blinds and Nick thinks he's going to lower them. He thinks Jimmy is going to turn on him and grab him by the collar and haul him out of the chair. Jimmy could do it, with those hands. He could take Nick apart and leave him bleeding. And whatever effort it took, it wouldn't affect him. It wouldn't raise his heart rate or make him breathe hard. It wouldn't show in his eyes.

The moment passes.

"I think he got the message too," Jimmy says. He's standing still and thoughtful by the glass. "Kelly can be a hothead," he adds. "But you stayed in control. He's going to resent you for a while. That's the way he is. You should watch yourself around him."

Just like that it's over, and Nick knows he's going to walk out of this room, though he wasn't sure before.

Nick gets up and looks through the glass to the lounge. The old lady is gone but the TV is still tuned to CNN. The anchor is there and he's talking, but whatever he's saying is just a murmur through the glass. Then he's gone—replaced by an image set against a blue background. It's a driver's license photo of a pasty man with thinning hair. The caption reads: HENRY ALAN KEEN, HOUSTON SHOOTING SUSPECT.

After a few seconds, the image goes away, replaced by another. This one is a closeup of a man's face, but it's not from a driver's license. It looks like a still frame taken from a video.

The caption reads: PERSON OF INTEREST.

The face means nothing to Nick Ensen. He sees a stranger with dark hair, intense eyes. There's something in the man's expression that could be sadness or anger. But Nick takes only a passing interest in him. He's never been able to care very much about strangers. He knows that all of them have their own lives, like he has his. But they're not fully real to him. Their problems are not his problems.

He turns to Jimmy and says, "Is it okay if I go now?"

Jimmy doesn't answer. His eyes are fixed on the screen. Nick watches his profile and realizes that something has changed. If Jimmy was empty and unreadable before, now he's alive. As if a charge were running through him. Nick can feel it even across the distance between them.

"Jimmy?" he says.

Suddenly the image disappears from the screen and the anchor is back. Jimmy frowns for a few seconds and then snaps into motion. He crosses to the office door and whips it open. Nick follows him into the lounge. Jimmy finds the remote, punches at it with his thumb. The cable news channels are clustered together. He flips from one to the next until he finds one that shows him the image again.

No name underneath. Just: PERSON OF INTEREST.

"Do you know that guy?" Nick says.

But Jimmy just stares at the screen and says nothing at all.

8

Jimmy Harper

At home, Jimmy takes a suitcase from his closet and opens it on his bed.

It's close to midnight. He left the auto shop hours ago, and he's been thinking ever since. About what he needs to do. As if it's a decision he has to make.

It's not though. It was settled a long time ago. He could trace it all the way back if he wanted to. Back to when he was ten years old and his parents brought his brother home from the hospital.

Cole.

He was a tiny thing: red faced, crying. Jimmy was unimpressed. He'd seen babies before. He had three younger sisters.

It was his father who set him straight, oddly enough. His father had never been what you would call sentimental.

"You're lucky," his father said to him.

The two of them standing by Cole's crib. Jimmy remembers it was nighttime. The only light was what came in from the hallway. Cole had finally stopped fussing and gone to sleep.

"You could have missed out on this," his father said. "I'll tell you a secret. You can't tell anybody else."

"Okay," Jimmy said.

"You love your sisters. I know. But it's different, having a brother. I was afraid you might not get to have one, but now you do."

It was warm in the baby's room, but there was snow falling outside. Frost on the windows.

"You're a lot older than he is," Jimmy's father said, putting a hand on his shoulder. "That's all right. You'll still be close. Your brother'll be your friend all your life."

The memory of that night is clear to Jimmy, even now. He can recall the smell of whiskey on his father's breath. Sometimes when his father drank, he talked nonsense or told lies. But what he said that night proved true. Jimmy was far closer to Cole than he was to any of his sisters.

It was Jimmy who taught Cole how to ride a bike, how to drive a car, what music to listen to, how to talk to girls. They had fights, but the fights didn't last. When Cole needed anything, he came to Jimmy. Right up till the end.

As he tosses clothes into his suitcase, Jimmy works it out in his head: five years and ten months. That's how long it's been since Cole died.

Jimmy lived in a house back then, with his wife and his son and his daughter, in Corktown in Detroit. He lives a mile away from that house now, alone, in a two-bedroom condo. His wife is his ex-wife. He still sees his kids, but not every day.

Back then Jimmy's mother had a clear mind; she worked part-time as a secretary at her church; she belonged to a book club. Now she can't focus long enough to read a book. She has to be watched, or she wanders. He caught her once trying to climb out a second-story window. He had to put her in a nursing home.

These are things that might have happened even if Cole hadn't died. Jimmy is careful not to link them all together. He can't blame them all on Sean Garrety. But he can blame Sean for what happened to Cole. That he can do.

As Jimmy packs his suitcase, he has CNN playing on the TV in the background. They show Sean's face periodically. They've got different pictures of him now. And they've got a name for him: Sean Tennant.

The rest is muddled. The police keep promising a press conference and keep delaying. But the news goes on. If there are no facts, there are always experts. There's talk, because there needs to be something. You have to fill the time.

Most of the talk is about Henry Alan Keen, the schlub who went on a shooting spree. But some of it is about Sean. There's a narrative being shaped: He took out Keen. He's a good guy with a gun. But there are dissenting voices too: Did he know Keen? Were they in on it together? Did Sean Tennant change his mind at the last minute?

And where is he now?

A commercial comes on CNN and Jimmy flips over to Fox News. There's a talking head speculating that the police might already have Sean in custody. They might be questioning him. That might be why they're holding off on the press conference.

It's hot air. Jimmy knows it isn't true. Because Sean is smart enough to run.

Jimmy's cell phone is on his bed. There's a pistol there as well, a Walther PPQ. The cell phone buzzes and the screen lights up. Jimmy recognizes the name. It's the third call tonight from that particular party. He hasn't answered so far, and he doesn't answer now.

He picks up the Walther and holds it over the open suitcase. You can carry a gun in checked baggage on a plane, but you have to fill out a form. So there's a record. Jimmy doesn't want there to be a record. He'll have to improvise when he gets to Houston.

He stows the Walther in the drawer of his nightstand.

When his phone buzzes again, the suitcase is full, the lid zipped shut. He picks up the phone and slides it into his pocket unanswered. He turns off the television and carries the suitcase downstairs. Drops it by the sofa in the living room and starts to pour himself a drink.

There's a knock on his front door.

Jimmy doesn't need to check the peephole to know who it is. He turns the dead bolt and opens the door.

"Come on in," he says.

Adam Khadduri nods a greeting and steps across the threshold. He's clean-shaven and wearing a tasteful dark Dunhill suit and a silk tie. His black hair is cut short and swept forward like a Roman emperor's.

There's another man with him, an ex-cop named Tom Clinton. Clinton's suit is JC Penney, and he's not wearing a tie. He follows his boss in but then fades into the background, quiet and watchful.

"I'm glad to see you," Khadduri says. "I feared something might have happened to you."

"No," Jimmy says.

"Perhaps you only mislaid your phone."

"I was about to call you."

"That's excellent then. I've saved you the trouble."

There's a foreign air about Adam Khadduri, though Jimmy knows he was born up in Pontiac. Khadduri has studied abroad and traveled extensively. English is his native language, but he speaks it with an accent that's vaguely European.

"You've been following the news?" he says.

"Yes," says Jimmy.

"It's difficult to avoid. Curious the way these shootings occur so frequently. Yet everyone talks about them so breathlessly every time, as if they're surprised."

Jimmy nods but makes no other reply. He pours Khadduri a drink: Johnnie Walker Black. He looks at Clinton and raises the bottle, a silent offer that Clinton refuses with a shake of his head.

"I confess I've become jaded," Khadduri says. "I don't blink anymore when I see news of these incidents." He pauses to sample his drink. "But it's different this time, isn't it? At least for you and me."

"Yes, it is," Jimmy says.

"Sean Garrety seems to have made his way to Houston. Do you suppose he's been there all along?"

"I don't know."

"You spent a long time searching for him."

"Yes."

"You had no inkling he was there?"

"Why would I?"

Khadduri sips his whiskey, watching Jimmy over the rim of the glass. Then he says, "You can think of no reason he would be drawn to Houston? He has no acquaintances in Texas?"

"None that I ever knew of."

Khadduri lowers the glass, shifts it from one hand to the other.

"Do you suppose *she's* still with him?" he asks.

"I have no idea."

"But if you had to guess?"

"I'm not going to guess."

Khadduri smiles weakly, letting the matter go. He glances at the suitcase by the sofa.

"You intend to travel to Houston," he says. "Or am I misreading the situation?"

"You're not," says Jimmy. "I'm on an early morning flight."

"Perhaps I could help you."

"I appreciate the offer. But I don't need help."

A flash of emotion crosses Khadduri's face. Disappointment. Frustration.

"I have interests here," he says. "Sean Garrety wronged us both."

Jimmy watches him coldly. Lets a moment pass. "Me more than you, I think."

"Undoubtedly," Khadduri says, raising his free hand to show he's not interested in debating the point. "Still, the things he took from me were not inconsequential."

"He may not even have them anymore."

"I'd like to know, either way. If you're going to pursue him, you needn't do it on your own. I can lend you Mr. Clinton."

Clinton, lingering by the door, looks up at the mention of his name.

"That won't be necessary," Jimmy says.

"I could give you Lincoln Reed, if you'd rather."

Reed is another ex-cop. He and Clinton handle all of Adam Khadduri's security. Khadduri is in the import business, and what he imports are antiquities and works of art. The people he buys from aren't always aboveboard.

"Or I could let you have the pair of them," Khadduri says. "Surely they would be useful."

If there's one thing Jimmy has learned in his life, it's that if you don't want to argue you don't have to argue. He stares at Khadduri, lets a few seconds pass, and holds firm.

"I don't want them," he says. Turning to Clinton, he adds, "No offense."

Clinton offers no reaction. Quiet in the room. Khadduri lifts his glass until it's under his chin. He doesn't drink. He looks troubled.

"I would like to believe that you and I respect each other," he says eventually.

"We do," says Jimmy.

"I fear that our interests may diverge in this matter."

"I don't see why they would."

Khadduri studies the whiskey in his glass, as if it might offer him counsel. "Then I can rely on you? To recover what is mine. If you can."

"If I can."

"I will pay you, of course. A finder's fee. A hundred thousand." No hesitation about the number, as if he's had it in mind all along.

"All right," Jimmy says.

"We have an agreement then?"

Khadduri wants to shake on it. Jimmy doesn't care to touch him, but it's worth it to send him on his way. It's over fast: Khadduri shakes like a European. He lifts Jimmy's hand up and brings it down and releases it.

Then it's a matter of letting him finish his drink and walking him to the door. Clinton goes out first. Khadduri turns back to Jimmy for a final word.

"It's odd."

"What is?" Jimmy asks.

"Sean Garrety has remained hidden all these years. It's strange he should reveal himself in this way. What could he have been thinking?"

Jimmy can only shrug. "I doubt he was thinking."

When they're gone and he's alone, Jimmy returns to the drink he poured himself. It's untouched, but he finds he doesn't want it now. He carries it to the kitchen and empties it into the sink.

He doesn't know if he'll be able to sleep, but he decides he should try. He has a few hours before he needs to drive to the airport for his flight.

He's not going alone. He's taking Nick Ensen with him. The kid has proved he can keep a cool head when things go wrong. Jimmy thinks he might be useful.

Adam Khadduri

Khadduri and Clinton roll away from Jimmy Harper's place, the tires gliding smoothly over cracks in the pavement. Khadduri is behind the wheel. He opens the vents to let in the cool night air. Clinton could drive, but Khadduri doesn't want a chauffeur. The car is a Maserati GranTurismo. There's no point in owning it, he thinks, if you're not going to drive it.

There's a stop sign up ahead. He brakes completely, then goes through.

Beside him Clinton says, "I could fly to Houston."

"You could," Khadduri allows. "But to what purpose?"

Clinton gestures back toward where they've come from. "To keep an eye on our friend."

"He wouldn't like that."

"Who cares what he likes?"

Silence for a while. Khadduri steers the Maserati onto the Lodge Freeway, which will take him home.

"We'll see what he does," Khadduri says.

"Do you think he'll get you what you want?" Clinton asks.

"Yes."

"Why should he?"

"He agreed. I believe he's a man of his word."

"You can't count on that."

"Time will tell. I've offered him a generous reward."

Tom Clinton chuckles softly. Leans his head back against his headrest. "That won't matter. He has a motive that's stronger than money."

Khadduri drives on in the dark without responding. He doesn't need to ask what the motive is. He knows. It's hate.

He has a certain measure of it himself, though not as much as Jimmy Harper.

9

Rafael Garza

Detective Rafael Garza feels like a latecomer, and he is. By the time he arrives at Sean Tennant's house in the city of Stafford outside Houston, the investigation of the mass shooting at the Galleria has been under way for sixteen hours.

In addition to being late, he's the odd man out. Partnerless at the moment. Garza used to be paired with Don Lefors, but Don got colon cancer. It was only a few weeks ago that Don told him the news. Crudely, the way he always talked: *Cancer of the shitter. Can you believe it? Do you know what they do? They cut out your insides. Sew up your asshole. You shit through a little tube that comes out of your gut. It goes into a bag you wear around your waist. Picture it.*

I'd rather not, Garza said.

No kidding. Anyway, that's what I've got to look forward to. You'll have to find a way to get along without me. I'm retiring.

But Don Lefors never did retire. He went in for the surgery and died on the table. The surgeon told Don's wife it never happened before, not to any of his patients. But it happened to Don.

There was a funeral with full honors, and when they lowered the box into the ground Garza came very close to laughing out loud, because he kept hearing Don's voice: *Cancer of the shitter. Can you believe it?*

He held himself together. In fact, he overcompensated. His lieutenant thought he looked depressed. The man pulled him aside and told him to take a week or two. Maybe go on a trip. Process what had happened.

Garza went to Vegas. Played blackjack. Won a little money and lost it all again. He asked a dealer to have a drink with him and wound up telling her his troubles. She went up to his room with him to help him forget. Don would have approved.

Garza was with the woman again, a second night, when his lieutenant called and told him to come back. He packed fast and headed for the airport. The last he saw of her she was naked in the shower.

Now, on Saturday morning, Rafael Garza is once again a cog in the machine that is the Houston Police Department.

He attended a briefing at 8:00 a.m., so he's more or less up to speed. He knows that Sean Tennant rents this two-bedroom house on Woodvale Drive from a woman named Carla Whyte, who lives next door. Tennant shares the place with Margaret Winter, also known as Molly. Tennant and Winter have drivers' licenses issued by the state of Texas. Tennant is thirty-one years old; Winter is twenty-nine.

DMV records show a Toyota Camry registered to Sean Tennant. No vehicle registered to Molly Winter. There's no car in the garage behind the house.

The house is peculiar. As Garza walks through it, his first thought is that something's missing. The house isn't empty, but it's not full the way people's houses tend to be full. There's no mess, no clutter. There doesn't seem to be enough stuff. But then Garza realizes there *is* enough. All the things that two people would need to live are here and not much more.

As he moves through the rooms, he finds himself counting things. The numbers are mostly even: twos and fours and sixes.

Two bath towels hanging on the shower rod, four more folded in the linen closet. Two sets of sheets and pillowcases: one on the bed and one in a drawer. Two laundry baskets on the floor of the closet: one for whites and one for colors.

In the kitchen: Four chairs around the table. Two placemats. In a cupboard: four dinner plates, four dessert plates; four soup bowls, four salad bowls; four mugs, four drinking glasses, two wineglasses. In a drawer: six knives, six forks, six spoons.

The spare bedroom has two desks and two chairs. There are no computers, but the assumption is that there were laptops and Sean Tennant took them with him.

Tennant was definitely in the house after the incident at the Galleria. The landlady, Carla Whyte, saw him.

There are papers, pens, and notepads on the desks. Other detectives have already searched here, and one of them, Glen Kirby, discovered a clue. He looked closely at one of the pads and saw that someone had written on it and then torn the page away—leaving behind the impressions of numbers on the page underneath: 1090 and 320.

Kirby did some checking and discovered that United Airlines flight 1090 flew nonstop from Houston's George Bush Intercontinental Airport to Mexico City. It was scheduled to depart this afternoon at 3:20 p.m.

When he heard about it at the morning briefing, Garza was skeptical. "Has Tennant made a reservation on flight 1090?" he asked.

"No," Kirby said. "But he must realize we can access airline reservations. He may be waiting to buy a ticket at the last minute."

"That's clever," said Garza. "It's a shame he gave himself away. Maybe he didn't realize we'd search his house."

He said it drily, sarcastically, and when Kirby heard it his cheeks flushed red. He started to respond, but Garza's lieutenant—Arthur Hayden—raised a hand to interrupt him.

"The flight number could be misdirection. That's understood. We'll still send people to watch the airport. We might get lucky."

Garza doubted it, and he doubts it still. Since the briefing, he's studied the videos of Sean Tennant at the Galleria. The department collected mall security footage as well as several cell phone videos recorded by witnesses at the scene.

Footage from the mall's parking garage showed Tennant walking to his car and driving away. It captured his license plate, which was how Garza's colleagues were able to determine Tennant's name and address.

But there's another video that Garza has watched over and over. He finds it revealing. It was recorded from the second level of the mall by a salesclerk who works at Zales jewelers. It shows Tennant approaching Henry Alan Keen, drawing a pistol from under his coat, firing two shots that drop the man to the floor. Tennant moves with an unhurried grace. There's no sign of panic in him. He looks calm and in control.

He doesn't look careless. He doesn't look like a man who makes trivial mistakes.

He wouldn't leave a flight number behind. Not accidentally.

Garza leaves Tennant's rented house and walks a dozen yards through rain-wet grass to the landlady's place next door.

Carla Whyte is a slender woman in her forties. She answers her door in yoga clothes, brown hair tied in a ponytail. She leads Garza to her kitchen, where there's a juicer on the counter and a glass of something green that she's been drinking. She offers to pour him some.

"It tastes better than it looks," she says.

He accepts a glass, takes a sip, does his best not to make a face.

She laughs. "It's good for you."

"I bet," he says.

"Seriously, there's kale in it. Kale will make you live forever."

Garza asks her about seeing Sean Tennant the night before. She tells him she's gone over the story already with another detective. Which is true: there were detectives here last night, talking to all the neighbors along the street. But Garza's impression is that the interviews were thin and rushed, and in any case he needs to get a better sense of Sean Tennant and Molly Winter.

"Let's pretend I'm brand-new," he says. "Let's pretend I don't know a thing."

Carla is willing to pretend.

She likes to sit on her back porch when it rains, she tells him. It rained yesterday after sunset, and she was out there watching it come down. Sean drove in, and she heard him before she saw him: she heard his garage door rising and his car rolling along the driveway.

She waved at him, but he didn't see. He seemed preoccupied. He left the garage door up and went into his house. He was in there for maybe half an hour. The rain let up and she was getting ready to go back inside when she saw him come out with a suitcase and a small travel bag. He put them in the trunk of his car, returned to the house, and came out again with a duffel bag and a backpack.

He started the car, backed it out, lowered the garage door, and drove away. He never spoke to her. She assumed he was going away for the weekend.

"Molly Winter wasn't with him?" Garza says.

"No," Carla tells him.

"When did you see her last?"

She looks off at nothing, trying to recall. "Thursday afternoon. She came over here. We did yoga."

"You didn't see her yesterday then?" Garza asks.

"No."

"Another neighbor, a retiree across the road, Mr. Henderson—"

"Hendricks."

"Mr. Hendricks. He remembers seeing them leave together yesterday morning, Molly and Sean. Do you have any idea where they might've been going?"

"I don't."

It's a question that needs to be answered: where Molly was yesterday, where she is now. She wasn't at the Galleria with Sean. She doesn't appear in any of the surveillance footage.

"Could Sean have dropped her off somewhere?" Garza asks. "An appointment—"

"I wouldn't know about her appointments," Carla says.

"Maybe a friend's house."

"I don't know her friends."

"You're her friend. You do yoga together."

"That's true. But I don't know her other friends."

"It would help if I knew what her life was like," Garza says. "What does she do with her time?"

"She's a writer."

"What does she write?"

Carla smiles and looks away. "This is where I tell you she writes novels and you say, 'What kind of novels?' And I say, 'Dirty ones.'"

"Dirty ones?"

"Kind of like those *Fifty Shades* books. Do you know about those?"

"They're about bondage, aren't they? You're saying she writes bondage novels?"

"There's some light bondage in them, but mostly they're just . . . erotic."

"And she sells them? They get published?"

"Self-published. She puts them out as e-books. You can read them on your Kindle. She sells them cheap—like four bucks apiece. But she's done a bunch of them."

Garza tips his head to the side, skeptical. "You think she makes much money that way?"

"I don't know," Carla says. "But you've been over there." She gestures in the direction of the Tennant house. "The two of them live pretty simply. They're not throwing money around."

"What kind of work does Sean do?"

"He makes furniture for people. Tables, chairs, dressers."

"Do you know the names of any of these people?"

She shrugs. Picks up her glass of green juice. There's one good slug of it left, and she downs it in one go.

Then she says, "Can I ask you something?"

"Sure."

"Why are you doing this?"

"What do you mean?" Garza asks.

"I've been watching the news. That guy, Henry Keen, he was crazy. They're always crazy. I heard one reporter say he was carrying a bunch of spare clips for his gun. He had almost two hundred bullets with him, and he only got to fire fifteen. Because Sean stopped him. And now you're going after Sean."

"I'm not *going after* Sean," Garza says. "I just want to talk to him."

"Somebody ought to give him a medal. But I don't think he wants a medal."

"What do you think he wants?"

"Isn't it obvious? He wants to be left alone. And that's the one thing he's not going to get."

Garza gives Carla a kindly look. "I'll be happy to leave him alone. But I need to talk to him first."

"Sure," she says. "You want to talk to him. All the newspeople want to talk to him. If he had stuck around, they wouldn't have left him alone. Not for a minute. Sean never hurt anybody, except for Henry Keen. And it looks to me like he deserved what he got. I hope Sean disappears, if that's what he wants. I hope he and Molly are together right now, off somewhere by themselves. I hope you don't find them. I hope nobody finds them."

*   *   *

As Garza leaves Carla Whyte's house, he's thinking he's inclined to agree that Sean Tennant deserves a medal for his actions at the Galleria. In fact, he would gladly buy the man a beer if given the opportunity. But he still needs to understand who Tennant is. It's in his nature; it's the reason he became a detective. He needs to figure the man out.

Not that he has a choice. The investigation of the incident at the Galleria has a momentum of its own. Garza couldn't control it if he tried. A mass shooting gets people's attention. They feel a need to make sense of it. Henry Keen is dead, but there are teams of detectives questioning everyone who knew him, trying to work out what led him to Brooks Brothers with his gun and his pockets full of bullets. They're working with profilers from the FBI to try to understand his motives. They're tracing his contacts and his movements to determine if he has any connections to terrorist organizations, foreign or domestic.

Sean Tennant is a part of it too. He'll need to be picked apart and analyzed, tracked down and questioned. There can be no loose ends.

Garza spends the rest of the morning at his desk in the homicide division, typing up his notes and making phone calls and searching databases. He knows from this morning's briefing that Sean Tennant has no criminal record in Texas or anywhere else. It was an obvious thing to check, and Glen Kirby checked it while Garza was on the plane from Las Vegas to Houston. But now Garza knows more: Sean Tennant has lived at his current address for somewhat less than six years. Garza can find no record of a previous address. Tennant's credit history is thin, which is consistent with someone who rents and lives cheaply and doesn't like to borrow money. The strange thing is that none of his accounts have been open for more than six years.

Tennant's driver's license fits the same pattern: he's held it for less than six years. If he held one before in another state, Garza can't find a record of it.

From the moment Sean Tennant left the scene of the shootings at the Galleria, it was plain that he was running from something. Carla Whyte believes he's running from attention, from notoriety, from being hounded by the media. But to Garza it looks more and more as if he's running from something else. It looks as if Sean Tennant may have a secret, and the secret may be that he's not really Sean Tennant at all.

It's an easy theory to test. Garza drives back to the house in Stafford, and Carla Whyte lets him into the garage. Tennant's workshop. There's a carpenter's square on the workbench—a tool for laying out right angles. It's made of steel and has smooth surfaces that would hold fingerprints. Garza picks it up with a latex glove and bags it. He gathers other small items that Tennant would have handled: a tape measure, a wood file, a utility knife. He bags those too.

From there Garza has more driving to do: First to the lab, where he delivers his finds to the fingerprint analysis section. Next to the airport, where he meets up with Glen Kirby. Kirby is still convinced that Sean Tennant might try to take flight 1090 to Mexico City, so the two of them spend their afternoon coordinating with airport security, making sure Tennant doesn't board that flight or any other.

Tennant never shows. Garza doesn't believe he's heading for Mexico City. Tennant has a car, and he could be far away by now. He could be in Dallas or Baton Rouge or Memphis or Little Rock. The department has received tips from each of those cities: people who called in to report seeing someone who matched Tennant's description. There will be more as the day goes on, and Garza will hear about all of them.

But he's not counting on tipsters to help him find Sean Tennant. As Saturday wears on, there's a part of his mind that's working the problem. He's thinking about Molly Winter and the old man across the street who saw her drive away with Sean Friday morning. He's thinking about the Tennant house and all those things he counted: twos and fours and sixes.

He's thinking about Carla Whyte, who saw Sean loading his car Friday night with a suitcase, a small travel bag, a duffel, and a backpack.

One suitcase.

Two people living together should have two suitcases. So there should be a suitcase left in the house. But when Garza walked through it, he didn't see one.

There are more than two dozen airlines flying out of George Bush Intercontinental Airport. Garza starts with the bigger ones. He visits United, then American, then Delta. It's early in the evening when the ticket agent at the Delta counter gives him the answer he's looking for. Molly Winter flew out Friday at 11:40 a.m. Her destination: Bozeman, Montana.

It's a solid lead, but there are no guarantees. Maybe Sean will go to Bozeman to meet up with Molly, but maybe he won't. Maybe the first thing he did was call her and tell her to meet him somewhere else. Even if Molly stays put in Bozeman, it's a city of forty-five thousand people. She won't be easy to find.

Still, it's a lead. It's what he has. His lieutenant takes some convincing, but by Sunday morning Rafael Garza is on a flight to Montana.

10

Jimmy Harper

Sean hid himself well, Jimmy thinks.

He might have done better if he had been willing to give up civilization. If he had built a little cabin in the wilderness. Maybe near a river. Then he could have fished for his supper. He could have grown food in a garden.

You could live like that if you were disciplined, Jimmy thinks. If you didn't mind all the things you missed. You wouldn't even need a name, if you were living out there on the edge.

But Sean took another path. He wanted a life in a city; he wanted to be connected. For that, you need a name, an identity.

He did well though. He made an effort. Sean Tennant had no presence on social media: no Twitter account, no Facebook page, no Instagram, no LinkedIn.

But no one can hide, not anymore, not if they want a civilized life. Once Jimmy had the name Sean was living under, he found his street address with a simple online search.

The house is bland and a little run-down. White siding. Gray shingles on the roof. There are concrete steps in the front, but the steps leading up to the back door are wood, and they're bowed in the middle.

Jimmy can feel them bend beneath his weight.

He walks up to the back door and goes to work on the locks with a pick and a tension wrench.

Jimmy's father was a locksmith, a mechanic, and a small-time thief. He taught Jimmy everything he knew.

There's a spring lock in the knob that takes about forty-five seconds. The dead bolt takes a bit longer. Jimmy works in the dark, but he doesn't need to see anyway. It's all about feel.

The dead bolt surrenders and he's in. He pushes the door shut behind him.

Easy. The hardest part was the wait.

He and Nick Ensen touched down in Houston around ten o'clock this morning, rented a car, and drove to Sean's neighborhood. Jimmy parked a few blocks away, left Nick in the car, and went on foot to scope out Sean's house. He spotted two police cars on the block, one marked and one unmarked.

Not so bad, he thought. He was afraid there might be reporters camped out on the lawn.

Jimmy walked back to the rental car and drove aimlessly for a while. He decided he needed someplace with a television: a hotel room or a bar or a diner. He settled for a diner with flat screens on every wall, two of them tuned to football games, the other two to cable news.

Nick sat across from him in a booth, eating french fries and sipping Coke through a straw. He had his phone out and his earbuds in. He'd been like that on the plane too. Listening to music.

An encouraging sign, Jimmy thought. The kid could entertain himself.

Jimmy drank coffee and watched the news. The story was still largely focused on Henry Keen. Reporters had interviewed his neighbors and tracked down some of the people he worked with at a printing plant where he was a press operator. They had found his sister, too, but she didn't want to talk. CNN had tape of her walking away from a camera crew with her head bowed. She looked as if she wanted to cry.

"She needs to wise up," Jimmy said.

He was talking to himself, but Nick plucked an earbud from his ear to listen.

"The shooter's sister," Jimmy said. "She should make a statement through a lawyer. Or better yet, find some uncle or cousin who likes to talk and make him the family spokesman. Have him read a statement in front of the cameras. 'We're shocked and saddened and praying for the victims.' There are rituals that have to be observed. Otherwise the newspeople will keep hounding her."

Nick nodded and went back to his music, and Jimmy flagged a waitress and got her to refill his coffee. Later on they ordered dinner—the kid had a cheeseburger and another order of french fries—and when it started to get dark they headed out. Jimmy let the kid drive the rental car, and when they cruised past Sean's house the police cars were gone.

They went around the block to a parallel street, and Jimmy had Nick park and told him to stay alert. On foot, Jimmy cut through someone's yard and came at Sean's house from the back.

Now he has worked the locks and he's inside. The place seems familiar, though he's never been here. Jimmy has known Sean since they were kids. Sean was his brother Cole's best friend. He was a near-constant presence in the Harper house; he and his mother lived down the block. Sean's father had never been around, and his mother drank, so the Harpers took responsibility for much of his care and feeding. Jimmy's mother bought Sean's school clothes. Jimmy's father fixed up a bike for him to ride. And when Sean's mother drove her Ford Focus into a tree one night in August when Sean was thirteen, he didn't go to relatives. He came to live with the Harpers.

They set up a place for him in a corner of the basement. Just a narrow bed and an old dresser. Jimmy can picture it: Sean's meager possessions lined up on top of that dresser, his clothes folded in the drawers, his bed made every morning. The compulsive neatness of it—striving to put things in order.

This house outside Houston is the same. Jimmy flicks on a small flashlight and makes his way through the rooms. He sees Sean everywhere: in the sparse furnishings, in the way a sofa and an armchair align at a perfect ninety-degree angle. In the strict organization: everything in its place.

Jimmy is looking for pictures and papers, and he's disappointed. There are framed photographs on the walls, but none of them show people. There's no address book left behind, no cards or letters, nothing to indicate what friends Sean might have made in his new city. And nothing to suggest where he might be now.

There are clothes in the closet that make it plain Sean was living here with a woman. It could be Molly: the sizes and styles seem right. But even that isn't a sure thing.

It's frustrating, but more or less what Jimmy expected. He never hoped to find easy answers.

He lingers in the house longer than he needs to. Outside, it starts to rain. He sits in Sean's kitchen and watches the drops collect on a window, sees them trail down the surface of the glass.

When he leaves, he's tempted to feel regret, but he tells himself the visit was necessary, even if it came to nothing. He engages the spring lock and steps out into the rain and pulls the door shut. He doesn't bother about the dead bolt.

There are lights on in the house next door. Jimmy didn't pay them much attention before. But as he descends the wooden steps he realizes there's someone sitting over there—a woman in a wicker chair under the eaves of the back porch.

She sits up a little straighter; her chin rises. It's plain: she sees him.

There's only one thing to do when you're caught red-handed: play it cool. Jimmy waves at her. Walks toward her.

As he gets closer to the light of the porch, the woman looks confused. He flashes her a smile.

Jimmy Harper is six feet tall and broad shouldered. He has a bruiser's build that he inherited from his father. But while his father put on weight as he aged, Jimmy has kept himself fit. While his father's hair thinned, Jimmy's has stayed thick and wavy.

When he smiles, he has dimples in his cheeks. He has straight white teeth from two years of orthodontia. He's a handsome rogue—a charmer, as his mother would say.

Carla Whyte sees him smile, and though he's a stranger, she's charmed.

When he's close, she calls out: "I thought you were someone else."

"And who would that be?" he says.

"Someone who was here before. A policeman."

Jimmy makes the smile bigger. "I'm not a policeman."

"Who are you?"

"An old friend of Sean's."

He doesn't step onto the porch. He stands in the rain. That's part of the charm.

"Did Sean give you a key?" she asks him.

He could lie, or he could tell the truth.

"No," he says.

"But you were in the house just now."

He spreads his arms. "I have a way with locks."

He puts some mischief in the words, and they work the way he intended them to.

The woman laughs.

"You're a reporter, aren't you?" she says.

"I'm a locksmith."

"There was a reporter here this afternoon. He tried to bribe me."

"What for?" Jimmy asks.

"To let him in that house. I own it. I don't know what he hoped to find there. I didn't let him in."

"As well you shouldn't."

"I don't approve of reporters."

"I don't either. They're scoundrels. I wouldn't help one if I found him wounded by the wayside."

Another laugh. Jimmy puts one foot on the lowest step of the porch. The woman beckons him up.

It's only courtesy, letting a stranger come in from the rain.

There's a second wicker chair. She waves him into it. There's a small table with a bottle of wine, about half full. Only one wineglass and nothing in it but the dregs. She has a glow about her. She's tipsy.

It's one reason she's not afraid of him.

There's another: her keys are on the table, and there's a canister of pepper mace attached to her key ring. A sad necessity for a woman living alone. She reaches for the keys and moves them to her lap, out of his reach.

Jimmy shows no interest in the move. "What's your name?" he says.

"Carla."

"I'm John. John Donne."

"Like the poet."

"He was a preacher too."

"You're not a preacher."

"No. Not me."

"You're a friend of Sean's," she says. "Did you think he'd be at home?"

"I had nowhere else to look for him." Jimmy says. "I saw this business on the news and thought he might need help. It can knock you back on your heels, having to shoot somebody. So I drove in."

"From where?"

"From Lubbock."

"That's a long drive."

"Sean's a good friend. Molly too."

He's taking a risk, because the woman living with Sean might not be Molly, or if she is, she might be using a different first name. But the risk pays off.

"You know Molly?" Carla says.

"If you know Sean, you know Molly. They're a pair. Like salt and pepper. Like sugar and spice. Like biscuits and gravy—"

"Like frick and frack," she says. "Like dogs and cats. You like to talk, don't you?"

"That I do."

"Unlike Sean."

"Yes. He's a quiet one, isn't he? A hard nut to crack. But you and Molly, you must be fast friends."

"Why do you say that?"

"The two of you living so close together. And both of you with a fondness for red wine."

She smiles, and Jimmy knows he's hit the mark.

"I'll tell you the truth," he says. "I don't know Molly well. But Sean I've known since we were kids. Our families lived on the same street. Here's what I can say for him, for what he was like back then. There was a dog on our street, an old, ragged thing with one eye. It didn't belong to anybody, but people would feed it. Sean always made sure it had water. Good cold water in a metal bowl, fresh every day.

"One afternoon in the summer, he saw that bowl tipped over. He went looking for the dog. And he found it. Tied with a length of clothesline to a telephone pole by a vacant lot. There were three boys around it with sticks in their hands, and they would dance in and crack those sticks over the dog's back and dance away again so they were out of reach. They didn't need to bother: there was no fight in that dog. It didn't try to bite them. It only suffered and whined.

"Sean ran up to those boys and tried to grab a stick away from one of them, but they were bigger than he was. They laughed at him and pushed him down. He had nothing to defend himself with but a jack-knife with a two-inch folding blade. I don't know how far he could have gotten with it, but he never tried to cut them. He stayed down on the ground and sawed through the clothesline. The boys kicked at him, but he managed to get the dog loose."

Jimmy pauses, and Carla says, "What happened then?"

"The dog ran, and Sean was left there with those three boys and their sticks. One of them knocked the knife away, and they did what boys like that do. Someone was going to get a beating. Sean or the dog. They didn't care."

The rain has tapered off to a patter. Random drops fall from the eaves, twinkling in the light that comes out to the porch from the kitchen. Carla adds wine to her glass and sips from it and watches Jimmy. The same light glints in her green eyes.

"You can tell a story," she says. "I'll give you that."

Jimmy grins.

She looks at her glass and remembers her manners.

"Are you thirsty?" she asks.

"I could stand a drink," Jimmy says.

She sets her glass aside, rises, and says, "Wait here." Then she's moving past him. The keys that were in her lap go into a pocket of the sweater she's wearing. The sweater covers a flowered dress that shows off her legs. Jimmy admires them as she goes by. She opens the screen door and slips into the house.

She returns with another glass and fills it and tops off her own, emptying the bottle. Jimmy takes the new glass and raises it to her in a silent toast. Both of them drink.

Then they're shy with each other, strangers who have run out of conversation. They tend to their glasses and look out at the rain. It's awkward, but Jimmy doesn't mind awkwardness. It can work for him, he thinks. All he needs is to be patient. She may have something to tell him, but he won't get it if he asks for it. He has to wait and let her be the one to talk.

She does. "In vino veritas," she says.

He gives her a quizzical look.

"We're drinking wine," she says. "So you have to tell the truth. Can we agree on that?"

He nods. "We can."

She stretches out her legs, crosses them at the ankles.

"You swear to me you're not a reporter?" she says.

"I swear."

"What do you do?"

"I own an auto repair shop."

"You fix cars?"

"Sometimes."

"Let me see your hand."

She wants the right one. He shifts the wineglass to his left and lets her have it. She examines his palm, touches the calluses. Turns his hand over and rubs her thumb over the scars on his knuckles.

He passes muster. She lets the hand go.

"You're really Sean's friend?" she asks.

"I've known him longer than anyone left on earth."

"Then you shouldn't have to look for him, should you?" she says. "He would come to you, if he wanted your help."

"I don't know what he'd do," Jimmy says. "It's been years since I've seen him."

Carla holds her glass by the stem, rolling it between her fingers. "You're hoping I can tell you where he is."

"Yes."

"I can't. I don't know where he is."

"But you know something," Jimmy says.

She doesn't deny it. He watches her playing with the glass.

"The way I see it," she says, "you should want what Sean wants, if you're his friend."

"Sure."

"If he wanted to talk to the police or to reporters or to anybody, he would talk to them. If he wanted to be found, he would let them find him. Don't you think?"

"Absolutely."

"So it's not for us to second-guess him. Right?"

"I see what you mean."

She leans toward him, her green eyes looking eager. "But I'm right. Aren't I right? If we're Sean's friends, then we should respect his wishes. I shouldn't tell you what I know, just like I didn't tell the police. And you shouldn't want me to tell you. We should just drink to Sean and wish him well."

She's happy with her little speech. She drinks, and Jimmy does too. The rain patters on the roof. An easy time passes. No words. The two of them looking out at the dark lawn.

Jimmy says, "You didn't tell the police."

She's somewhere else, in her own thoughts. She turns to him, looking serious.

"Hmm?"

"There's something you know," Jimmy says. "But you didn't tell the police."

She smiles a little and shakes her head, as if he's being naughty. "You won't get it out of me," she says. "I'm determined."

"But there's something. But not about Sean. You don't know where he is."

She gives him a sly look over the rim of her glass. "Not him. *Her.* Molly. But that's all you get. I'm not telling you any more. You might as well give up. I'm stubborn."

"What if I'm stubborn too?"

Her smile grows wider. "I bet you are. But let's be nice. No more prying. You can have one more glass of wine. And then off with you."

She reaches for the bottle. Remembers it's empty. She plants her feet and rises from her chair. Rests a hand on his shoulder as she passes him. "I'll be right back," she says.

Then she's through the screen door and into the kitchen. Jimmy Harper watches her go, and he's pleased. He thinks he can get what he needs from her if he plays it right.

He gets up, draws open the screen door, and passes in. Carla is standing at the kitchen counter with her back to him. She's got a corkscrew; she's opening a fresh bottle of wine.

She hears the door, and his footsteps on the kitchen tile. She glances back at him.

"I didn't say you could come in."

The words are playful. She's not afraid of him. She's not alarmed.

"You didn't say I should stay out," he offers.

It makes her laugh. She's back to twisting the corkscrew.

He likes the shape of her, the way the sweater drapes down from her shoulders, the look of her bare calves.

He crosses the room until he's standing behind her, close enough to touch. He lays his right hand on her hip.

"Well, I don't know about that," she says.

Her voice is smooth and low. Flirty.

He takes in some of the details of the room: white cupboards, black tiles on the wall above the sink. There's a plaque above a window that reads: THIS IS WHERE YOU ARE NOW.

He puts his other hand on her other hip.

"I definitely don't know about *that*," she says.

But she leans back against him, the wine bottle forgotten.

His hands move up to her waist. He takes in the smell of her hair. Strawberries.

She tips her head back on his shoulder and it's an offer. He accepts: kisses the side of her neck. She turns until they're facing, and then her mouth is on his, her lips parting, her tongue sliding over his teeth.

Jimmy pulls the sweater off her shoulders and she gets her arms out of the sleeves and tosses it away. Then the two of them are tangled together: he can feel her fingers at the back of his neck, twisting into his hair. He moves his hands down her body over the dress, and lower, until they're under the dress and moving back up again. Her body is warm and firm.

He can feel her pressing against him, her arms around him and one leg, too, trying to encircle him. His hands find her panties, silk and lace, and he hears her gasp as he tugs them down. He lifts her up in one smooth motion and sits her on the counter. The dress is up around her waist now and her legs are parted.

He steps back to look at her. Because he's human, and whatever else he's doing here, she's an attractive woman. He wants to see her. As he looks her over, his fingers are working the buckle of his belt. It's a mistake. He's moving too fast.

"Whoa. Easy," she says. And slides down from the counter.

She's looking around, at her panties on the floor, her sweater. She pulls her dress down to cover her thighs. Jimmy steps close to her, trying to salvage things. Tips her chin up with one gentle finger and leans in. She pushes him back. She's starting to be nervous.

"I don't even know you," she says.

A simple fact, and it has all of her attention now. She tries to step around him; she wants her sweater. The key ring is in the sweater—and the pepper mace. He takes her by the arm.

"You're fine," he says.

He's not even holding her tight, but it's wrong. He's got it wrong. She pulls away from him and there's an inkling of fear in her eyes. That's the end. No going back from here. Jimmy grabs her shoulder and spins her around. She struggles, but she's not so strong. Tries to plead with him instead of screaming—*Please don't, I don't want to*—but nothing she says matters. He pushes her against the counter and gets an arm around her neck.

It's something else his father taught him, though Jimmy never had an occasion to use it on a woman. A sleeper hold. Pressure on the carotid arteries. It scares her, and that helps. She resists, but it's feeble. He feels her go limp and suddenly she's heavy in his arms.

Carla Whyte

The cold comes up through the floor.

It's a hard floor. Carla can feel it against her back. She's in her basement. She recognizes the ceiling, the rough wood of the joists. Gray ductwork. She turns her head, and she can see her washer and dryer. There's a dent at the base of the dryer. She's never looked at it from this angle.

She wants to reach out and touch that dent. There would be something reassuring about it. But she can't. Her hands are bound.

There's a smell, a bad smell, and for a few seconds she thinks it's gasoline. She thinks he's going to burn her, the strange man she let walk into her house.

But it's not gasoline. It's the tape that's covering her mouth. Carla knows the smell. It's from an old roll of packing tape. Her tape. He must have found it in a drawer.

She's not going to burn then. She's going to live. That's what she tells herself.

She hears a tread on the stairs. It's him, coming down. He's carrying something small. A picture frame. She recognizes it. It makes her want to scream.

There's a click as he lays the frame on top of the dryer. He steps over her and stands by her feet and bends down. When he comes up again he's holding a thick orange cord, an outdoor extension cord she uses to plug in her electric hedge trimmer.

She doesn't know what he's doing with the cord. Her legs are already tied. She can feel it.

There's a steel I-beam that's supporting the floor above. He runs the end of the cord over the beam until it dangles down on the other side. Then he pulls on it. Puts his weight into it.

Carla's legs come up off the floor. The orange cord is wrapped around her waist, over her dress. It's wound around her hips and her legs. It's knotted around her ankles.

He pulls the end of the cord, and her back is dragged along the floor. She's lifted up until only her shoulders are touching the cold concrete. Then the back of her head. Then she's hanging in the air. The cord bites into her ankles. He ties off the end. She's suspended upside down. It's a peculiar sensation, swaying from the beam.

He retrieves the picture frame from the dryer and sits on the floor with his legs crossed, facing her. He bends forward, but still they're not on a level. She has to look up to see him.

He had dimples when he smiled before, but now he's not smiling. He stares at her with empty eyes, and she feels the pain of the cord on her ankles and the rush of blood to her head. And the swaying, the swaying is disorienting. She thinks it's going to make her sick.

"That story I told you," he says. "About Sean and the dog. That wasn't true. I mean it *was* true, but it didn't happen to Sean. It happened to me. I was the one who took the beating for the dog. I don't know why. I wouldn't do it now, if it happened today. That kind of loyalty, that's something kids have."

He looks off, as if he's lost interest in the subject, and when he looks back he seems to remember that she's hanging upside down. He waves a hand at her, at the cord, at the situation.

"This is over-the-top," he says. "I know. It's dramatic. I don't like drama. I really don't. But I need to get through to you. I need you to know I'm serious."

He stops, and it takes her a moment to realize he's waiting for her to respond.

She nods once for him.

"Good," he says. "That should make this easier. I need to find Sean. My reasons, well, they shouldn't matter to you. I have to find him, so you have to tell me what you know. You don't know where he is. Right?"

She nods again.

"But you know where Molly is. And if I can get to her, I can get to him. So you need to tell me where she is."

He's waiting again. She gives him another nod.

"You're conflicted right now," he says. "You're thinking I'm going to hurt Sean. That's true. I won't lie to you. I'm going to hurt him. You think he's your friend, and if you help me find him you're betraying him. But that's wrong. Sean is not your friend. He doesn't care about people. He only thinks about what they can do for him. This is what you need to understand: Sean knew that I would come here to look for him. He could have warned you about me. But he didn't. He doesn't care about you."

Carla stares at him, this strange man sitting on her basement floor. From her perspective, he's upside down.

"This is the deal we're going to make," he says to her. "You tell me where to find Molly, and I cut you down and untie you and walk away.

"You don't think that's real, but it is. You're afraid of what I'm going to do to you. But that's why this is going to work. You need to be afraid of me. That's going to keep you alive. If you're not afraid of me, you're going to make a mistake. Because I *am* going to hold up my end of the bargain."

He's perfectly still, and Carla realizes that she is too. She's stopped swaying.

"You're going to tell me where Molly is, and I'm going to leave," he says. "When I'm gone, if you're not afraid of me, you're going to think, *He's not so bad after all.* You're going to think you can go to the police and tell them about me, and they'll protect you."

He leans in toward her. "If you do that, they might find me, they might arrest me, but that won't save you. Even if they put me in prison. Because I know people. People who owe me favors. People who would do whatever I ask them to do."

The picture frame is lying on the floor beside him. He picks it up now and looks at the image. Carla reaches for it instinctively with her bound hands. The movement sets her swaying again.

"Here's a difference between you and Sean," he says. "There are no pictures of people in his house. Only pictures of things. But you have pictures of this girl. Lots of them. She's your daughter, isn't she?"

She is. But Carla doesn't nod. She tries to give him nothing.

"You don't have to answer," he says. He turns the frame around so she can see, and taps the glass. In the picture, Carla's daughter is wearing a T-shirt with the logo of the University of Texas.

"You understand how easy it would be for me to find her," he says.

The fear she's feeling must show in her eyes, Carla thinks, because he reaches out to touch her cheek as if to comfort her.

"It's all right," he says. "It's good. You need to be afraid. That's the only way this works." He puts the frame aside. "This is the bargain I'm offering you: You tell me what I need to know and then you forget about me. And then you're safe, and she's safe. That's fair, isn't it?"

Carla closes her eyes. She can feel herself trembling. But she nods at him.

He reaches for the tape and starts to peel it from her mouth. His touch is surprisingly gentle.

"Good," he says.

Jimmy Harper

It's an easy walk back to the rental car. The air feels cool and the rain has trailed off to nothing. Nick is waiting with the engine idling and the radio tuned to a country music station. He turns the volume down when Jimmy slides into the passenger seat beside him.

"Airport," Jimmy says.

Nick switches on the lights and pulls away from the curb. Jimmy takes out his phone and opens Google Maps. He enters the name of the town that Carla gave him: Clyde Park. The nearest big cities are Bozeman and Billings.

He opens another app and starts searching for flights.

Nick leaves him alone. He drives along in the dark, two hands on the wheel. He doesn't speak until they reach the exit for the airport.

"Where are we going?"

"Montana," Jimmy says.

11

Sean Tennant

Saturday night. Interstate 25, an hour north of Cheyenne, Wyoming.

There's an eighteen-wheeler stopped on the shoulder up ahead, with a state police cruiser settled in behind it, blue lights flashing. Sean moves into the passing lane to give them a wide berth.

He's wary for the next twenty miles, watching for those lights to appear in his rearview mirror.

"Getting paranoid again," Cole says beside him. "They've got better things to do up here than look for you."

It's seventeen hundred miles from Houston to Clyde Park, Montana. Sean has covered twelve hundred already. Cole has been keeping him company.

He's there now in the passenger seat, one black boot braced on the dash, the white bandage glowing at his throat.

"It's late," Cole says. "You should think about stopping."

"Not yet."

Sean drove for seven hours last night, from Houston to Chillicothe. He kept himself going until four in the morning with vending machine

Coke, but then his eyelids started feeling heavy and he thought he should get off the road. He found a motel and paid cash for a room. The night clerk looked too bored to take any interest in him.

Sean set an alarm to wake himself in four hours and heard Cole's voice say, "Make it eight. Don't screw around with your sleep. You've got a long way to go."

He compromised and slept six hours and was back on the road by eleven Saturday morning. Now he's been driving for twelve hours, going on thirteen—through Amarillo and Denver and Cheyenne.

"Another hour," Cole says. "Then you stop."

"We'll see."

"One hour. That'll get you to Casper."

There's a burner cell phone resting in one of the cupholders between the seats. Sean bought it before he left Houston. He powered down his own phone and popped out the SIM card. He doesn't know how far the police will go to track him down, but he's seen the news reports. He knows they're looking for him.

He picks up the burner cell and tries calling Molly, and when it goes to her voicemail he leaves her a message. He tells her about what happened at the Galleria and assures her that he's okay. She shouldn't worry. He's coming for her.

He thumbs the red button to end the call.

"How many times have you left her that message?" Cole says.

"Three or four."

"More like six," Cole says. "She won't get it. They take everybody's phone. How did she put it? *They tie them in a sack and throw them down a well.*"

Sean makes another call, this time to a number he found on the website of Long Meadow Ranch, the place that's hosting Molly's retreat. No one answers there either, and he has to leave another message. He says it's an emergency and asks them to have Molly call him as soon as possible.

"Long Meadow Ranch," Cole says. "Bunch of hippies on horseback doing sun salutations. They probably don't even have voicemail in Montana. They're still using answering machines. Right now there's a little red light blinking in the farmhouse, but nobody sees it. They're all dancing around a fire outside, chanting about their chakras."

Sean puts the phone away and turns on the radio and keeps driving.

Sunday morning. A motel room in Casper, Wyoming. Sean wakes to the sound of the burner cell phone ringing. He snatches it from the bedside table, thinking it's Molly.

It's the alarm he set before he went to sleep. Seven o'clock.

He turns it off and closes his eyes. Only for a minute, he thinks. When he wakes again it's almost nine.

At the diner next to the motel, he orders breakfast at the counter: eggs and bacon. He eats fast. When he looks up, the waitress is staring at him, and he thinks she may have recognized him from the news. He lets her have a big smile. People on the run don't go around smiling. She smiles back and gives him the check.

Then it's gas at the Exxon station and back on I-25. It's a clear morning when he leaves Casper, but after an hour he's driving under high white clouds. Another hour and I-25 has joined up with I-90. The clouds are lower and grayer. There's a Taylor Swift song on the radio when the rain starts. Little pinpoint drops on the windshield. Sean turns on the wipers to clear them away.

The wipers move sluggishly, as if time has slowed down.

"That's not good," Cole's voice says.

Sean switches the wipers off, then on again. Now they're moving at the customary rate.

"That's your alternator," Cole says.

"It's fine," says Sean.

"My dad was a mechanic," Cole says. "But what do I know?"

Fifteen minutes later Sean is coming up on an exit for a town called Ranchester. The wipers go sluggish again and the radio cuts out. The car starts to slow. Pushing the accelerator doesn't help. Sean steers for the exit and feels the engine stall. He lets the car roll down the ramp and eases it to the shoulder as the momentum runs out. When it stops, he shifts into park, turns off the ignition, and tries to start it again. Nothing.

"Battery's dead," Cole says. "That's what happens when your alternator craps out."

Sean uses the burner phone to search for towing services. There seem to be only two within thirty miles. He manages to get through to one of them, and the man says to sit tight. He can be out in forty minutes. It takes him more than an hour.

He's a thirtysomething guy with a ruddy face. Unshaven. Wearing blue jeans and a gray uniform shirt with his name on the pocket: EUGENE.

He listens to Sean's story as he's hooking the car up to the tow truck. The rain has moved on.

"Sounds like your alternator," Eugene says.

"That's what I thought," says Sean.

Cole chuckles.

"Your best bet," Eugene says, "I take you into Sheridan."

"How far is that?"

"Twenty minutes back the way you came."

"There's nothing closer?" Sean asks. "Maybe in Ranchester?"

"Ranchester has a campground and a bar. And the T-Rex Natural History Museum, which is one room and kind of a letdown. What it doesn't have is a repair shop."

"Then I guess we're going to Sheridan."

The cab of the tow truck smells mildly of sweat and grease. There's a picture of a curvy blonde taped to the dash. Eugene says it's his girlfriend. It seems improbable.

Eugene drives at the limit on I-90, but to Sean it feels slower. When they reach Sheridan, it's bigger than Sean expected. He counts three hotels on Main Street. There's a Mexican restaurant and a Domino's Pizza. The auto shop is on a side street off Main. The sign says: BENSON'S. It's a cinderblock building with two repair bays, and the whole thing looks to be shut up tight.

"It's closed," Sean says.

"Yeah," says Eugene. "It's Sunday."

"I can't wait," Sean says. "I need my car. I need to keep moving."

"That's what I figured. I could take you to other places, but none of them are gonna be open. Art Benson is the guy you want. Tell you the truth, he's in his sixties and his hands have started to shake. But what you need, it's not brain surgery. He can replace an alternator. No problem."

"Can he do it today?" Sean asks.

"He can if he's in the mood and if you offer him a little extra. I'll call him for you. He'll be in church now and he generally has Sunday dinner at his daughter's, but with any luck . . ."

It's three o'clock when Art Benson turns up, driving a Ford pickup freshly washed and waxed. Eugene is long gone, and Sean is leaning against the hood of his car. Benson is thin and stooped and gray. When he walks over to Sean, his left foot drags a little. He sticks out a hand and says, "Hello, Texas."

Sean is startled, but only for an instant. His car has Texas plates.

Benson raises the door of one of the bays, and Sean puts the car in neutral and pushes it in. He pops the hood while Benson fetches a socket wrench and rolls up his sleeves. "Well, let's see," the man says.

He disconnects the battery cable and loosens the belt and moves it aside. There are four bolts holding the alternator in place, and he goes to work on them with the wrench. His hands seem steady enough.

"Texas," he says. "You wouldn't be from Houston, would you?"

A casual question. Maybe too casual.

"No," Sean says. "Dallas."

"Hell of a thing, what happened in Houston."

"That's the truth."

Benson goes quiet, bent over under the hood, turning the bolts. Then he finds something more to say: "That fella Keen, he needed to be put down. Some men, they're like rabid dogs. The only thing to do is shoot them. It's an act of mercy."

"I guess so," Sean says.

All the bolts are loosened now. Benson starts spinning them off with his fingers.

"Where you headed, son?" he asks.

Sean has a lie ready. "Washington State. I've got family in Spokane."

"When my second wife left me, she moved to Spokane. Never been tempted to visit."

The last bolt comes off and Benson unplugs the alternator. He carries it with him through a gray steel door into a back room out of sight. When he returns he's shaking his head.

"You don't have a replacement?" Sean says.

"Thought I did. But no. Have to take a run down to O'Reilly's. It's not far."

"And they'll have it?"

"Should."

Sean would like something more definite, but he surrenders and watches Benson limp to his truck and drive away.

He's alone in the repair bay. And then Cole is beside him.

"The guy's wily," Cole says.

"Maybe," says Sean.

"He knows who you are."

"Seems to."

"Or he's just making conversation. You have to wonder: Was he telling the truth about not having the part?"

"Yeah, I wonder."

"You could check. If he left the door unlocked."

Sean walks to the steel door and tries the handle. It's locked.

"Huh," Cole says.

Sean leans against the fender of his car with his arms crossed. He can feel the shape of the Glock in its shoulder rig. He ditched his gray jacket back in Houston. Now he's wearing a blue one.

The clouds have drifted off and the sun is out, but it's cool in the repair bay.

Ten minutes later Sean is looking out at the parking lot and the street, waiting for Benson. He sees a sheriff's cruiser glide by.

"Well, shit," Cole says.

The cruiser doesn't stop. It disappears down the street.

"Another thing you have to wonder," Cole says. "Would you shoot a cop, if it came to it?"

Sean frowns. "I'm not shooting any cops."

A few minutes pass and the cruiser comes back. It rolls to a stop across the street. Benson's truck appears a moment later. It pulls up beside the cruiser and there's a conversation Sean can't hear. Then the truck draws into the lot.

Benson climbs out. He's carrying a cardboard box with a new alternator in it. He looks sheepish.

"I owe you an apology," he says.

Sean can feel the weight of the Glock underneath his jacket. "What for?"

Benson nods in the direction of the cruiser. "My son-in-law," he says. "I told him you were here in my shop. He didn't believe me. Said he'd have to see for himself."

Sean uncrosses his arms. "Now he's had a chance to see."

"I wouldn't want you to misunderstand," Benson says, setting the box on a workbench. "You're safe here. He only wants to shake your hand, for what you did down there in Houston."

Across the street, Benson's son-in-law waits in the cruiser with the window rolled down.

"Can I wave him over?" Benson asks.

"Be careful," Cole says. "Next they'll have you down at the Legion hall, high-fiving with the veterans and the Elks and the Knights of Columbus."

Sean ignores him. "That's fine," he says to Benson. "But then I'll need to be on my way."

By four thirty he's back on the road. Benson didn't want to take any money for the work on the car, but they compromised. Sean paid a hundred fifty for the part and nothing for the labor.

The only other cost was a few minutes of talk with Benson and his son-in-law. They wanted to know what it was like, shooting Henry Keen.

Sean told them it happened fast and didn't seem quite real. When that didn't sound like enough, he told them he felt as if something had been guiding his hand—like it was meant to happen.

They nodded at that. Both of them solemn and thoughtful.

"You got away easy," Cole says in the car. "I was sure they were gonna make you show them the gun."

Sean puts the radio on, but he can't find any music he likes. He turns it off and cracks the window and feels the air on his face. Before long he crosses the state line into Montana.

There's still a long way to go. Two hundred thirty miles to Long Meadow Ranch and Molly.

12

Jimmy Harper

Jimmy and Nick spend Saturday night at the Airport Marriott in Houston. Sunday morning they're on the first flight to Bozeman. There's a stopover in Salt Lake City, and they're in Montana by one in the afternoon.

They rent a car and their first stop is a sporting goods store. Jimmy sends Nick in with a pocket full of cash. He comes out with a shotgun and a box of shells and two carbon-steel hunting knives.

Their second stop is at a hardware store for a bag of zip ties and a hacksaw. Then they get lunch at a McDonald's drive-through and head for Clyde Park.

Nick takes the wheel. Jimmy, in the passenger seat, saws off the barrel of the shotgun. The drive takes less than an hour, the first half running east on I-90, the rest running north on a two-lane highway labeled Route 89. It's farm country, rolling hills, mountains in the distance.

Route 89 turns into First Avenue when it passes through Clyde Park. There are a handful of streets branching off from it. Jimmy and Nick take Brackett Creek Road, which curves west and crosses the Shields

River by way of an old wooden bridge. Five miles on, there's a turnoff for Long Meadow Ranch. Jimmy has Nick drive by and turn around and come back again. He knows from the Long Meadow website that there's a farmhouse and a stable for the horses and a barn that's been converted to a yoga studio. There are cabins where the guests stay and a dining hall where they eat. But the only thing visible from the road is the barn. Jimmy doesn't know the layout, and the map on his phone is no help. The satellite image isn't detailed enough.

"Are we driving in?" Nick asks.

That would be the worst option, Jimmy thinks. He doesn't know if Molly's still here; Sean might have already come and gone.

They'll need to do some reconnaissance.

"No," he says.

They drive back into town. Jimmy is hoping for a visitors' center but he's disappointed. There are only a few shops and the Clyde Park Tavern. But there's a post office, and in the lobby they find a rack of brochures meant for tourists. There's one for a canoe livery and another offering guided hikes in the Gallatin National Forest. There's a place that rents mountain bikes by the day or by the hour.

The most promising item is a foldout map of nearby horse trails. Long Meadow Ranch shows up on the map, with a couple of rectangles that seem to represent buildings. It's not much use in itself, but it gives Jimmy an idea. He turns to Nick and says, "When's the last time you rode a bike?"

Molly Winter

Kate rides up beside her and says, "You holdin' those reins right?"

Molly laughs.

There are twelve women on horseback spread out along the trail, and Kate and Molly are in the middle of the group. At the front of the line is Barbara Holland, the woman who's running the retreat. She's lean and leathery and wears her silver hair cut short under a wide-brimmed hat. Barbara has very particular ideas about how the reins should be held: one in each hand, looped around the first three fingers (pointer, middle, and ring); thumbs pointed up and slightly toward each other; hands five inches apart and a little above the saddle; elbows bent about ninety degrees.

Molly and Kate got it wrong at first. Barbara wasn't shy about correcting them. Now it's a joke between them. Kate is especially good at imitating Barbara's voice; she gives it a bit of rasp, as if she's been breathing too much trail dust: *You holdin' those reins right?*

Kate is a real estate agent from San Diego. She's ten years older than Molly and had a child when she was young. Now that her son is off at college she's trying things she always wanted to try: surfing and hang gliding and riding horses.

Molly likes her. Which is a good thing, because they're sharing a cabin. The other women arrived here already paired up: they're friends or sisters or mothers and daughters. Molly and Kate, the only two singletons, wound up together by necessity.

The trail runs alongside a pasture for a while and then climbs up into a forest of pines and birches. At odd intervals, a space opens up between the trees, providing a view of distant mountains. Kate keeps pace with Molly for a quarter mile, then moves up along the line to chat with a schoolteacher from South Carolina.

Molly stretches tall in the saddle and breathes. She takes things in: the scent of pine needles and the earthy smell of her horse; the feel of the reins laced through her fingers; the chill in the air that hints of the coming winter, even though it's only October. She thinks of Sean and the last time they talked. She told him she was going on this retreat to breathe, and it's true. He's a cautious man, with good reason, and his caution has rubbed off on her. She used to love riding horses when she was a girl, and for that reason, paradoxically, she almost didn't come here. Because riding horses was something from her past, and she and Sean have made a break with their pasts.

But that way of thinking will do you in, if you let it. It's confining, and Molly doesn't want to be confined. She wants to breathe.

She's fallen into the rhythm of this place: meditation before break-fast; long yoga sessions that start mid-morning and last till noon; trail rides after lunch; stretches of free time throughout the day and in the evenings, with lectures here and there that you can attend or not as you please. She slips away when she wants to. Sometimes she walks down to the pond on the north end of the ranch; sometimes she watches the horses run free in the field near the stable.

The horse they've given her to ride is a brown mare named Maggie. Which is only logical, Molly thinks. Maggie is short for Margaret, which is her name too. The horse is gentle and sure-footed, and Molly believes they've developed an understanding. She's not worried about being thrown off.

She would like to get Maggie up to a canter or even a gallop to see what she can do. She remembers what it felt like when she was a kid: the freedom of riding fast. But all the trail rides here are conducted at a stately walk. The teacher from South Carolina tried to trot her horse around the paddock once, and Barbara gave her a scolding.

She was afraid the woman might be injured, no doubt. She was wor-ried about liability.

Molly wonders what Barbara would say if she knew she was preg-nant. It's a hypothetical question, because Molly's not going to tell her. She hasn't even been to a doctor yet; she's only taken a drugstore test. She's a few weeks along and very far from showing. She's not going to let it prevent her from riding.

A twenty-year-old from Boston moves up alongside her on the trail. The girl's name is Robin and she's here with her mother; the two of them are wearing matching cowboy hats and denim jackets. A lot of the women brought digital cameras, because they knew they'd have to give up their phones. Robin has a camera in her right hand and the reins of her horse gathered in her left. Barbara would probably frown on the arrangement, but Barbara isn't looking.

Robin raises the camera to shoot a selfie. She takes some time to get the angle right, because her mother is riding behind her and she wants her in the frame too. The shutter clicks. Afterward she glances at Molly and looks concerned. Molly smiles to let her know it's okay.

It's a problem that Molly has thought about: showing up in pictures. Because pictures get posted online, and you never know who might see them. She found a solution on her first night here. She had a talk with Kate and made up a story about an ex-boyfriend who was sort of a stalker and prone to harassing her online. Even seeing her picture was enough to set him off. Kate spread the word, and now everyone knows that Molly is camera shy.

Robin holds up the camera again, but Molly doesn't mind. She can tell she's not going to be in the frame. Up ahead on the trail, there's some commotion, and Barbara's voice calls out for everyone to stop.

"You're caught," Molly says to Robin. "I don't know why you thought you could get away with that, holding two reins with one hand."

The girl smiles.

That's not the reason they're stopping, of course. Molly pats Maggie's neck gently and looks ahead. There's someone else on the trail. They've encountered other riders before, but this is different.

It's a young guy with a bike.

Nick Ensen

He was never any good at riding a goddamn bike.

He didn't tell Jimmy that. What he told Jimmy was: *Sure, I can ride. It's been a while, but you don't forget, right?*

Nick thought he could manage. He always did okay on a flat, level surface. A street or a parking lot. No sweat. But if he had to weave around potholes or go down steep hills, he got skittish.

And he never once rode in the fucking woods.

It started out okay. He found his balance and got the bike into the right gear. He felt good, picking up speed, flying along the trail. Then he bumped over a tree root or some damn thing and slid on a patch of mud and *bam* he's sprawled on the ground with his arm torn up. A strip of skin scraped off, four inches long.

One good thing: it's not bleeding much, just sort of seeping. Nick picks himself up, and one knee hurts like hell from the fall, but he'll live. He stands the bike up and doesn't see any damage, so after a minute he climbs on and starts to pedal. Right away he knows something's wrong. The front tire's gone soft.

He hops down and walks the bike along the trail. On top of everything else, he thinks he's lost. He should call Jimmy, but it's not a call he wants to make.

Turns out he doesn't have to. He hears voices up ahead on the trail, and before long the first rider comes into view: a tough-looking old woman who fixes him with a dark stare.

She gets down from her horse and Nick thinks she's going to give him a hard time. Maybe he's not supposed to ride a bike here. But what it is—she's concerned. Because he looks like hell. His clothes are dirty from the fall and there's a trickle of blood running down his arm.

He finds himself telling her what happened, and she washes his arm with water from a canteen. Out of a saddle bag comes a big pad of gauze and she lays it on the wound and tapes it down. All the while, there's a line of other women behind her on the trail, looking on.

This is where his luck turns. The old woman is from the ranch, which is right where Nick wants to go. She tells him they're heading back there now and he's welcome to come with them as long as he follows at the end of the line and doesn't spook the horses. She'll find someone to help him with the bike or give him a ride into town.

Nick accepts her offer and stands at the side of the trail, waiting for the women on horseback to file by. They're friendly and open and curious about him. They look him over and he looks back.

And there she is, in the middle of the group. She's dark haired and slim and not exactly what he expected, because he's only seen her in an old photo that Jimmy showed him on his phone.

But it's definitely her. Molly. The woman Jimmy's looking for.

Molly Winter

The guy with the bike bothers her, though she can't say why.

She tries not to think about him on the ride back to the ranch. There's a place where the trail comes down out of the forest, and she has to focus on keeping her balance in the saddle while the horse negotiates the descent. It's a good excuse for putting all other thoughts out of her mind.

After the ride, there's a whole ritual to go through: tending to the horses. First there's a cool-down walk around the paddock, and each rider gives her horse water. Then the bridles and the saddles come off, and it's time for grooming: with a currycomb and a stiff brush and a soft one, all under the direction of Barbara Holland and a woman named Arlene who works for her. Arlene never goes on the trail rides, but she seems to know everything there is to know about the horses.

When the grooming's done, Molly leads Maggie to her stall and slips off her halter and hangs it on a hook. She kept some slices of apple from lunch, and she feeds them to the horse and whispers that she's a good girl.

She wants a shower, so she walks to the cabin where she's staying. She finds that Kate got there ahead of her and had the same idea; she's in the bathroom with the shower running. Nothing to do but wait. Molly steps outside again and sits in a rocking chair; there are two in front of every cabin. The afternoon is fading and growing cooler. She looks across the yard at the main house.

The guy from the trail is there by the front steps, drinking from a bottle of water. He looks at her and looks away, and she spends a good five minutes thinking about whether he looked away too fast.

Silly.

He pays her no attention after that. He's tinkering with his bike, and Arlene comes along with an air pump to help him. Kate finishes her shower and Molly goes inside. Afterward, when she's clean and dressed and thinking about dinner, she looks out the window and the bike guy is gone.

13

Jimmy Harper

When Jimmy hears the results of Nick's recon mission, he's quiet for a long while. He's thinking about how to approach things.

One option is to wait, on the theory that Sean will come here sooner or later. That means staking out the entrance of the ranch, and there's only the two of them, Jimmy and Nick, and no telling how long the stakeout would last. Even if it were practical, it might not pay off. Suppose Sean doesn't come. Suppose he gets word to Molly and she slips away in the night. According to Nick, there are several cars parked on the ranch. One of them could be Molly's. Are they going to stop every car that drives out?

There is, of course, a second option. It seems desperate, but the more Jimmy considers it, the more he thinks it might be the best way.

He knows that Molly's here. He could take her.

Then Sean would have to come to him.

There are risks, but Jimmy thinks it could be done. He knows the layout of the place, because Nick has drawn him a map. He knows which cabin Molly's staying in and that she's got a roommate. Which makes it more complicated but not impossible. He might even be able to use the roommate as leverage. *Come with me or your friend dies.*

Jimmy thinks it over in the car, parked by the side of Brackett Creek Road, Nick in the passenger seat. If they go in after dark, if they're lucky, they might get away before anyone figures out what's happening.

He looks at the kid and wonders if he's going to be a problem. Jimmy has been cautious so far. He's paying Nick well for this little trip: five thousand dollars, with the promise of more if it goes on longer than a week. But he hasn't shared his mind with Nick any more than he's had to. Nick knows they're looking for Sean, but he hasn't asked what will happen when they find him. He hasn't asked many questions at all—even today, when Jimmy sent him to buy the shotgun.

Time to see what the kid's made of. He lays out the plan and Nick listens with his head bowed. He's fussing with the bandage on his arm.

When Jimmy comes to the end, Nick says, "We're not gonna hurt her?"

"No."

"Or the roommate or any of the others?"

Jimmy gestures in the direction of the ranch. "I've got no quarrel with anyone in there," he says.

"Okay."

"I can count on you?"

"Okay."

He sounds reluctant, but it's no more than Jimmy expected. He thinks Nick will come through.

"Good," Jimmy says. "We'll go when it's dark. That gives us a couple of hours. I want to stay here and keep watch, but you should return the bike to the rental place."

"Now?"

"We won't have time later. We'll be in kind of a hurry. While you're gone, pick up something for us to eat."

Nick nods and both of them get out of the car. They take the front wheel off the bike and stow it in the trunk. Jimmy slips the sawed-off shotgun under his coat and crosses the road. He finds a place along the tree line where he can watch the entrance to the ranch unobserved.

The tires stir up dust when Nick pulls off the shoulder and onto the road. After he's gone around ten minutes, Jimmy starts to think about the risk he's taking. If the kid has second thoughts, he can just keep on driving.

Jimmy smiles and shakes his head. There's nothing he can do about it now.

He thinks the kid'll come back.

Thirty minutes go by, then forty, and things begin to look grim. Jimmy takes out his phone to check his messages. Nothing from Nick, but there's a text from Adam Khadduri.

Progress? it says.

He ignores it. Slides the phone back into his pocket.

Five minutes later Nick pulls up with fish-and-chips from the Clyde Park Tavern.

Molly Winter

There's a bonfire after dinner.

It's brush cleared from the ranch and old wooden pallets. When it gets going, the flames rise ten feet in the air.

Fourteen women gather around it, guests and staff. They're sitting in the yard behind the farmhouse in folding chairs, drinking wine and beer. Kate tells a story about jumping out of a plane: being harnessed to her instructor and watching the ground coming toward her and wondering what it would be like if the parachute didn't open. The teacher from South Carolina has a guitar, and she plays songs by Patty Griffin and Mary Chapin Carpenter. Someone asks if she knows Don McLean, and suddenly there's a chorus of tipsy women singing "American Pie."

Molly is happy. She takes in the smell of the fire, and the sparks and the smoke rising up into the dark sky. Someone touches her shoulder and she turns to see Barbara Holland, who's just come out from the house. The woman never looks happy, but now she seems distraught.

She draws Molly aside and hands her something she hasn't seen for more than two days: her cell phone.

Barbara trips over the words of an apology. She's never there to answer the house phone during these retreats, but she tries to keep on top of the messages. This time it got away from her. There's a message—more than one—for Molly from Sean, and he says it's an emergency.

Molly powers up her phone, imagining the worst. There are only a few things that Sean would consider an emergency.

One in particular.

Barbara is rambling on next to her. "I'm so sorry. If there's anything I can do—" But Molly wants nothing from her, just wants to get away from her. "I'm sure it's fine," she says. "Sean exaggerates sometimes."

She walks away, toward the farmhouse, and Barbara stays behind. Molly types her password into her phone and there's a long string of voicemails waiting from a number she doesn't recognize. She listens to the latest one: Sean's voice, sounding weary and almost mechanical. As if he's practiced the story and has it down to essentials.

The story is bad: There was someone killing people at the Galleria, and Sean had to shoot him. Now his picture is all over the news on TV.

Walking along the side of the house, Molly calls him back. He answers after a single ring.

"Thank god," he says. "Where are you?"

"Still at the retreat," she says. "I just got—"

"It's okay. I'm coming. I'm almost there. Maybe thirty minutes away."

She rounds the corner of the house, and the cabins come into view. Something's not right. Each cabin has a light above the door, with a sensor to make it come on automatically after sunset.

The light above her door is out.

"Someone's here," she says to Sean.

"Who?"

The cabin is fifty yards away, but even with the light out she can see someone there, a shadowy figure standing in front of her door, his back to her.

"Who?" Sean says again.

"I don't know. But he's at my door."

"Get out of there."

"No, I'm not in the cabin. I'm watching from outside."

The shadowy man pushes the door open. He reaches up and the light comes on. He must have loosened the bulb before, and now he has twisted it back in. He moves inside and the door closes.

"I think it's Jimmy," Molly says.

"You're not sure?"

"I only saw him from the back."

"Did he see you?"

"No," Molly says. She has slipped back around the corner of the farmhouse, so even if he looks out the window now, he won't be able to see her.

"I'm coming," Sean says. "But you need to get away. The car you rented—can you get to it?"

It's parked alongside the driveway of the ranch. She would have to cross a lot of open ground to reach it. In any case, it doesn't matter.

"The keys are in the cabin," she says.

There's a beat or two when Sean is quiet on the line. Then he says, "You need to go where there are other people. You'll be safe. He won't come after you in a crowd."

It's a comforting thought, but Sean doesn't sound convinced. Molly isn't convinced either. She remembers the guy on the bike. It could be a coincidence that he showed up today, but she doesn't think so. If he's with Jimmy, there might be others. Who's to say what they might do?

Molly can hear the women at the bonfire singing. She likes them. She doesn't want to bring this trouble down on them.

"I'm not staying here," she says to Sean. "I don't need a car. I can find another ride."

Jimmy Harper

The lock on the cabin door was child's play.

Jimmy's inside now, sitting in the dark at a thrift-store writing desk by the window. Through a gap in the curtains he can see the farmhouse in the distance. There's a hedge between him and the backyard, but he can make out the glow of a fire on the other side.

That's where everyone must be. The other cabins seem deserted.

Nick is waiting in the car at the side of the road near the turnoff for the ranch. He's taken off the license plates.

If all Jimmy's wishes come true, it'll go this way: Molly will come to him. She'll walk through the door and he'll grab her. He has zip ties to bind her wrists. He has a hunting knife to control her. He has the sawed-off shotgun.

He's cutting strips from a bedsheet right now. He'll use them to improvise a gag.

Once he's got her, he only has to make a call. Nick will be here in half a minute with the car. Then Jimmy pushes Molly into the back seat and jumps in with her and they're gone.

That's the easy version. It might not happen that way.

Watching through the window, Jimmy sees someone emerge from the far side of the farmhouse. In the dark, at a distance, it's only a silhouette. It could be Molly, or it could be one of the other women.

Whoever it is, she walks from the farmhouse to the barn and disappears inside.

Jimmy waits for her to come out again. She doesn't. If it's Molly, she could slip away through a different door and he wouldn't be able to see her.

He takes out his phone and dials Nick.

"I need you to check something out."

Molly Winter

There was no way to avoid it, crossing from the farmhouse to the barn out in the open.

But once Molly is in the barn, she has cover. She passes through the yoga studio to a side door. From here, there's no line of sight to her cabin. The stable is in the way.

That's where she wants to be.

She jogs across the grass and slips between the rails of the paddock fence. The stable doors have nothing holding them shut but an iron latch. The hinges make hardly any noise.

It's dim inside, but there's a row of switches on the wall. She flips one of them and a single bulb flicks on up in the rafters. It's all the light she wants to risk, and it's enough to see the rack on the wall that holds the grooming tools: combs and brushes and picks for cleaning horses' hooves.

Molly takes down one of the picks. It's a sharp metal hook—the closest thing to a weapon she's going to get. She tucks it handle first in her back pocket.

Maggie's stall is the fourth on the left. The horse shifts around when she opens the door.

Molly touches her neck. Whispers, "Good girl. Will you take me for a ride?"

She puts Maggie's halter on first, then the bridle. Drapes the saddle pad over the horse's back, then lifts the saddle into place. The girth is next—the straps that secure the saddle. Molly's had practice with it; she knows how tight to cinch it.

Maggie is breathing a little heavy with the saddle on. Nervous. Molly touches her flank to soothe her.

"We'll be all right," she whispers.

She plans to ride around the far side of the barn, down to the pond on the northern edge of the ranch, then pick up the trail that leads through the woods. If she's lucky, no one will see her. There's a branch of the trail that leads to Brackett Creek Road, and she considered going that way, but the turnoff for the ranch is on Brackett Creek Road and for all she knows Jimmy might have someone watching it. She'll take a different branch, a longer route, south and east to Castle Mountain Road. She'll meet up with Sean there.

"There's a place where the horse trail crosses the road," she told him. "It has a yellow sign to mark it. You won't miss it. That's where I'll be."

She walks the horse down the broad aisle between the stalls. The other horses stir as they go by. Molly listens at the stable doors without opening them. She hears nothing but the huff of Maggie's breathing.

There's a row of lead ropes hanging in coils by the doors. Molly takes one down. She doesn't need it now, but she'll want it at the end of the line. She'll need to tie the horse to a tree so she doesn't wander off and the people from the ranch can recover her.

Molly puts her left arm through the coiled rope and brings it over her head. She wants both hands free.

Now she's ready. But as she's about to open the stable doors, she sees the flaw in her plan. She's been focusing on her need to get away, but not on what will happen when she's gone. If Jimmy doesn't realize she's gone, he's bound to search the ranch for her. Which could put the other women in danger.

She can't leave without warning them.

She'll have to tell them a story. Not the truth, but something convincing enough to put them on guard. It dawns on her that she's already laid the groundwork with her story about an abusive boyfriend. She can tell Barbara and the others that he's found her somehow and he's here.

She'll say she's in fear for her life, which is true. Then she'll ride off, with or without Barbara's blessing. Barbara will handle things as she sees fit. She'll probably call the police. By the time things get sorted out, Molly will have met up with Sean.

It's not as clean a getaway as she had hoped for, but it should work. She opens the doors and leads Maggie out of the stable. A light grip on the bridle is enough to guide her. The paddock gate is off to the right, and Molly is ready to go that way when she hears someone singing.

Bye, bye, Miss American Pie . . .

She turns left instead and moves along the side of the building. She reaches the corner and pokes her head around it. From here she can see the cabins.

There's Kate stepping up to their cabin door, drawing her key from her pocket.

Molly's heart sinks. She's about to call out to Kate, but at that moment Maggie lets out a snort and pulls away. The bridle slips from Molly's fingers. And before she can react, a hand claps onto her shoulder from behind.

Jimmy Harper

Jimmy sees the woman approaching the cabin, and he's ready.

She walks through the door, eases it shut behind her, and tosses her key onto the writing desk. Jimmy comes out of the bathroom with a pillowcase. He pulls it over her head before she can turn around.

He pushes her onto one of the beds, tells her not to struggle or he'll kill her. He has the zip ties ready, two of them looped together. He slips them around her wrists and tightens them. He's got two more for her ankles, but they're harder to get on. She tries to kick him. He has to punch her to settle her down.

He ties the gag on under the pillowcase. Tells her to be still and she won't get hurt.

She seems docile enough now, but for good measure Jimmy takes out another zip tie and secures her bound wrists to the headboard of the bed.

He can hear her crying as he returns to the window.

When he looks out, he sees Molly running past the cabin toward the woods.

Molly Winter

It's the bike guy.

She slips free of him and chases after the horse, but Maggie is already halfway across the paddock.

The bike guy catches Molly, gets both his arms around her from behind, and tells her to stay calm, he's not going to hurt her. Molly tries to break free, but he's stronger, so she follows his advice. She stays calm.

Molly has given thought to this moment. She's known for years that someone might come for them, for her and for Sean. She remembers everything Sean told her.

When they come, they may be stronger than you. They probably will be. But sometimes you can use their strength against them.

The bike guy pulls at her, but this time Molly doesn't try to get away. She sets her feet and bends her knees. Launches herself back against him.

He goes over—both of them go over together—but he lands on his back on the ground and she lands on top of him. He lets out a grunt that turns sharp at the end like a squeal, and she rolls off him and scrambles to her feet. He's clutching at his stomach. There's something silver there.

The hoof pick. It was in her pocket.

Molly looks around. Maggie is trotting along the paddock fence. Spooked. Wild. In the distance, the door of Molly's cabin is closed. Kate must be inside. And Jimmy's in there.

The bike guy is still on the ground. He plucks the hoof pick from his stomach. The tip of the hook is dark with blood.

He starts to get up. And Molly runs.

14

Jimmy Harper

Jimmy picks up the sawed-off shotgun. His knife is in a sheath on his belt. The extra zip ties are in his coat pocket. There's nothing else he brought with him.

He wipes his fingerprints from the doorknob with a strip of bedsheet on his way out.

The moon floats in the sky, half-full, over the peak of the barn. Molly has disappeared into the trees. Nick runs up from the direction of the stable. There's blood on his shirt.

"She stabbed me," he says.

"Come on," says Jimmy.

There's a footpath that leads into the woods. It climbs up a slope and bends around to the southeast. Jimmy runs along for almost a quarter mile with Nick behind him. The path is a dark ribbon unfolding ahead of them, and it passes through a small clearing and joins up with a wider trail: a horse trail running roughly north to south.

Jimmy follows the trail south, thinking that momentum would have carried Molly along this way. He slows and fishes his flashlight from his pocket and scans the ground. It's soft here and he can make out footprints. They look fresh. He clicks off the light and keeps going.

Another half mile or so and the trail rolls down into a shallow depression and rises up again. A little farther on, it splits into two trails, one bending west and the other east.

"Which way?" Nick says.

Jimmy gets his flashlight out, but the ground is harder here. No telling which branch of the trail Molly followed.

"We split up," Jimmy says.

Nick Ensen

It hurts to run.

Nick had a cousin once who got stabbed with a steak knife, all the way to the handle. Right about the same place, next to his belly button. It fucked him up, cut through his muscles. For a long time, he couldn't walk around without moaning.

This is bad, but it's not *that* bad.

Nick feels it with every stride he takes, but it's not wrecking him. Which means the wound isn't too deep. He thinks he'll be okay.

He wants to be the one to catch her now, the girl. He won't make the same mistake, being all nice about it, thinking she'll surrender. Next time it's going to go hard. Nick has one of the knives Jimmy had him buy. It's on his belt. Anybody gets cut next time, it won't be him.

He tears along the trail, downhill now in the dark. He picks up speed. The trail winds back and forth, and he expects to see the girl around every bend. She can't be far ahead. If she came this way.

If.

He keeps on, but he's starting to have doubts.

Then he thinks he hears her.

Molly Winter

It was reckless, running past the cabin. Molly knew.

But all she could think of was Kate in there. She wanted to lure Jimmy away from her.

If nothing else, she hopes she's done that.

Her breathing is heavier than it should be. Molly ran track in school, but that was ten years ago. Her endurance is not what it was then. Still, she thinks she's going to make it. It can't be much farther to Castle Mountain Road.

Another mile? Less, she thinks.

She'll make it, and Sean will be there.

Up ahead, something darts across the path. A mouse or a chipmunk. Molly takes in a sharp breath. Cool air.

She feels it even before she hears it—someone behind her.

She dodges right, off the trail, into the woods. She stops and listens. Perfectly still. She can feel her heart pumping.

With the moonlight, she can see him through the trees. The bike guy. He slows to a jog and then to a walk. Hands on his hips. Listening for her.

He walks past the spot where she left the trail.

She looks around. Pinecones on the ground, some bigger than her fist. A few feet away: a broken branch, long as a walking stick, sharp on one end. Molly takes a slow step toward it, then another. She bends to pick it up. The bike guy turns in a circle on the trail.

Molly waits for him to move on. He doesn't. She picks up a pinecone. Feels the weight of it in her hand.

She thinks of another thing Sean told her once.

When they come for us, you should run if you can. But if you have to fight, you fight. You're a good person. You don't want to hurt anyone. They'll count on that. It will make you hesitate. But they won't hesitate. They'll be ruthless. So you have to be ruthless. You have to be willing to do damage.

With the branch in her right hand, Molly tosses the pinecone across the path. It lands in the brush and the bike guy turns toward the sound. He takes something from his belt. A knife. He moves toward the far side of the trail. Molly charges at him, two hands on the branch now. He hears her and spins around, and she jabs the sharp end at his left eye.

He jerks his head back at the last moment and the branch misses his eye, but it tears a gash in his cheek. His scream breaks the quiet of the woods. She goes for the eye a second time and once again he jerks away, but the effort throws him off balance. He falls over backward, landing hard, dropping the knife. His hands move to shield his face.

Molly stands over him and hears Sean's voice in her head: *You have to be ruthless.* The bike guy is covering his face, but his neck is exposed. She brings up the branch again, but her heart is racing, she's trembling.

She's not that ruthless.

She can't leave him like this though. She hasn't done enough damage. She doesn't want him coming after her.

The lead rope she took from the stable is still coiled around her. She thinks about tying him up, but it would be a struggle and would take time, and she doesn't know where Jimmy is.

Instead she reverses the branch in her hands, holds it like a baseball bat, and brings it down hard on the side of the bike guy's head. He groans and tries to get away from her, sliding along the ground. Molly lifts the branch again and brings it down, four more times, the last time across the bridge of his nose. By then he's begging her to stop.

She drops the branch and picks up his knife and runs.

Jimmy Harper

Jimmy hears the scream and it stops him.

First he thinks it's Molly, that the kid caught her. But before long he's hearing his own name. It's Nick, calling for him. It sounds pitiful.

Jimmy leaves the trail he's on and cuts through the woods. It's rough going, and he wonders if he should have doubled back to the fork instead, gone the long way around. But he stays on course, weaving through the trees. He's got Nick's voice to guide him.

He finds him sitting cross-legged on the ground, one hand in his lap, the other covering his cheek. Blood running between his fingers. He's rocking forward and back.

"Jesus, Jimmy," Nick says.

"Where is she?"

"She tried to poke out my fuckin' eye. With a stick."

Jimmy crouches down. Lays the sawed-off shotgun on the ground.

"Let me see," he says.

"She cut my face."

"Let me look."

Eventually the kid takes his hand away and Jimmy looks. The wound on Nick's cheek is deep and ugly.

"It's not bad," Jimmy says.

"Fuck you, it's not bad. It hurts like hell."

There's a smaller cut on Nick's forehead, and his face is a collection of bruises starting to swell.

"We'll get you fixed up when this is over," Jimmy says. "I promise you."

"When it's over? I think it's fuckin' over."

Jimmy's not in the mood to argue. "It's over when I say it's over, kid." He picks up the shotgun and stands. Looks down the path, orienting himself. "Did she go this way?" he asks.

Nick doesn't answer. He's covering his cheek again, rocking.

"This way?" Jimmy says again.

"Yeah," Nick says.

"On your feet. Let's move."

"I'm done running after her."

"Then you can walk," Jimmy says. "But we're going. Now."

He doesn't wait. He starts off at a jog, the shotgun in his right hand. He builds up to a run. The trail slopes downward. The night air feels cold in his lungs. The muscles of his legs burn. He pushes on.

He's heading roughly east now, he thinks. He left the trail map behind in the car, but he can almost picture it. If he keeps on in this direction, he'll come to a road. Castle something.

Castle Mountain Road. Maybe that's where Molly's heading.

Jimmy covers half a mile and he believes he's going to catch her. She's younger, but his stride is longer and one thing he's always had is endurance. He gets his second wind and puts on a burst of speed. He's running steadily downhill now and he feels good. Strong. Like a wild animal, leaping.

Another quarter mile and out of nowhere something tears at his ankle. He pitches forward, airborne, and lands on knees and elbows, his chin scraping the ground. He loses his grip on the shotgun and it skitters along the trail ahead of him.

Molly Winter

She watches him from the cover of the trees and she thinks he might leap over it—the lead rope that she's tied low and taut across the trail. But it snares him and he's undone. He lands with a groan and his face in the dirt. Molly steps out onto the trail and stops the shotgun with her foot.

She bends to pick it up. Stands straight again. Aims it at him.

"Hello, Jimmy," she says.

He turns onto his side, wipes blood from his chin with the back of his hand.

"Jesus," he says.

He plants his palms on the ground and tries to get his feet under him. His shoes skid over the dirt.

"Take it easy," Molly says. "Stay down."

He gets one foot set and starts to rise.

"I'm serious," Molly says. "Stay down or I'll blast your face off. Try me and see."

He goes still. Eases himself back down until he's sitting, one arm braced on the ground to hold himself up.

She keeps the gun trained on him. "Why did you have to come here?"

"You know why," he says.

"That's over," she says. "We can't change it. Let it go."

He's peering up at her in the moonlit dark. His eyes look black.

"Where's Sean?" he says.

"It's over," Molly says. "You don't even want him. You want somebody else, from years ago."

"Where is he?" Jimmy says again.

Molly takes a step back and shakes her head. "He's not the same," she says. "He's a different person now. What he did back then—he wouldn't do it now. If you want revenge, you might as well go after a random stranger. It would make about as much sense."

Jimmy's been breathing hard, but he's starting to get it under control. There's a line of blood running from his chin down his neck, but he makes no effort to wipe it away.

"I know who I'm after," he says.

Molly fades back another step. The road is behind her, only a few yards away. She hears a car's engine, faintly at first and then growing closer. She hears the car come to a stop.

Jimmy hears it too. His black eyes are watching her.

"That's my ride," she says.

She moves slowly backward down the trail, keeping the gun leveled on him.

"It's all over, Jimmy," she says. "Forget about us, and we'll forget about you."

He's still on the ground when she turns. She covers the final distance to the car at a run. Gets the passenger door open and slips inside. She shifts the shotgun to her left hand so she can close the door.

"Where'd that come from?" Sean asks her.

All the tension that's been built up inside her comes out in a laugh.

"Drive," she says.

15

Rafael Garza

Nobody ever holds still.

Something Garza's late partner used to say. Don Lefors.

Lefors liked to tell stories. Sometimes they rambled, but generally they had a point. There was one about a bricklayer named Art Charlemagne who called 911 on a late summer night to report that his wife had fallen down a flight of stairs. She was still breathing. He hoped someone would come fast.

The call came in at one in the morning, and by the time Lefors arrived at the scene it was closer to two. Art Charlemagne was long gone. His wife might have been breathing when he made the 911 call, but she had stopped before the EMTs arrived. The medical examiner opined that the fall had probably killed her, but there was more to it than met the eye. There were bloodstains on the carpet in the Charlemagnes' bedroom—along with three of Mrs. Charlemagne's teeth. They'd been knocked out with a masonry hammer. Lefors found the hammer under the bed.

Garza heard the story years later on a stakeout one night, the two of them in a car that smelled of coffee and fast-food hamburgers.

"I interviewed the Charlemagnes' friends and neighbors," Lefors said. "And they all told me the same things about Art. He liked to drink, and he liked to fish. He didn't much like to work or to get nagged by his wife. He had a temper that he usually kept under control, until he couldn't anymore. No one was surprised that he killed his wife, though some raised an eyebrow when they learned he'd used a hammer. They figured his bare hands would be enough."

Lefors drank from his takeout coffee and went on. "Took me two weeks to find him. One of his friends told me that whenever Art got hold of some money, he'd go down to the coast and rent a cabin. I put together a list of the places he'd rented before and checked them out one by one. I ended up at this little shack ten miles south of Corpus Christi. Green clapboard rotting away, and the shingles falling off the roof. I found the front door locked and the curtains closed, but when I walked around to the back I saw him: Art Charlemagne in cutoff jeans and a ball cap, sitting on a blanket in the sand with the Gulf of Mexico in front of him and a cooler of beer by his side.

"I told him where I'd come from and why, but it wasn't news to him. He knew someone would come. He started talking, without any prompting from me. He wanted to justify himself. It really was an accident, he said. His wife had tripped down the stairs trying to get away from him. I told him I had to take him in, even so. He wanted to bargain: just a few more minutes to feel the wind coming in from the ocean. That's all he wanted. Long enough to finish his beer. He turned his face out toward the waves and closed his eyes, but I kept mine open. I watched him.

"While I was watching him, a waitress he'd picked up at a truck stop came out of the cabin and crept up behind me. She went barefoot in the sand, and with the *shussh* of the waves I didn't hear her. Didn't know she was there until she clocked me on the back of the head with a cast-iron pan."

Lefors frowned, his coffee forgotten. "I was probably out for less than a minute, but I woke up in a hazier world. Blood in my hair and sand in the blood. The waves coming in slower than before. I rolled up to my feet and set off down the beach. I don't know why. I made it about a quarter of a mile before I stumbled through some kid's sand castle. His father started to give me hell, until he realized there was something wrong. I had a concussion."

"What happened to Art Charlemagne and the woman?" Garza asked.

"They got away, for a while. A month later they got picked up in New Mexico when Charlemagne tried to rob a convenience store. He'd run out of money. The point is he didn't hold still. I wanted him to, so I could catch him. But he didn't. Nobody does. You see what I'm saying?"

"Sure."

"I don't just mean that he ran. People keep living their lives, even when you're not watching. Charlemagne picked up that waitress and convinced her to run off with him to a cabin on the beach. He told her what happened to his wife—his version anyway—and she still fell for him. I didn't expect that. It never entered into my calculations. And it cost me."

Nobody ever holds still.

It's the first thing Garza thinks of Monday morning when he drives out to Long Meadow Ranch and sees a sheriff's cruiser parked at the roadside.

Garza has kept busy since his arrival in Bozeman. He's been tracking down passengers and flight attendants who might have spoken to Molly Winter on her flight from Houston to Montana. No one was any help—until this morning, when he found the woman who'd been in the aisle seat across from Molly's.

She was in her sixties, retired. She'd been flying home from a visit with her granddaughter. And she remembered Molly.

"People don't talk on planes anymore," she said to Garza. "They've got a laptop open, or earphones in their ears. They're in their own little world. It's a shame."

"But you spoke to Molly."

"Oh, yes. She had a book with her, but she kept it closed in her lap as much as she kept it open. Something about her, she seemed happy. Eager to get where she was going. I asked her if she had family in Bozeman."

"What did she say?"

"She shook her head. Told me she was on vacation. Heading to a retreat, at a ranch."

"Did she tell you the name of the ranch?" Garza asked.

"She might have," the woman said, looking off, trying to remember. "I don't recall. But it was a yoga retreat. With horses. Does that help?"

It did. Garza steps out of his car onto the dusty driveway of the ranch. There's a farmhouse in the distance with a throng of women gathered on the porch. Two men as well, in uniform. Sheriff's deputies. One of them catches sight of Garza and breaks away. Garza reaches into a pocket for his badge, and the deputy's hand goes instinctively to the gun on his belt.

Garza spreads his arms out. Offers his name with a big friendly smile. Lets the deputy study his badge.

"You're a long way from home," the deputy says, handing it back.

"I'm here on business," says Garza. "Looking for a woman named Molly Winter."

The deputy's eyes narrow. "That's interesting. What do you want her for?"

"Is she here? Did something happen?"

The deputy looks up at the sky, as if it might hold the answer. But there's nothing there, just a lot of clouds with the sun somewhere behind them.

"I guess you could put it that way," the deputy says. "*Something* happened."

It's a mess.

Molly Winter is gone. That much is clear. She's left behind her clothes and possessions and the car she rented at the airport in Bozeman.

Garza gathers the details—some from the deputies, some from the women. He talks first to Barbara Holland, who's running the retreat. But all she can give him are bits and pieces, and they don't fit together into anything that makes sense.

There's a series of phone calls from Sean Tennant to Molly, which Molly only learned about last night.

There's a horse that was saddled and bridled and left wandering in the paddock by the stable. Molly's horse—the one she'd been riding.

There's a tool found lying in the grass of the paddock. A hoof pick, stained with blood.

No one knows whose blood it is.

"Not Molly's," Barbara Holland says.

"What makes you say that?" Garza asks.

"Molly called me after she left," Barbara tells him. "She wouldn't say where she was, but she said she was okay. She wasn't hurt. She wanted us to check on Kate."

She's referring to Kate Domenico, the real estate agent from California who shared a cabin with Molly. Garza talks to her next, and she tells him a harrowing story about being attacked in the night, bound to a bed with zip ties, a pillowcase over her head.

She remained there for more than an hour, until Barbara and the other women found her after Molly's call.

When Garza asks her about her attacker, Kate looks frustrated. She never saw his face.

"What about his voice?" Garza asks. "Did he say anything?"

"'Stop struggling or I'll kill you.' It was sort of a whisper."

"Nothing more? He didn't ask you about Molly?"

"No," Kate says. "But I wondered if it could have been her stalker."

"She had a stalker?"

"An old boyfriend."

"Did she tell you his name?"

"No. It didn't seem like something she wanted to talk about. I think she only mentioned him to explain why she didn't want anyone to take pictures of her, in case they ended up online. She was afraid he would see them."

"Right."

"But her current boyfriend would know, wouldn't he?" Kate says. "The guy she lives with. Sean."

Garza smiles. She's been out of touch, he thinks. She doesn't know about the shootings in Houston.

"I'll ask him when I see him," Garza says.

He talks to the other women as the morning shades into the afternoon. By two o'clock he's no closer to figuring out what happened here. He doesn't know where to look for Molly or Sean. He calls in to his lieutenant, who listens to his report and tells him he should get on a plane and come home.

Garza ends the call and walks to his car. The drive back to the airport in Bozeman is fifty miles. He's halfway through it when his phone rings. His lieutenant, calling him back.

"This is loopy," the man says. "This whole damn thing."

"What?" says Garza.

"You sent some of Sean Tennant's tools to the lab, so they could lift prints."

"Yes."

"Well, they got a hit. Tennant grew up in Detroit. He served in the army, in Iraq."

"Must be where he learned to shoot."

"And his real name isn't Tennant. It's Garrety."

Garza feels a rush run through him. The road is straight and flat ahead of him and he's moving fast. He glances at the speedometer, sees the needle well past eighty. He eases back a little.

"There's one other thing," his lieutenant says.

"What's that?"

"There's a warrant out for Garrety in Michigan, from six years ago. It's worth looking into, I think. So maybe you don't come home yet. Maybe you take a detour instead."

16

Nick Ensen

Jimmy has the TV on again. It's getting on Nick's nerves.

The hotel room is a grim place: gray walls and brown carpet. The pillows are thin, and the sheets are stiff. It's not even a chain; it's something called the Blackfoot Inn. Named after the town—Blackfoot, Idaho.

There are two things in the drawer of Nick's bedside table. He looked. A Gideon Bible and a brochure for the Potato Museum.

Jimmy's sitting on the other bed, flipping through the cable news channels. They're all reporting on Molly Winter's disappearance from Long Meadow Ranch. They've made the connection between Molly and Sean, but they don't quite know what to say about this development. They've all hit on the same words to express their bewilderment: it's a "bizarre twist" in the Houston shooting story.

Nick lies back on his bed. The pillowcase is scratchy on his neck.

"My face hurts," he says.

"Take some more Tylenol," says Jimmy.

The Tylenol is useless, but there's no point in saying it. He's said it before.

Nick casts around for something else.

"I can't smell anything."

Jimmy chuckles. "You're not missing out. All I can smell is smoke."

"I thought this was a nonsmoking room."

"I guess somebody broke the rules."

Nick closes his eyes, tries to fall asleep. Minutes crawl by. He rolls sideways and sits up. Pain shoots through his abdomen. He winces, and the wincing hurts. He gets up and stalks off to the bathroom.

One yellow bulb in there, over the sink. Nick stands beneath it and looks in the mirror. His nose is a purple lump. His eyes are black and puffy. But at least he can open them now.

It's been twenty-four hours since Molly bashed his face with a tree branch.

When he caught up with Jimmy in the woods, his eyes were starting to swell shut. Jimmy had to take his arm to get him back to the car. A long walk in the dark. Nick thought it would never end.

He remembers getting a little hysterical in the car.

"Jesus, Jimmy," he said. "I'm bleeding. You gotta take me somewhere."

"Calm down," Jimmy said.

"I can't see. I can't see a goddamn thing."

"All right."

Hard to tell how fast Jimmy was driving, but Nick could feel every bend in the road in his gut. He thought he would throw up.

"I can't *see*. Do you get that? You gotta take me to a hospital."

"All right."

"You gotta take me *now*."

Jimmy's voice sounded bland and distant. "I'm taking you."

Nick couldn't count the time. It might have been twenty minutes. Not long enough to get to Bozeman. But Jimmy was slowing down. Nick felt the car turn, and it sounded like they were rolling over gravel.

Jimmy cut the engine and came around and opened the passenger door. Nick reached out and Jimmy's hand caught him and pulled him up.

"This way," Jimmy said.

It felt wrong. Stones under his feet, not pavement. No sound of other cars. No people. If they were at a hospital, there would be other people. There would be activity.

Nick felt a fear that almost made his knees buckle. He broke out in sweat.

His voice sounded like a child's. "I'm sorry, Jimmy."

He couldn't open his eyes. He didn't know where they were going or what Jimmy might do. His fear filled things in: any second now, Jimmy would grab his hair and pull his head back. Draw a knife across his throat. Leave his body by the side of the road.

"I'm sorry, Jimmy," he said, freezing in place. "Don't. Please don't."

Jimmy tried to pull him along. "Come on, kid. What's wrong with you?"

"I'm sorry. I promise I'll be good. I won't complain anymore."

Jimmy's grip tightened on his arm and they were moving again.

"I'm trying to help you. Come on."

They came to a set of steps and went up, and Jimmy knocked on a door. Time passed, and Jimmy knocked again, pounded this time. Nick heard the door rattle in the frame.

More pounding and a voice behind the door said, "Yes, yes. Hold on." An old man's voice. Nick heard a bolt turn. The door opened.

Now the voice was close and clear.

"Lord in his heaven. What happened to you?"

"We ran into some trouble," Jimmy said.

"So I see. But it's not my kind of trouble. There's an urgent care in Livingston, twelve miles down the road. They're open twenty-four hours."

"You're open twenty-four hours," Jimmy countered. "It says so on your sign."

"Look closer. It says twenty-four-hour emergency service. That's meant for farmers who call me in the middle of the night when their cows go into labor. Otherwise I open at nine in the morning and close at six."

"Well, we're here now," Jimmy said. "And this *is* an emergency."

Nick frowned. "Wait. Did he say 'farmers'?"

"Shut up."

"Did he say 'cows'?"

In the bathroom at the Blackfoot Inn, Nick leans close to the mirror, turns his head, and studies the stitches that run along his cheek. Courtesy of Richard Weatherby, doctor of veterinary medicine. The black thread stands out starkly in the yellow light.

He has no idea what Weatherby looked like, but he remembers the heat of the old man's breath on his skin. The bite of the needle. The tug of the thread.

Nick lifts his T-shirt and bares his stomach. He's got a bruise as big as a peach, just to the left of his navel. And more stitches, a line of them, shorter than the line on his face. He wonders if this is the end or if there's more sewing in his future. If he stays with Jimmy, how much more damage will there be?

Jimmy Harper

The kid comes out of the bathroom and lies down again, sulking.

Like he's been doing all day.

Jimmy has tried ignoring the problem. He's tried feeding it too, but Nick seems to have no appetite. The pizza and wings Jimmy ordered for dinner remain mostly untouched.

If this goes on, the kid will be useless.

Jimmy is the oldest of five children, and he has two of his own, so he's accustomed to dealing with childish behavior. When he was young, his father handled the discipline, and it generally went in two stages. If you acted up, you got yelled at, and if the yelling didn't work, you got hit.

Jimmy's ex-wife doesn't believe in hitting, so when it comes to their kids he tries to do things her way. Everything is a discussion. You talk about the kids' feelings, explain to them why things have to be a certain way. If that doesn't solve the problem, you put them in time-out.

One thing Jimmy knows: he isn't going to talk to Nick about his feelings. But yelling isn't likely to do any good either, and he needs to do something.

He switches off the television and swings around so he's facing Nick's bed.

"Sit up," he says.

Nick doesn't move.

"Please," Jimmy says.

It's a big production with a fair amount of sighing, but Nick sits up and plants his feet on the floor.

Jimmy takes a long look at the kid's face.

"It's getting better," he says.

Nick makes a noncommittal noise through closed lips.

"It is," Jimmy says. "And once we're back home, I'll make sure it gets taken care of properly. I give you my word."

No reply. Nick looks down at the floor.

"Hey," Jimmy says. "When I give you my word, that's solid. It's serious. Do you hear me?"

Nick nods, but he doesn't mean it. He lifts his head and looks around the room, at the door, the TV, the heavy curtains on the window, the painting of a sailboat on the wall. He's got something to say, and he's working his way up to it.

Eventually he gets there. "I don't know why we're doing this," he says.

It's a fair question, Jimmy thinks. And in a sense, the answer's simple. *Because I didn't break Sean Garrety's neck when I had the chance.*

But he knows he'll need to explain it better than that.

"It goes back a long way," Jimmy says. "Sean used to live with my family. He was my brother Cole's best friend, and we took him in because he had nowhere else to go. My mother and father were generous people. Then my father died. From a heart attack, from smoking and drinking all his life. I was twenty-eight years old and Cole was seventeen. Our three sisters were in between us.

"I had to step up. I'd been helping my father run his business, and now it was mine. My sisters were either married or away at college, but I had to look after them too. And Cole, who was still in high school. And Sean.

"The thing about Sean is, he was reckless. I'm not saying there was malice in him, but he didn't care about himself or about other people. He drank too much, and he drove too fast, and he hung around with deadbeats. And Cole was devoted to him, so Cole followed his lead.

"After they graduated, I hired them to work for me at the auto shop. Cole liked the work. But Sean, I don't know, maybe he thought it was beneath him. He quit after a couple of weeks. Ended up working at a home-improvement store instead.

"Next I heard, he wanted to go to college. I didn't think he had the temperament for it, but I helped him anyway. He got into Wayne State. Whether he went to any classes, I couldn't tell you. I think he was more interested in living in a dorm and partying. Cole met up with him every weekend, the two of them getting drunk and trying to get laid.

"Sean failed his classes and dropped out, and I stopped caring about what happened to him. I ignored him, until one night my mother came to me and told me Cole had enlisted in the army.

"It wasn't his idea, of course. Sean enlisted first. I imagine he thought it would be a big adventure. Now they were both going. In five weeks they would have to report to basic training.

"I tried to convince Cole he was being an idiot. I told him I'd get him a lawyer. We could say he was drunk when he signed up. Or something. If we couldn't get him out of it, I would have sent him to Canada. But he wouldn't listen to me.

"One night I went to see Sean. He was living in this dumpy apartment with peeling paint on the ceilings and scarred linoleum on the floors. I made him the same offer I'd made Cole. I'd hire a lawyer and get him out of it.

"'I don't want to get out of it,' he said.

"'How much are they paying you?' I asked him.

"'It's not about money,' he said.

"'But there's a signing bonus. Right?' I said. 'How much? Five thousand? Ten? Whatever it is, I'll match it.'

"'I'm not doing it for the signing bonus,' he said.

"I was already angry, and he was making it worse. 'Jesus,' I said. 'You're not really this dumb, are you? There's no reason to do it, if not for the money. Do you think it's gonna be like a movie?'

"'No,' he said.

"'You do,' I said. 'Look, I don't care what happens to you. But I can't have Cole going with you.'

"'I never asked him to,' Sean said.

"'You didn't have to,' I said. 'You know how he is. You need to stop him. This is not a game.'

"'I can't stop him,' Sean said."

Jimmy pauses. He takes a deep breath that's tinged with stale cigarette smoke.

"That wasn't true," he says to Nick. "Sean could have stopped him. And I could have stopped the whole thing. Sean and I were alone in his apartment, and I hadn't told anyone I was going to see him. I could have killed him without too much trouble. Snapped his neck. I could have disposed of the body. People would have thought he ran off. Cole never would have gone into the army on his own. The problem would have been solved.

"But I did nothing. I let Cole go to basic training. They both went. And later on, they went to Iraq."

Jimmy rubs his palm over his chin. There's a stillness in the room. The only sound is outside: an eighteen-wheeler idling in the parking lot.

Nick is watching him. Working up his courage again. He has another question.

"What happened?" he says. "Did your brother die over there?"

Jimmy bows his head and shakes it slowly side to side.

"No," he says. "Not over there."

17

BEFORE

Sean Garrety

Sean's tour of duty in Iraq lasted fifteen months, but out of all that time, what stuck with him was a few hours on a night in September. The night his platoon went to search a house in a slum neighborhood in Baghdad called Kamaliyah.

The owner of the house was Munir Zaman, a college professor who was having an affair with one of his former students. Zaman lived with his wife and four children in Sadr City. The Kamaliyah house was where he kept his mistress.

Sean saw a picture of her at the briefing before the mission. She had brown eyes and clear skin. A round face framed by a scarf that covered her hair.

A pretty girl. Munir Zaman's secret.

But not his only one. According to an informant, Zaman had welcomed the American invasion of Iraq in 2003 because he hated Saddam Hussein, but as the war dragged on he had become disillusioned. Now,

the informant said, he had thrown in his lot with the Jaish al-Mahdi—
the Shia insurgency—and he was allowing them to store weapons in
his house in Kamaliyah.

The informant was a cabdriver who sold marijuana on the side, but
he had provided good leads before. So at midnight Sean and Cole and
twenty other soldiers from their platoon rolled out of the main gate
of their base in a convoy of five heavily armored Humvees. They were
joined by the captain in charge of their company, a farm boy from
Indiana named Dalton Webber.

They drove north and east, crawling along at twelve miles an hour
with their headlights dark, using night-vision gear to scan the road
ahead. Looking for signs of roadside bombs.

Captain Webber brought the convoy to a halt a block away from
Zaman's house, and they approached it on foot. The temperature stood
at 96 degrees, down from a high of 108. They passed a series of squalid
houses with patchy roofs and torn-off siding. The lawns were nothing
but dirt.

"Aizdihar," Cole said.

Sean remembered the word from the mission briefing. It was the
name of the street. In Arabic it meant "prosperity."

They came to a section of chain-link fence with a bicycle resting
against it. Zaman's house was the second one past the fence.

Sean and Cole took the lead, with Captain Webber and the others
behind them. As they walked to the door, Cole went right and Sean
went left. Cole tested the knob, shook his head, and stepped back. Sean
moved in with the battering ram and swung it at a spot just above the
lock.

It should have sent the door crashing inward. But the door was
cheap. Hollow. The ram punched a hole through the wood.

"Shit," Sean said.

He wrestled it back out and tried again, aiming below the lock. This
time the door swung in and slammed against a wall.

Too much noise, Sean thought.

Ten soldiers entered the house: five moving through the first floor, five charging up a narrow staircase to the second. The rest set up a perimeter outside. Sean was the last one up the stairs. He moved along a cramped hallway that ran from the back of the house to the front, the floorboards creaking under his feet.

"Bathroom back here," someone shouted. "It's clear."

"Got something," said another voice in a different room. Sean stepped in and found a sergeant named Ross standing by a stack of wooden crates. Ross lifted the lid from one of them and inside were artillery shells. A dozen. Each one could be used to make an IED.

Sean reached for the lid of another crate, but before he could remove it he heard a scream from down the hall.

He ran toward the sound, came to a bedroom at the front of the house. The source of the scream was Zaman's mistress. Sean recognized her, even through the green tinge of night-vision goggles.

She'd been awakened by the noise of the front door crashing open and tried to hide under her bed. Cole had found her and dragged her out. She was still struggling with him.

He pushed her down to the floor and she sat there with her back against the bed. She was quiet for a moment, eyes wide, and then she let out a steady stream of Arabic that started out frightened and soon turned angry and indignant.

She'd been sleeping in a long nightshirt and her legs and arms were bare. Cole handed her a blanket to cover up.

"Take it easy," Cole said. "No one's gonna hurt you. I need to know if you're alone. Is anyone else in the house? Is Zaman here? Munir Zaman?"

She shook her head fiercely, said something sharp that no one understood. Sometimes when they rolled out, they brought a translator. But not tonight. The plan was to bring the woman back to the base to be questioned.

Cole tried to calm her. Explained to her in English that she needed to come with them. She might have understood some of it, Sean thought. If she'd been panicky before, she seemed to be getting it under control. Sean found her clothes on a chair and handed them to her, and she pulled them on over her nightshirt while he and Cole and two other soldiers stood by and made an effort not to stare.

They took her down to the ground floor, and Sean kept watch over her. While he'd been upstairs, his platoon mates had been searching the downstairs rooms. Now they rolled back a rug in the sitting room and discovered a trapdoor that opened into a crawl space less than four feet high. Captain Webber sent a young private named Park down there, and Park began passing up AK-47s. Twenty-five of them. After they came through, Park started handing up boxes of ammunition.

But the house had other secrets, apart from the trapdoor and the crawl space.

The sitting room opened into the kitchen, and the kitchen was where they found the safe.

It was next to the refrigerator and almost as large. A hunk of black steel with gold lettering on the door:

MOSLER SAFE & LOCK CO.
CINCINNATI, OHIO

"Cinci-fuckin'-nati," the captain said.

Sean heard him through the doorway. He was standing with his M4 pointed down and away from the woman. She was in a chair in a corner, hands folded in her lap.

"Bring her in here," Captain Webber said.

Sean brought her. Cole came, too, and lingered in the doorway.

The captain pointed to the safe. "Do you know the combination?"

The woman looked at him blankly.

He spun the dial back and forth. "The com-bi-na-tion," he said. "What is it?"

Her blank look gave way to a shrug.

The captain sighed. He tapped the safe with a gloved hand. "What's in there?" he said. "What's inside?"

Another shrug.

The captain crossed his arms and stood staring at the safe as if he could will it to open.

"How much do you suppose the damned thing weighs?" he said softly.

Sean had no answer.

Cole said, "Seven hundred pounds, at least."

Captain Webber nodded. "Well, somebody got it in here. I imagine we could get it out. But I don't think we'll fit it in a Humvee." He turned to Sean and Cole. "Do you?"

"No, sir," Sean said.

"You'd need a truck," said Cole.

"I guess you would," the captain said. "And if I send for a truck, we'll be here half the night." He glanced back at the safe. "But I would dearly like to know what's in there."

He reached for the dial and spun it right, then left, then right again, as if he might hit on the combination randomly.

"One in a million," Sean said.

The captain looked back at him.

"The numbers on the dial go from zero to ninety-nine," Sean said. "If there are three numbers in the combination, that's a million possibilities."

The captain gave the dial a final twist. "Do you know something about opening safes, Corporal Garrety?"

Sean shook his head. "Not really, sir." He looked at Cole, who was still in the doorway.

The captain saw him looking. "Do you have something to add to this conversation, Corporal Harper?"

"Sir?"

"Garrety seems to think you have something to add."

Cole gave Sean a dark look. "My father was a locksmith, sir."

"And?"

"He taught me a few things."

Captain Webber let out an impatient breath. "Did he teach you how to crack a safe?"

"He did his best," Cole said. "I never practiced on a Mosler, though."

The captain looked up at the ceiling, laughing. "Never practiced," he said. "Well, now's your chance."

Cole tried to teach him once.

Sean remembered: sneaking into the repair shop late at night, when they should have been sleeping. Cole had a key to the shop and another to the door of his father's private office.

The safe was in a corner behind the desk. A black hulk with a silver-gray dial.

They were fifteen years old.

They'd go into the office and find the bottle Cole's father kept in his desk drawer: Jack Daniel's. They'd drink a little at a time, because Cole's father was gruff and scary and mean. You wouldn't want him to catch you drinking his whiskey.

Sean remembered pressing his ear against the door of the safe, turning the dial, and listening. Cole telling him to picture the wheels that were in there—the tumblers. Each one had a notch, and if you could line up all the notches you could open the door. You had to turn the dial and search for the notches, and if you knew what to listen for, the sound would tell you when you found them.

Sean couldn't do it. But Cole could. His father changed the combination of the safe every month. With practice, Cole reached a point where he could open it every time.

In the house in Kamaliyah, he worked on the Mosler safe for more than an hour.

Captain Webber cleared the house so Cole could work. The other soldiers carried out the AK-47s and the crates of mortar shells, and the only people who remained were Sean and Cole and Sergeant Ross and the captain and Zaman's mistress. They were gathered in the kitchen with candles burning around the room because there was no electricity. Zaman's mistress sat at the table, her face unreadable. The captain sat with her. The sergeant leaned against a counter by the sink. Cole, with his gloves and helmet off, had pulled a chair up to the safe. Sean stood nearby, watching.

No one spoke, because Cole needed quiet. He laid his cheek against the black door to listen and turned the dial, sometimes fast, sometimes slow.

After almost half an hour, he pushed himself away and exhaled as if he'd been holding his breath. He ran the fingers of both hands through his hair and over his face.

"I got one," he said softly. "Fifty-seven."

"Fifty-seven," the captain repeated.

"Could be fifty-six or fifty-eight. But I'm pretty sure it's fifty-seven."

"Good," the captain said.

Cole went back to work, looking for the other numbers. Sean listened to the sound of the moving dial—but there were other sounds, too, and other movements: Zaman's mistress picking at her nails. Sergeant Ross drumming his fingers on the stock of his M4. Captain Webber shifting in his chair. The candle flames flickering.

Another forty minutes passed before Cole found the second and third numbers.

Thirty-one and twelve.

The final step was to put the numbers in the right order. There were six possible combinations and nothing to do but run through them. Cole worked the dial with a smooth confidence now.

Fifty-seven, thirty-one, twelve. Try the handle.

No.

Fifty-seven, twelve, thirty-one.

No.

Thirty-one, fifty-seven, twelve.

No again.

This part didn't require silence, but no one said anything and no one moved. Cole spun the dial four times to the right and started in on the next combination.

Thirty-one . . .

The candle flames wavered in the air.

Twelve . . .

Sean heard the crackle of the wicks burning.

Fifty-seven.

Cole worked the handle, and the black door opened.

Somewhere overhead, a floorboard creaked.

"What was that?" Sergeant Ross said.

"Fuck," said Sean, looking up at the ceiling.

Captain Webber looked up too. "You cleared those rooms."

"Yes," Sean said.

"Definitely," said Cole.

The captain grabbed Zaman's mistress by the arm. "Who's up there? Is someone up there?"

She turned away from him, her hair falling over her face.

The captain looked at Sean, then at Ross. "Go," he said.

Ross made it to the stairs first. Sean was close behind. Zaman's mistress slipped free of the captain's grip and tried to follow them. She passed from the kitchen to the sitting room, screaming in Arabic. The captain caught her and shoved her to the floor.

When Sean hit the top of the stairs, Ross was in the doorway of the bathroom. "It's clear," he said.

They moved together to the middle room—the one where they had found the mortars. It was empty now. Nowhere to hide but a small closet covered by a curtain. Sean tore the curtain away. "Clear," he said.

Which left the bedroom at the front of the house.

It held a full-size bed with a metal frame and a thin mattress. Space to hide underneath—that's where Cole had found the woman.

Sean took hold of the frame and jerked it upward, slamming the mattress into the wall.

There was no one underneath.

He dropped the frame to the floor. Sergeant Ross was standing by the closet. This one didn't have a curtain; it had a door. Ross reached for the knob. Sean got into position, took aim with his M4. "Ready," he said.

Ross swept the door open.

Clothes on hangers. Dresses. Blouses.

Sean lowered his rifle, then stepped forward and started tearing the clothes out and throwing them on the floor behind him.

Munir Zaman was a small man. Short and thin.

He was there at the back of the closet.

He was holding something in his right hand. Something silver.

Sean had learned a few phrases in Arabic. He'd never had a chance to use any of them, but he did now.

"Iisqat albunduqia!" he yelled. "Drop the gun! Drop it!"

Zaman looked terrified. He was a middle-aged man with a sheen of sweat on his face. His hair was a mess from hiding in the closet. It hung limply over his forehead.

And the silver thing in his hand was definitely a gun. It was down at his side—but it was a gun.

He began to lift it up. Maybe to shoot, maybe to toss it from the closet. Sean didn't know. He would never know.

He brought up his M4 and put two rounds in Munir Zaman's chest.

*　*　*

For the next little while, Sean felt numb. Zaman bled out fast on the floor of the bedroom, wild-eyed and gasping, reaching up like he wanted someone to hold his hand.

Sean stepped back from him, but he couldn't look away.

You should have stayed quiet, he thought. You should have been better at hiding.

Sergeant Ross patted Sean on the shoulder, told him he'd done the right thing.

"Could have been either one of us," Ross said. "I would have shot him too."

There was something comforting about the idea. That it could have gone either way. Later on, Sean would give a lot of thought to what might have been—to the alternate history where he had been the one to open the closet door and Ross had been the one to pull the trigger.

Random chance. That's all it was.

The same was true of the ride back to the base. Five Humvees in a convoy. On the trip out, Sean had ridden in the third one, with Cole and Captain Webber and a private named Ortiz. On the trip back, they took Zaman's mistress with them. She got Sean's seat, and Sean rode in the fourth Humvee.

Musical chairs.

It saved Sean's life.

The ride started smooth, Sean in the left rear seat with a cardboard box on his lap—the haul from the safe. Full of loose papers, a ledger, a laptop, and three hard drives. The captain hoped they might yield some useful intelligence.

Sergeant Ross was in the seat next to Sean. Keeping an eye on him, Sean thought. But he felt better even now. Less numb.

A mile from Zaman's house the convoy turned onto a wider street—a commercial street with two- and three-story buildings on either side. They passed a grocery store and a boarded-up restaurant, and then a taller building loomed up: brick and stone on the facade and the ruins of a marquee. A movie theater. Abandoned, because they weren't showing movies in Kamaliyah these days.

As the convoy passed the theater, Sean saw a flash like lightning at the roadside. A boom of thunder came with it, the shock wave pulsing through him. Up ahead, the third Humvee jerked sideways and rose up. Almost tipped, hung still for a moment. Came down again.

When it came down, it was on fire.

Chaos then. Sergeant Ross barking orders. Sean hit the door and was out on the street before his Humvee rolled to a stop. He started running, still gripping the cardboard box. Then tossed it away. The papers spilled out over the ground.

The boom of the explosion still echoed in his ears, but there were other sounds with it: the *clip-clip* of rifle fire, someone screaming. Up ahead, the driver's door of the third Humvee swung open. Cole leaned out. Fell into the street.

Sean got to him. Pulled him clear.

"Ortiz is burning," Cole said.

"Okay," said Sean.

"I don't think it's okay." Cole said. "Am I burning?"

His sleeve was. Sean slapped out the flame with a gloved hand.

"You're all right," he said.

He scanned around for cover, saw a narrow alley between the movie theater and a tea shop. He dragged Cole into it.

"I'm hot," Cole said, pulling his night-vision goggles off. "Why does it always have to be so goddamn hot?"

"I don't know," Sean said, distracted. He tore his own goggles from his face and slipped off his gloves. Unsnapped a pocket on his thigh and drew out a tourniquet.

"What are you doing?" Cole said.

"Never mind," said Sean.

At the mouth of the alley, a bullet struck the wall of the theater, chipping off splinters of stone. Another struck the ground.

"Jesus," Cole said. "Are they shooting at us? Why would anyone want to shoot at us?"

Sean squatted by Cole's right leg and pulled the tourniquet over Cole's calf. It was simple. There was no boot in the way. And no foot.

Sean tightened the tourniquet, taking out all the slack. He twisted the plastic rod to close off the artery. Used the Velcro strap to secure the rod in place.

"Am I bleeding?" Cole said.

"You were," said Sean. "Now you're not."

Cole was sitting against the wall of the theater, his head leaning against the stone. He took a breath in through his nose and bent forward to look at his leg.

"Aw, shit," he said.

"You'll live," said Sean.

"I hate this fucking place."

"I know. I'm starting to not like it either."

Cole's body shook, and Sean thought he was coughing. But it was something else: a laugh, quiet and bitter. Cole tipped his head back against the wall.

"How are we getting out of this alley?" he said.

"Beats me," said Sean.

"I wish they'd finish shooting all those motherfuckers."

Sean listened to the gunfire. Heard the *chut-chut-chut* of the M50s, the big guns mounted on the Humvees.

"They're working on it," he said.

He crouched low and moved closer to the mouth of the alley.

"What are you doing?" Cole said.

"Trying to see what's going on."

"There's a war out there. That's what's going on."

Sean reached down and ran his fingers through the dirt. Rubbed it between his palms.

"Come back here," Cole said.

Sean didn't move.

"I'm serious."

Sean brushed the dirt from his palms and walked back.

"It was probably one guy, don't you think?" he said.

Silence for a few seconds. Then Cole said, "What are you talking about?"

"I bet there was one guy, on a roof across the street, who saw the two of us come down here and tried to shoot us. But he's not shooting now."

"So?"

"Maybe they got him," Sean said. "I think they got him."

"There's other guys," said Cole.

"I know," Sean said.

"There's no end of guys in this city who would be happy to kill you."

"Yeah. I know."

"So stay here. Don't go out there."

Sean leaned against the stone wall of the theater.

"Okay," he said.

A bead of sweat rolled down his forehead and along his nose. He wiped it away.

"Okay," he said again, softly. "But what about Ortiz?"

"He's dead," Cole replied. "He was on *fire*."

"Right," Sean said, nodding. Then: "What about Zaman's mistress?"

"Who gives a fuck about Zaman's mistress?"

Sean moved his fingers over the surface of the stone. "No, you're right."

"She's dead anyway. They're all dead."

Sean let himself slide down the wall until he was sitting on the ground. But he kept staring at the mouth of the alley.

"The captain though," he said.

"The captain's dead," Cole told him.

"He was on the left side of the Humvee," Sean said. "Like you were. Away from the blast."

"He's dead. And if he's not, then somebody else already pulled him out. You go out there, you're gonna get shot."

"Yeah. You're right."

Sean listened to the sound of the guns. Felt the wall against his back. The sweat on his face. The air dense around him. Time passing.

"Fuck," he said.

He pushed himself up till he was standing. Eased forward along the wall toward the street.

"Jesus," Cole said. "Stop it. Stay here."

"Yeah."

"I mean it."

"I know."

"Then stop."

"Okay."

"*Stop.*"

18

NOW

Sean Tennant

It's beautiful, Sean thinks: The chill in the morning air and the black silhouettes of pine trees rising out of the fog. The gentle slope of the hill rolling down in front of him.

The wild grass of the hill is broken by scattered boulders and logs. The logs are smooth-sawn on the ends. They must have been felled on purpose, though why they were left here Sean doesn't know. Maybe for people to sit on.

Molly is sitting on one of them, down toward the bottom of the slope. She's talking to a woman named Claire. They met only yesterday, but they're getting along like old friends. Claire is from Seattle, and she's traveling with her fiancé, a skinny, bearded kid named Travis, who used to write code but quit his job—*Because what's the point, if you don't like what you're doing, right?* What Travis likes doing is climbing rocks, and he's off doing it now. He picked a good place for it: the Wrinkled Rock Climbing Area, a campground southwest of Rapid City, South Dakota, down the road from Mount Rushmore.

Sean and Molly have spent three nights here. After he picked her up from the ranch in Montana, they drove two hundred fifty miles to a Motel 6 in Sheridan, Wyoming. They slept there for a few hours— Molly paying for the room and dealing with the night clerk. In the morning they went to Walmart and bought a tent, a pair of sleeping bags, some groceries, and two new burner phones. From there, they headed east.

The accommodations at Wrinkled Rock are primitive. It's essentially a parking lot for cars and RVs and a field where you can pitch a tent. But there's no clerk to check you in and no TVs tuned to CNN. Cell reception is spotty. There are restrooms but no showers. There's a spigot where you can draw water that's supposed to be drinkable, but Sean doesn't like the taste. He's drinking bottled water instead, sitting in front of his tent on a camp chair borrowed from Travis, admiring the beauty of the fog.

Sean hasn't heard Cole's voice for days, but now it's there, to his right and a little behind him.

"You need a shave," Cole says.

It's true. Sean has six days' worth of stubble. He touches his neck and says nothing.

"Or maybe not," Cole says. "That could be your disguise."

"That's what I'm thinking," Sean says.

"You should buy a razor. Clean it up around the edges. Give it some shape. Otherwise you'll end up looking like coder boy."

Travis has a thick unruly beard like a lumberjack's.

"Yeah," Sean says.

He reaches down until his fingers touch the dewy grass. Out of the corner of his eye he can see Cole settling onto the ground beside him, legs stretched out, bootless. Two intact ankles and two perfect, bare feet. There are always two when Sean sees him these days.

"How long are you gonna stay here?" Cole asks him.

"I don't know," he says.

"Your car is sitting in the parking lot. A cop could pull in there anytime."

"It's a silver Camry. There are a lot of them on the road."

"Uh-huh."

"And there are stolen plates on it. I picked them up in Wyoming."

"Criminal mastermind," Cole says. "That's what you are."

Down the slope of the hill, there's a chipmunk on the log where Molly and Claire are sitting. It's entertaining them: creeping closer, then running away.

"How long are you gonna keep *her* here?" Cole says.

Sean doesn't answer.

"Gets cold at night," Cole says. "Sleeping in a tent."

"It's not too bad."

"Yet."

"I figure we'll head south," Sean says. "Find another camping spot."

"Sure. How much cash have you got?"

Sean knows the number, but he doesn't say it. He started with a little over three thousand dollars—money he and Molly had hidden away at their rented house in Texas, in case they had to run. Sean has it stashed in a money belt around his waist. What's left.

"We've got enough," he says.

"It'll go fast," says Cole. "You have to eat, even if it's drive-through food. Unless you're gonna live off the land. Maybe all you need is a fishing pole."

"Maybe."

"You never caught a fish in your life. You know that won't work. She's gonna have your kid. Is she gonna have it in a tent?"

The idea makes Sean frown. "No."

"So what are you doing? What's the plan?"

Sean doesn't answer. He focuses on the chipmunk in the distance, putting on its show.

"I know what the plan is," Cole says. "You think you can do it again. Start over. New life. New identities."

That's exactly what Sean has been thinking. "It worked once," he says.

"True," Cole replies. "But last time your faces weren't plastered all over the news."

Sean nods. That's the problem, and the only solution he sees is to wait it out.

"It won't last," he says. "Something'll happen. Some idiot will shoot up a school or a church, and the news will move on. There's always another thing."

It sounds reasonable when he says it out loud. People have short attention spans, and their memories fade.

Sean wants to believe it. He breathes the cool air and watches the fog drifting off through the pines. It's quiet beside him and he thinks Cole is gone, but he's wrong. Cole has one more thing to say to him.

"The news might move on, but Jimmy won't."

Sean waves the words away with a flick of his hand.

"You know it's true," Cole's voice says. "You should have dealt with him the other night when you had the chance."

Sean is tempted to agree. He wonders what he would have done in Molly's place. If he had been holding the shotgun, with Jimmy on the ground in front of him. Would he have ended it then?

But that's hypothetical. Sean made his choice that night. Molly telling him to drive. Telling him that Jimmy was in the woods only a short distance away. He could have stopped and gone back, but he didn't.

Sean tells himself now that it was the right decision. It would have been too risky, chasing after Jimmy in the dark. But that's an excuse.

The truth is he didn't want to kill Jimmy that night. He didn't think he had the stomach for it.

"I don't need to kill him," he says.

He gets no answer. Cole is gone.

Molly Winter

The chipmunk leaps from the log and vanishes into the grass. Claire takes it as her cue to leave, saying she's going to meet up with Travis. Molly watches her climb the hill, sees her wave at Sean as she passes him.

The fog is thinning fast now. Molly stands and stretches. She's wearing hiking boots and jeans, a flannel shirt, a fleece jacket. Clothes Sean brought for her from Houston. She steps up onto the log and walks along it with her arms held out for balance. She feels light.

She and Sean have worked it out between them, how they're going to start over again, with new names and new IDs. The main obstacle is money: it will cost far more than the cash they have. But they're not without resources. Last Friday night, before he left Houston, Sean drove to Bear Creek Park and dug up the box in the woods. He's got fourteen cylinder seals right now, resting in the pockets of his jacket. There are two more boxes they can dig up if they need them. One in Kentucky and one in upstate New York.

The seals are just pieces of stone: amethyst, obsidian, lapis lazuli. It's strange that they should be worth so much, Molly thinks. Strange that they've had such an impact on her life.

The other night, when he picked her up from the ranch, Sean told her he was sorry for getting her into this. He's said it many times over the last six years. But it's not right. The fault is hers as much as his. They decided together to steal the cylinder seals. They were both reckless.

Molly was the first to see them. Adam Khadduri showed them to her. They were dating, and he liked to play the charming older man. He liked to impress her with his wealth.

The seals meant something to him. Molly remembers him holding one up—a small one, about the size of a double-A battery. He showed her the intricate images carved into its surface. "There are three figures here," Khadduri said. "The first is a god. The sun god, Shamash." He rotated the stone slightly. "The second is a man. He's asking for the sun god's blessing. But you can't approach Shamash on your own. That's what the third figure is for. The woman. She's a goddess called Lama. She's there as a kind of guide."

Khadduri weighed the seal in his palm. "This belonged to someone who lived thousands of years ago. When you touch it, you're reaching back into history."

Molly liked that about him, that he could be moved by a piece of art. She liked the things they did together: plays and concerts, weekend getaways, exhibits. She recognized the differences between them. He had far more experience than she did. He had an ex-wife who lived in New York and a son who was a sophomore at U of M in Ann Arbor.

Molly didn't dwell on those things. Adam Khadduri was good company, even though she knew the relationship wouldn't last. But it didn't end the way she expected.

They were at dinner one night at a place in Detroit called Cliff Bell's. Dark wood, live piano music, speakeasy lighting. Khadduri finished his meal and got up to use the restroom, and fifteen seconds later Sean slid into his empty seat.

Sean was eight months out of the army then. Lean and solid. He had long, unruly hair, bright eyes, three days' stubble on his face. He had an energy about him that was slightly manic.

Molly had never seen him before.

"We don't have much time," he said.

Mischief in his voice. It made Molly smile.

"We don't?" she said.

"No. So I'll just say it: You look bored. Are you bored?"

"Am I—?"

"I get it if you are. That guy you're with has to be, what, fifty?"

Molly felt her smile fading. "He's forty-three."

"And you're all of twenty-two."

"Twenty-three."

"Close enough. Forty-three minus twenty-three. I can do that math in my head. It comes out to *dull*."

"Do I know you?"

Sean shook his head. "Not yet. But you could. We could leave right now. I've got a car. But you have to decide."

Molly leaned forward, playing along. "Because we don't have much time," she said.

"Exactly. If you're worried about being rude, you can text him from the car. Tell him you ran into a friend and not to worry."

"You've got it all worked out."

"I've been thinking about it, over at the bar. He'll be back any second. We have to go right now."

She looked at him across the table. The bold, handsome stranger, trying to lure her away.

"Right now?" she said.

"Right now."

And it worked. She left with him.

But leaving Adam Khadduri wasn't as easy as she hoped it would be.

19

BEFORE

Molly Bowen

Molly worked in an art gallery in midtown Detroit. Sean had been doing odd jobs since he left the army.

The night they met, he wanted her to pack a bag and run away with him. She laughed and told him to slow down. But before long they were spending every night together, at her apartment or his.

She learned about him gradually. Discovered his quirks. Bright lights and sudden noises could make him jump. Crowds of people bothered him, but he made himself go out anyway. Sometimes when they went to bed, he couldn't sleep. He said he saw things when he closed his eyes.

"What things?" she asked.

He shook his head. "Things I'd like to forget."

She was lying on her side. He was tracing his fingers over the curve of her hip.

"You can tell me," she said.

"It doesn't matter. It's getting better. You and I are going to be happy."

And they were, as the weeks went by. It was autumn and the days were getting shorter, but Molly didn't care. The only thing that troubled her was Adam Khadduri.

In the days after she ran out on him at the restaurant, he tried to contact her. Angry at first, then calmer. Conciliatory. Wanting to meet. Molly put him off, gave him vague answers by text. She hoped she could slip out of the relationship without the drama of a confrontation.

When he persisted, she left a message on his voicemail: she wished him well, but it was time for her to move on.

She received no reply. Thought it was over. Until the night Khadduri came to see her at the art gallery.

He came around closing time. The owner of the gallery, a woman named Karen Tierney, had left early, and Molly was alone. No customers.

When Khadduri spoke to her, he started out gentle. He had missed her. They'd had such lovely times together, hadn't they? He didn't know what he'd do without her. Wouldn't she change her mind?

When Molly told him she wouldn't, Khadduri's mood turned darker.

"You're seeing someone new," he said.

There was an edge in his voice she didn't like. Molly didn't want to tell him about Sean.

"I'm not seeing anyone," she said.

They were standing together near the back of the gallery. She wanted to get away from him, but when she moved he followed her and grabbed hold of her wrist.

"You little liar," he said.

"I'm not lying."

"You are. The waiter at Cliff Bell's saw you leave. You left with a man."

"A friend. That's all."

Khadduri's grip on her wrist tightened. "Liar," he said. "Are you afraid of me? Do you think I care about some boy you're running around with? Do you think I'm jealous?"

"Adam, please—"

"You're a child, working in a shop. What do I care about you? You want to sell your life out cheap? Do it. Do it while you can. You're not bad looking, I suppose, for now. Give it a few years, and then we'll see."

She tried to step away from him again, but he kept hold of her. He pushed her until her back was against a counter.

"I can see your future, darling," he said. "You'll trick some boy into marrying you, and he'll want babies. You'll give them to him. Lucky him. You'll get fat. He will too. He'll disappoint you. You won't want him anymore. You'll divorce him. You'll think you can find another. A better one. But you won't."

His face was inches away from hers. Eyes dark, mouth twisted. Molly tried once more to break away from him, but Khadduri pulled her back harshly and squeezed her wrist. The pain made her cry out.

"*Adam*—"

He laughed. "You really are afraid." Suddenly he spun her around and bent her over the counter, pressing his body against hers. "Well, there's no one here," he said. "I suppose I could take you right now."

She struggled, but he held her down. Eventually the struggling stopped and she froze, aware of nothing but the heat of his breath falling on the back of her neck.

"I could," he said. "But why would I? I've already had you."

He released her and walked out. Molly stayed frozen for a time. When she could move again, she went to the door and locked it, her fingers trembling. She slid down to the floor and sat there until the trembling stopped.

She felt better in the car on her drive home. When she got to her apartment, Sean was waiting. She didn't want to tell him what had happened, but she didn't want to lie either. And when he saw the bruise on her wrist, he wanted the whole story.

It made him angry. His first impulse was to find Adam Khadduri and shoot him.

"You can't shoot him," Molly said.

"I can," Sean told her. "I've got a gun."

"Then I'd rather you didn't shoot him."

He took some convincing, but she settled him down. "It's over," she told him. "He needed to get mad, and he got mad. It's his pride. But now it's done. Trust me."

"I trust you," Sean said. "That's not the point."

"What's the point?"

"He hurt you. So I want to hurt him."

Molly laid her palm on his chest, over his heart.

"I know," she said. "But you won't, because I don't want you to."

That night, after he fell asleep, she stayed awake in the dark, listening to little noises: the wind outside, the heat coming on in her apartment.

Khadduri's voice in her head, saying one word: "Liar."

The word stung her, because she had told Sean a lie.

She wanted to see Khadduri hurt.

Not because of the bruise he had given her, but because he had frightened her and made her feel weak. She hated feeling weak.

When she finally got to sleep, it was close to 3:00 a.m. She woke at 10:00 to the smell of coffee. Sean brought a mug of it and put it on her nightstand. He was wide awake, happy, playful. He got into bed with her, straddled her on hands and knees. Put his face close to hers.

"I've been thinking," he told her.

"Uh-oh," she said.

"No, this is good. Ask me what I've been thinking."

"What?"

"I've been thinking there's more than one way to hurt him."

Sean Garrety

There was more to it than wanting to hurt Khadduri, of course.

When Sean thought about it, he acknowledged that it was mostly about money: needing it and not having it.

In a larger sense, it was about debt. Cosmic debt, you could call it. There were books that needed to be balanced. Sean was owed something for what he'd seen in Iraq, for what he'd done. For fifteen months of misery, breathing air that reeked of smoke and sewage. For watching Munir Zaman bleed to death on the floor.

In exchange for that, Sean wanted a new beginning with Molly. It wasn't too much to ask. Stealing from Adam Khadduri to pay for it seemed like justice.

Even so, he might not have gone through with it. But the more he talked about it with Molly in the weeks that followed, the more it made sense. Sean knew Khadduri was rich, but he never realized how rich until Molly told him about the cylinder seals.

The thing that clinched it was learning that Khadduri kept the seals in a safe in his house. It was a sign, Sean thought. It was the universe telling him to go right ahead.

Because he knew someone who could crack a safe.

Khadduri lived on Elgin Avenue in Huntington Woods, one of Detroit's northwestern suburbs. Sean and Cole drove there on the second Saturday in December. They parked on the street under tall, stark, leafless trees. It was snowing.

"I don't like it," Sean said.

"You worry too much," said Cole.

"We'll leave footprints."

"Not if it keeps falling. It'll cover everything up."

Sean switched off his car's headlights. Drummed his fingers on the steering wheel.

"One thing," Cole said.

"What?"

"Is that the only suit you own?"

Sean touched the lapel of his jacket. "What's wrong with it?"

"Black suit, black tie, white shirt. You look like a hit man."

"Funny."

Cole had on a blue blazer and khakis. His tie seemed like something from another decade: polyester with red and yellow stripes.

"You look like you want to sell me a Buick," Sean said. "And you'll throw in the floor mats for free."

The suits were meant to be camouflage. No one expects a burglar to wear a suit.

Cole looked out his window at a sprawling house with a single light on in one of the rooms on the second floor. The same light had been on for three nights in a row, which was why they had chosen to park here. They thought the owners must be out of town.

Khadduri lived four houses down, on the other side of the street. From here, they had a good view of the end of his driveway.

"How much do you think these houses run?" Cole asked. "Half a million?"

"At least," Sean said.

"But not a million? Right?"

"Maybe a million."

"No shit."

A green Ford Taurus appeared at the end of Khadduri's driveway. It pulled into the street and drove off. They watched its taillights until it turned around a corner.

"That's the housekeeper," Cole said.

"Yup."

"Off to bingo night."

"Backgammon."

"Whatever. And the son is in Ann Arbor."

"U of M. He lives in a dorm on campus."

"Which leaves the Khadduri house empty. Except for good old Adam."

Another half hour passed before Adam Khadduri drove out in his Maserati and disappeared down the street.

Sean and Cole had watched him three Saturday nights in a row. He always went out.

"Perfect," Cole said.

Sean turned off the engine and pulled the key from the ignition. He reached for his door handle, but Cole stopped him.

"One of us at a time," Cole said. "We'll look less dodgy. Wait three minutes and follow me."

"Will that be enough time?"

"Should be."

It was. Three minutes later, Sean reached behind the passenger seat for the briefcase that was resting there. He carried it with him across the street and walked to the side door of Khadduri's house. Cole was waiting for him in the mudroom, latex gloves on his hands, Tyvek booties over his shoes. He had picked the locks on the door and punched the code into Khadduri's alarm system.

Molly had given them the code. She had seen Khadduri's housekeeper enter it once.

Sean handed Cole the briefcase, then pulled his own gloves and booties from his pockets and slipped them on.

With the door closed behind them and the dead bolt turned, they walked through the house to make sure it was empty. Cole clicked on a penlight and led the way. Khadduri lived well. His kitchen had terrazzo tiles on the floor and marble on the countertops. He had a huge farmhouse sink and a stovetop with eight burners. His refrigerator looked as wide as a tank.

The rest of the house was equally extravagant, from the formal dining room to the basement entertainment center, which had a pool table, a wet bar, a leather sectional sofa, and a ninety-inch TV.

The housekeeper had her own suite at the back of the second floor, with a separate staircase leading down to the pantry. There were five bedrooms in all, and Adam Khadduri had the largest. His closet was as big as a bedroom itself, and they found his safe where Molly said it would be: behind a sliding panel in the back wall.

Cole aimed his penlight at the gray steel door. The dial was a few inches below eye level. The handle looked like a small steering wheel.

"What do you think?" Sean said.

"I think we could be out of here quick," said Cole. "If Khadduri left this unlocked."

"Does that ever happen?"

"My dad said he found one unlocked once. But he liked to tell stories."

Sean reached for the handle and tried to turn it. It didn't budge.

"Ah, well," Cole said. "This could take a while."

He opened the briefcase and set it on the long, cushioned bench that occupied the middle of the closet. There were two empty backpacks inside, along with a pad and a pen.

Cole loosened his tie, unbuttoned his collar. Shed the blue blazer and laid it on the bench. He had a Colt Defender in a holster clipped to his belt. He unclipped it and tossed it onto the blazer.

Sean lingered nearby with his hands on his hips.

"Is that what you're gonna do?" Cole said. "Hover?"

Moving to the safe, Cole pressed his ear against the door and began working the dial. Sean picked up one of the backpacks and wandered into Khadduri's bedroom.

Opulent, he thought. That would be the word for it.

The room held a king-size bed at one end and a seating area at the other, with two armchairs and a wall of built-in bookcases. The color scheme was gold and crimson. It carried over from the bedspread to the curtains to the rug.

Sean saw a pair of wristwatches on top of a bureau: Bulgari and Rolex. There were others in one of the drawers: high-end brands he'd never heard of. Vacheron Constantin, Tag Heuer, Girard-Perregaux. Nine watches in all. Sean stowed them in his backpack. In a different drawer, under piles of neatly folded socks, he found a bundle of cash held together with a silver clip. He took that too.

In the next thirty minutes he covered the whole house, gathering up anything small and valuable. When he came upstairs again, the backpack was full.

From one of the guest rooms at the front of the house, he looked out at the street. Tiny snowflakes drifted through the air. He could see his car halfway down the block, undisturbed.

He thought of Molly. She should be on the road now, driving to Toledo, where she would check in to a hotel. He would meet her there after this was done.

He spent another minute looking at the snow and headed back to Khadduri's bedroom. He found Cole in the walk-in closet with his ear against the door of the safe. Cole had put away his penlight and switched on the light overhead.

Without turning, he said, "Close the door."

Sean closed it and walked to the bench in the center of the room. Looked down at the pad where Cole had written two numbers: 17 and 82.

"You're making progress," he said.

Cole grunted a reply and spent another five minutes working the dial. Then he pushed himself away from the safe and let out a frustrated breath. He stepped to the bench, favoring his right leg, and sat down.

"Are you all right?" Sean asked.

"Yeah."

"Does it hurt?"

Cole flexed his right knee, bringing his leg up parallel to the floor. He wobbled his shoe from side to side, the one that covered his prosthetic.

"If it hurts—" Sean began.

"It doesn't," Cole said sharply. He looked away from Sean and back again. "It doesn't hurt. The problem is, it's asleep."

"Your leg's asleep?"

Cole laughed quietly. "Not my leg," he said. "My foot. It's not there, but it's asleep."

He wobbled the shoe some more, bent his knee, bounced his heel on the carpet. He glanced up and caught Sean watching him.

"Don't give me that look."

"What look?" Sean said.

"Pity."

"I'm not—"

"Or whatever. Remorse. I don't want either one." Cole got up from the bench. "You're not responsible for every goddamn thing."

Sean searched for a reply, but he never found one. A sound from outside set him moving.

The rumble of a car pulling into the driveway.

He skirted around the bench, snapped off the overhead light, and opened the door. Passed through to Khadduri's bedroom and parted the heavy curtains on one of the windows so he could look down.

Cole trailed behind him. "Is it Khadduri?"

"No," Sean said.

"The housekeeper?"

"I think it's the son."

"What's he driving?"

"Would you believe a Ferrari?"

Sean watched the doors open, saw a young guy climb out on the driver's side. He wore a gray wool coat that looked expensive. A young woman climbed out on the other side. Black haired, beautiful, well dressed.

She walked around behind the car to Khadduri's son and slipped her hands inside his coat.

"I'm *cold*," she said.

He got his arms around her and kissed her, and she tossed her head back, laughing. Snowflakes fell through the air around them like fairy dust.

"They're coming in," Sean said. "He'll see that the alarm's not on."

"He won't care," said Cole.

"Yeah?"

"All he's thinking about is getting laid."

They listened to the side door opening down below and closing again. Muffled voices from the kitchen.

I can hang up your coat.

Leave it.

Quiet after that, punctuated by giggles.

Cole headed back to the safe. Sean followed him, drawing shut the closet door.

"This is bad," Sean said, whispering.

"Could be worse," said Cole.

"They'll come up here."

"Maybe."

"This is where the beds are."

"There's booze in the basement, and that leather sofa," Cole said. He clicked on his penlight and pressed his ear against the steel door of the safe.

He passed the light to Sean. "Hold this."

"What are you doing?"

"I've only got one number left. And you know what the best part is?"

"What?"

"My foot's not asleep anymore."

"This isn't funny."

"It's a little funny," Cole said. "Hold the light. And get your gun out."

Sean had his Beretta in his jacket pocket. He could feel its weight at his side.

"I'm not shooting them," he said.

"If you show them you've got it, you won't need to shoot them."

Sean left the gun where it was. Cole's fingers spun the dial of the safe.

"They won't come up here anyway," Cole said. "They'll go down to the basement."

He turned out to be right. After a few minutes Sean heard music rising up faintly from below. A woman's voice. "Is that Adele?" he said.

Cole nodded. "'Daydreamer.' Told you they were gonna screw."

Sean forced himself to stand still and hold the light.

"We should leave," he said. "While they're distracted."

"You should shut up," Cole said. "I'm almost done."

The dial clicked along under Cole's fingers. Sean started shifting his weight from one foot to the other. After a few minutes, Cole said, "Thirty-nine. Probably."

"Probably?"

"I'm almost sure."

He had three numbers now, six possible combinations. Sean watched him go through them. When the fifth one came around and the handle wouldn't turn, he saw Cole scowl.

Cole spun the dial to the right. Four times around. Then he stepped back.

"You do the last one."

Sean moved closer and reached for the dial. The light threw the shadows of his fingers over the steel. He found the first number: 82.

The second: 39.

The third: 17.

He passed the light to Cole. Gripped the wheel with two gloved hands.

It turned.

"Hot damn," Cole said.

The door was heavy. Sean drew it open and Cole aimed the flashlight inside. The beam found a tray of gold coins. Beside it: stacks of cash. On another shelf, there were three carved wooden boxes.

Sean opened one of them. It held sixteen cylinder seals.

Cole picked one out and held it up to study it in the light.

"So these are what all the fuss is about," he said.

He slipped the stone into his pocket. Sean loaded the wooden boxes into the second backpack. The cash and coins fit neatly into the briefcase.

Sean shut the door of the safe and spun the dial as Cole got into his jacket and clipped the holstered Colt to his belt.

They moved the sliding panel back into place, and the closet looked the way it had before.

Sean took the lead now, moving through Khadduri's bedroom and into the hallway. They each carried a backpack, and Sean had the briefcase. He stopped and listened in the dark and heard only the music from the basement.

He motioned for Cole to follow him to the housekeeper's room, and from there they went down the back stairway, through the pantry and the kitchen to the mudroom.

Khadduri's son had engaged the dead bolt after he came in. Sean turned it and eased the door open. He stepped out and took the Tyvek covers off his shoes, peeled the gloves from his hands.

Cole came out after him and got out his lock pick and tension rod to reengage the dead bolt.

"Leave it," Sean said.

Cole waved him off. "It'll take thirty seconds."

It seemed longer. Sean felt snowflakes gathering in his hair. Finally Cole said, "Done," and stripped off his gloves. He leaned on Sean for balance and removed the covers from his shoes, and the two of them made their way down Khadduri's driveway, leaving footprints they hoped the snow would blanket over.

Two things struck Sean as they reached the end of the driveway: The empty house in front of which he'd parked his car was no longer empty; there were lights on in the downstairs rooms. And a man was standing in the street by the car with a cell phone to his ear.

"Don't panic," Cole said softly.

"I won't if you won't," Sean said.

They kept walking and the man on the street put his phone away and waved at them. He was dressed for the weather: winter boots, corduroys, a hooded parka. As they got closer, Sean saw that he was older, maybe sixty, with thinning gray hair and a neatly trimmed mustache.

Sean noted something else too: a scrape ran all along the driver's side of his car, and the side mirror had been clipped off.

"I saw who did it," the man in the parka said.

Sean reached the car, popped the trunk, and laid the briefcase inside.

"Couple of kids in a Chevy van," the man in the parka said. "I saw them from my driveway. Just got home from a trip."

Sean slipped his backpack off his shoulder and placed it beside the briefcase.

"They stopped at the end of the block there, to check the damage to their van," the parka man said. "Never thought twice about your car. Just drove off. I got their license number."

He had written it in ink on his arm. He pulled up the sleeve of his coat to show Sean.

"That's great," Sean said.

It came out dull. Mechanical. The man in the parka seemed disappointed. As if he'd been hoping for a more enthusiastic reaction.

"Ticks me off," he said. "No one takes responsibility anymore. Punks. I called the cops on them."

Cole stepped in. "Really?" he said.

"Absolutely," said the parka man. "They're coming out. I hope you fellas don't mind waiting."

"I wouldn't think they'd bother," Cole said. "For something minor like this."

"Ordinarily they might not," the parka man said with a wink. "But I know some guys on the force. My wife worked as a dispatcher for twenty years."

"The thing is," Sean said, "we don't want to be here all night." He gestured at the damage. "I'd rather take care of this myself."

The parka man gave him a disapproving look. "It won't take long. They'll just need your information, for the report."

"Even so—"

"People around here take pride in this neighborhood. You let the small things go, pretty soon the whole world goes to hell."

"Isn't that the truth?" Cole said.

Cole swung his backpack into the trunk and closed the lid. Looked Sean in the eye and said, "Why don't you go find the mirror."

Sean tried to read his expression. Cole saw him doing it and smiled, relaxed. "Go on," he said. "We're good."

The mirror wasn't hard to find. It had traveled a little way down the street, and the snow had dusted it lightly. Sean picked it up and brought it back. The man in the parka was telling Cole stories of suburban crime.

"This past spring, somebody broke into my wife's car and stole a bag of groceries and a phone charger. Smashed a window to do it. Who breaks a window for a bag of groceries?"

"I hear you," Cole said.

Sean opened the door and tossed the mirror onto the back seat.

"Are we all set?" Cole asked him.

"Yes we are."

"Let's go."

Simple. Should have been simple.

But the man in the parka didn't cooperate. He tried to block Cole's way.

"Hold on now," he said.

Cole leaned into him. Spoke in a low voice. "Listen to me. I'm not interested in being part of this power trip you're on. You want to get some kids arrested over nothing, over an accident, good for you. But we're going now. Back off."

The man's eyes went wide. He took an uncertain step back.

Cole went past him, around the rear of the car to the passenger side. Sean reached for the handle of the driver's door. The snow fell. White flakes glimmering in the light of the streetlamps.

Sean saw Cole grinning at him across the roof of the car.

And the man in the parka made a decision. He must have put things together. Maybe he'd been puzzling it out all along: wondering what was in the briefcase and the backpacks and why these two strangers felt the need to leave before the police came. Anger might have had something to do with it too—anger and humiliation, because of the way Cole had talked to him.

The reasons didn't matter. What mattered was that he drew a revolver from somewhere under his parka and brought it up into a two-handed grip.

"Freeze!" he shouted. "Don't move!"

Cole looked at Sean across the roof of the car. Half-amused. Half-disbelieving.

"Did he say 'Freeze'?"

Cole's left hand was braced on the car. His right hand was out of sight.

"Don't," Sean said. "Don't do it."

It seemed unreal. Sean witnessed it, but the images were blurred; the sounds were muffled. Everything moved slow.

Then things sped up to normal again and they were in the car. There was a hum in Sean's ears, separate from the hum of the engine. Cole's voice seemed to reach him from far away.

"Didn't see that coming," Cole said. "I really didn't."

"Me neither," said Sean.

"That old guy, packin'."

"Yeah."

Sean was driving fast, away from Khadduri's street. He had his phone out, looking at a map. As he rounded a corner, he fishtailed in the snow.

"Tell you one thing," Cole said. "That guy can shoot."

"I suppose," said Sean.

"You don't think so?"

"I've seen better."

"You always were hard to impress."

"The way I see it, he had six chances," Sean said. "He only hit you twice."

Cole, in the back seat, snorted and shook his head from side to side.

"Jesus," he said. "Don't make me laugh."

Stop sign up ahead. Sean slowed and rolled through, picking up speed on the other side. Two blocks on, he came to Coolidge Highway, which would take them north to Beaumont Hospital.

The humming in Sean's ears was getting quieter—the memory of the gunshots receding into the past.

"You must be disappointed," Cole said.

Sean glanced at him in the rearview mirror. "Why?"

"'Cause I only hit him once. Barely. Winged him."

"He had the drop on you."

"Still."

They came to a red light and Sean had to stop or risk slamming into traffic. He stopped. As soon as the way cleared, he went through.

Cole said, "You shot him, though. Right?"

"Nope."

"Seriously?"

"He was empty."

"*Empty*. Did you punch him at least?"

Sean had come close to shooting him. The Beretta in his hand, his finger on the trigger. The old man running from him, tripping on the curb. Sean had kicked him in the ribs, rolled him over, bashed him in the face with the barrel of the Beretta.

"I broke his nose," he said to Cole.

"Guess that's something."

Sean had left the old man lying in the snow. Had gone to find Cole sitting slumped against the car, bleeding from his neck and his chest. Thought he was dead. Until his eyes opened.

"Can you get up?" Sean asked him.

"You're funny," Cole said.

"I have to move you."

"I don't want to scare you, but I can't feel my legs."

Sean grabbed him under the arms and hauled him up. Hefted him onto his shoulder. Managed to get the car door open and wrangle him into the back seat. Laid him down at first, and then decided it would be better to sit him up. He wanted to keep the neck wound higher than Cole's heart.

He used the seat belt to strap him in. Cinched the shoulder harness tight in the hope that it might help to slow the bleeding of the chest wound. He slipped the knot of Cole's tie and tugged it free. Rolled it into a pad and pressed it over the hole in his neck. Put Cole's hand over it and told him to keep it in place.

The bleeding worried him, but not as much as it might have. The blood seeped; it didn't spurt. Sean thought the bullets must have missed the major arteries.

"You're good," he said to Cole.

He said it again, speeding north on Coolidge Highway, a light turning green just in time for him to breeze through: "You're good."

Cole smiled at him in the mirror. "Where are we going?"

His breathing had been rough all along. Now it sounded rougher.

"We're going to get you some help," Sean said.

"I want to see my mom."

"You'll see her."

"I want to see her now. You should take me to her now."

"It's too far. We have to go to the hospital first. But I promise you'll see her."

Cole's smile faded. "You're not very smart."

Sean shifted his attention back to the road. The snow fell more quickly than before. It was harder to see.

When he looked in the mirror again, Cole's eyes were closed. His hand, holding the tie, had fallen away from his neck.

"Hey," Sean said. "Don't go to sleep."

Cole's hand came up, hovered, and fell away. His eyelids fluttered open.

"You know I love you, right?" Cole said. "Otherwise I wouldn't do the things I do for you."

When they reached the hospital, Cole's head had fallen to the side. His eyes were closed again. Sean braked to a stop in front of the emergency room doors and leaned on the horn as he got out of the car. Two paramedics who had just made a drop-off ran out. When they saw Cole, one of them ran back in for a gurney.

The one who stayed behind said, "What happened?"

"Couple of kids," Sean said. "They tried to steal our car." A lie, but he made it sound true. "Punks," he added. "One of them had a gun."

The paramedic nodded in sympathy. The other came out with the gurney, a young doctor jogging along behind him. Sean stepped back and let them work. The doctor, checking for a pulse, seemed surprised to find one.

The paramedics hauled Cole from the car and rolled him inside. The sliding doors opened for them and stayed open for Sean. He heard the doctor calling out to a nurse, telling her to get a resident down from surgery.

Sean grabbed the doctor's sleeve. "His name is Cole," he said to her. "His blood type is A positive."

She patted his arm. "Good. That's good."

She punched a button on the wall, and a pair of gray doors swung open. The paramedics rolled Cole through and pushed him down a bright hallway. Sean followed them. Saw them make a right turn into an exam area. The doctor swept a curtain into place to block his view.

Sean stood still in the middle of the hall, and the world moved around him. Two nurses hurried in to join the doctor behind the curtain. The paramedics cleared out.

One of them brushed Sean's arm as he passed.

"You shouldn't be back here," he said.

Sean ignored him. He needed to stay, even though he knew what was going to happen.

Voices narrated for him from behind the curtain. Calm and professional. They called it out when Cole's left lung collapsed, when his blood pressure crashed. Sean knew the exact moment when Cole went into cardiac arrest. He heard the doctor asking for a shot of epinephrine. Heard the tone of the defibrillator charging.

They shocked Cole three times, trying to revive him.

The doctor sounded heartbroken at the end. "That's enough," she said. "Time of death, ten oh four p.m."

Sean didn't wait for her to come out. He retraced his steps down the hall, to the ER waiting area. A nurse from the reception desk spotted him. She told him his car had been blocking the ambulance bay. One of the paramedics had moved it. She handed Sean his keys.

"You should have a seat," she said. "The police will want to talk to you about your friend."

She pointed him to a bank of chairs. He walked past them toward the sliding glass doors.

"Sir," she called after him.

He went out through the doors into the cold night. No one tried to stop him.

He found his car in the visitors' lot. The snow drifted down all around him. He started the engine and put the car into gear. Drove out of the lot and kept on driving.

20

NOW

Molly Winter

Molly misses the campground at Wrinkled Rock. It felt like autumn there, and she loves autumn. But she saw the wisdom of moving on. There's risk in staying too long in one place.

She and Sean have covered almost fifteen hundred miles in three days. They camped one night at an RV park near Lincoln, Nebraska, and once by a lake in southern Illinois. They would have stayed longer at the lake, but they got spooked by a middle-aged dude who spent hours pacing along the shore with a metal detector. He never approached them, but every once in a while he would stop and stare. Molly couldn't decide if he recognized them or if he was thinking about how he would murder them.

She didn't want to wait and find out. Neither did Sean. They took to the road again, and it brought them here: Cumberland Avenue in Knoxville, the northwest edge of the campus of the University of Tennessee.

Knoxville feels like summer. It's seventy degrees on an October afternoon. The sidewalks are filled with students in T-shirts and short pants.

The sun is shining, and it feels good to be out of the car. Molly is walking arm in arm with Sean. They're older than the college kids around them but young enough to blend in.

"It should be here," Sean says.

"Let's try the next block," Molly answers.

They're looking for a place called the Vienna Bar and Grill. They found it once, a long time ago, when she was Molly Bowen and he was Sean Garrety. Someone told them you could go in there and ask for Steve Z., and Steve Z. could start you over clean. He could give you a new name, a new birth certificate, a new Social Security card, a new driver's license. Everything you needed.

Steve Z. helped them once. They're hoping he can help them again.

They walk two more blocks and there's no Vienna Bar and Grill. There are no more businesses here, only academic buildings.

"It's back there," Sean says. "We missed it. Or it's gone."

They go back, strolling along the sidewalk on the north side of the street. They pass a Chipotle and a Chinese restaurant and a bar called the Copper Cellar. There's a sandwich shop, and across the street Molly can see the Taco Bell. They left Sean's Camry in the Taco Bell parking lot. There's a skinny shirtless guy standing in front of the drive-through window. He looks agitated. He's waving his arms.

Sean is looking at the door of a restaurant called Rusty's All-American.

"This," he says. "It was this building. I recognize the brickwork. This used to be the Vienna Bar and Grill."

Molly pokes him on the shoulder. "If only there were a way to know for sure," she says.

He laughs and takes out his burner cell phone. Does a Google search and finds a listing for the Vienna. Under "Hours of operation," it says "Permanently closed." The address is the same as the address of Rusty's.

"We can still go in and ask," she tells him.

When they enter they find a late-lunch crowd: a few big tables with groups that look like office workers or staff from the university. There's a waitress doing double duty as a hostess. They ask her if she knows Steve Z. She gives them a warm smile. "I sure don't. Will he be joining you today?"

Molly asks her a few more questions. Does she remember when this used to be a bar? She sure doesn't—must have been before her time. Is there anyone who might remember? Maybe Bonnie. Is Bonnie working today? She sure is. But Bonnie turns out to be no help. She doesn't know anyone who used to work at the Vienna, and she doesn't know Steve Z.

Molly thanks her and takes Sean's hand, and they go back out into the afternoon. From the sidewalk outside Rusty's, they see something troubling: a blue-and-white car turning into the Taco Bell parking lot across the street. The letters on the door read: CAMPUS POLICE.

"Huh," Sean says.

The car pulls into the space next to Sean's Camry. A campus cop steps out and walks to the drive-through. The shirtless guy is there—the one they saw before. He's sitting on the ground now, blocking the lane.

The cop crouches down by the shirtless guy. Friendly. As if he knows him.

Molly squeezes Sean's hand. "I'm hungry," she says. "Are you hungry?"

"I could eat," he says.

They head back into Rusty's. The waitress gives them her warm smile again and leads them to a booth with a view to the street.

"Is this okay?" she asks.

"Perfect," Sean says.

She brings them water and iced tea while they look at their menus. The special is meat loaf, she says, but people like the rib eye steak too. Molly orders a Caesar salad with chicken. Sean gets the steak.

Across the street at Taco Bell, the campus cop has persuaded the shirtless guy to get out of the way of the drive-through. The pair are still talking on a patch of grass near the curb.

The food comes, and Molly realizes she really is hungry. She ignores what's going on outside and focuses on her salad. The next time she looks up she sees Sean frowning.

He chose the side of the booth that put his back to the wall. It gives him a view of the customers at the other tables.

"What's the matter?" Molly asks him.

He looks down at his plate. "People are staring at us."

"How many people?"

"More than I'd like."

"Do they seem friendly or hostile?"

"Not hostile. Curious."

"Okay. Let them be curious."

Across the street, an ambulance pulls into the lot of the Taco Bell. Casually: no lights, no siren. Two EMTs get out and walk over to the campus cop and the shirtless guy.

Sean nods in their direction. "This could go bad for us," he says.

"It's got nothing to do with us," says Molly.

"Not yet. But it might. Keep your purse handy."

Her purse is on the seat next to her. Sean's gun is inside.

"If things go bad," she says, "I don't know what good my purse is gonna be."

He stabs a piece of steak with his fork. "Yeah. I don't know either."

Across the street, the shirtless guy is sitting in the grass. The EMTs are checking his heart rate. One of them slips a cuff around his arm to take his blood pressure.

Molly hears a group of diners at another table getting up to leave. One of them breaks away and tells the others he'll meet them outside.

He approaches Sean and Molly's booth. Stops at a respectful distance.

"I don't mean to disturb you," he says.

Smooth voice, gray suit, no tie. The suit is expensive without being flashy. Molly puts his age around fifty. A distinguished fifty.

"My friends and I saw you here," he says. "And we were going back and forth. *Is it them? It can't be them.* And I wanted to know." He smiles at himself. Rueful. "Now that I'm here . . ."

He trails off and Molly says, "What can we do for you, Mr.—?"

"Frazier," he says. "Howard Frazier. And you've got it backward. The question is: Is there anything I can do for you? If you're in trouble—"

"We're not in trouble," Sean says. He sounds calm and looks relaxed, though Molly can't help noticing his right hand resting on the table, within easy reach of the serrated knife the waitress brought him with his steak.

"Perhaps I'm wrong," Frazier says. "But if you were in trouble, legal trouble, I would be happy to advise you. You may have options you haven't considered."

He holds up a business card and leans in to place it on the table.

HOWARD J. FRAZIER, ATTORNEY-AT-LAW.

Molly picks it up. "That's lovely. Thank you."

She thinks he's going to want to shake her hand or Sean's, but he only nods and says, "Well. Pleasure meeting you."

Sean nods back and watches him walk away.

When he's gone, Sean says, "We need to get away from here."

"We're fine," says Molly.

"You don't know what he'll do. Or what his friends might do."

"They won't do anything," Molly says, looking out the window. "Besides, we can't go. Not yet."

Across the street, there are two fresh cops on the scene. City cops: Knoxville PD. Their cruiser is parked haphazardly in the Taco Bell lot. It's blocking in Sean's Camry.

The shirtless guy is still sitting on the ground, scratching at the side of his head. The cops try to coax him up. One of them reaches for his elbow. The shirtless guy slaps his hand away.

It goes on, the two city cops trying to get the guy to stand. Patient, even when he swats at them. The campus cop looks on. About a dozen people gather to watch. Most of them look like students, but one woman stands apart. She's dressed professionally in a skirt and blouse. She's holding up her phone, shooting video. She's trying to talk to the cops. They mostly ignore her.

Molly finishes her salad. Sean fusses with his steak. Outside, one of the city cops finally persuades the shirtless guy to come along peacefully. The cop guides him by the arm and deposits him in the back seat of the cruiser.

The cruiser backs out of the lot and drives away. The ambulance follows suit a minute later, and so does the campus cop. The crowd disperses until there are only a few people left. One of them is the woman in the skirt.

The waitress comes to the booth and Molly tells her they're ready for the bill.

She doesn't have the bill.

She's got a whole speech ready. She delivers it in a soft voice but with an edge of excitement, like she's telling them a thrilling secret.

"When you first came in, I didn't recognize you. But now, I mean, *obviously*. I've been seeing you on the news, we all have, me and Bonnie and everybody, and we're just so grateful for what you did out there in Houston." She reaches out and her fingertips graze Sean's shoulder. "God bless you, both of you. It's a real treat to have you here. And your lunch, well that's covered, don't you give it another thought. In fact, we took up a little collection, the staff and some of our regulars." She draws a sheaf of cash from the pocket of her apron and lays it on the table. "It's not a lot, some gas money, but maybe it'll get you on the way to where you're going."

She pats the money, nervously. Molly looks across at Sean and knows his pride will make him want to refuse it. She slides out of the booth, smiling, and pulls the waitress into a hug. "Thank you," she says. "That's the most generous, sweetest thing. We need to go, but you'll thank everyone for us, won't you?"

"I sure will," the waitress says.

Sean hugs her, too, but Molly, watching him, knows he's not comfortable. They wave at the other waitresses as they make their exit. Outside, a robin hops along the sidewalk. The sun feels warm. Sean says, "We didn't need to take that girl's money."

Molly slips the cash into her pocket as they cross the street. "It was the right thing to do, and the smart thing. If we had said no, she would have soured on us. This way she loves us. She wouldn't turn us in now in a million years."

Jennifer Linsey

Standing in the Taco Bell parking lot, Jennifer Linsey is reminded that her job is not as glamorous as she once hoped it would be. She's a crime reporter for the *Knoxville News Sentinel*.

On the upside, if you want to look at it that way, Knoxville has a crime rate much higher than the national average and the average for Tennessee. But it's still not a big city. With a population of less than two hundred thousand, it's not Chicago or Baltimore or Detroit.

There are twenty murders in Knoxville every year, give or take, so most days Jennifer isn't looking at dead bodies. Most days are like today: the police get called out to deal with some joker acting up at Taco Bell. There's a real story here, because the joker in question is someone Jennifer has heard about before. He's a kid who got diagnosed with schizophrenia at nineteen, who had to drop out of UT as a sophomore, who's been in and out of psych wards for years, on and off his medication. He has tried going back to the university, but he can't hold himself together for longer than a semester.

That's a story Jennifer would like to write, but whether the paper would print it is another question entirely. So she does what she can. She tries to talk to the cops, but they're not in the mood. All they want is to get the kid off the street. They give her nothing. She lingers afterward and interviews some members of the crowd. One of them knows the kid. She gets some quotes she might use someday. Not today. Today, on this, her editor won't want more than a paragraph or two.

She's ready to head back to her car when she sees something that alters the course of her afternoon.

It's two people crossing the street. Normally she wouldn't give them a second glance, but this time she does. She's been following the Houston shooting story, and the man in the street looks like a scruffy version of Sean Tennant, the guy who shot Henry Alan Keen.

The woman with him looks like Tennant's girlfriend, who went missing from the yoga retreat in Montana.

There's no earthly reason for the two of them to be in Tennessee, but the closer they get, the more Jennifer is convinced: it's them.

Jennifer has the presence of mind to raise her phone. Her camera app is already open. She starts shooting video.

"Sean!" she says. "Molly!"

They see her, and Sean puts out a hand to block her view, like a celebrity annoyed by the paparazzi. Molly gives a faint smile and shakes her head, as if Jennifer has made a mistake.

It's no mistake. Jennifer is sure. The two of them get into a silver-gray Toyota Camry. The same color and model that Sean is said to own.

They back out of the space and roll toward the street. Jennifer runs along beside the car, still capturing video. "Wait!" she says. "What are you doing in Knoxville?"

Brilliant question, she thinks. You'll get a Pulitzer with that.

Then they're gone, west on Cumberland Ave.

Jennifer runs to her car, but by the time she pulls into the street they're out of sight. She drives west and then north, thinking they might head for I-40, but she doesn't spot the Camry again. They might have turned off at any of a dozen intersections.

She pulls off the road at an Exxon station and reviews the video on her phone. She should share it with the police, but that can wait. The police have done her no favors today, and she has larger responsibilities. As a journalist.

The first call she makes is to her editor at the paper. The second is to CNN.

21

Adam Khadduri

His housekeeper tells him about the story on CNN.

She's a quiet woman, which is why he likes her. She's in her sixties, a second cousin on his mother's side of the family, the Lebanese side. Never married, she keeps to herself. Khadduri doesn't know what she does with her off time, and he doesn't care. She keeps the house immaculate, and if he wants a home-cooked meal she can provide it. Shish kebab, spiced perfectly. Rice pilaf. Tabbouleh and fattoush.

She makes no comment about the story, just lets him know it's on and leaves him alone to watch it. At first it's sketchy: a piece of video shot by a newspaper reporter in Knoxville, Tennessee. The CNN anchor is slightly noncommittal: *We're showing this to you now, exclusively,* he says, *because we believe it to be footage of Sean Tennant and Molly Winter. We're confident of the identification, though as yet it has not been confirmed by any official sources.*

Khadduri doesn't need confirmation. He recognizes them. He hasn't seen Molly in six years, but she hardly seems to have aged.

The story develops over the next hour. Or rather, it stretches out. There's nothing new, only talking heads speculating on what Sean and Molly might be doing in Knoxville. Commentators filling time.

The closest thing to a new development comes when a TV reporter from a local station in Knoxville does a piece from outside a restaurant called Rusty's All-American, the same restaurant that can be seen in the background of the video. It's believed that Sean and Molly spent some time inside. In fact, they might have hidden out there to avoid the police, who were called to investigate an unrelated incident nearby.

What are the people in the restaurant saying? the anchor asks the reporter. *Have you spoken to the customers or the staff?*

That's the strangest part, the reporter says. *They're not saying a thing. I only heard one comment, from a waitress who wouldn't give her name or be interviewed on camera.*

What did she say? the anchor asks.

She said Sean and Molly are good people, and they have friends here in Tennessee.

Khadduri mutes the television, shaking his head.

He takes his phone out and calls Tom Clinton. Tells him the news and asks him to come over.

He makes a second call to Jimmy Harper but gets no answer.

The situation bothers him. He's spoken to Harper only once in the past few days and only for a few minutes—long enough to hear an account of the fiasco at Long Meadow Ranch in Montana. Khadduri regrets not sending his own men to hunt for Sean. They might have had better luck.

Jimmy Harper has proved overconfident and unreliable. Now Khadduri can't even raise the man on the phone.

By the time Tom Clinton arrives half an hour later, Khadduri has made up his mind.

"I'd like you to go to Knoxville," he says.

Clinton nods.

"See what you can find," Khadduri says. "Take Lincoln with you."

"Sure."

"It might be too late, I suppose." Khadduri looks at the muted television. CNN is playing the video again. "Those two can't stay on the run forever," he says. "If the police bring them in, I may never recover what's mine."

"You think they'll get caught?" Clinton says.

"Don't you?"

Clinton stares at the screen. "I don't know. I'm hearing things, from friends in Detroit. From cops who are in touch with folks in the FBI. It's a strange case." He nods at the image of Sean and Molly getting into their car. "There are lots of people who don't want them caught."

"The police don't want to catch them?"

"Not the police. People. There's a flood of calls coming in, from Seattle to Miami, New York to LA, Sean and Molly sightings in hundreds of different cities. Some of them are sincere: people who really believe they've seen them. Others want to gum up the works. It's intentional. It's coordinated."

"What do you mean, coordinated?"

"It started on Twitter," Clinton says. "Do you pay attention to Twitter?"

Khadduri shakes his head. He bought stock in the company when it went public, and he sold it at a profit and never thought about it again. He knows how Twitter works but doesn't understand why anyone would waste their time with it.

"Probably some high school kid got it going," Clinton says. "There were hashtags, very early on. #HoustonHero was one. #ImWithSean was another. That turned into #ImwithSeanandMolly. People expressing their support and encouraging each other to phone in false tips." Clinton shrugs. "A lot of people admire Sean for what he did in Houston, and now they're trying to provide cover for him. There's no telling how long he and Molly might be on the loose. That's good for us. It gives us a chance to find them."

It's a comforting thought, and Khadduri holds on to it after Clinton leaves him. That night, before he goes to bed, Khadduri opens a browser on his phone and searches Twitter for #ImwithSeanandMolly. Fascinating, what people will do to fill up the emptiness in their lives. They'll latch on to strangers, talk about them as if they know them. Call them by their first names. Sean and Molly. Butch and Sundance. Bonnie and Clyde.

They're folk heroes now, Khadduri thinks. Outlaws on the road.

If they stay out there long enough, if they stay free, then his people will find them. He'll get what he wants: the treasure they took from him.

After that, he doesn't care what happens to them.

22

Tom Clinton and Lincoln Reed

Eighteen hours after his meeting with Adam Khadduri, Tom Clinton is in Knoxville, Tennessee. Searching for two people who, in all likelihood, are far away by now.

There are worse ways he could be spending his life, he thinks. He used to be a police officer in Detroit. Joined up when he was young and idealistic. He figured he could make a difference, getting lowlifes off the streets.

After a few years, he figured out that the lowlifes were winning. They had the numbers, and they weren't confined to the streets; they were everywhere. Most of the calls he responded to were domestic: men doing violence to the women they lived with. You could arrest them, even send them away for a while, but they'd come back. You'd see the same ones over and over.

Clinton played the game for almost a decade, until he started having bad dreams. In his dreams, he never arrested anyone. All the violent men he saw, he let them off with gentle warnings. Then he watched them, followed them, came at them at night when they were alone. He brought a metal pipe with him, as long as his arm, and he beat them until they were bloody and begging for mercy.

One day, in waking life, he came across a metal pipe in a vacant lot. He picked it up and threw it into the trunk of his car, thinking he might find a use for it.

A week later he quit the force and went to work for a friend who had a private security company. The bad dreams went away. His friend introduced him to Adam Khadduri, and he's been working for Khadduri ever since.

Clinton has no official title. He tells his wife he's a security consultant, but bodyguard might be more accurate. Or right-hand man. Or jack-of-all-trades.

Whatever he is, he has a partner: Lincoln Reed, another former cop from Detroit. Reed put in almost twenty years, advancing from patrol to detective before he decided to leave the job. Clinton has never gotten a clear answer on why he left. One rumor had it that Reed got caught planting a gun on a suspect he had shot. Another said he got caught sleeping with his lieutenant's wife.

Clinton wouldn't care either way. He gave up on idealism a long time ago. The only thing that matters is that Reed is reliable.

This morning they're driving together through the streets of Knoxville. It's a college town with some nice architecture, and Clinton is taking in the view. Beside him, Reed is complaining about their boss.

"Khadduri's strange," Reed says. "You've got to give me that."

Clinton yawns and offers no comment. He realizes, too late, that he should have let Reed drive. Reed is quiet and focused when he's behind the wheel, but if you put him in the passenger seat he gets restless.

"Stuffy," Reed says. "That's what he is. Talks sometimes like he's got a stick clenched between his teeth. Don't know what his accent is supposed to be. I've been to Plymouth. They don't talk like that there."

Clinton makes a turn onto Cumberland Avenue. "Pontiac," he says.

"What?" says Reed.

"Adam is from Pontiac, not Plymouth."

"Shit. They don't talk like that in Pontiac either. Another thing, they don't move the way he does. You ever notice the way the man walks around? Back stiff, trying to stand up taller than he is. Like somebody took that stick from between his teeth and shoved it up his ass. You walk around like that in Pontiac, it'll earn you a beating."

Clinton stops for some college kids crossing the street. Says nothing.

"*Adam*," Reed says. "Listen to you, callin' the man Adam. Like he's your pal. He's not. You don't mean a thing to him, except what he can pay you to do. Sends you chasing after fugitives. For what? So he can get back some rocks that he likes. He cares more about those rocks than he does about you."

Definitely should have let him drive, Clinton thinks. Reed drove for most of the trip down here: eight hours on the road, five hundred miles from Michigan to Tennessee. They listened to oldies stations and NPR and arrived in Knoxville around 3:00 a.m. Checked into the Holiday Inn downtown. Clinton got up at nine this morning for a jog and a swim in the pool. Knocked on the door of Reed's room around 11:00, and now they're cruising along Cumberland, trying not to run over college kids.

Clinton spots the restaurant—Rusty's All-American—and parks the SUV in the lot of the Taco Bell on the other side of the street. The SUV is a black Ford Explorer, and it doesn't belong to Clinton or Reed. It's registered in the name of someone long dead. Better this way, in case it gets noticed at a crime scene.

Not that they intend to get noticed. If all goes well, any crimes they commit will go under the radar.

As Clinton cuts the engine of the Explorer, Reed says, "This is stupid."

Clinton doesn't need to be told. He's been thinking the same thing.

"Seriously," Reed says. "Unless Sean and Molly waved goodbye to the people in this restaurant and said, 'We're off to Albuquerque'—I don't know what we're doing here."

"We're here to find out what we can," Clinton says. "Because that's what Adam wants."

"Seems to me *Adam* wants miracles."

Clinton is about to tell Reed he can stay in the car, but the words drift out of his head. He's looking at the entrance to Rusty's, and what he sees is Jimmy Harper strolling along the sidewalk, opening the door, and walking in.

Reed sees him too. "Is that—?"

"Yes, it is."

"No shit. Now what do we do?"

Clinton isn't sure. He imagines Jimmy's here for the same reason they are. So they could go in now, like they're all playing on the same team. Or they could hold back. Maybe find an advantage that way, if Jimmy doesn't know they're here.

Reed is silent. Waiting.

"Let's sit tight," Clinton says. "We'll see what he does."

Jimmy Harper

It's probably a waste, coming here.

Jimmy feels like he's wasted the last few days. He and Nick have been driving around in the same rental car they picked up in Bozeman. They spent a night in Idaho, then drove back through Montana, Wyoming, Colorado, Kansas. With no leads to follow, they stopped at random motels along the highway: dingy, off-brand places where you could pay cash and they wouldn't care much about seeing an ID.

The same routine in each place: Hold up a cell phone, flash pictures of Sean and Molly. Watch tired clerks shaking their heads. Jimmy knew it was futile. But he needed to keep moving, to keep trying.

They were in St. Louis last night, checked into a Red Roof Inn, when Jimmy caught the news about Knoxville. Nick crashing on one of the hotel beds, Jimmy on the other, flipping through channels. He came to CNN and saw Sean holding his hand up, palm out toward the camera. As if he knew Jimmy was watching.

Jimmy woke Nick and they drove through the night to Knoxville and checked in to another hotel. They slept late; Nick was still snoring when Jimmy left to come here—to Rusty's on Cumberland Ave. He figured he could give the kid a break. Nick's face is healing, but the stitches are conspicuous. It's not the kind of face you want to take out in public.

It's twenty minutes after eleven, but Rusty's is already starting to draw a lunchtime crowd. Sean and Molly must be good for business.

Jimmy scans the room and settles on a booth in a corner. He asks if he can sit there, and the waitress leads him over. With his back to the wall, he can see everyone else in the restaurant, and he can watch the street.

He knows instinctively that this is where Sean sat.

The decor is old-fashioned: wrought iron light fixtures and rough-hewn wood. There are flags framed behind glass on the walls: the Stars and Stripes and the state flag of Tennessee.

The waitress gives him some time with the menu, then comes and asks him what he'd like.

Jimmy grins at her. "What did *they* have?" he asks.

"I don't know who you mean," she says. But she's playing. She knows. She has a pretty smile, and he's surprised not to see a ring on her hand. She looks like nothing so much as someone's young wife.

"You can tell me," he says. "I bet they had the fish fry."

"No," she says.

"Turkey with gravy and mashed potatoes."

"No."

"Meat loaf? Steak?"

She looks around as if someone might overhear. Then says, "*He* had a steak."

"I knew it," Jimmy says. "What's your name?"

"Denise," she tells him.

"Denise, I'll have a steak too. Rare."

"Yes, sir."

"And a beer. Is it too early for a beer?"

"I don't see why."

"Exactly. I like you."

The steak is fine, and it comes with a baked potato and green beans. Jimmy digs into it; he hasn't eaten anything since the night before.

Denise comes by and asks him if he'd like another beer. He says he would, but she should sit down with him first.

"Oh I can't," she says.

"Sure you can. For a minute."

She perches on the edge of the seat across from him.

"There you go," he says. "Now tell me about them."

"About who?" she says. Playful again.

"You know who. You talked to them."

It's a guess, but it's true. She turns shy. Blushes.

"Everybody keeps asking me," she says.

"What did you think of them?"

"They're sweet. Just . . . nice."

"Did they talk to anyone else while they were here?"

She shakes her head, as if she's already revealed too much. But Jimmy catches something, a glint in her eye. This might not be a waste.

"Come on," he says. "You can tell me."

She's teetering on the edge, but when she falls she doesn't fall his way. She gets up and winks at him and says, "Back to work."

A little later she delivers the beer he wanted. Jimmy finishes his steak and orders fish-and-chips to go, for Nick. He leans back, nurses the beer, feels the warmth of the sunlight through the window. More people come in. It's a lively place. Jimmy looks them over, wonders if any of them were here yesterday.

A busboy clears his plate away and fumbles with the silverware, dropping a knife on the floor. He's slightly skeevy looking, with a tattoo on his neck that the collar of his shirt can't hide. Denise arrives with the fish-and-chips in a Styrofoam box. She lays the bill facedown on the table.

"What if I need to see you?" Jimmy asks her.

There's the blush again. "I guess you'll have to come back," she says.

He taps the bill. "Write your number on there, in case I need to call."

She gives him a look that says, *Oh you, you're trouble,* and she writes her number down.

Tom Clinton and Lincoln Reed

Jimmy Harper stays in Rusty's for an hour, and when he comes out he's carrying a takeout box. Clinton watches him walking west, until he reaches the end of the block and turns a corner onto Twenty-First Street.

Reed got hungry, waiting. He bought a sack of tacos and he's eating the last one.

"Now what?" he says.

Clinton starts the engine and pulls out onto Cumberland. He drives past Twenty-First and turns onto Twenty-Second, which brings him around to the street that runs behind Rusty's. Clinton stops well short of the lot behind the restaurant and sees Harper walk to a blue sedan and set his takeout box on the hood.

Then nothing. Harper doesn't get into the car. He stands there, staring at the back of the restaurant.

"What's he doing?" Reed says.

"I don't know," says Clinton.

Jimmy Harper

Twenty minutes. That's how long Jimmy waits.

He spends the time thinking about how to handle Denise and what he might have to do to her if she won't tell him what he needs to know. He doesn't like the images that come into his head. But maybe there's another way.

After twenty minutes, the busboy comes out for a smoke. He stands by the dumpster with his head bowed. He looks up as Jimmy approaches.

"What do you want?"

"I want to talk to you," Jimmy says.

"I don't know you."

"Doesn't matter. You work yesterday?"

The busboy takes a drag on his cigarette. "I work every damn day."

"So you saw when that couple came in, the ones on the news?"

"Those rock stars, Sean and Molly? Sure."

"You talk to them?"

"Nah."

"You overhear anything they said to each other?"

The kid shakes his head. "I just clear the tables, man."

"I bet you heard something," Jimmy says. "Or saw something."

There's a plastic milk crate on the ground near the dumpster. The busboy kicks it with the toe of his shoe.

"How much would you bet?" he says.

"How much?"

"Yeah. You play high stakes or is it just nickels and dimes?"

He's trying to be clever.

"How about fifty bucks and you tell me what you know?" Jimmy says. "Are those stakes high enough?"

"I don't think so," the busboy says. "Sounds like penny ante to me."

Jimmy laughs. "Where'd you get that ink on your neck?"

The kid looks away, evasive. "My cousin—"

"No. It wasn't your cousin. It looks like something they gave you in prison. Some skinhead with a needle and a ballpoint pen. Am I right?"

No answer, but Jimmy knows he's hit the mark. He says, "You ever take a beating in prison?"

The busboy drops his cigarette and grinds it out. "From tougher guys than you."

"I wouldn't count on it," Jimmy says. "But let's not find out. How about I give you a hundred bucks?"

A hundred is the magic number, Jimmy thinks. But the kid plays coy, lighting up another smoke and pretending to mull it over.

"That guy, Sean," he says. "He's a good shot."

"You think so?" Jimmy says.

"He did all right in Houston. You're not his friend, are you?"

"No."

"Or hers either."

"Nope."

"Maybe he'll shoot you."

"We'll see."

The busboy turns his head to let out a stream of smoke. "They talked to two people yesterday, far as I know. That waitress, Denise, she was one of them."

"Who was the other?"

"A lawyer. But he was only with them for a minute."

"Do you know this lawyer's name?"

"Yeah. He comes in a lot. Let me see the hundred."

Jimmy takes five twenties from his wallet and holds them up. The busboy reaches for them. "Howard Frazier," he says.

Tom Clinton and Lincoln Reed

They watch Harper from the SUV, see him talking with the smoking kid. Clinton is intrigued when Harper's wallet comes out.

When Harper returns to his car, they let him go. As soon as he's out of sight, they swing into the parking lot. The kid is still working on his cigarette by the dumpster.

Clinton and Reed approach him on foot. The kid looks them up and down and says, "Five hundred bucks. That's what it's gonna cost you."

"Is that right?" Clinton says.

"Five hundred. No less. That's what the last guy paid."

"What did he get for five hundred?" says Reed.

"He got a name."

"That's a lot, for a name."

"He seemed happy."

"We could give you two hundred," Clinton says.

"Or we could break your arm," says Reed.

"Tough guys," the kid says. "He threatened me too. Didn't work."

"Two fifty," Clinton says. "That's as high as I go."

The kid tips his head up and blows smoke. "All right. Let's see the money."

23

Rafael Garza

When Rafael Garza learns that Sean and Molly have been spotted in Knoxville, he's in bed with a pretty, thirty-three-year-old FBI agent named Rachel Massoud.

He met her on his second day in Michigan. On the first day, he met Len Palmer, a police detective in an upscale Detroit suburb called Huntington Woods. Palmer dug through a file cabinet and dropped a green folder in front of Garza. The contents were slim. They had to do with a burglary from nearly six years ago.

Back when Sean Tennant was known as Sean Garrety.

"He was a suspect?" Garza said.

"He was," said Palmer. "Along with a friend of his, Cole Harper. Garrety lived in Detroit back then, and he skipped town before we had a chance to interview him. I haven't thought about him in years. I didn't connect him to Sean Tennant until you called."

Palmer drove Garza out to the scene on Elgin Avenue and walked him through what happened.

"Our only witness was a retiree named George Monahan," Palmer said. "He saw Garrety and Harper carrying two backpacks and a briefcase, coming around the side of that house." Palmer pointed across the street. "He spoke to them. He wanted to let them know their car had been damaged. Monahan was sort of a wannabe cop, active with the neighborhood watch. He had a concealed carry permit, and he was carrying that night. He got suspicious of Garrety and Harper when they didn't seem concerned about their car. He thought they must be up to something. They were too eager to leave. They didn't want to stay and file a police report. 'They seemed off' is what he told me. So he drew down on them."

Palmer shrugged, as if to acknowledge that people are unpredictable. "'A citizen's arrest' is what he called it. But they had guns too. Monahan put two bullets in Cole Harper, and Harper put one in him. Sean Garrety loaded Harper into the car and sped off. They ended up at Beaumont Hospital, about ten minutes away. Harper died. One of his wounds was to the chest."

"And Garrety?" Garza asked.

"Disappeared from the hospital."

"You're sure it was him?"

"Monahan picked him out of a photo array."

Garza gestured at the house across the street. "Let's go back to the burglary. What did Garrety and Harper come away with?"

"That's where things get interesting," Palmer said. "The loot disappeared with Sean Garrety. The owner of the house is an art dealer named Adam Khadduri. At first he said all they took was some wristwatches and a few hundred dollars he had lying around. When we told him about the backpacks and the briefcase, he looked again and said they had made off with a set of sterling silver flatware he had inherited from his parents."

"Two backpacks full?" Garza said. "That's a lot of spoons."

"It gets better," Palmer said. "When we went through Cole Harper's possessions the night he died, he was carrying lock-picking tools, which is how they gained entrance to the house. But he had something else too. Something odd."

"What?"

"A hunk of amethyst as big as your thumb, with carvings on it. Looked valuable, but we didn't know what the hell it was. We had to ask the FBI."

"Did they know?"

"Yes they did. You should talk to them."

The next day Garza drove to the FBI field office in downtown Detroit. He waited an hour in the lobby and then got passed from office to office until he ended up with Rachel Massoud.

She had long black hair and skin the color of cinnamon, and if she had been taller he would have thought of her as exotic. She wore a well-tailored suit in charcoal gray, the skirt ending just above her knees, and the heels on her shoes brought her up to maybe five foot three. If you were an awkward boy in high school, Garza thought, you would have a crush on Rachel Massoud. She would be the friendly girl who talked to you in your art class. You would see her sitting alone in the library, and you would imagine that you could have a special connection with her, because you were both serious, sensitive people. And if you worked up the courage to ask her out, you would discover that she was dating a football player. But she would be sweet about turning you down.

"You came all the way from Texas?" she said when he introduced himself.

"By way of Montana," he said.

"Sounds like the Houston PD has money to burn. Why don't you buy me lunch?"

They walked four blocks to a Thai place called Go Sy, and over plates of fried rice she told him about the stone found in Cole Harper's pocket.

"It's a cylinder seal, an artifact from the Akkadian empire dating back to the twenty-third century BC. They were common back then. The Sumerians used them, too, for signing contracts. You'd roll the seal over a clay tablet, and the image on the stone would be pressed into the clay."

"If we're assuming Harper took it from Adam Khadduri's house," Garza asked, "where would Khadduri have gotten it?"

"That particular seal was one of several stolen from the British Museum in London. Khadduri would have picked it up on the black market."

"And then it got stolen from him," Garza said. "Did Cole Harper and Sean Garrety break into his house at random, or did they know what he had?"

"There's a good question," said Rachel Massoud.

"How would they know? What's the connection between Garrety and Harper and Khadduri?"

Rachel rested her chin on her hand and looked at Garza across the table. Her eyes were a rich, deep brown.

She said, "You really are in the dark, aren't you?"

"Help me out," he said.

"The connection is a woman, and her name is Molly."

Garza frowned. "Molly Winter?"

"She was Molly Bowen at the time."

Garza felt a flush of heat on the back of his neck, something that happened when he was embarrassed, ever since he was a child. He'd been so focused on Sean, he had never wondered about Molly's past.

"Molly Bowen dated Adam Khadduri," Rachel said. "And she disappeared at the same time as Sean Garrety."

"You're certain about this?"

"Absolutely."

"How long have you known?"

The words held a trace of an accusation. Garza heard it himself, as soon as he uttered them. Rachel heard it too.

"Let's not go down this path," she said.

"What path?"

"The one where the police complain about the FBI withholding information. I've been figuring this out myself. Sean Garrety and Molly Bowen were names and pictures in a file to me. It wasn't even my case back then. I inherited it. I only made the connection after the news started talking about Molly and her sudden departure from that ranch in Montana. I shot off an email to your people last night. To Arthur Hayden."

"My lieutenant."

"And you showed up today. Seemed awfully fast. I thought I had conjured you. But now that you're here, I'll do what I can."

The offer seemed sincere. Garza said, "You mentioned a file. I'd like to see it."

Rachel nodded. "That could be arranged."

"How much do you know about Adam Khadduri?"

"Quite a bit."

"Is he violent?"

Rachel raised an eyebrow. "Why would you ask me that?"

"What happened in Montana is sketchy, but someone may have been trying to abduct Molly Winter," Garza said. "If you saw the news, you know that the woman who shared a cabin with her wound up tied to a bed frame with a pillowcase over her head. I spoke to her. She said Molly was afraid of an old boyfriend. A stalker."

"You think Adam Khadduri went to Montana and tied someone to a bed?" Rachel asked. "That's not his style."

"Maybe he hired someone to do it," said Garza. "I don't know. The stalker story could have been a lie. Something Molly invented so people wouldn't take pictures of her and post them online, because she and Sean were trying to minimize their exposure. They would have been afraid of the police, because they knew the police would be looking for Sean in connection with the burglary. But maybe they were afraid of Khadduri too. I might need to talk to him."

A pained expression passed over Rachel's face. "I would have to discourage that course of action," she said.

Garza smiled. "You would?"

"And if discouraging didn't work, I would have to forbid it. Do I need to say why?"

"I think you do."

She was silent for a moment, then pitched her voice low, so as not to be overheard. "Adam Khadduri is under investigation for trafficking in stolen works of art, in violation of federal and international law. Preserving the integrity of that investigation takes priority over some shootings at a mall in Houston."

"Does it?" Garza said.

"It certainly does. No matter how sensational the shootings might be. We can't have you blundering around, spooking Khadduri before we're ready to move on him. That's the message I've been instructed to convey to you. But I'm hoping that even if you resist the message, you'll see that talking to Khadduri is not the smart move for you."

"Why not?"

"It wouldn't get you what you want. You think you're going to question him and he's going to confess to an attempted kidnapping in Montana?"

"Hardly," Garza said. "I could approach him with some subtlety. He knew Molly before. He might have some insight into what she would do now, where she would go. He might even be in contact with her. What if she went to him for help?"

Rachel gave him the raised eyebrow again. "A minute ago you were saying he was her stalker."

"I don't know what he is. But if I were in a room with him, I could get a sense of him pretty quickly. Without any 'blundering around.' Then I would know more than I know now."

She shook her head. "We can't have it. Too risky. And unnecessary. Khadduri won't help you find Sean and Molly. You know how you're going to find them. There's only two ways."

"Tell me."

"The first way: dumb luck. A civilian spots them and phones it in, or a cop pulls them over. There's no glory in that for you, but it gets the job done."

"And the second way?" Garza said.

"You get ahead of them. Figure out where they're going to be. Talk to people they used to know, people they might turn to now. That's what you need to do. I can give you some names. Get you started."

She did more than give him names. She accompanied him over the next few days as he drove around southeast Michigan in a rented car tracking down old friends and relatives of Sean Garrety and Molly Bowen.

She was with him when he spoke to Molly's mother in a town called Flat Rock, twenty-five miles south of Detroit. Janice Bowen answered her door in a taffeta dress, dark green and formal, as if she'd been hosting a cocktail party and they had turned up unexpectedly.

She lived in a tiny apartment, an efficiency with a curtain to hide her bed away. There were stacks of magazines and unopened mail on the seats of the chairs. Garza counted three birdcages and eight parakeets—some of them not confined to the cages. The air in the place held a sour smell.

Mrs. Bowen seemed not to notice. She was eager to talk about Molly. She hadn't seen her in six years and hadn't heard from her in all that time. "But I keep hoping," she said. "I always did my best for that girl. She knows I'd do anything for her. I'd give her my last dime."

"Did Molly have brothers or sisters?" Garza asked. "Or any other family she would reach out to?"

"No," Mrs. Bowen said. "I always wanted more babies. Molly was such a beautiful baby. But her father thought one was enough, and when he passed, that was it for me."

"Did you ever meet Sean Garrety?"

A flash of yellow passed through the middle of the room—a parakeet swooping from one corner to another. It made Garza flinch, made Rachel raise a hand to shield her face. Mrs. Bowen showed no reaction.

"Molly never introduced him to me," she said. "She was always very private. A strong-willed girl. She left home young. I never blamed her. But I'll tell you one thing—"

She broke off suddenly and turned toward the corner, where the yellow bird had been joined by a green one. Both of them perched on a lampshade. The green bird lunged at the other, chattering and flapping its wings.

"Hush now," Mrs. Bowen said. She took a step toward the corner and the green parakeet fluttered away, alighting on top of one of the cages.

"I'll tell you," Mrs. Bowen said, as if there'd been no interruption. "If Molly's in trouble now, she's not to blame. She was always a fine girl. It's his fault. Sean's. That's what I told them."

"Who?" Garza asked.

"The newspeople. They came here to interview me. From Channel Four. I talked to them for an hour, but they only used a minute or two. Do you think they're saving the rest?"

"I don't know," Garza said.

"I thought they'd use more. I wouldn't mind doing it again. I could do it better." Mrs. Bowen paused and stared off at nothing. When she spoke again, her voice had a faraway quality. "I could show pictures, from when Molly was a girl. I could make an appeal to her, ask her to turn herself in. If you want me to."

The yellow parakeet dived down from the lampshade and swept upward in a smooth arc to land on her shoulder.

"I don't think we'll need that," Garza said.

He spent a few more minutes with her and got the names of some of Molly's friends. When he stepped outside into the sunlight, he felt relief. The air smelled clean. He breathed it in.

"Was she drunk?" he asked Rachel. "I looked for booze in there. I didn't see any."

"That's not drunk," Rachel said. "That's crazy."

Most police work is a slow accumulation of facts. It might lead nowhere, or you might think it's leading nowhere until unexpectedly it takes you somewhere. These were truths Rafael Garza had learned early on.

As he spoke to friends of Molly and Sean, the impression that emerged was of two people well suited to each other: pleasant, intelligent, attractive, but perhaps a little aimless. Molly had earned a bachelor's degree from Eastern Michigan University. She wasn't a standout, but she had done well. Her professors remembered her, vaguely. Most of the friends she made lost touch with her after graduation, and when they realized she had moved away without saying goodbye, none of them were hurt. "That's Molly," one of them told Garza. "That's a very Molly thing to do."

Sean had attended Wayne State in Detroit, but he had dropped out after one semester. If he'd made friends there, Garza couldn't find them. Rachel Massoud hadn't been able to come up with a name for Sean's father, and his mother had died when he was thirteen. Afterward, he had gone to live with Cole Harper's family. Cole had three sisters—Georgia, Nancy, and Evie—and a brother, Jimmy. Garza talked to Nancy and Evie and got the impression that Sean had been an odd, shy kid and that he and Cole had usually been off in their own little world. The sisters were glad to be rid of Sean after Cole died; they thought he'd been a bad influence on their brother.

The other sister, Georgia, had moved out of state, and though Jimmy still lived in the area, Garza had no luck finding him at either his home or his business. He left phone messages for both of them.

Cole Harper's mother lived in a nursing home, and the sisters Garza spoke to warned him that she was suffering from dementia.

"She has good days and bad," Nancy told him. Garza found out for himself. He and Rachel drove a few miles south of Detroit to Harmony Senior Living in Lincoln Park, and a nurse led them to a patio with a woodland view. Aileen Harper sat in a wheelchair with a shawl draped around her.

The nurse introduced them and then left them alone. When she had gone, Aileen Harper said, "That one's tricky."

"She seemed nice enough," Garza said.

"That's how they fool you. But that little bitch is a thief. She stole my glasses."

"My dear lady," Garza said. "Your glasses are on a chain around your neck."

"Not these, you fucking moron. My other pair."

Garza smiled. Beside him, Rachel stifled a laugh.

"You have an accent," Aileen Harper said. "Where are you from?"

"My mother was from Juárez," Garza said. "But I was born in this country."

"Mexican. I should have known. What do you want?"

"I'd like to ask you about someone you knew once. Sean Garrety."

"Who?"

"Sean Garrety. Your son Cole's friend."

"Cole's dead."

"I know. I'm very sorry—"

"Got himself shot. Idiot."

"Do you remember his friend Sean?"

The woman pulled her shawl close around her as if she were cold. "There's nothing wrong with my memory, you dirty greaser—"

"I apologize if I've upset you—"

"I remember Sean, that little prick. I wish he'd never moved in with us. I'd stab him in the heart, if I knew where he was. Do you know where he is?"

"No," Garza said. "I'm looking for him."

Aileen Harper stared out at the woods. "Well, if you find him, bring him here. I'll rip his fucking head off. Then I'll bury him and piss on his grave."

Her voice rose on the last lines, and the nurse came and gave Garza and Rachel a withering look. As they left, the nurse was speaking softly to Aileen Harper, trying to calm her.

Walking back to the car, Rachel poked Garza with her elbow. "Don't let her get to you," she said. "I like your accent."

Sean had enlisted in the army a few months after he dropped out of college. The people who knew him from that time, his fellow soldiers, were scattered across the country. Some were still in active service; some had moved on to other things.

Garza contacted as many of them as he could. He spoke to them by phone from Rachel's office or his hotel room near the Detroit airport. The picture they painted of Sean was of a good soldier, a quiet guy who didn't talk much about himself. Few of them had heard from Sean after he left the army, and none in the last six years.

When Garza asked them if they had seen Sean's picture on the news after the mall shooting, some of them claimed they hadn't made the connection between that Sean and the man they had served with. Others acknowledged they had known him right away. None of them had called in to the Houston police. "I figured Sean knew what he was doing," one man said. "Why should I make trouble for him?"

All the people Garza spoke to told him they would help Sean now if he came to them. But they didn't expect to hear from him. "He's not that kind of guy," they said. "He wouldn't ask for help."

One night in his hotel room, after a dozen calls that led nowhere, Garza got through to a master sergeant named Leland Ross who was stationed at Fort Jackson in South Carolina. He remembered Sean Garrety well.

"I think he was twenty when we got him," Ross said. "Most of the kids I see are eighteen or nineteen when they enlist. But even at twenty, they're still kids. Some of them come in thinking they're ready for a fight. They want it, but then you put them in a situation where they're under fire and they choke. Others, like Sean, you take one look at them and they look scared. You think they'll break. But they come through for you. That's what I want around me, guys that'll come through. They don't have to be fearless, because nobody's fearless, not really. And they don't have to be perfect, because nobody's perfect either. You understand what I'm saying?"

"I think so."

"Seems to me Sean came through in Houston," Ross said. "If he didn't want to stick around after, that's his decision. This stuff I'm hearing now, that he's running from some trouble he got into years ago, that doesn't matter to me. I don't know if he would come to me or not. If he does, I'll give him your number. But I won't turn him in. No way."

"I'm not asking you to," Garza said. "I only want to talk to him. I'd like to help him if I can."

Ross turned quiet, and Garza thought he might have hung up. Until he said: "Dalton Webber. That's who you should talk to."

"Webber?"

"He was captain of our company at Rustamiyah in Baghdad," Ross said. "He retired as a major, I think. Lives on his family's farm in Indiana. He's who I'd go to, if I were in trouble. I don't know if Sean would. But if he did, Webber would help him. He'd feel like he owed it to him. Sean saved his life."

It was late when Garza got off the phone with Ross. He stood at his hotel window, his own vague reflection in the glass. Dots of light moving in the distance: planes coming in for a landing and headlights floating along I-94.

Ross had given him a number for Dalton Webber. Garza dialed it, got no answer, left a short message. He felt tired. He brushed his teeth and lay down on his bed. The ceiling looked gray in the dark.

Garza closed his eyes and glided along the edge of sleep. He thought about Indiana. There was something about Indiana in the file—in Rachel's file on Sean Garrety. But the file was in her office. It would have to wait.

The next morning Garza tried Webber again, without success, and made some other calls. In the afternoon he and Rachel drove west to Ann Arbor to interview Karen Tierney, a woman who had once known Molly Bowen.

They met up with her at a park along the Huron River, a place with slides and swings where soccer moms brought their young children to play. Karen was one of the moms, blond hair tied back in a ponytail, yoga pants and a fleece top, running shoes. She had a four-year-old daughter, a cherub dressed warm to ward off a mild October chill, darting around on the grass with the other children.

Karen watched her daughter from a bench. Rachel and Garza joined her there. She laughed when Garza asked her if Molly had been in contact with her.

"You're imagining a more exciting life for me than the one I have. Desperadoes showing up on my doorstep. No, I haven't heard from her."

"But you were close once," Garza said.

"Sure. We were friends, and she worked for me. I opened an art gallery in Detroit. Not the smartest financial decision I ever made, but it was fun while it lasted."

"Did you ever meet Sean?" Garza asked.

"No, but I heard about him. Molly fell for him hard, and fast."

"I understand she was involved with someone else when she started seeing him. Adam Khadduri."

"That's right," Karen said. "Adam used to come into the gallery. He had good taste. That's how Molly met him."

"What was it like when their relationship ended? Did Khadduri take it badly?"

Karen gazed out at the river. People in canoes floated by on the water. "I'm not sure," she said.

"Molly didn't talk to you about it?"

"No, but I got the sense that something happened. *Because* she didn't want to talk about it."

"Do you think he got angry?" Garza asked.

"Maybe. If I had to guess. But it's only a guess."

"Could he have turned violent?

"I thought he might have, at the time. But I never saw Adam that way, as someone who would be violent."

"How did you see him?"

"I only knew him from the gallery," Karen said. "He was always a gentleman. Courteous, soft-spoken. Of course, people can be one way in public and another in private. But none of the stories Molly told about him raised any alarms."

"What stories did she tell you?"

Karen looked down at the ground. "I remember Adam took her on a trip once, up north, around Kalkaska—to a place called Grass Lake. I guess there used to be a summer camp there. It's abandoned now. All that's left are some cabins and an old chapel at the end of an unpaved road. But it meant something to Adam. He had gone there as a teenager. That's what he told Molly. He'd been happy there, and he wanted to show her. They bought lunch in some town nearby and brought it out there and ate it at one of the old picnic tables. They spread a blanket in the grass after and lay down and looked at the sky."

She turned toward Garza, a trace of a smile on her lips. "I thought it was sweet. He was too old for her, but there was a younger man inside him, someone who wanted to get back what he used to have."

*　*　*

Garza got stuck in rush hour traffic, driving from Ann Arbor back to Detroit. The eastbound lanes on I-94 were packed for as far as he could see, cars creeping forward a few yards at a time. Rachel, in the passenger seat, scanned through the radio until she found NPR. She listened to the news for a while, then switched it off.

"What do people call you?" she said. "Rafael?"

The question took him by surprise. "My old partner used to call me Ray."

She laughed. "Ray? That doesn't suit you at all."

They covered half a mile before she spoke again.

"What are you thinking, Ray?"

"What do you mean?"

"Back at the park, with that woman, you steered the conversation toward Adam Khadduri. You've been good so far, leaving Khadduri alone, like I asked you. But he's been on your mind."

Garza shrugged. "I think Khadduri had something to do with what happened in Montana. He has a motive to want to find Sean and Molly."

"You think it drove him crazy, when Molly left him. But you've got no evidence of that. Were you listening to the lovely tale we just heard? Adam Khadduri's a big softy. He wants to recapture his lost youth."

"I don't know if he cares about Molly anymore. But I'd say there's something he wants to recapture. Sean stole from him. There's his motive. How much do you think Sean took?"

"Nobody knows." Rachel said.

Garza glanced over at her. "I think you know more than you're telling me," he said. "If you're investigating Khadduri for trafficking in stolen art, you must have more evidence against him than the single stone they found in Cole Harper's pocket."

"Of course I do," Rachel said. "Khadduri's been operating for years. Most of his business is legitimate, like any other art dealer. But some of the stuff he buys has been stolen from museums or archaeological sites, often in war-torn countries. It's hard to track. And he's careful about who he sells to. He has connections to private collectors who have no interest in ratting him out."

"How do you go after someone like that?"

"The same way you go after anyone. You look for his weaknesses."

"What are his weaknesses?"

"People who are close to him, who know his business."

The interstate widened to three lanes and the congestion eased. Garza got his speed up to fifty.

"Do you have someone close to Khadduri?" he said. "An informant?"

"You're a clever one," Rachel said, slipping off her shoes, putting her feet up on the dash. "But forget about Khadduri, or you and I won't get along. And I want to get along with you."

Something strange in the way she said it—not like a warning from an FBI agent. Something softer and so subtle that Garza assumed he must be imagining it. He had another half hour in the car with her to think about it. He had planned to drop her at her office, but it was after five o'clock, and she asked him to take her home, directing him up Woodward Avenue to an apartment building in midtown.

He wasn't sure of her intentions, even when she told him he should come up for dinner. He went up in the spirit of an experiment. She put on music but nothing romantic. She poured him soda instead of wine. She moved around her apartment in her bare feet, toenails painted red, tidying here and there. In the kitchen, she put some rice on to boil, then covered it and turned down the heat to let it simmer. She got out a cutting board and an onion. A yellow pepper and a red one. She started chopping the red one.

Garza stood behind her and took her hair in his hands. Gathered it together and drew it away from her neck.

"Well, all right then, Ray," she said. "That's good."

He touched the skin at the back of her neck, with his fingertips first, then with the palm of his hand. She went on chopping. He slipped his fingers under her collar, then his whole hand, rubbing her back between her shoulder blades. After a while, he withdrew his hand and combed his fingers through her hair again.

She was still chopping when he tugged her blouse free of her skirt and laid his palm against the small of her back.

"Jesus, Ray."

She laid the knife down and he kissed her neck. His hand slid around to her stomach and she turned to him. She lifted her face up and he kissed her mouth. Both hands on her waist now, feeling the heat of her. Her breath smelled sweet. She was surprisingly aggressive with her tongue.

He started to pull up her skirt.

"Not here," she said.

They made it to her bedroom, leaving her blouse and her underwear behind. The skirt went last. He unzipped it and it fell to the floor. He laid her down on her stomach and traced his fingers over her, starting at her neck, working all the way to her ankles and back again. She turned over and parted her legs and put his hand on her. She guided him, then let him go on his own. She buried her face against his shoulder as he gave her an orgasm.

She got on top of him after, her long hair falling down to brush his chest as she leaned over him. Her hips moved in a rhythm that built over time, turning fierce, insistent, until the only thing he could do was let go.

He's still inside her and it's a sweet, hazy feeling, the weight of her against him, the touch of her cheek on his chest. He doesn't know if she's asleep or awake.

Until she says, "I want a bath. Do you want a bath, Ray?"

"Yes."

"I've got a tub big enough for two. We can have a soak. But I should turn off the rice first. It might be overcooked."

She doesn't move, though. Not until there's a chirp from a phone.

"Is that yours or mine?" she says.

"It's mine," says Garza. "But it can't be as important as what we're doing now."

She laughs. "There's a nice thought. But you can get it. Go ahead."

It's only a text. His pants are on the floor by the bed. He digs the phone from a pocket and reads the message with Rachel sitting cross-legged beside him.

Turn on CNN.

It's from his lieutenant.

There's a TV on Rachel's dresser. She grabs the remote from her bedside table and clicks it on.

Video of Sean and Molly, getting into their car and driving away. The chyron at the bottom of the screen says: KNOXVILLE, TENNESSEE.

Garza calls Lieutenant Hayden and gets the whole story, thin on detail as it is. A discussion follows. Hayden thinks Garza should go to Tennessee. Garza wants to stay in Michigan. He remembers something Rachel said.

"I need to get ahead of them," he tells Hayden. "Figure out where they're going to be. I won't do that by going to Knoxville. I still have leads to follow here."

Hayden seems skeptical, but he agrees. Garza can take another day or two.

When he finishes the call, Rachel is running a bath. She's wearing an open robe. Garza slips a hand inside, rests it on her hip.

"You've got leads," she says. Teasing him. "Tell me about these leads."

But he does have a lead: Dalton Webber, Sean's captain from Iraq. And the image of Sean and Molly in their car has jogged his memory.

"Cars," he says to Rachel. "When they disappeared six years ago, they each had a car. But they couldn't keep them. Someone could trace them."

"They abandoned them," Rachel says.

"Where?"

"One of them was left in a hotel parking lot in Ohio. The other one in—"

"Indiana."

"That's right."

"There's someone Sean knew from the army who lives in Indiana," Garza says. "A man named Webber."

"Could be a coincidence."

"Maybe it's not. Webber lives on a farm outside a town called Elkhart. It's only a three-hour drive from here. We could go tomorrow."

"That's your lead?" Rachel says.

"That's my lead."

She hangs her robe on a hook and gets into the tub. "All right, Ray. That's what we'll do."

24

Rafael Garza

The Saint Joseph River winds through the middle of Elkhart, Indiana, and the streets bend to accommodate its course. But when you drive a few miles south of the city you reach farm country and the roads are all long and straight and at perfect right angles. The major ones have no names, only numbers.

Dalton Webber's farm is off County Road 7. It has a driveway long and straight like the road—covered in gravel and wet with morning rain. When the driveway reaches the farmhouse, it takes a ninety-degree turn, widens, and runs past a garage to a barn.

Rafael Garza makes the turn and parks just short of the garage. He and Rachel step out into the early afternoon. Before they reach the farmhouse porch, Webber's wife comes out to greet them. She's wearing denim and flannel, and her honey-blond hair is gathered in a thick braid that runs halfway down her back.

She brings them around to a deck at the rear of the house. Sits them at a table. Goes inside and returns with glasses and a pitcher of lemonade. The sun is obscured by a cover of clouds, but it's mild. Sixty degrees.

She leaves them there with an apology for being a bad hostess. She needs to look in on her twelve-year-old son, who's home from school with a cold.

She goes in through a sliding glass door and Dalton Webber comes out.

Garza does his best not to stare at him, though he senses that Webber is used to people staring. Webber is tall, wide shouldered, and from a distance he would put you in mind of a high school quarterback all grown up. You'd have to get closer to see the damage.

It's most obvious on the right side of his face. It's nothing grotesque, but the skin is stiff and waxy. The eyebrow over his right eye is only half there, and the hair on that side of his head is a patchwork. His earlobe looks shrunken.

He walks with a cane, but confidently. He crosses the deck to Rachel and Garza, shakes their hands, and joins them at the table.

There's small talk over lemonade. The farm has been in Webber's family for five generations. They grow corn and soybeans and keep a few chickens and cows for the eggs and milk. Webber and his wife have four children. The oldest will turn sixteen in a month.

Garza asks him about his time in the military, intending to work his way around to Sean Garrety, and soon Webber is talking about Iraq.

"I was in charge of a company of two hundred soldiers, part of a battalion of eight hundred on a base called Rustamiyah. Our area of operations amounted to about sixteen square miles of Shia neighborhoods in Baghdad. This was in 2007, when the Shia insurgency was at its worst. Every time we left the base we were taking our chances. We traveled in Humvees and our biggest problem in that war had always been IEDs, roadside bombs. The armor on our Humvees was good—not like at the beginning of the war. But all it meant was that the bad guys had to come up with better ways to blow us up. Have you ever heard of an EFP?"

"No," Garza says.

"It stands for 'explosively formed penetrator.' They'd take a big metal pipe and put a concave copper disk at one end. They'd pack explosives behind the disk. They'd detonate it remotely as a convoy passed by, and the explosion would turn that copper disk into a molten slug that would burn through the armor on a Humvee."

Webber pauses and scratches the side of his face. "We were coming back from a mission in the middle of the night when we got hit. Five vehicles in a line, and the EFP hit the third one. The one I was in. That copper slug tore through an Iraqi civilian who was sitting next to me. Tore through my legs, too, though I didn't realize it at first. And it set the vehicle on fire. A private named Ortiz never got out.

"Sean Garrety was in the next Humvee in line. He ran up and dragged Cole Harper clear. Cole had been driving. He'd lost a foot. Sean hauled him into an alley between two buildings and fastened a tourniquet around his leg.

"Private Glen Park pulled me out. A skinny kid but tough. He did it under fire too. We had driven into an ambush. There were insurgents with rifles on the rooftops. All around us, other soldiers were returning fire. I was in shock. I'd lost both legs: one above the knee and one below. Park put tourniquets on them, but he had never done it before. I mean he had practiced, but it's different when you're being shot at. He couldn't stop the bleeding from my right leg, couldn't get the tourniquet tight enough.

"We were exposed. He wanted to move me. He lifted his head to call for help, and a bullet tore through his throat."

Webber closes his eyes for a moment. "Park slumped on top of me, bleeding out," he says. "I couldn't move, couldn't speak. I was barely awake. Which was good, because it meant I didn't realize I was slipping away. I would have died there. But Sean came out of the alley where he'd been tending to Cole. He pulled Park off me and dragged me away. Into the alley. Where he tightened my tourniquets and kept me alive until the firefight ended and they could get me back to the base."

Webber runs a hand over his patchy, close-trimmed hair. "I was twenty-nine then, and I had a wife, a daughter, and a son back home. Now I'm thirty-nine and I have two more daughters. Because of Sean." He looks at Garza candidly across the table. "That should tell you something. But ask me whatever you want to ask."

Garza says, "Six years ago, when Sean was in trouble, did he come to you for help?"

Webber nods. "They both came here. Molly too."

"And you helped them?"

"Of course."

"What did you do for them?" Rachel asks.

"I did as much as I could, as much as they would let me."

"What about this time?" Garza says. "Have they contacted you?"

"No."

"But you would help them if they did."

"What do you think?"

Garza leans forward. "I think you would probably do anything for Sean Garrety. Even if it meant lying for him."

Webber sits with his eyes fixed on Garza's and makes no reply.

"I admire your dedication to your friend," Garza says. "We are not at odds, you and I. You have nothing to fear from me. I have no wish to disturb you or your family. I won't ask to search your home, even though Molly and Sean might be hiding in there at this very moment. I only ask that if they are or if you see them or speak to them, you deliver a message for me."

"What message?" Webber asks.

"That Sean should turn himself in. I'll take him into custody personally, and no harm will come to him or to Molly. What he did in Houston, I believe he did in defense of himself and of others. There's no reason he should be charged, but he needs to talk to me, to give me his account. The burglary in Michigan six years ago is another matter, of course. It's a problem for him, but it can be overcome."

"Is that right?" Webber says.

"Absolutely," Rachel says. "We're optimistic that a deal can be made."

"What kind of deal?"

"It's hard to say without knowing exactly what Sean took. Did he ever tell you?"

"No."

Rachel has a photograph of the cylinder seal found in Cole Harper's pocket. She brings it out and places it on the table.

"We found this stone on the body of Sean's friend," she says. "Have you ever seen one like it?"

Webber pulls the photo toward him, shakes his head.

"I'll tell you something about these stones," Rachel says. "They tend to come in sets. They're like stamps or coins. If you collect them, you don't have just one. So Sean might have taken a number of them, and if he still has them, or even if he knows where they are, that's worth something."

"How much would it be worth?" Webber asks.

"It's hard to say, until we know what Sean has. But if he cooperates, if we can recover what he took, then it could be worth a lot. He might do no jail time. He might not even be charged with the burglary."

"That sounds . . . optimistic," Webber says.

Garza takes a card from his wallet, writes his cell phone number on the back, and sets it on the table. "We're looking for a good outcome here," he says. "The way I see it, we're all on the same side."

Driving away from Webber's farm, Rachel says, "That wasn't bad, Ray."

"You think so?" he says.

"You played it cool. I could tell you really wanted to search the house. Do you think Sean and Molly are in there right now?"

"They could be. Their car could be in the garage or in the barn."

"I wonder if we could get a warrant. Webber admitted to helping them before."

"It's probably not enough," Garza says. "And if we tried to execute a warrant, someone might get hurt. And if they're not there, we would lose whatever goodwill we've managed to build up."

"What do you want to do?" Rachel asks.

"I want to park on the side of the road and watch the house, but there's no cover anywhere, and Webber would catch on in a second. So instead we'll drive into Elkhart and find a place to have lunch. We'll wait and see if Sean and Molly call."

"And if they don't?"

"How much time can you spare? Maybe we'll hang around for dinner."

25

Molly Winter

It's well after dark when they drive into Elkhart, Indiana.

Molly is at the wheel. Sean is sleeping beside her. He's clean-shaven now, after Knoxville, and his face looks as soft as a boy's. Molly's hair is gathered under a ball cap.

These minor alterations are all they've had time for. They've been moving.

They headed west after Knoxville, because they'd been driving south and east before and they wanted to break the pattern. They stole a Tennessee license plate for the car at a rest stop on I-40 and Missouri plates just before they stopped for the night at a campground outside Cape Girardeau. The plates they have now are ones they picked up this afternoon in a supermarket parking lot in Kankakee, Illinois.

Little crimes they're leaving in their wake.

It's peaceful, driving in the dark, no radio. They glide over a bridge, the Saint Joseph River down below, and Molly sees the lights of Main Street stretching out ahead of her. She stops at a red light, and there's a woman crossing with a chocolate Lab on a leash. There's an antique shop that's closed for the night and a bookstore that's still open. Farther south on Main she passes restaurants. There's a couple standing in front of one called Artisan. Both well dressed, the man much taller than the woman. They look happy. The woman takes hold of the man's coat to pull him close and turns her face up for a kiss.

Then they're gone. Molly has passed them by. After a few more blocks she comes to County Road 9 and lets it lead her out of town. There's less and less light as the miles tick by, eight of them, and she starts looking for the turn. It's on the left: a narrow lane that runs between two fields.

It takes her to Dalton Webber's farm. The back way, less conspicuous than driving up to the front door. She cuts her headlights and rolls to a stop, a hundred yards away from the rear of the house. Sean is awake now.

"We're here," Molly says.

Outside, it's dead quiet. She's aware of every sound: the engine ticking, the car doors shutting, Sean's footsteps and her own. She looks up, and there's a clear sky full of stars. She picks out the Big Dipper. The shape of the barn looms ahead of them. There are lights on upstairs in the house.

They leave the lane and cut across the grass. There's movement on the patio deck as they approach. A shadow separates itself from other shadows. It moves stiffly, descending three steps to the yard.

"About time you showed up," Dalton Webber says. "I've been expecting you for a week."

Sean Tennant

It's the first shower he's had in what seems like forever, and he stays in it a long time. His muscles ache from days in the car and nights spent sleeping on the ground.

He towels off in a cloud of steam, cracks open the bathroom window to help it clear. He wraps the towel around his waist and crosses the hall to the bedroom where Molly is waiting. It's one of the kids' rooms, the oldest girl's.

The detective's card is on the dresser. Webber handed it over as soon as they came into the house. Sean picks it up now and wonders about Rafael Garza of the Houston police.

Molly is sitting on the bed, running a brush through her hair. She's already showered and dressed in a T-shirt and shorts. She sees him fiddling with the card and says, "You're obsessing. Stop."

Maybe he is. Webber filled them in about Garza and the FBI agent, Rachel Massoud. He told them everything, sitting with them at the kitchen table with the curtains closed, while his wife, Yvette, made them bacon and eggs.

Sean is thinking now what he thought then: Garza and Massoud could be fake. Imposters. Jimmy might have sent them to flush him out. If he arranges to meet them, to surrender, he might end up meeting Jimmy instead.

It's paranoid, he knows. But sometimes paranoia keeps you alive.

He wonders even now if he and Molly should leave. Get back on the road and away from here. But Webber has urged them to at least stay the night. Webber already moved their car into the barn.

"We'll hash it all out in the morning," he said.

Sean hears Molly stir. She comes up behind him and touches his shoulder, takes the card from his hand.

"Tomorrow," she says. "You can worry about everything then."

She leads him to the bed, lays him down, curls up against him under the covers. It takes effort to make himself lie still, and he's sure he won't fall asleep. But there's a clock on the night table, the old-fashioned analog kind, with a big hand and a little one. He had one like it in his room, his own room in his own house, when his mother was still alive.

He never had trouble sleeping there.

He listens to it ticking. On and on, the same sound. He closes his eyes and gets lost in it.

It's bright out when he wakes in the morning. A patch of sunlight falls on the foot of the bed. Molly is already up. Sean dresses and goes down and finds her in the kitchen, drinking coffee with Yvette.

Dalton Webber is shuffling around in sweats, mixing batter, making pancakes.

It's the second batch. The kids got the first. They've already caught the bus to school.

Webber's been up since dawn, and he's been busy. He searched out Rafael Garza and Rachel Massoud online and confirmed, with pictures, that they are who they say they are. "So that's one less worry for you, Garrety." Beyond that, he's been making inquiries, calling up friends from his army days. He's located Steve Z.

It was Webber who put them in touch with Steve Z. the first time, when they came to him after Cole died. When they needed to start over with new identities.

"He's still in business," Webber tells Sean. "He moved out of Knoxville and set up shop in Florida. Three years ago, when his son enrolled in college there. He's in Miami now, works out of a bar called Churchill's."

It's a long way to Miami. Sean left his burner phone upstairs, but Molly takes hers out and looks it up: almost fourteen hundred miles.

"Steve's rates have gone up over the last six years," Webber says, naming a figure that's more than twice what they paid the first time. "I can't cover the whole thing, but I can loan you part of it."

Sean waves the offer away. "I won't take your money, Dalton."

Molly punches him lightly on the arm. "What he means to say is that we're grateful for the offer, but we'll manage."

Sean nods, distracted. He hopes it's true: that they'll manage. The first time, they had the cash and gold coins from Adam Khadduri's safe to pay Steve Z. Now what they have are the cylinder seals.

They're in Sean's coat, which is on the back of one of the kitchen chairs where he left it last night. He reaches for it and takes one of the seals from a pocket. It's rolled in a handkerchief. He unrolls it on the table.

"Do you think Steve would make a trade?" he asks Webber.

Webber leans over the table, examining the stone without touching it.

"I don't know," he says. "I've never talked to him directly. I think you'd have to go and see."

"Couldn't we call him?" Molly asks.

"My understanding is he never discusses business over the phone," Webber says. To Sean, he adds, "How many of those do you have?"

"Fourteen here," Sean says. "Another thirty hidden away."

"How much are they worth?"

"All together? Seven figures, I hope."

"No kidding."

Webber busies himself at the stove, and a few minutes later he sets plates of pancakes in front of Molly and Sean. There's sausage, too, and sliced cantaloupe and grapes.

Sean eats everything that's offered to him, but his mind is on other things. The taste of the food is lost on him.

After the meal he clears the plates and runs water in the sink to wash them. Yvette tells him to leave them, but he keeps going until he starts on the pans and she gets up and shoos him away.

Webber takes him to a small room in a corner of the house. His study. It's got a desk and bookshelves and a window with a view of the backyard. Sean imagines Webber sitting in here working, watching his kids play.

"You've got a good thing going, Dalton," he says.

"I know."

"I shouldn't have come here. But I didn't know where else to go."

"I don't want to hear this speech, Garrety."

"It's not—"

"It's bull," Webber says. "You're where you belong. Tell me what you're thinking, and we'll work it out. You've got those stones."

"Yeah."

"You could turn them over to the cop and the FBI agent. Garza and Massoud. Take the deal they offered."

"I'm not sure what that gets me."

"No jail time is what they said."

Sean turns away from the window. "Jail's not the only thing I'm worried about."

Webber nods. He eases down into the chair behind his desk. "Cole's brother."

"That's right," Sean says. "Jimmy Harper won't be making any deals with me."

"Maybe Garza and Massoud can help you with him. Put you into witness protection. New identities for you and Molly. That's what you're looking for anyway."

"I don't know them. I don't know if we can trust them. Even if they come through, we'll have to do what they say and live where they tell us."

Webber brushes his fingertips over the side of his face. "So you go with the other option. Steve Z. But you're taking a chance. A lot could happen between here and Miami. I could go instead."

"No," Sean says.

"I already talked it over with Yvette. You stay here, and I go and negotiate with Steve—"

"No. You're not doing it. You don't want me staying here. The cops have already been around. If they come again and find me, that's trouble for you."

"It's small trouble."

"It's too much of a risk."

Webber smiles. The damage to his face makes the smile crooked. "I knew a guy who took a risk once. Worked out okay for me."

Sean closes his eyes. Puts his hands on top of his head, the fingers interlaced. "Don't do that, Dalton," he says. "You don't owe me. If you ever did, you already paid."

"That's not how I see it."

"It's how it is. You don't know how close a call it was, me coming out of that alley."

Webber's smile leaves him. "I've heard this before. It was a load of crap then, and it still is."

"It's not."

"Whatever. You came out. I don't care how long it took or how scared you were."

Sean moves away from the window. He wants to pace, but the room is too small. "Fine," he says. "I saved you. And I like thinking about you here on your farm with your family. So if you want to pay me back, live your life. Milk the cows. Plant some corn. Buy some more acreage. Have another kid."

Webber starts to laugh. Sean stands still in the middle of the room and brings his hands down off his head. "We're having one," he says.

It takes Webber a second to put it together, but then he uses his cane to lever himself out of his chair and comes around the desk. He's grinning.

"She's not showing yet," he says.

"It's early," says Sean.

Webber grips his shoulders, pulls him in, pats him on the back. "Good for you, kid."

"I don't know what I'm doing."

"Yeah, that's how it goes."

"I really don't."

"All right."

"Maybe I could go to Miami and Molly could stay here. Would that be okay?"

Webber laughs softly and pats his back again.

"Why is that funny?" Sean asks.

"She's welcome to stay as long as she likes," Webber says. "But I've seen the way she is around you. Good luck trying to convince her."

26

Jimmy Harper

The lawyer, Howard Frazier, has an office in downtown Knoxville.

It's on the ground floor of a four-story building. The main entrance is on Market Street, but there's another in the back that you can access from the parking lot. That's the entrance Frazier uses.

If Jimmy had to guess, he would say it's the one Sean and Molly will use. If they come here.

It's a shaky foundation to build his plans on, but guesses are all he has right now.

He's guessing the busboy at Rusty's All-American was telling the truth when he said that Howard Frazier spoke to Sean and Molly. He's guessing Sean and Molly won't want to run forever. He's guessing that when they get tired of it, they might decide they need the advice of a lawyer. So he's watching Howard Frazier's building for the second day in a row.

Sometimes he watches from a Starbucks on Walnut Street that has a view of the back entrance. At the moment, he's parked in the lot, watching from his rental car. Nick is curled up on the back seat, napping.

Jimmy says, "Wake up."

He says it twice more, then crumples an empty coffee cup and tosses it at Nick's shoulder. Nick sits up, groggy.

"Stay alert," Jimmy says. "I'm gonna take a walk."

It's 11:00 a.m. and the sun is out. He walks to Market Street and crosses it, and a block north there's a small park with trees and benches. A homeless man sits on a low concrete wall with his bedroll beside him. Jimmy leans against the same wall a dozen feet away and watches the front entrance of Frazier's building.

Five or six minutes pass and the homeless man approaches him. Asks for a dollar. Jimmy puts his hand in the pocket of his coat and shakes his head. The guy goes away.

Another five minutes pass before Jimmy realizes he's holding tight to the gun in his pocket.

He lets go of it and withdraws his hand.

The gun is a recent acquisition. He decided he needed it yesterday and wasn't sure how he would get it, but it turned out to be simple. He went back to the busboy at Rusty's and slipped him another hundred dollars, and the busboy put him in touch with a friend of his named Troy. Troy sold Jimmy two Ruger nine-millimeter pistols and two boxes of rounds out of the trunk of a cherry-red Chevy Camaro.

"Is that all, hoss?" he said. "Or do you need somethin' else?"

"That should do it," Jimmy told him.

"I got more. You'd be surprised what I got."

"What have you got?"

"Got what you need, if you plan to get into a fight. Hold on, let me show you."

He dug around in the trunk, pulled out something heavy. A black vest. Kevlar.

"Just your size," Troy said. "I got you covered, hoss. You put this on, you ain't gotta worry about shit."

Jimmy bought it, and now he's wearing it—with a black button-down shirt to conceal it and a lightweight coat over the shirt. He thought it would be uncomfortable, but it's not bad. The worst part is that it makes him sweat. But it's a cool day, even with the sun. He can deal with it.

He leaves the park and walks toward Walnut Street. Gets back to the parking lot and sees his rental car. Nick is in the front passenger seat now, nodding along to whatever music he's listening to. Jimmy scans the other vehicles in the lot. One of them is a blue Mercedes: Howard Frazier's car. But there's another that Jimmy recognizes. A black Ford Explorer.

It's the second time he's seen it. The first time was last night.

Last night he followed Frazier when he left his office. The man drove west for around twenty minutes, to a big house with a well-tended lawn on Wesley Road. The house had a facade of red brick and two tall, white columns supporting the roof of the porch. A row of arched windows on the second floor. A horseshoe driveway and a two-stall garage.

The other houses in the neighborhood were equally prosperous. They were all alike without being too much alike. Jimmy parked along the curb across from Frazier's house and kept watch on the place as the night grew dark. There were other cars parked on the street, so he didn't stand out.

Around 10:00 p.m. he felt ready to fall asleep. He got out and stretched and took a stroll through the neighborhood. Passed a teenager walking a dog and nodded to her like they were neighbors.

As he was walking back to his car, he saw a black Ford Explorer parked a block away from Frazier's house. He watched as the headlights flared on and the Explorer came away from the curb and drove off down the street.

Half an hour later, the same vehicle returned and parked in front of a different house. It was still there when Jimmy left for the night around 2:00 a.m.

He never saw who was inside, but he didn't need to. He knew. And he didn't do anything about it. But now, seeing the Explorer again in the lot behind Frazier's office, he thinks he should.

From a distance he can tell the vehicle is empty. When he gets up close, he sees fast-food wrappers on the floor, and discarded coffee cups.

From Starbucks.

That's where he finds them. Khadduri's men: Tom Clinton and Lincoln Reed.

They're sitting by a window with a view of Walnut Street, drinking lattes and eating muffins. They're dressed in khakis and plaid shirts.

Jimmy remembers the first time he encountered them, a week or two after Cole died. They sought him out one night when he was working late in his office at the repair shop.

They were an interesting pair. Clinton was white and Reed was black, but they were similar in build: tall and solid with thick necks and square jaws. They carried themselves the same way, with a kind of casual arrogance.

The night they came to Jimmy's shop, they wanted to know if he had been involved in the burglary of Adam Khadduri's house. Jimmy convinced them that Sean and Cole had acted on their own; he'd had no knowledge of what they'd planned to do.

Which wasn't quite true.

He hadn't planned it with them, but he had found out about it. A few days before the burglary, he had caught Cole practicing on their father's old safe. Jimmy knew something was up, and he wouldn't leave Cole alone until he got the truth.

He warned Cole not to go through with it, but he knew it wouldn't be enough.

The next day, he went to Sean's apartment. Told him he was crazy. He and Cole were amateurs, and they'd end up getting arrested or killed.

Jimmy made it as plain as he could. He took Sean by the throat, shoved him against a wall.

"If anything happens to Cole, I'll kill you," he said.

He thought the threat would be enough.

Now, in Starbucks, Jimmy orders a venti dark roast and brings it over to the table where Clinton and Reed are sitting. Reed pulls a chair out for him.

"We've been waitin' on you, Jimbo," he says.

"We could have talked last night," Jimmy replies. "At the lawyer's house."

"Seemed like the wrong time," Reed says. "And the wrong place."

"What about now?"

Reed looks at Clinton. Clinton says, "We'd be happy to hear whatever you have to report."

Jimmy turns his coffee cup in a slow circle on the table. "I don't report to you."

"Whatever you tell us, we'll pass along to Adam."

"I don't report to him either."

"That's becoming more and more clear," Clinton says. "Adam has lost confidence in you. That's why we're here."

Jimmy stops fidgeting with the cup, takes a sip. Says, "What will you do, now that you're here?"

"Same as you. Watch the lawyer. See if our friends show up."

"And then?"

"Depends on when they show up and where. I figure we'll have to improvise."

Jimmy turns the cup again. Clockwise. Three hundred sixty degrees. "Could be a waste of time. They might not come here."

"Could be," Clinton says.

"Doesn't make sense for all of us to watch at once," says Jimmy. "We could take shifts."

"Yeah? How would that work?"

"You could go and get some rest, and I'll stay here. When I get tired, I'll call you."

"And if you see them?" Clinton asks.

"Well then I'll definitely call you."

Clinton smiles and looks at Reed. "He'll definitely call us."

"And we get to rest," Reed says. "He's generous."

"What about this?" Clinton says, turning back to Jimmy. "Lincoln and I will stay, and you can go. When we get tired, we'll call *you*."

Jimmy chuckles and pushes his chair back from the table. He can recognize an impasse when he sees one. He keeps his eyes on Clinton's, which are gray and cold. They're a cop's eyes—unsurprising, since Clinton used to be a cop. He's waiting, and Jimmy can guess what he's waiting for: a parting line, a threat. *Stay out of my way.*

But some things don't need to be said. Some things, it's better if you *don't* say them.

Jimmy stands and takes his coffee and leaves the two of them there.

He hears Reed's voice as he walks away.

"Nice talkin' to you, Jimbo."

Outside, the sun seems brighter, but the wind is cool. Jimmy circles the block again and returns to the rental car. He slides behind the wheel and Nick nods at him without taking out his earbuds.

After half an hour, Clinton and Reed come out of Starbucks, cross Walnut Street, and climb into the Ford Explorer. Jimmy watches them through his open window. They don't start the engine. They're not going anywhere.

Nick says, "Who are those guys?"

Jimmy didn't think he was paying attention. Sometimes the kid surprises him.

"They're trouble," Jimmy says.

"What kind?"

"I don't know yet. Where's your gun?"

Nick pats his coat. "Right here."

"Good," Jimmy says.

"We gonna shoot them?"

"I hope not. But who can say?"

Nick goes back to his music and doesn't ask any more questions. He's been like that since they arrived in Knoxville. Quiet. Going with the flow.

It's just as well, Jimmy thinks. If he had to explain what they're doing, he'd have a hard time of it.

What if he saw Sean right now? What if he spotted him walking across the parking lot? He wants Sean dead, but could he do it here, in the daytime? Walk up to him and shoot him. One bullet to the head and it's done.

Even if he could get away with it, would it be enough?

It seems too quick. Unsatisfying. He should say something to Sean before he does it, and he doesn't know what he would say.

It bothers him, not knowing.

But not too much. Because Jimmy doesn't really think it will happen here. He doubts Sean will come here, to the lawyer's office. There are too many people around who might see him. He would feel out of control.

It's more likely that Sean will arrange to meet the lawyer somewhere. Somewhere he can feel comfortable. That's the real reason Jimmy's here, to keep tabs on the lawyer. To follow him wherever he might go.

If Clinton and Reed follow the lawyer, too, Jimmy will have to deal with it. He can't guess how it might play out; there's no sense in trying to make a plan. Things never happen the way you expect.

He doesn't know how he's going to kill Sean.

All he knows is that he needs to be ready when the time comes.

27

Molly Winter

When they reach Lebanon, Kentucky, Molly is feeling optimistic.

She likes Sean's plan, the one he worked out with Dalton Webber this morning. When she heard it, she approved it right away, except for the part where she was supposed to stay behind.

They argued about that, but not for long. Sean gave in when Molly made it clear that if he left without her she would find a way to follow him.

So they're together, which is what she wants. And they've left the silver Camry behind, which means they haven't had to worry about state troopers pulling them over.

They're driving a pickup truck, a white Dodge Ram the Webbers lent them. All their stuff is in the cargo bed under a waterproof cover: their tent and sleeping bags and everything Sean brought with him from their house in Houston. There's food back there too: a cooler full of sandwiches and drinks.

Sean is driving. Molly trimmed his hair before they left, and dyed her own with a kit Yvette Webber gave her. She's honey blond now, like Yvette.

Little differences, but Molly feels like they're making progress. They're on their way to being different people. That's the goal, after all. That's why they're going to Miami to find Steve Z.

They have a stop to make first. It's out of their way but not too far. An hour's drive on winding country highways takes them from Elizabethtown, where they left the interstate, to Lebanon. From there they drive south a few miles more to a lake that as far as Molly can tell doesn't have a name. They park on the south shore on a lane overgrown with weeds and hike north and west into a forest of lindens and beech trees.

Sean is carrying a backpack and a folding camp shovel. He's got his gun in its holster under his coat. Molly is carrying a bottle of water and wearing a denim jacket that Yvette gave her. It's faded and comfortable. In the right-hand pocket there's a nickel-plated thirty-two-caliber pistol. Another gift from Yvette.

Sean seems sure about the trail, although to Molly it seems barely there. She's only been here once before, but there are markers she committed to memory. She sees one of them up ahead. It's a beech with a trunk damaged from some long-ago storm: it's split a few feet from the ground, and it bends like an arch.

Sean ducks under it, leaving the trail behind. Molly follows him, stepping over brambles. A dozen yards on, they come to a clearing with a cedar tree on its northern edge. Sean shrugs off the backpack, unfolds the shovel, and starts to dig.

Sean Tennant

Sean used to have a great-uncle who lived in Lebanon, so technically he's violating his rule about staying away from people and places he used to know.

He figures it's safe, because he only visited his uncle once, with his mother when he was seven, and the man was ancient even then. He must be dead by now.

Sean remembers coming to the lake during that visit, his uncle towing a motorboat on a trailer. Backing it into the water. There were five or six other boats on the lake that day, cruising around in long loops, from the south end to the north. Some of the people driving them were reckless, tearing past the others, seeing who could leave the biggest wake.

Yahoos, his uncle called them.

Sean has a very clear memory of sitting in the back of the boat in an orange life jacket. His mother wearing sunglasses and a wide-brimmed hat. His uncle bringing the boat around in a sharp turn, laughing over the sound of the motor.

When they were back on land, Sean asked his mother if his uncle was a yahoo.

"He is," she said. "But we mustn't tell him."

Sean thought of the lake years later, when he needed to hide the cylinder seals. He didn't want them all in one place; he thought it would be safer to spread them out.

Now he's digging in the clearing at the foot of the cedar tree. He's got the fourteen seals from Houston, and there are another fourteen here. He shouldn't need twenty-eight of them to pay off Steve Z., but he doesn't know what will happen when he gets to Miami. It's better if he has them. He doesn't want to have to come back here.

Almost six years have gone by since he buried the cylinder seals, and he can't remember the exact spot. He has dug two holes already, eighteen inches apart, with nothing to show. The sun's going down. He jabs the blade of the shovel into the earth between the two holes, bears down on it with his boot.

A minute later he finds what he's searching for: a cigar box wrapped in a plastic bag. With a little more work, he pulls it clear, but it's too late. He should have been faster. Everything might have gone differently if he had been faster.

Molly touches his shoulder. Says, "Sean."

He looks up as they step into the clearing: two hunters, one in jeans and one in camo pants, both wearing fleece jackets with orange safety vests over them. Hard to guess their ages: somewhere in the twenties. One is stocky, one thin; both have patchy beards.

"You lost?" the stocky one says. He's carrying a bow and a quiver of arrows. The other one has a shotgun resting on his shoulder.

"They ain't lost," the thin one says. "They're digging."

"Digging for what?" says the stocky one.

Sean stands up, leaving the box on the ground. He holds on to the shovel.

Molly says, "We're geocaching."

"Come again?" the stocky guy says.

"Geocaching. Somebody buries a package and puts the location online. Latitude and longitude. Then other people can come and find it. It's like a game."

"Like digging for treasure?"

"Sort of," Molly says.

The stocky guy steps closer, intrigued. The other one does, too, but he seems distracted. He's staring at Molly. Sean doesn't like the look of him.

"What's in the package?" the stocky guy says.

"Could be anything," Molly tells him. "Sometimes it's a book, and you can sign your name to show that you were here."

"It's a game, huh? You play it a lot?"

"All the time," Molly says.

The stocky guy is looking down at the box, which is still wrapped in the plastic bag.

"Let's open it up," he says.

The thin guy hasn't stopped staring at Molly. "Where are you from?" he asks.

"Elizabethtown," she tells him.

"I feel like I've seen you before."

Molly smiles. "I don't think so."

The stocky guy pokes at the box with the toe of his boot. "Open it up," he says again.

"Go ahead," Sean says. "You do the honors."

"Oh, I've definitely seen you," the thin guy says, laughing suddenly, showing his teeth. "You changed your hair."

He looks from Molly to the box and back. Sean watches him, tries to guess what he's thinking. It's not hard. The thin guy doesn't seem smart, but he seems cunning. He's not exactly sure what he's stumbled into, but he's searching for a way to turn it to his advantage.

Sean knows what the thin guy is going to do before he does it. He's going to bring the shotgun down from his shoulder.

The stocky guy is bending to reach for the box. Oblivious. Not a threat.

Sean steps between Molly and the thin guy and brings up the camp shovel. He slams the flat of the blade on the knuckles of the thin guy's right hand before he can bring the shotgun to bear. The guy howls and Sean drops the shovel and wrenches the shotgun away from him. He sweeps the stock of the gun across the guy's jaw and then jams the butt hard into his sternum. The guy falls backward onto the ground.

Molly Winter

When Sean makes his move, Molly focuses on the other hunter, the one with the bow. He's picking up the box. Molly pulls her gun from her pocket just as he straightens up and turns to see what all the commotion is about.

She levels the gun and tells him not to move, but her voice is soft. He's not paying attention to her. He drops the box, takes his bow in two hands like a club, and moves toward Sean.

Molly shifts her aim and fires a shot. It's meant to go over the hunter's shoulder, to warn him, but it comes a little closer than she intended.

Sean Tennant

Sean hears the shot and spins around. Watches the stocky guy drop his bow and raise a hand to his neck. There's blood, but it's a trickle, like he cut himself shaving. He gets some on his fingers and stares at it.

Molly has him covered with her pistol. "Sit down," she says.

The stocky guy looks bewildered. "What the fuck? You shot me. I didn't do anything."

"Sit."

The guy sits on the ground with his back to the cedar tree.

"Are you good?" Sean says to Molly.

"You bet," she tells him.

Sean collects the cigar box and stows it in the backpack. He does the same with the camp shovel. The thin guy is lying on his side groaning and rubbing his jaw. Sean nudges him with the muzzle of the shotgun.

"You never saw us," Sean says.

When the guy doesn't answer, Sean nudges him again. "Say it."

"Never saw you," the thin guy mumbles.

"You're gonna stay here for twenty minutes," Sean says. "If you come after us, we'll kill you." He turns to the stocky guy. "Understood?"

"I ain't goin' anywhere," the stocky guy says.

Molly picks up the bow and carries it with her as they leave the clearing. Sean is alert for the sound of following footsteps all the way back along the trail to the truck. He stashes the shotgun behind the driver's seat. Molly leaves the bow in the weeds at the side of the lane.

Sean can feel his heart racing as they drive away from the lake, heading for Lebanon so they can get back on the highway. As he passes through the town, he can feel himself getting things under control.

When he turns to look at Molly, she's staring straight ahead. She's breathing through her nose. Slowly, deliberately.

"Are you okay?" he says.

"I'm fine."

He finds a place to pull over, kills the engine of the truck. He reaches over and lays his fingers against her neck. Finds her pulse. It's throbbing fast.

"Did I do good?" she asks him.

"You were perfect."

He gets free of his seat belt and unclips hers, and she leans into him and he holds on to her, rubbing her back.

"Perfect," he says. "Perfect." Over and over.

He remembers what Dalton Webber told him: *A lot could happen between here and Miami.*

Sean has just seen a sample. And it could have been much worse, because if he hadn't had the shovel in his hand, he knows what he would have done. He would have drawn his gun and blasted those two yahoos.

He weighs it all out over the course of a few minutes while they're parked at the roadside and he's listening to Molly breathe. There's a thousand miles to cover between here and Miami, and when he gets there he might find that Steve Z. isn't interested in cylinder seals, that he doesn't want to be paid in anything but cash.

There's Rafael Garza, the detective from Houston, who says he's willing to make a deal if Sean turns over the seals. The idea seems more attractive now than it did before.

If Sean were on his own, he might keep the deal in mind as a last resort and take his chances with Steve Z. But he's not on his own.

He strokes Molly's hair, kisses her cheek.

"I made a mistake," he says.

He draws away so he can look into her eyes.

"We shouldn't be here. What just happened shouldn't have happened. You should never have had to go through that."

"Sean—"

"I won't let it happen again."

"I'm fine," Molly says. "I told you."

"I know."

"I can handle a lot worse."

Sean touches his forehead to hers. "I know you can. But I don't want you to. This needs to end. I'll talk to Garza. I'll take whatever deal he offers."

She sits up straight, traces her thumb over his chin, takes a long look at him.

"You're forgetting something," she says.

"What?"

"We're in this together. *We'll* talk to Garza."

He smiles. "Okay."

"And we'll be smart about it," she says, reaching for her handbag, rooting around. "We'll talk to a lawyer first."

She finds the card and holds it up for him to see: HOWARD FRAZIER, ATTORNEY-AT-LAW.

28

Jimmy Harper

It's after seven o'clock when Frazier leaves his office.

Jimmy is by himself in the rental car. Nick was whining about being hungry, so Jimmy gave him twenty bucks and told him to get something. That was ten minutes ago. No sign of him coming back.

Frazier's blue Mercedes drives out of the lot, and Clinton and Reed follow in the black Ford Explorer. Jimmy starts his car and trails after them.

He phones Nick as he goes. "Frazier's moving."

"Shit," Nick says.

"Don't worry about it," Jimmy tells him. "Go back to the hotel."

Frazier takes the same route he took the day before: west for eight miles on I-40, then north to his house on Wesley Road. Clinton and Reed handle the tail professionally. They hang back, giving Frazier plenty of room.

When Jimmy reaches the house and drives past it, he sees the garage door closing on the blue Mercedes. He finds the spot where he parked before: north of the house on the opposite side of the street. Clinton and Reed take up their position to the south.

It's dark and getting darker. Jimmy settles in for a long night of nothing. Around eight thirty there's movement at the side of the house, but it's not Frazier. It's a woman, presumably his wife. All she does is walk out to the mailbox and back.

At ten o'clock, Jimmy starts to get restless. He holds out until ten thirty, then takes a fifteen-minute stroll. He doesn't run into anyone. Nobody's walking their dog.

He's barely back in the car when he sees headlights coming up the road from the south. A white pickup truck slows as it approaches the Frazier house. It swings into the horseshoe driveway and comes to a stop.

The driver's door opens, and Sean climbs out.

Tom Clinton and Lincoln Reed

"Would you look at that," Clinton says.

Reed whistles beside him.

Molly's out of the truck now on the passenger side. She joins Sean and they walk to Frazier's front door. After a few seconds, it opens to admit them.

"Bet you're glad I'm here about now," Reed says.

Clinton doesn't answer him.

"Because I had the foresight to bring ski masks."

Clinton sighs. "We're not using the ski masks."

"Are you going in without a ski mask? 'Cause I'm not."

"We're not going in," Clinton says.

Reed clicks his tongue against his teeth. "What would *Adam* say? You think he'd want you sittin' on your ass? Are we gonna observe and report?"

"I know he doesn't want us shooting up a lawyer's house."

"Might not have to shoot if we do it right."

Clinton turns to him, eyes narrowed. "Do you believe that? Really?"

"No, I don't," Reed says. "You know why? Because I'm a sensible fuckin' man. I know when I've been given a job that's impossible to do. When are you gonna figure it out?"

Molly Winter

The Fraziers have been expecting them. Molly called Howard Frazier when she and Sean were still an hour and a half from Knoxville.

Frazier greets them at the door in a red cardigan sweater that makes him look like Mr. Rogers. He ushers them into the living room. There's a wood fire burning in a big stone fireplace.

Frazier's wife comes in from the kitchen. Theresa. She has auburn hair and tortoise-shell glasses. She's wearing an apron over a blue cotton dress. She's been baking cookies: chocolate chip. There's a plate of them set out on a long mahogany coffee table.

Other things too: cheese and crackers, apple slices, honey-glazed almonds. As if they're old friends getting together.

Molly appreciates the kindness. Sean seems uneasy, perching on the edge of the sofa when Howard Frazier invites them to sit. Theresa offers wine. Molly asks for water instead. Frazier wants to start with the shootings at the mall in Houston, and soon Sean is telling the story— Frazier interrupting him occasionally to ask for details, writing notes on a yellow pad.

As the story goes on, Sean seems to relax, leaning back into the cushions. Theresa excuses herself; she has another batch of cookies to check on. Molly follows her and asks if there's a bathroom she can use. Theresa points her down a hall.

It's a modest powder room, hardly bigger than a closet, but there are little homey touches that remind Molly of the Webbers' farm: lace curtains on the window, a clamshell bowl of scented soaps. Hard to believe she was there only this morning.

Afterward she looks in on Sean and Howard Frazier, still talking, and wanders into the kitchen. Theresa has a tray of cookies cooling on the counter. She's pouring herself a glass of red wine.

"You look lost," she says to Molly. "No. Lost is the wrong word. You look like you're not sure you should be here."

"Do I?"

Theresa nods. "For one thing, you haven't taken off your coat."

It's true. Molly smiles sheepishly. But she doesn't make a move to take it off.

"You can relax," Theresa says. She gestures at the wine bottle. "Are you sure you wouldn't like some?"

Molly's right hand moves reflexively to her stomach. "I can't."

Theresa looks her over, understanding. "For heaven's sake," she says.

Then she's asking how far along Molly is. All Molly has is a guess: two months, she thinks. Theresa wants to know if there's anything she needs, how long she was on the road today, if she'd like to lie down.

"I don't want to put you out," Molly says.

"You silly girl," Theresa says. "I've already fixed a room for you."

Tom Clinton and Lincoln Reed

Clinton looks out through the windshield of the Explorer and it's as if everything's frozen: the house and the garage and the white truck in the driveway. Four people in the house, at least, and he can imagine them frozen too. But they're in there, doing something, and time is ticking away.

"I'm waiting." Reed says.

Clinton keeps his eyes on the house. "For what?"

"For you to come up with a big idea."

Clinton has one, but it's far from big. "Open the glove box," he says.

"What's in the glove box?" Reed asks.

"What I brought along, instead of ski masks."

It's a GPS tracker. Reed takes it out and weighs it on his palm.

"What are we doing with this?" he says.

"It's linked to my phone," Clinton tells him. "We put it in the truck and we'll know where they go when they leave here."

"That's smart," Reed says. "Or it would be, if there was any reason to think they're gonna leave in the truck."

"They might."

"If you're in trouble and you go to a lawyer," Reed says, "that generally means you're ready to turn yourself in. So my money's not on them leaving in the truck. When they go, they'll go with Frazier or in the back of a cruiser."

Clinton knows it's probably true. But the tracker is the best chance they have. Their other option is to call Adam Khadduri and admit defeat.

"Go on," Clinton says. "Put it in the bed of the truck or in the cab behind one of the seats."

"Seriously?" says Reed. "Why do I have to do it?"

Molly Winter

"I've already fixed a room for you," Theresa Frazier says. "Howard will want to go over everything three times at least, and your young man seems very intense. They'll be up half the night, I'm sure. But you don't need to be. My advice is to have a bath and go to bed."

Molly doesn't know if she'll be able to sleep, but the prospect of a bath is tempting. She decides to give in.

"I need to bring some things in from the truck," she says.

There's a side door off the kitchen. Theresa unlocks it for her. "I'll help you," she offers.

"No, no," Molly says. "I can do it myself."

Jimmy Harper

It's an act of discipline, staying in the car.

Jimmy wants to get closer. Wants to creep up to a window of the Frazier house and see what's going on inside. But he bides his time. His chance will come, he thinks.

He doesn't know how, but not knowing is part of it. He has to be patient.

Clinton and Reed seem to have the same idea. The black Ford Explorer sits on the street, in the shadows under a tree.

Jimmy doesn't see the Explorer's passenger door open. He doesn't realize anything's happening until he sees a tall figure walking along the sidewalk.

It's Lincoln Reed. Jimmy recognizes him when he turns to follow the curve of the Fraziers' driveway. A bold move, nothing furtive about it. Reed steps to the back of the pickup truck as if it belongs to him. He lifts a corner of the bed cover and reaches into his pocket.

Then his head snaps toward the house, as if he's heard something. Whatever's in his pocket stays there. Three quick strides take him to the front of the Fraziers' garage. He stands with his back pressed against the garage door.

And Molly comes out from around the side of the house.

Lincoln Reed

The girl comes right to him and there's no time for planning or finesse.

Reed rushes her as soon as she steps into view, maneuvers to get behind her, one arm around her waist, one hand clapped over her mouth.

She bites him.

He pulls his hand away and punches the side of her neck, but it's a weak blow. She's squirming. He realizes at the last moment that she's reaching for something in the pocket of her coat. He grabs her wrist and yanks it out. Sees the gun, a little silver lady pistol.

He jerks her arm so that when she fires, the gun is aiming at the ground.

Just one shot and then he spins her around and slams her gun hand against the corner of the garage. The pistol flies from her grip and into the grass.

Jimmy Harper

Jimmy watches things unfold from across the street. The gunshot, when it comes, makes him flinch. It's followed shortly after by a revving engine: the Ford Explorer rushing up the street and into the Fraziers' driveway.

It brakes to a stop behind the pickup, and Lincoln Reed lifts Molly onto his shoulder and scrambles into the back with her.

Frazier's wife is the first one out of the house. She's just in time to see the Ford Explorer reverse out of the driveway and tear off southward.

Then Sean charges from the front door, with Frazier trailing behind him.

Sean Tennant

The gunshot makes him fear the worst.

He expects to see Molly lying on the ground, but she's not there and there's no blood. There's only Theresa Frazier, apologizing. *Shouldn't have let her come out here alone.*

A black SUV, she says. *I didn't get the license plate. I'm sorry. It went so fast.*

She's pointing south down the street. *That way.*

Howard Frazier has his cell phone out, calling 911.

Sean runs to the pickup truck, Frazier shouting after him to wait.

Jimmy Harper

Jimmy has a moment of indecision.

As soon as he sees Sean, he gets out of the car. His Ruger pistol in his right hand.

Sean is maybe thirty yards away. It's a shot Jimmy could make. But he doesn't raise the gun.

If he kills Sean now, will he need to kill the lawyer, too, and the lawyer's wife?

It's too much to process, and things are happening too quickly. Jimmy watches Sean climb into the pickup, and there's a second when Sean is pulling the truck's door shut and he stops.

Sean sees him.

They're locked together.

Jimmy can see Sean waver.

Then the door closes, and the pickup truck is on the move. It swings along the curve of the driveway and speeds off down the street after the Ford Explorer.

Sean Tennant

"You're okay. You're okay. You're okay."

Sean doesn't know how many times he hears the words before he realizes he's the one saying them.

He's talking to himself out loud, the way he used to do when he was a child.

He makes himself stop and focus on the road ahead. He's driving too fast and not fast enough. There's no black SUV in sight.

He comes to the southern end of Wesley Road and has to make a decision. It's a T junction with Kingston Pike. He has to go east or west. He chooses west.

After a little more than a mile, there are signs for Interstate 40. He follows them and takes the ramp: I-40 westbound.

"You're guessing," a voice says. Not his own this time.

Cole's.

Sean glides into the passing lane. Gets his speed up to eighty.

"Brilliant," Cole says. "Don't know where you're going, but you're making really good time."

Sean ignores him, scanning ahead for a black SUV.

"So many questions," Cole says. "Like, how did Jimmy find you? That one's easy. Somebody at the restaurant squealed about the lawyer. You thought all those people were on your side."

Sean passes a little red Mazda, a semitruck, a lime-green Volkswagen Beetle. No SUVs.

"Another question," Cole says. "Why didn't you shoot Jimmy back there? That's a puzzler. Maybe you didn't want to do it in front of your lawyer."

"He's not my lawyer," Sean says.

"No. Not now, I guess. But you never really wanted a lawyer. You were doing it for her. That's ironic, isn't it?"

"Shut up."

"What do you think they'll do to her? There's a question. And who are they? Who took her?"

"People working for Jimmy," Sean says.

"Maybe."

"Or for Khadduri."

"There you go. If it's Khadduri, maybe you can get her back. You've got something he wants. Forty-four somethings."

Sean spots a dark SUV, though it looks more blue than black. He accelerates to draw up alongside it. There's a white-haired woman driving.

"She looks sinister," Cole says. "But I wouldn't peg her as a kidnapper."

There's a U-Haul van up ahead. Sean slides into the right lane to pass it. He hopes he'll find what he's looking for on the other side, but there's nothing but gray highway stretching out ahead of him. He wonders if he should exit and go back. Maybe the SUV drove east.

He lets a minute pass, and another. He looks in the rearview mirror and sees a set of headlights, close.

"He's back there," Cole says. "You knew that, right? He's been following you. What are you gonna do about him?"

Jimmy Harper

Jimmy doesn't know which way Clinton and Reed went, and it seems clear to him now that Sean doesn't either.

He glances at his fuel gauge: his tank is three-quarters full. He can drive a fair distance without stopping. He wonders if Sean can do the same.

It's tempting to try to make something happen: to speed up and tap the bumper of the pickup, to flash his high beams. He doesn't do either.

There's an exit coming up. Sean zips across the right lane and onto the ramp. Jimmy does the same, slipping between a VW Beetle and a semi.

At the light at the end of the exit ramp, Sean turns south. Onto Campbell Station Road, heading into a city called Farragut.

Less than a mile later, there's another traffic light. Jimmy watches it turn yellow. Sean's brake lights flare, as if he's going to stop. But at the last instant he races ahead and makes a left turn through the intersection.

Jimmy has to stop to let a tow truck pass, but when it's through he runs the red light and follows Sean.

He doesn't need to go far. Up ahead there's a sign: FARRAGUT HIGH SCHOOL. Jimmy sees a long, single-story building. Brick and steel and glass.

The white pickup is there, in front of the building.

Jimmy stops behind it, a dozen feet back. Cuts his engine, takes the key. Outside, the night is quiet.

The windows of the building are dark, but there are security lights up high on the corners.

Jimmy approaches the pickup with his gun held down at his side. He reaches the tailgate and moves cautiously to the driver's door. The cab is empty.

"We don't have to do this, Jimmy."

Sean's voice, coming from a distance. From the northern end of the building. Around a corner. Out of sight.

"Act like a man," Jimmy says. "Don't hide from me. Come out."

He walks to the corner of the building. Waits for a few seconds. Listening. Then rounds the corner suddenly with his gun raised, his finger on the trigger.

No one there. Just a length of brick wall.

Sean's voice comes to him across the distance, from around the next corner.

"Who took her, Jimmy? I need to know. Was it your people?"

"It was Khadduri's," Jimmy says.

"Are you working with them? Can you get her back?"

"Khadduri and I want different things," Jimmy says, moving slowly along the brick wall. "You know what he wants. He wants what you took from him."

"I still have the cylinder seals," Sean says. "He can have them. But I need her back."

"Don't talk to me about it," Jimmy says. "You know I don't give a damn about those stones."

He listens for a reply as he comes to the next corner of the building. Nothing.

He stops with his back against the brick wall.

"You still with me?" he says.

When there's no answer, he spins around the corner.

No Sean. Just more wall. This time the brick surface is broken up by windows. Black squares of glass leading to a covered alcove in the distance: one of the entrances to the school. There's more brick and glass on the other side of the entrance, leading away to the building's south end.

Jimmy makes his way toward the alcove. He moves slowly with his gun up. Sean could be there, hiding by the entry doors. From this angle, Jimmy wouldn't see him.

"I'll make a bargain with you," Jimmy says. "You tell me where the seals are, and I'll take them to Khadduri myself. I'll make sure Molly goes free. You have my word. All you have to do is come out."

Jimmy listens for an answer, but there's nothing. Just nighttime sounds: the low buzz of the security lights, the hum of crickets somewhere far away. He's coming up to the alcove and he believes that Sean is there, waiting.

Jimmy has been keeping close to the wall, but now he angles away from the building, taking the last few steps at a jog and aiming his gun at the entryway. He sees movement and he almost fires, but it's not Sean. It's his own rough reflection in the glass of one of the entry doors.

The alcove is empty.

Which means Sean went on to the south end of the building.

Jimmy spins that way just as Sean emerges from around the corner. Jimmy has time to bring his gun around for one wild shot. Then the first slug hits him square in the chest and drives all the air from his lungs.

Sean Tennant

Sean hears a shattering of glass, but he doesn't let it distract him. He fires his Glock three times and watches Jimmy drop to the pavement at the entryway to the school.

Afterward, a few remaining shards of glass come loose from their frame and fall away. Sean looks left and sees the broken window. The result of Jimmy's stray bullet.

At that point, Jimmy is still moving.

He's lying on his back and his gun is on the ground nearby. His right arm stretches out away from his body. His fingers walk over the surface of the pavement, searching for the gun. But it's out of reach.

Sean steps closer to him. Not too close.

He doesn't want to be too close.

"I told you we didn't have to," Sean says. "This is not what I wanted."

He stands in the dull yellow glow of the security lights. He knows he can't stay, though he thinks he should. He's not quite looking, not directly, but he sees when Jimmy's fingers go still.

"I'm sorry," he says.

29

Sean Tennant

"How do you feel?" Cole asks.

He wasn't there at the school. But now as Sean drives away, he's back.

"You did it," Cole says. "I know how you are. You had it all built up in your head. The big bad wolf. But he hit the dirt just like anybody else. Three to the chest—"

"Shut up," Sean says.

"You're making too much of it is all I'm trying to say."

Sean sees the sign for I-40. He steers the truck up the ramp and gets on. Eastbound.

"I don't blame you," Cole says. "If that's what you're worried about."

Jimmy Harper

Jimmy hears sirens.

He's sitting up. He has his jacket unzipped and he's working on the buttons of his shirt.

He wants to take the vest off. As if that's the thing that's hurting him.

A long time ago he used to play baseball. Center field. Once, the star hitter on the other team slammed a high fly ball his way. Jimmy got under it but didn't bring his glove up in time. The ball bounced off his chest.

This is maybe a thousand times worse. Like being hit by a train.

Focus.

The sirens are faint, but he can't ignore them.

He decides to take one thing at a time. Forget about the buttons. There's his gun. He scoots over, still sitting. Picks it up. Pockets it.

Good.

Now to stand. Anybody can do it. Little kids. Toddlers. Jimmy rolls sideways onto his hands and knees. Feels like the muscles of his chest want to tear apart.

Better to keep the vest on then. Could be the only thing holding him together.

One foot under him. The ground seems solid.

The other foot. Nothing wrong with his legs.

One good push and he's standing. Like a champ.

The sirens are closer.

Jimmy's breath is steady. It sounded wrong before. Wheezy. He didn't think he'd be able to hold it. But he did. Playing dead, so Sean would go away.

Now, as Jimmy walks to his car, his breathing seems almost natural. Not normal, but no worse than a guy winding down from a long run.

Getting into the car is a challenge. He backs in, then swivels his legs around. Panics when there's no key in the ignition.

It's in his pocket.

The engine sounds smooth. The steering wheel turns hard, like it's attached to weights and pulleys. Jimmy gets himself aimed in the right direction. Reaches the main road and turns north.

He sees the lights of patrol cars in his rearview mirror. Two of them. The sirens are incredibly loud.

The cars turn toward the school.

Jimmy drives on, heading for the interstate.

Sean Tennant

He doesn't expect to find the black SUV. Not now. But he needs to be moving. East is as good a direction as any.

Cole has gone silent, but he's still there. Sean can see him out of the corner of his eye. Slouching in the passenger seat, one booted foot against the dash.

Sean is looking at the first exit sign for Knoxville when his burner cell phone rings.

He slows reflexively, pulls the phone from his pocket. Molly's name on the screen.

Her voice when he answers.

"I'm not hurt," she says. "I love you."

He has time to say "Thank god. Where are you?" before the second voice comes on the line. A man's voice.

"That's so you know we've got her," it says. "Now we'll talk about what you're going to do."

"If anything happens to her I'll kill you."

"Of course. I don't doubt it. But let's talk about the stones."

"You can have them," Sean says. "Forty-four of them. I never tried to sell them."

"I know. Molly and I have been having a conversation. A very civil conversation."

"I have twenty-eight right now. The rest I have to get."

"I've heard about that too. She says there are sixteen buried in the woods in Maine. I don't quite believe her. I think she'd lead us on a wild-goose chase if she could."

"I'll get them," Sean says. "It won't be a problem."

"I'm glad to hear it."

"I'll need a couple days."

"I have your number. I'll call you back and we'll talk about delivery."

"If anything happens—"

"You don't have to say it again. When we get the stones, you get her."

Tom Clinton and Lincoln Reed

Clinton ends the call and hands the phone to Reed, who's in the back seat with the girl.

"Sloppiest ransom call I ever heard," Reed says.

"What did I miss?" says Clinton.

"Forgot to tell him not to get the cops involved."

"He knows," Clinton says, adjusting the rearview mirror so he can see Molly. "Right?"

Her eyes look hateful, but she nods at him. They've got her sitting up, belted in, hands cuffed behind her back, ankles bound with duct tape. And it's true: they haven't hurt her, not in any major way, though Reed had to slap her a little to get her to calm down.

They're in good shape, Clinton thinks, checking his speed. They'll be in Michigan in seven hours. Easy.

Reed holds up Molly's burner phone. "If he does go to the cops, they could trace this."

"Ditch it," Clinton says.

Reed finds Sean's number on the burner and punches it into his own phone. When he's done, he lowers his window and tosses the burner out into the dark.

Nick Ensen

He's having a dream where he turns on a light, the kind with a pull chain, and he's looking in a mirror and his face is back to normal. No wound, no stitches.

Suddenly he's awake, the glare of a table lamp in his eyes, somebody shaking his shoulder. He reaches for the pistol Jimmy gave him, but it's in his coat and his coat is across the room.

"Get up," Jimmy says.

He sounds mad and Nick wonders: What now? What fresh new thing has gone to hell?

"Up," Jimmy says again. "We're leaving."

Nick yawns and sits up. Drinks from a half-full can of Coke on the night table. It's warm.

Jimmy is moving stiffly around the hotel room. He gets out of his coat like an old man. Drops it on the floor. Sheds his shirt the same way.

He stands in front of the full-length mirror on the closet door. Picks at the Velcro straps on the Kevlar vest.

Nick didn't get one of those. He got a gun, but no vest. Tells you something.

Jimmy gets the thing off and it thuds on the floor. His white T-shirt comes off last, soaked with sweat. Nick moves closer. Sees a big purple bruise across Jimmy's chest, reflected in the mirror.

"What the hell happened to you?" he says.

30

Molly Winter

They've got her in a room that's maybe twelve by fourteen, with a double bed and two chairs. It's daytime. Three in the afternoon, if she had to guess, which means that roughly sixteen hours have passed since they grabbed her in Knoxville.

She's in Michigan, as far as she can tell. That's the way they were headed last night. When it started to get light this morning, they were on I-75 in northern Ohio. At that point they made her lie down in the back of the Ford Explorer. So they might have changed course without her knowing.

But she doesn't think so. Michigan is Adam Khadduri's home base. That's where they would take her.

The room where they've put her has a window, and when she looks down she can see a paved driveway. The driveway loops around a ring of stones, and in the center of the ring there's a flagpole with no flag.

It looks like there were flowers planted around the pole, but now they've all died off.

The Ford Explorer is down there in the driveway. And one other vehicle: Adam Khadduri's Maserati.

He's here, but wherever this is, it's not his home.

They've taken her up north, Molly thinks. At least two or three hours outside Detroit. Someplace out of the way. Up north is where city people go in the summer to escape the heat. Khadduri took her on trips up north when they were together, but they always stayed in hotels. Never here. She doesn't know this place.

But from the window she can see a garden shed with a kayak leaned up against it. So there might be water close by.

"Are we near a lake?" she says.

Tom Clinton ignores her. He's in the chair by the bed. There's a television mounted on the wall that's playing episodes of *MASH* back-to-back. He was watching it before, but now the sound is muted. He's looking at his phone.

"How many bars do you have?" Molly asks.

Clinton doesn't answer.

"On your phone," Molly says. "You get a good signal up here?"

Finally he lifts his head. "I could fetch the duct tape from the car," he says.

She takes the hint and doesn't say anything more.

They've both been like this, Clinton and Reed. They've taken turns guarding her: Reed going first, Clinton relieving him about an hour ago. Neither of them wants to talk to her, as if they're afraid she might bewitch them.

Molly rises from the chair by the window, crosses to the bed, and lies down. When they got here they cut off the tape they'd used to bind her ankles, and they uncuffed her hands and recuffed them in front. Reed made a big deal of it, like he was doing her a favor, but it was a practical decision. They wanted her to be able to feed herself.

She's been acting docile so they won't change their minds. Staying quiet. No sudden moves. Now she closes her eyes and pretends to sleep, testing Clinton, seeing if he might leave the room.

Without meaning to, she really does fall asleep. When she wakes, there's a fresh episode of *MASH* on the TV. Clinton is in the same spot as before. He must be getting bored, she thinks. She's being held captive, and *she's* getting bored.

The one bit of excitement came this morning, about an hour after they arrived. Reed was guarding her, and he had the TV tuned to ESPN—the sound turned up. Some show where they played highlights from football games and talked about them with a panel.

Molly was at the window looking out, wondering if she could open it and climb through before Reed could cross the room. Wondering if she would break her legs if she jumped.

She decided she would probably only sprain her ankles. Just then a car came along the driveway and stopped behind the Ford Explorer. A woman got out: Noura Ibrahim. Adam Khadduri's housekeeper.

Noura opened the trunk of her car and lifted out two bags of groceries. As she approached the house, Molly thumbed the lock on the window. Khadduri appeared below, walking out to meet Noura. Molly pushed up on the sash, but it was stuck. It was wood, and it must have swollen in the frame. She pounded the glass with the side of her fist, trying to catch Noura's attention.

Lincoln Reed pulled her from the chair and threw her onto the floor.

"Don't do that again," he told her.

Molly didn't fight. She didn't scream. It wasn't the right time.

Lying on the floor, she listened to the car driving away. She wondered if Noura had seen her or if it mattered. She had never been Noura's friend. Didn't even know if the woman liked her.

That was hours ago. Molly hasn't heard the sound of a car since. She thinks about Sean and hopes he's safe. She knows if her salvation comes, it won't come from Noura Ibrahim. It'll come from Sean. Or from herself.

She glances at Tom Clinton. He's eight inches taller than her and probably eighty pounds heavier. She wouldn't be much use against him in a fight. Not if it was fair anyway. Not if they started on a level playing field.

But if she could trip him, if she could get him on the ground, things might even out a little.

The handcuffs are a problem, but there are still moves she could make. She's had years to practice. One of the benefits of living with Sean.

We look ahead, he told her more than once. *We prepare. That's our advantage. Because we know the battle's coming.*

She pictures Clinton on the ground. Pictures herself jamming her thumbs into his eyes, or driving her elbow into his throat.

He keeps the keys to the Explorer in the right front pocket of his pants. He keeps his phone in the left. Those are the two things Molly needs to escape and call Sean.

She'll take them if she can. She only needs to wait for the right chance.

31

Jimmy Harper

Seven hours of sleep in his own bed and Jimmy feels better. Or at least less awful.

He slept some in the car as well, with Nick driving through the night, arriving in Detroit as the sun came up. The painkillers Jimmy's taking seem to be helping. Time is passing at its customary rate, not sluggishly like before. He's moving more like himself again.

He showers and dresses and phones Adam Khadduri. No answer. Same as when he tried to call last night.

It's around three thirty in the afternoon and breakfast seems inappropriate. Jimmy makes himself a thick sandwich of ham and provolone and yellow peppers. Eats it at his dining room table with a cold beer to wash it down.

He grabs his gun when he leaves the house and drives to Khadduri's office in Royal Oak. Khadduri's not there, and his secretary doesn't know when he'll be in. Next stop is Khadduri's house in Huntington Woods. No one answers when Jimmy knocks, and when he peers through the windows, the house seems deserted.

Which is what he expected. He needed to try, but he's pretty sure things with Khadduri are not going to be resolved by talking.

He drives back home to Corktown and stops in at the repair shop. He left his cousin Kelly in charge, and when he walks in he finds Kelly in the customer lounge watching reruns of some zombie show on the flat-screen TV.

Jimmy waves him into the office and listens to what he has to report, which is mostly that things have been good, business as usual, though he does complain about one of the mechanics.

"Demitri. He came in late three days in a row. Got a mouth on him too. I'm not saying you should fire him—"

"Demitri's fine," Jimmy says. He knows Demitri is one of his most reliable guys. "Is there anything else?" he asks Kelly.

Kelly shakes his head but then remembers. "A cop came by here, with a Fibbie."

That's Kelly being clever. Fibbie.

"An FBI agent?" Jimmy says.

"They asked about Sean. Said they were talking to people who used to know him."

"What did you tell them?"

"Nothing," Kelly says. "He was never a friend of mine."

"Did you get their names?"

"They left cards. I put them in the desk."

Jimmy opens the center drawer and finds them. Rafael Garza and Rachel Massoud.

Garza tried to call him at home too. He found out earlier when he checked his messages.

"The Fibbie was hot," Kelly says. "Small, but curvy. Looked foreign. Massoud is an Arab name, isn't it?"

"Right," Jimmy says. "You can go."

Kelly looks disappointed. "You need me to keep covering things? Or are you back?"

"We'll see. I may need you for something else."

Kelly leaves and Nick comes in a few minutes later.

"I didn't think you'd really be here," Nick says. "You feel all right?"

Jimmy ignores the question. "What did you find out about Khadduri's son?"

Nick looks at the chair in front of Jimmy's desk, like he needs permission to sit.

Jimmy waves him into it, impatient.

"He's still in Ann Arbor," Nick says. "Still at the university."

"You sure? He was a student there six years ago."

Nick shrugs. "Unless there's another Matthew Khadduri. Six years ago he was an undergrad. Now he's a grad student. Working on a PhD in French literature. Writing a dissertation on Victor Hugo." Nick waits a beat and adds: "That's the guy who wrote the book about the hunchback."

"I've heard of him," Jimmy says. "Where did you find all this?"

"The U of M website and Facebook. He has an Instagram account too."

"Yeah?"

"Lots of pictures of him and his car. And at parties. With girls. His dad's rich, right?"

"Definitely," Jimmy says.

"I think Matthew gets laid a lot."

Jimmy is not at his best, but he figures it can't wait. He goes after Matthew Khadduri that night.

The kid's house is easy to find. It's a small wood-frame place in a historic district on the west side of Ann Arbor. A gabled roof, casement windows, granite steps leading up to the front entrance.

The house is dark when they get there. Matthew Khadduri is out. He arrives home at twenty minutes after ten in a metallic blue Lamborghini that seems a little out of place. His neighbors are families with kids; they have minivans parked in their driveways.

Matthew puts the Lamborghini away in a detached garage and goes into the house through a side door—with a short, stylish blond woman in tow. She's wearing a suede jacket, a leather skirt, and knee-high boots. A college student, Jimmy thinks.

"What did I tell you?" Nick says. "Matthew gets laid."

They're observing from Jimmy's car across the street. Kelly is in the back seat.

An hour and forty minutes later, Matthew and the girl emerge from the house. The girl looks as well put together as she did when she went in. They might have been having sex, or they might have been discussing French literature.

Matthew gets the Lamborghini out of the garage again and the two of them drive off.

Matty K. is a gentleman, Jimmy thinks; he's driving the girl home.

Jimmy crosses the street and walks to the side door of the house. The locks aren't even a challenge. He's inside in under two minutes.

When Matthew Khadduri returns half an hour later, Jimmy and Nick and Kelly are waiting inside in the dark.

Nick went down to the basement and turned the power off at the breaker, so when Matthew flips the switch in the kitchen the overhead light stays off. He comes through to the living room, and Nick and Kelly knock him to the floor. He tries resisting, but he's not a fighter. Soon enough they've got him straightened out: zip ties on his wrists and ankles, a blindfold over his eyes. Not much damage beyond a bloody lip.

They empty his pockets and sit him on the sofa. Jimmy takes a chair across from him.

"I'm not going to kill you," he says.

Matthew is unnaturally calm, as if he gets bound and blindfolded every day. "There's three hundred dollars in my wallet."

"I don't care," Jimmy says.

"There's more upstairs. Top drawer of the dresser. About eight hundred, I think."

"You need to listen," Jimmy says. "I won't kill you, but my friend"—he doesn't use Kelly's name—"has a violent streak. If I have to ask him to hurt you, he might get carried away. He could break your ribs. Or other things."

"What do you want?" Matthew says.

"That's better. I need information about your father. Do you know where he is?"

"He doesn't live here."

"I know where he lives. He's not there. Where would he go, if he had to hide for a while?"

"He has apartments in London and New York."

"What about someplace closer, where there wouldn't be many people around?"

Matthew hesitates, bows his head. Jimmy watches him in the gray dark.

"There's no place closer," Matthew says.

Jimmy nods once at Kelly. Kelly leans over Matthew Khadduri and punches him hard in the stomach. Matthew doubles over and Kelly drags him off the sofa and pushes him to the floor. He kicks him once in the small of the back.

"You heard what I told you about broken ribs," Jimmy says.

Matthew tries to crawl. Kelly kicks him again. Jimmy gets out of the chair. He's got the gun he bought in Knoxville. He crouches down and presses the muzzle against Matthew's cheek.

"When I said I wouldn't kill you, that was more a prediction than a promise. I meant I wouldn't kill you if you told me what I needed to know."

Matthew lies still on the floor. His breathing is a little crazy, but he gets it under control. "There's a lodge up north, on the Au

Sable River. Near Grayling. Sand Hill Road. The closest neighbor is a mile away."

Something hollow in his voice. Defeated. It sounds like truth.

"Good," Jimmy says, moving the gun away from the kid's cheek. "Help him up," he says to Nick. "Get him some ice for his lip."

32

Sean Tennant

Cole's voice sounds faint and distant, like it's being carried on the wind.

"You need to straighten up," it says.

It's three in the afternoon. The day after Molly got taken in Knoxville. Sean is in upstate New York, on the outskirts of a town called Rome. He's walking on a long, straight path beside a remnant of the old Erie Canal.

"You need to get your shit together," Cole says. "That's what she told you, way back when."

Sean frowns. "She never said that to me."

"She used prettier words. But it amounts to the same thing."

Sean remembers the words: *Today a new sun rises and we start again.*

Fragments of memory—that's all he has from the days after Cole died. He remembers meeting up with Molly in Toledo. Leaving his car behind because Cole had bled there, in the back seat. Traveling east in Molly's car and spending a night in a seedy motel in Pennsylvania.

On the road again the next day, crossing into New York State. Slush on the Thruway. A gray sky. Sean leaned his head against the window beside him while Molly drove. When she tried to talk to him he gave her one-word answers.

She left the Thruway in the early afternoon. Exit 34. Took a two-lane highway north. She didn't say where she was going. Half an hour later, a few random turns, and she pulled over on a patch of wet gravel and melting snow and got out.

"Come on," she said. He didn't ask why. It felt easier to follow along.

There was a wooden barrier and a sign that read: NO MOTORIZED VEHICLES. And beyond: a path with trees on one side and a canal on the other. A thin blanket of snow on the path. The water in the canal was murky black.

They walked half a mile and Molly said, "Today a new sun rises and we start again."

Sean kept walking and made no reply.

She got ahead of him, turned around, stopped him with a hand on his chest.

"Did you hear me?" she asked.

"I heard you," he said. "I don't want a pep talk."

She hit him lightly with the side of her fist. "It's not a pep talk. It's a deal you have to make with me. Ask me why."

"Why?"

"Because I need you, and because you and I are alive. Aren't we?"

He took his time answering. It was a serious question.

"Yes," he said.

"Then say the words."

He wasn't the sort of person who cared about rituals. But she was waiting.

He said the words. "Today a new sun rises—"

She finished it with him: "—and we start again."

Afterward she watched him. Solemn. As if she was wondering if he would come through for her.

"Where do we start?" he asked.

"Anywhere," she said. "We just have to pick a place." She looked up at the gloomy sky. "But not here. Somewhere warm."

They made a few decisions that day: They would go to Dalton Webber for help. They would spend the cash and the gold coins Sean had stolen from Adam Khadduri, but they wouldn't try to sell the cylinder seals.

Sean remembers the spot where he made his deal with Molly. There's an ash tree by the side of the trail. Back then, he carved an X in the trunk with his pocketknife. He finds the tree now and leaves the trail. He counts off twenty paces, due north.

Here's a stone the size of a softball, half sunk in the ground. Here's another, six feet away. He drops his backpack on the grass and unfolds his camp shovel. Starts to dig midway between the two stones.

Five minutes later he has the box. The last of the cylinder seals. The first ones he buried. He puts the box in the backpack.

Cole's voice is with him as he hikes back to the pickup truck.

"You need to pull it together."

"Yeah," Sean says.

"How long have you been wearing those clothes?"

"I don't know."

"Too long. Put on something clean. Brush your teeth."

"Sure."

"Do it. You'll feel human again. Then we need to talk about sleep."

"I slept last night," Sean says.

Technically, it was this morning. He found a hotel parking lot around 7:00 a.m., in Hagerstown, Maryland, just off the interstate. He slept sitting up in the truck.

"Two hours," Cole says. "Doesn't count."

"Closer to three," says Sean.

Cole goes silent, but he's still there. Off to Sean's right and half a step behind. Sean can hear the tread of his boots in the mud.

There's no snow now, not like the last time. The trail is littered with fallen leaves. The wind is blowing more of them down from the trees. Red and orange. They spin slowly through the air.

Sean comes to the wooden barrier. The end of the path. He sees the white pickup. And a cop standing behind it, looking at the license plate.

The cop looks up and sees him.

For a handful of seconds, they're balanced on the edge of a knife. The cop moving closer and taking him in. Sean sees everything play out over the cop's face: *No, it can't be. Holy shit, it is.*

"What's your name?" Sean says.

It throws the cop off. He's used to being the one asking the questions. But he can't be too used to it, Sean thinks. The cop is young. Maybe twenty-one.

"Brian Cole," he says.

Sean's laugh surprises both of them.

"Is that funny?" the cop says.

"No," says Sean. "I used to have a friend named Cole."

The cop nods. He's maybe ten feet away now. "I need to see some ID," he says.

"No you don't," Sean says. "You know who I am."

It's not the response the cop expected. He runs his tongue over his teeth.

"What are you doing out here?"

Sean glances back along the path. "There was something I needed. I had to dig it up."

The cop's eyes narrow. "What was it? What did you dig up?"

Sean slips the backpack from his shoulder and lowers it to the ground. The cop reaches for the pistol on his belt. He unsnaps the holster. But he doesn't draw.

Sean holds still. Arms down at his sides. "I could show you," he says. "But honestly it wouldn't mean anything to you. It's just some rocks."

"Rocks?" the cop says. "Like diamonds?"

"No. Not diamonds."

The wind picks up. A leaf floats down through the air between them.

The cop says, "You're not making sense."

"Well, I haven't been sleeping enough," Sean tells him.

"You drove here from Knoxville."

"Yes."

"They briefed us this morning about you. Said you were driving a white pickup now. Be on the lookout. And I thought, *Right. Like he's gonna come here*. There's a warrant out for you in . . . where is it?"

"Michigan," Sean says.

The cop nods. "Michigan. You're supposed to be armed and dangerous." His hand is resting on the grip of his pistol. "Are you armed?"

"I'm not dangerous."

"That's good. I like you."

Something a kid would say. It makes Sean smile.

The cop blushes. "I mean I like what you did in Houston. I respect it. But I have to take you into custody."

"I understand."

"I need you to get down on your knees," the cop says, drawing the pistol from his holster, "and place your hands on top of your head with the fingers interlaced."

"On my knees?" Sean says.

"That's right."

"No."

The cop raises the pistol and takes a step closer. "Keep your hands where I can see them."

"I haven't moved my hands, Brian."

"Get down on the ground," the cop says. His voice is deeper than before. Harsher.

"Doesn't matter how you say it, Brian. I'm not gonna do it."

"On the ground. Now."

"I'll tell you what," Sean says. "I've got a Glock under my coat. The same one I used to plug Henry Keen. Go ahead and shoot me. You'll be fine. You can say I reached for it."

"Do *not* reach for your weapon."

"Take it easy. I'm not reaching. We're not gunslingers, Brian. We're not gonna shoot it out. I've got someplace I need to be."

The cop holds his pistol steady. "Where?" he asks.

"A long way from here. You know what happened in Knoxville."

The cop's expression softens. "Somebody abducted your girlfriend. Molly."

"Yes they did," Sean says. "And the only way I get her back is if I leave here, with this." He points at the backpack on the ground. "If you won't let me leave, you might as well shoot me."

The cop takes a step back. Sean can see him thinking. His patrol car is on the other side of the pickup. He'll have a radio there, and no doubt he has a phone in his pocket.

"You can call for backup if you want," Sean says. "It won't change anything. Backup only means more people who might make the wrong decision."

Silence between them, and then Sean hears a vehicle approaching. The cop lowers his pistol. A yellow school bus comes around a curve in the road. They both wait for it to pass.

"Rocks," the cop says when it's gone. "That's what's in the backpack."

"Yeah."

"And you're gonna trade them for her?"

"That's the plan."

Sean keeps his eyes on the pistol. The cop is tapping it against his thigh. An unconscious gesture. He's working things out in his mind. Deciding.

"You're not just telling me a story?" the cop says.

"No."

The cop sighs and lifts the pistol up and slides it into his holster.

"I guess it's not my problem. We're not in Michigan, are we?"

33

Rafael Garza

Garza heard the news of Molly Winter's abduction in the middle of the night.

His phone woke him, and he sat up. Rachel Massoud was asleep beside him, her black hair spilling over her pillow. Garza grabbed for the phone, trying to answer before it rang again. Knocked it from the nightstand to the floor.

Two more rings and eventually he found it—under the bed. By then, Rachel was awake and laughing.

"Jesus, Ray. You make a racket."

The name on the screen was Arthur Hayden, his lieutenant. When he answered, Hayden said, "You need to go to Knoxville."

Garza packed his bag and drove there. Eight hours on the road, the first four in the dark. Now, after a day spent interviewing witnesses and consulting with the Knoxville police, he still knows frustratingly little about what happened.

He knows that Sean went to a lawyer, Howard Frazier, with the aim of turning himself in. He knows Molly was taken by two or more men in a black SUV. He knows Sean pursued the SUV in a white pickup truck.

He knows that Frazier first spoke to Sean and Molly earlier in the week, at Rusty's All-American Restaurant. Garza went there and questioned the staff—and discovered what led the men in the SUV to Frazier's house.

The busboy looked squirrelly from the start. A skeezy ex-con with a razor-wire tattoo on his neck. Garza had to push him, but in the end he talked. He told Garza that two men in an SUV had come around asking about Sean and Molly. Both tall, late forties: one black, one white. The busboy gave them Frazier's name.

"I thought they might be cops," he said.

"Why?" Garza asked.

"They had the look," the busboy said. "And they acted like pricks."

Garza learned that a third man had spoken to the busboy too—before the others. Another white guy, early forties with curly hair. "A tough guy," the busboy said. "Not a cop though."

"No?"

"Looked more like a boxer."

Garza shared the information with the Knoxville police, then called in to his lieutenant and made a report. "I want to go back to Dalton Webber," he told Hayden. "Maybe he's got a way to contact Sean. Maybe we can still get Sean to turn himself in."

Hayden was skeptical. "You tried that route."

Four words, but Garza heard a larger message in them. *You tried, and you failed.* In hindsight, Garza knew it was true. He wondered what might have happened if he had come to Knoxville earlier, if he had talked to the busboy sooner. He might have figured out that Sean would go to Howard Frazier.

Hayden seemed to be thinking the same thing. "It's time for you to come home," he said.

Now Garza is at the Knoxville airport, waiting to board a flight for

Houston. It's six in the morning. He's sitting near an outlet, charging his phone. He's thinking about Rachel Massoud when it rings.

It's her.

"I was wrong," she says.

"About what?"

"Adam Khadduri," she says. "I really didn't think it was his style."

"Khadduri?"

"I think he's got Molly."

The story comes out, all in a rush. It's about Rachel's informant, the one who's been helping with her investigation of Khadduri. She's a woman named Noura Ibrahim. Khadduri's housekeeper.

"She owns a place up north," Rachel says. "Khadduri paid for it. It's his, but it's in her name. He uses it to get away in the summertime. But she takes care of it. He can't be bothered with trivia. This time of year, if you're not using it, you have to turn the water off or the pipes can freeze. Noura closed the place down weeks ago, but yesterday Khadduri wanted her to open it again. Make sure the furnace was running. Stuff like that.

"She drove there yesterday morning and got the place ready for him. She went to buy groceries so he'd have something to eat, like she always does. When she returned, Khadduri was there, but he wasn't alone. She saw his car and a black SUV."

"Did she see Molly?" Garza asks.

"No," Rachel tells him. "Noura didn't stay. Khadduri sent her home. Which was strange, because usually she stays to cook for him. But she didn't think much about it until later, when she saw the news about Molly's abduction. Even then, she wasn't sure. She went back and forth about it until finally she called me. Since then I've been busy. But I think we'll be able to get a warrant."

"Based on the SUV?" Garza says. "That's thin."

"There's a little more. Noura heard a noise while she was there. Like someone pounding on a window to get her attention."

"That's still thin."

"I know. I had to exaggerate when I explained things to my boss. I got him to sign off. I plan to go up there to search the place, but it'll take some time to get organized. You've got a couple of hours to get here, if you want in. Knoxville has an airport, right?"

"I'm already there," Garza says. "I'm supposed to go to Houston."

"It's up to you, Ray. But I bet they've got a flight to Detroit."

34

Jimmy Harper

When Jimmy heads north, it's four in the morning.

The trip is two hundred miles, from Detroit to the city of Grayling. Nick driving, Kelly riding shotgun, Jimmy grabbing some sleep in the back seat.

After Grayling there's ten more miles to go and then a hike through the woods. By seven forty-five, Jimmy is standing near the shore of the Au Sable River, looking at Adam Khadduri's vacation house on the other side.

The sun won't rise for another twenty minutes, but there's a pink glow in the eastern sky. There's a fine mist rising from the water.

Jimmy sees something dark break the surface near the bank. It's not a fish, and it's too small for a beaver. A muskrat, he thinks.

It goes under again and he puts it out of his mind. He slides his phone from his pocket and shoots off a text to Demitri Stamatopoulos, one of his mechanics, the one Kelly wanted to fire for being late.

Everything okay?

The reply comes a few seconds later: *No sweat.*

Demitri lives alone in a house with a basement. He's watching over Matthew Khadduri.

Jimmy delivered the kid to him last night. Matthew talked the whole way from Ann Arbor to Detroit, trying to persuade Jimmy that he was going about things all wrong. "Call my father. He'll pay you whatever you want. He loves me. Do you know how much money he has?"

"I don't care about his money," Jimmy said.

"What do you want?" Matthew asked him.

"I want him not to see me coming," Jimmy said.

Before he left Detroit, Jimmy made a stop at home to pick up some things he needed: mostly weapons and ammunition.

And a pair of binoculars. He raises them now and aims them across the river at the house. A lodge, Matthew called it. It's big: two stories, four bedrooms on the top floor, according to the diagram he made the kid draw. The house is set back from the shore, and there's a porch that runs from one end to the other. There are five wooden steps leading down from the south end of the porch and then another series of steps cut into the earth and shored up with old railroad ties.

Those steps lead down to a deck that overlooks the water.

By quarter after eight the sun is up, and the mist is starting to burn away.

Jimmy is still watching from the cover of the trees when Lincoln Reed comes out of the house with a big red coffee mug and walks down to the deck. Reed stands there with one arm braced on the railing and looks at the river.

Jimmy brought an AR-15 rifle with a scope. He could take Reed out from here, one shot, but not without alerting the others. That would defeat his purpose. He'll have to get closer, which means hiking back to the car and driving three miles north to the nearest bridge. Crossing the river and approaching the house from Sand Hill Road.

One good thing: the yard around the house is relatively small. The woods come up close, within twenty feet on either side. And since he has Nick and Kelly with him, they can come at the house from different directions.

Time to go. Jimmy turns to Kelly, who's been restless, shuffling around, tromping over dead leaves. In a low voice, Jimmy tells him to head back to the car. He gestures for Nick to do the same, but Nick shakes his head and points across the river.

When Jimmy looks again, he sees that Lincoln Reed has left the deck and is climbing the steps back to the house. But there's someone else coming down: Adam Khadduri, carrying a tray laden with food. He brings it to the deck and puts it on a table there.

Breakfast by the water.

He won't be eating alone. As Jimmy watches, Reed reaches the back entrance of the house. There's a screen door, and he holds it open. Molly walks out, in handcuffs, with Tom Clinton right behind her.

Molly Winter

They cuffed her to the bed frame last night.

Left her alone in the room and looked in on her every hour or two. She slept on her back with her arms stretched over her head. Not the best sleep she's ever gotten. But they look well-rested: Clinton and Reed.

There's a chill in the air when Clinton brings her out. Molly sees dew on the wooden steps and on the railroad ties farther down. This might be the place to fight, where the ground is uneven. But not yet. Not with Reed watching from the porch.

She marches down to the deck with Clinton behind her. He pulls out a chair for her, like a waiter at a restaurant. Adam Khadduri is smiling.

"Good morning," he says. Like he means it.

And it is, if you go by the glimmer of sunlight on the water.

"I'm sorry we haven't had a chance to talk," Khadduri says. "I've been busy."

He wants to act as if they're having a normal conversation. Molly is willing to play along.

"I've wondered what it would be like to see you again," she says.

"What's it like?"

"Not what I hoped for."

Khadduri laughs and waves a hand at the food spread out between them. "Help yourself," he says. "You must be hungry."

She is. Clinton and Reed have been feeding her, but nothing like this. There's bacon and hard-boiled eggs. Buttered toast. Blueberry muffins. Oranges and grapes and slices of melon.

"Finger foods," Khadduri says. "No metal implements, they told me. Or hot drinks. Nothing you could use as a weapon. I hear you're a fighter now."

He's amused. As if it's the funniest thing in the world. Molly takes a glass of orange juice from the tray. She could break it and slice an artery in his neck. But it wouldn't get her out of here. Reed has gone into the house, but Clinton is standing only a few feet away.

"Poor Lincoln said you tried to shoot him," Khadduri says. "Is that true?"

Molly drinks from the glass before delivering her answer.

"You can't blame a girl for trying."

Khadduri claps his hands, delighted. "Oh, I like this Molly. I really do."

He's leaning back in his chair, laughing, repeating the line. *Can't blame a girl . . .*

She pops a grape into her mouth, starts to peel an orange. "You're in a good mood, Adam. Not like the last time I saw you."

He turns serious suddenly. Looks away at the water, then back.

"I owe you an apology," he says. "There's no excuse, except that I was wounded then. You wounded me. You see, I fell in love with you.

I didn't realize it until I lost you. A foolish thing, getting attached to a woman. It wouldn't happen now. I've had so many. I've learned that no single one of them makes a difference. You can always find another."

He pauses, as if he's said something profound. Molly keeps her eyes on him, but she's listening to the rush of the water flowing by.

"I bear you no ill will," Khadduri says. "All this"—he holds up his left hand and wiggles the fingers—"unpleasantness will soon be over. I've spoken to Sean. He says he has all the stones. He'll meet us in a few hours and we'll trade. I have no desire to keep you or harm you. I only want what's mine."

Khadduri's voice sounds dull and his eyes are hard to read. He might think he's telling the truth. But Molly doesn't believe he'll let her go or let Sean walk away unharmed. Not in the end, when the time comes to keep his promise.

She doesn't believe in this version of Adam Khadduri. The magnanimous version. She's seen his other side. She's not going to trust him.

She's heard all she cares to hear, and the only thing left is to get away. But first she eats, because she knows she'll need the energy. She eats the orange she's peeled and three strips of bacon and two hard-boiled eggs while Khadduri talks to her as if they're friends. He talks about his business. He's been branching out into modern art: abstract sculptures and paintings and installations. He shied away from that stuff before because he didn't understand the market. Now he has studied it, and he's more confident. It's a larger and larger share of what he sells.

All she hears is the boasting of a mobster: *In a few years all my business will be completely legitimate.*

He rambles on for twenty minutes, until she's wondering how to excuse herself. He saves her the trouble, pulling out his phone, saying he needs to make some calls.

He tells Tom Clinton to take her back inside the house.

Molly picks up a slice of toast as she rises from her chair. Bites into it as she's walking up the steps. They're broad and shallow, the ones that are cut into the hill and reinforced with railroad ties. Six steps and there's a swath of grass and a forty-five-degree turn before the next one.

Five steps in the next group. Clinton follows close behind her. She counts them silently—five, four, three, two, one—then drops the toast and throws herself backward.

It doesn't unfold the way she imagined it. She imagined Clinton falling like a tree and landing on his back. Her landing on top of him, knocking the breath out of him. Then, before he could recover, driving her elbow into his throat.

But Clinton is bigger than her and stronger. When she throws herself into him, he wraps his arms around her middle. He loses his balance but not the way she hoped. They topple over sideways together into the grass. The elbow she aims at his throat hits his chin instead. She pulls away from him and tries to scramble up the hill.

He grabs her ankle, tripping her. She rolls onto her back and tries to kick him, but then he's on her, straddling her stomach. Pinning her arms above her head. He grabs one of her thumbs and bends it until she screams.

"Don't make me hurt you," he says.

His face is inches from hers. Until it jerks back suddenly. Molly has time to register a hand that's not hers or his. It's tangled in his hair. Another hand appears, drawing the blade of a hunting knife across his neck.

She turns her face away, feels blood spurting onto her cheek. Then Clinton's weight is lifted from her. When she turns back, she sees Jimmy Harper standing over her. The knife is gone. He has a gun in his hand.

"You've got some moves," he says. "I'll give you that."

Nick Ensen

Nick hears Molly scream, but she's Jimmy's problem, not his. He's focusing on Adam Khadduri.

Khadduri is running from the deck, trying to make it to the house. He doesn't use the steps, because the steps would take him toward Jimmy. He climbs the grassy slope at the north end of the house. When he sees Nick coming down the same slope, he freezes.

The only place Khadduri has to go is back. He retreats to the deck and, when he reaches it, boosts himself onto the railing. He's going to jump over, into the river.

If he goes in, Nick will have to go in after him, and Nick is not a great swimmer. He fires a warning shot that strikes the railing, breaking off a splinter of wood. Khadduri changes his mind and hops down. He looks sullen.

Nick is on the deck with him now. Tells him not to move or he'll blow him away.

Which is bullshit. Jimmy wants Khadduri alive.

Nick gets between Khadduri and the river and holds the muzzle of his pistol against the man's back. He looks around and sees that Clinton is lying motionless on the ground and Jimmy has Molly under control.

Which leaves Reed. Who's walking along the north side of the house with his gun drawn.

Kelly was supposed to take care of Reed, but Kelly is nowhere to be seen. Just like him to turn chickenshit at the last minute, to hang back in the woods.

Nick grabs Khadduri by the collar and moves him between himself and Reed. He holds his pistol to Khadduri's head. Reed is yelling at him, telling him to drop it.

Jimmy has Molly on her feet now, but he's at the south end of the house. He can't see Reed, and Reed can't see him.

Reed creeps forward, staying close to the side of the building. He's holding his gun with two hands, aiming at Nick. For a moment Nick feels sure that Reed is going to take the shot. That he doesn't care about hitting Khadduri.

The shot, when it comes, sounds as loud as a cannon. It makes Nick close his eyes. He opens them again to see Reed leaning against the house, clutching a wound on his thigh.

And there's Kelly Harper, stepping out of the woods. Kelly takes a second shot that slams into Reed's shoulder and a third that hits his stomach. Reed falls against the house and tries to raise his gun, but Kelly fires a fourth shot that tears off the top of his skull.

35

Jimmy Harper

Jimmy takes them inside: Molly and Khadduri. Puts them in one of the bedrooms upstairs. Nick brings him the key to the handcuffs from Tom Clinton's key ring and Jimmy makes use of it, uncuffing Molly's wrists and recuffing them behind her back.

He doesn't bother binding Adam Khadduri. It seems unnecessary. Khadduri is shell-shocked.

"I want to see Tom," he says.

"There's nothing to see," Jimmy tells him.

Khadduri sits in a chair leaning forward, staring at the carpet. "You killed him."

"That's right."

"And Lincoln. Who was it that shot him?"

"It doesn't matter."

Khadduri rubs his face with both hands. "They were honorable men. Family men."

"Did they tell their families they were coming here?" Jimmy asks.

"No. I don't believe so."

"That's good."

"This was senseless," Khadduri says.

"I gave them a chance to back off. In Knoxville."

"They were following my instructions."

"I understand."

"You and I could have come to an arrangement."

"We *are* going to come to an arrangement," Jimmy says.

He's standing in the doorway where he can watch them both: Molly on the bed and Khadduri in his chair by the window.

"Part of this is my fault," Jimmy says to Khadduri. "There's something I should have made plain. It goes back to the night Sean and Cole robbed you. The night Cole died. I got a call from a nurse around eleven o'clock. She found my number in Cole's phone. She broke the news to me. In stages, the way they do. *Your brother was shot. His injuries were very serious. We did all we could for him. I'm sorry to say he didn't survive.* I drove to the hospital through a blizzard, and they showed me his body. They had a sheet over him, pulled up to his chin. His wounds were covered. He looked perfect. Unharmed. He could have been asleep."

Jimmy leans against the door frame, holding his gun down by his hip. "I got back home around one in the morning. Stood in my front yard with the snow falling. I didn't want to go inside. My cell phone rang, and for a moment I believed it might be the hospital again, telling me they'd made a mistake. That Cole had woken up.

"But it was Sean on the phone. He could barely speak, but he managed to tell me what had happened. Said he was sorry. Afterward he was silent. I think he wanted me to forgive him. I told him his life was over. All he could do now was run—as far as he could for as long as he could. But I would find him. I told him nothing would stop me from finding him."

Jimmy moves from the doorway into the room. Khadduri sits up straight in his chair. Jimmy leans over him and taps his knee with the gun.

"That was a vow," Jimmy says. "Do you understand?"

Khadduri's nod is almost imperceptible. "Yes."

"You say that, but I wonder if you do." Jimmy brings out his cell phone and opens his text messages. He finds an image that Demitri sent him. He shows it to Khadduri.

It's Khadduri's son tied to a post in Demitri's basement.

The color drains from Khadduri's face. "What have you done?"

"Nothing yet," Jimmy says.

"Why—"

Jimmy puts the phone away. "Do you understand now that I'm serious?"

Khadduri closes his eyes. "Yes."

"I need to know you won't try to cross me again."

"I won't."

"Good," Jimmy says. "Now tell me what arrangements you've made with Sean."

Nick Ensen

It freaks him out, moving the bodies.

Nick has never thought of himself as a killer, and in the literal sense he still hasn't killed anyone. But he has definitely thrown in with killers. He has aided and abetted.

It's not like Jimmy didn't tell him what was going to happen.

And Nick didn't bow out. He didn't walk away. So he's a killer now, and a killer can't afford to be squeamish.

The dumbest thing: he can't help thinking about his high school biology class.

His teacher made the students break into pairs one day, and every pair got a frog. A dead frog, smelling of formaldehyde. They were supposed to dissect it.

Nick picked up the scalpel to make the first incision, and swear to god he thought he saw the frog move. He thought he would cut it open and it would come to life.

He couldn't hold the scalpel steady.

"Let me do it," his partner said. "You're shaking like a leaf."

When he and Kelly pick up Tom Clinton, it's the same. Nick takes the arms and Kelly takes the legs. Nick can feel himself trembling. Clinton's eyes are halfway open, and any second Nick expects them to come open all the way.

They carry Clinton into the woods south of the house. Lay him down next to a fallen tree. They cover him with leaves and branches.

Lincoln Reed gets the same treatment, but Nick takes the legs this time. Because Reed's head is blown open, and Nick doesn't want to look at it.

When Reed is covered and they come out of the woods, Nick sees that there's blood on the side of the house. He moves closer and scans the ground. Sees pieces of Reed's skull.

He points them out to Kelly. "You need to get those."

Kelly laughs. "I took the guy out, Nicky. Cleanup is your job."

Kelly sits on the porch at the back of the house and sorts through the things they collected from Clinton's and Reed's pockets. Plucks the cash from their wallets. Nick goes inside and brings back a paper towel from the kitchen. He folds it in half and uses it to pick up the remains of Reed's skull.

He carries them down to the deck and drops them into the river. Drops the paper towel after them.

He saw keys in the kitchen, hanging on a hook. He goes back for them and finds one that opens the lock on the shed in the front yard. The usual stuff in there: shovels and rakes, a lawn mower. Nick finds a garden hose and brings it out. Hooks it to a spigot by the back porch and sprays Reed's blood from the side of the house. Sprays the blood from the grass too.

He cleans his hands under the water. Then brings the hose around and sprays the place where Clinton died.

Kelly watches him from the porch. "Look at you," he says. "Stone-cold criminal."

Nick returns the hose to the shed. Sees the shovels and thinks about burying the bodies, even though Jimmy didn't tell him to. Nick wonders how long it would take. Probably too long. He doesn't want to linger here. He doesn't think it's safe.

Four shots. Kelly's such a fuckup that it took him four shots to kill Reed.

Maybe no one was close enough to hear. Maybe people are used to gunshots, out here in the country. But it makes Nick nervous.

He stands in the front yard looking at the driveway. Realizes he's been listening for the sound of an approaching car. But there's nothing. No sound at all except the wind.

Behind him, the front door of the house opens. Adam Khadduri comes down the steps. Then Molly. Then Jimmy.

Jimmy says, "Are we all set?"

Nick nods.

"Go get Kelly," Jimmy says. "Tell him we're leaving."

36

Rafael Garza

In the FBI raid on Adam Khadduri's vacation house, Rafael Garza is more or less a bystander.

Six agents make the trip north from the field office in Detroit, including Rachel Massoud and her boss, a stern-looking man in his fifties named Wayne Jansson. Garza follows them in a rental car he picked up at the Detroit airport.

They drive for three and a half hours to the town of Frederic, Michigan, where they're joined by six deputies from the Crawford County Sheriff's Office in nearby Grayling. The two groups meet at a staging area on Sand Hill Road: the gravel lot of an ice-cream shop that's gone out of business. Rachel briefs them on the operation and everyone suits up. The deputies are young. Some of them could be fresh out of high school. Their equipment looks new: body armor and helmets and Colt M4 carbines.

They take a knee in the gravel and say a prayer, and when they come up they're energized. They give each other high fives.

Garza is worried for them, but his worry is misplaced. None of them suffers so much as a scratch.

The operation unfolds precisely as Rachel planned it. The FBI agents take the lead, driving south on Sand Hill Road in a UPS delivery van they brought up from Detroit. A bit of subterfuge. Their aim is to get right up to Khadduri's front door without arousing suspicion.

The sheriff's deputies follow in a van of their own.

Garza brings up the rear in his rental car. He's got his service weapon, a Glock 19, and he's wearing a Kevlar vest on loan from the FBI. But Jansson has made it clear that he's being allowed to tag along as a courtesy. He's supposed to stay out of the way.

It's four miles from the staging area to Khadduri's house. The UPS van makes the turn into the long driveway. The deputies hang back a little. They time it perfectly, entering the driveway just as the FBI agents breach Khadduri's door.

The agents go into the house. The deputies deploy around the perimeter.

Garza stays out of their way.

It's over quickly. The house is empty.

Garza walks through it after the agents have cleared all the rooms. It's plain that someone has been here recently. Several someones. There are four bedrooms on the second floor. Four beds. All of them have been slept in.

Three of the rooms have travel bags in them. Men's clothes scattered around.

No clothes in the fourth room. Molly Winter might have been held there. You don't get spare clothes if you're being kept against your will.

Or maybe Garza is seeing what he wants to see.

There's a kitchen at the back of the house on the ground floor. Evidence that someone cooked breakfast. The smell of bacon lingers. The sink holds unwashed pans and dishes.

There's a table outside, on a wooden deck by the river. A tray and plates. Glasses of orange juice. At least two people ate out there, and they left some food behind. It's gathering flies now.

It's unusual. Suggestive even. But it's not evidence of a crime.

Wayne Jansson says as much. He's not pleased. He takes Rachel aside for a private conversation. Garza observes it from a distance. It looks grim.

To top everything off, there's no black SUV in the driveway. The only vehicle present is a dark blue Maserati GranTurismo, which is registered to Adam Khadduri.

Garza walks through the yard to the front of the house. The sheriff's deputies are milling around there. Disappointed. The adrenaline rush fading. They've got their helmets off. One of them is sitting cross-legged on the ground, pulling up blades of grass.

Others are stripping off their body armor. Looking like kids again. One has a blue-and-white T-shirt on. School colors. The logo reads: KALKASKA HIGH.

When Garza sees it, there's something familiar about it.

Kalkaska.

Garza's suitcase is in the trunk of the rental car. He digs out his notebook and pages through it. Finds his notes from his interview with Karen Tierney, Molly's old boss. The one who owned the art gallery. She told him a story about Adam Khadduri—how he once took Molly to the site of a summer camp he attended when he was young.

At Grass Lake. Up near Kalkaska.

The camp is abandoned now, she said. Nothing but some cabins and an old chapel.

Garza takes his phone out and opens Google Maps. He finds Grass Lake. It looks remote. Only one road leading in.

If you were looking for a place to keep a captive, it might be ideal.

It's only fifteen miles away.

Garza returns his notebook to the suitcase and closes the trunk.

He's already behind the wheel when he sees Rachel and Jansson walking along the north side of the house. Jansson breaks away to talk to the deputies.

Rachel approaches Garza's car.

He rolls down his window. "I don't think you were wrong," he says.

She smiles faintly. Puts on a patronizing tone. "We're all stewards, Ray. Stewards of Bureau resources. And Bureau resources are not to be wasted." She's imitating Jansson.

"This wasn't a waste," Garza says. "She could have been here."

"I think she was," Rachel says with a shrug. "But she's not now, and I don't know where to look for her."

Garza fidgets with his car key, turning the key ring around his finger.

"I have an idea," he says. "It's probably a long shot."

He tells her about Grass Lake.

"That's a stretch," she says.

"I know."

"Kind of a big stretch. To think Khadduri would take her there."

"It's a place he feels connected to."

"Sure."

"And it's not far," Garza says. "It's worth a look. I'm going to drive by there, just to satisfy my curiosity."

She studies him through the open window, her brown eyes thoughtful.

"Well, you're not going alone, Ray."

37

Molly Winter

She's been here before.

Camp Antioch is the name of the place. Adam Khadduri brought her here once on an August Saturday for a picnic and a swim in the lake. Molly remembers him grinning as he showed her around, leading her by the hand like they were kids.

It's about a mile off the main road. A collection of long, low, wood-frame buildings. All of them are run-down, and some have been damaged by fire.

One building is set apart from the others, farther back from the road. It stands near the southern shore of the lake, and it's taller: a chapel with a steeple rising from its peaked roof. Its clapboard walls were once painted white, but time and weather have stripped the paint away.

Most of the chapel's windows are broken, and the altar lies in ruins. Nearly all the pews are gone, hauled away by scavengers. If you look down from the choir loft, you can see three of them left, arranged to face each other in a rough triangle.

Molly is up there now, in the choir loft. But she's not looking down. They've got her sitting on the floor with her back to a wall, hands cuffed behind her, ankles bound with zip ties.

Khadduri is sitting a few feet away. He's got zip ties on his ankles, too, and on his wrists.

Jimmy comes and goes. The last time Molly saw him, he disappeared up a set of winding stairs at the back of the loft. She climbed those stairs herself, years ago. They lead up into the steeple.

Molly knows what Jimmy's doing up there. He's watching for Sean.

Sean is coming here with the cylinder seals. That's the arrangement Khadduri made with him. A simple trade. But Sean doesn't know Jimmy's here, and Molly has no way to warn him.

She feels powerless. Quite literally.

She's been thinking about the handcuffs. They're loose on her wrists, but not so loose that she can slip free of them. It would help if she could shift them from the back to the front; it would put her in a better position to fight, when the time comes. And it's possible. She and Sean used to practice now and then. The maneuver is simple, if you're limber enough. You lie on your back and scoot your cuffed hands down past your bottom until they're behind your knees. From there, with some effort, you can bring your legs through—but only one at a time. Molly has never been able to do it with her ankles bound.

She's desperate enough to try anyway, but unfortunately she's being watched. Jimmy's men are standing guard over her and Khadduri. There's Nick, the one who was with Jimmy at the ranch in Montana. And there's Kelly.

Kelly is short and wiry, dressed in black jeans, a silk shirt, and a leather jacket. He has a face you would call ill favored. Pale and heavy browed, with a bent nose and a blunt, ugly mouth. Molly has caught him staring at her off and on since they arrived here. But *caught* is the wrong word. Kelly's stare is open and hungry; he doesn't try to hide it.

Molly makes herself relax. Tries to estimate how long they've been here. Two hours at least. She sees Kelly staring at her again and watches as he moves closer to her. He squats down so their eyes are on the same level. But when he talks, he's not talking to her. He's talking to Nick.

"I'll tell you something," he says. "You're a better man than I am, Nicky."

Nick is standing at the railing of the loft, looking down into the chapel.

"That's a pretty low bar," he says.

The corners of Kelly's mouth turn up. "That's funny. But I'm serious. You're a saint. I mean, here she is, your enemy. The girl who wrecked your face. And it seems like you're willing to forgive and forget."

"How about you give it a rest, Kel."

"If it were me," Kelly says, "I'd want some payback." Without taking his eyes off Molly, he reaches into the pocket of his leather jacket and pulls out a folding knife. He opens the blade. "I'd want to mark her up a little."

Nick has turned around now. He sees the knife. Says, "Put it away."

Kelly scowls. "Don't tell me what to do, Nicky. You know I don't like it."

He scrapes the tip of the knife across the wooden floor. "I think I get what you're doing," he says to Nick. "You're biding your time. When this is over and Sean's dead, Jimmy won't need her anymore. I bet if we asked him, he'd let us have her. I bet she'd be fun."

Nick steps away from the railing. His hands have been in his pockets, but now they come out. The right one has a gun in it.

He doesn't aim it, just holds it. Kelly sees it and looks away as if he's bored.

"I know you're not gonna threaten me, Nicky."

"Let it rest," Nick says.

Kelly tosses his knife in the air and catches it on his palm. Molly has her legs extended in front of her, and he's been squatting by her feet, but now he rises and approaches her on her left side. He goes down on one knee. Brings his face close to hers.

"Nicky's torn, don't you think?" Kelly says to her. "I mean, he can't be happy when he looks in a mirror. But he likes to pretend he's a nice guy. I bet he's thought about seeing you bleed, even if he doesn't want to admit it."

He brings his right hand up to her cheek. The hand that's holding the knife. Molly forces herself to remain still.

"We could show him some blood," Kelly says. "I wouldn't have to cut too deep."

Adam Khadduri has been sitting silently, staring at the floor. He raises his head and says, "Leave her alone."

Kelly laughs and lifts his eyebrows to show Molly his surprise. "Look who's here," he says. He looks over at Khadduri and his voice turns cold. "Shut the fuck up," he says. "I could carve you into little pieces and I can't think of anyone who'd care."

"You're not as frightening as you suppose, you little hoodlum," Khadduri says.

Kelly turns back to Molly and flashes her a big smile. He brings the knife close to her face again, but when he touches her it's not with the blade. He uses his index finger. Draws his nail along her cheek.

"What about you?" he says. "Are you frightened?"

He's close enough that Molly can see the blood vessels in his eyes. She doesn't answer him. She holds still, even as he traces his fingertip along her neck. It takes all the control she has not to shudder.

No telling what his next move might be. Molly doesn't find out. There's the sound of heavy footsteps on the spiral stairs: Jimmy coming down from the steeple.

Kelly and Nick hear it, too, and they react in different ways. By the time Jimmy reaches the bottom of the stairs, Nick's gun is back in his pocket. He looks sheepish: a child caught misbehaving. Kelly withdraws his finger from Molly's neck, but he keeps his knife out and doesn't move away.

"What are you doing?" Jimmy asks him.

"Nothing," Kelly says.

"Seems like something."

Kelly winks at Molly as if they've shared a secret. Then turns away from her and stands.

"We've been talking," he says. "That's all."

Jimmy's carrying a pair of binoculars and a rifle with a scope. He props the rifle against the wall on the other side of the loft. Approaches Kelly and hands him the binoculars.

"Make yourself useful," he says. "Go keep watch."

Kelly goes, and as Molly listens to the trudge of his steps on the staircase, she feels a change in the air. It's not exactly relief. It's more like trading one menace for another. Like when the wild dog that's been stalking you gets chased off by a wolf.

Jimmy stands near her feet staring down at her. He's got a sheath on his belt that holds the hunting knife he used to kill Tom Clinton. Molly half expects him to draw it out and kneel beside her, like Kelly did. Jimmy has rough hands. Thick fingers. She doesn't want to feel them on her face.

The knife stays in its sheath. Jimmy comes over to the wall and leans against it. Eases himself down until he's sitting beside her.

"What did Kelly say to you?" he asks.

Molly answers in a quiet voice. "He's wondering if you'll let him rape me after Sean's dead."

Jimmy nods. "That's about his speed." He lets out a sigh and brings his knees up. The heels of his boots scrape along the floor. "Do you think I'd let him do that?"

"I don't know," Molly says.

"I wouldn't. I'm not a savage."

Molly is staring straight ahead, but she can feel him beside her, and she can smell his sweat.

"It's tempting though," Jimmy says. "The idea of hurting you. It's crossed my mind. As a means to an end, as a way to hurt Sean. All those years you were gone, I had a lot of time to think about ways to hurt him."

"What have you come up with?" Molly asks.

"Nothing good. I can let my mind go to dark places, but the things I see tend to be crude. Cutting off limbs. Cole followed Sean to war, and he came back missing a foot. Now I've got you. I wonder what it might be like to give you back to Sean without your feet."

She turns to look at him, and he seems almost embarrassed. She watches him shrug.

"I told you," he says. "Crude. It's only an idea. I'm not going to act on it. Imagination is always better than the real thing anyway. When we came here, when I saw this place from outside, I pictured a heavy wooden cross over the altar. I thought I might tie you to it. So that when Sean walked in here, you would be the first thing he'd see. But there's no cross. We'll have to get along without it."

He reaches over to pat her shoulder. "You shouldn't worry about this. It'll go quickly once Sean gets here. It used to be, when I pictured it, I thought I would need to make a speech. But that's wrong. Sean knows what this is about. There aren't any words that can make it better or worse. It just needs to be done."

It's clear to Molly what he's doing: trying to sound reasonable. She isn't buying it.

"That's a lie," she says. "It doesn't need to be done. That's something you've told yourself. It's not what Cole would want. Cole loved Sean, and Sean loved him. Like a brother."

Jimmy makes a face like he's been stung. She sees it in profile.

"You don't know anything," he says.

"I know Sean."

He shakes his head, angry. "You only see what he shows you. I know him. He wasn't Cole's brother, or mine, but we tried to make him part of our family. We did that for him, after his mother died. It should have meant something."

"It did," Molly says.

"No," says Jimmy. "Not when it counted. Not when it came to that idiotic burglary." He turns and meets Molly's eyes. "I tried to stop it," he says. "Did Sean ever tell you?"

"Yes," she says. "A long time after."

"It was around a week before Cole died. I learned what they were planning. I went to Sean's apartment to talk him out of it."

"The way I heard it, you did more than talk," Molly says. "You just about knocked him through a wall."

Jimmy is quiet for a moment, and when he speaks his voice is almost gentle. "I wanted him to listen. Sean was never good at listening. I wanted to make him understand: He could do what he wanted with his own life, but it was wrong to risk Cole's life for nothing. For money. I thought I'd gotten through to him. He promised he would call it off, and I believed him. But it was a lie."

He seems sad, and in the silence that follows Molly searches for a way to reach him. To defend Sean.

"He never thought Cole would die," she says. "He thought they would both be safe."

"I know what he thought," Jimmy says, tipping his head back against the wall of the choir loft. "I know what both of them thought. They were children, but they had been to war and they had come back alive. They thought they were invincible. Cole was always like that, even as a little kid. But Sean should have known better. I warned him."

His voice is turning hard again. Molly tries one more time to get through to him. "I was with Sean after," she says. "What happened to Cole broke him. He wasn't the same—"

Jimmy lifts a hand to cut her off. "Don't try to tell me he's paid."

"He has."

"Not enough."

"This feud between you, it's all one-sided," Molly says. "He's never wanted to hurt you."

Jimmy laughs, and the laughter goes on a long time. At the end of it he says, "You have no idea. He already killed me once. Down in Tennessee. Shot me three times. I'd be dead now, but—" He raps his knuckles on his chest and hits something hard.

She should have realized before. His shirt is bulkier than it should be. He's wearing a bulletproof vest underneath.

She wants to hear what happened in Tennessee. But before she can ask, Kelly calls down from the steeple.

"Jimmy. Someone's here."

Then Jimmy's up off the floor. He crosses the loft and reaches the bottom of the spiral staircase as Kelly is coming down.

"Is it Sean?" Jimmy says.

Kelly is shaking his head. "It's the cop and the Fibbie."

38

Rafael Garza

He was right about one thing: the place is remote.

Garza steps out of the car and onto the broken road. As he looks around, he's thinking no one's been here in a very long time.

There are wooden poles at intervals along the roadside. They would have carried power lines once, but now they lean empty at drunken angles.

Farther off, beyond them, the trees have lost all their leaves. Their branches stand out black and twisted against the sky.

Rachel comes around the car and stands at Garza's side, close enough that her arm brushes his.

"We should have come two weeks ago, Ray," she says. "We missed the fall colors."

The road is faded gray. It's been years, maybe decades, since anyone bothered to maintain it. Cracks wind through the surface in crazy patterns. Some of them are filled with the dark green of moss.

The chapel stands off in the distance with the lake behind it. The other buildings, closer by, look like bunkhouses. They're on the eastern side of the road: long cabins with patchy shingles on their roofs. Rachel sets off toward the nearest one, and Garza follows. There's litter in the road: a flattened soda can, a length of bicycle chain, half a Frisbee.

There's a cool wind blowing, but the midday sun feels warm on Garza's face. It shines on Rachel's black hair.

The windows of the bunkhouses are all boarded over. The walls are painted with graffiti. None of it looks fresh. The messages range from the banal to the profound.

God is watching, one says.

Kiss my ass, says another.

The most striking is written all in caps, in letters two feet high: EVERYTHING BAD GETS WASHED AWAY.

The door of the nearest cabin is swollen in its frame. Garza shoves it inward with his shoulder. Inside, it's murky dark. There's nothing but trash and rusted bed frames and a pile of burned mattresses.

Jimmy Harper

Jimmy is back up in the steeple.

There's a platform at the top of the winding stair, with room enough for three or four people to stand. Jimmy's there alone with his AR-15 and his binoculars. Around him are four windows of stained glass, one facing in each direction of the compass.

The south-facing window has an image of Saint Peter holding a staff and a key, but there's a chunk punched out that's roughly the size and shape of a football.

Jimmy watches the cop and the FBI agent through this empty space, first with the binoculars, then without them. He has trouble making sense of what he's seeing.

Initially he thought Sean must have sent them here—that he'd been caught or had turned himself in. But if that were true, there should be more of them. As far as Jimmy can tell, there's just the two. From his vantage point, he can survey the whole length of the road.

So maybe the cop and the FBI agent found out about this place on their own. Maybe they discovered that Khadduri used to come here as a kid. Which makes them smart or lucky or both.

In that case, they're just taking a chance. They don't know anyone's here.

They're being cautious though. Both of them wearing Kevlar. They have sidearms, though they haven't drawn them.

Maybe they'll be sloppy. A quick look around and then they'll take off. Jimmy hopes so. If they take more than a quick look, he's in trouble.

There are six bunkhouses in all, lined up in rows. The cop and the FBI agent have already checked out two of them. There are two more behind those. Then two more farther on, closer to the lake.

If they get as far as those last two bunkhouses, there's a good chance they'll spot Jimmy's car—because it's parked behind one of them.

The black Ford Explorer is parked behind the other. Jimmy had Nick drive it here from Khadduri's vacation house. He thought they would need it later. He hasn't worked out all the details, but he knows he doesn't want to transport bodies in his own car.

The cop and the FBI agent have moved on to the second row of bunk-houses. They duck inside one of them, come out again, duck inside the other. Jimmy steps to the eastern window of the steeple, which gives him a better view. He watches as the two figures head for the third row of bunkhouses. They're taking their time, strolling in the sunlight. There's something sweet about the scene. Jimmy wouldn't be surprised if they held hands.

They reach the last cabin and the cop pushes the door with his shoulder. They step inside, but only for a few seconds. When they come out again, they walk along the front of the building. Now, Jimmy thinks, they'll either circle around to the back and see the cars or they'll come to the chapel.

Neither option is good for him.

They round the corner of a cabin. They're going to look in back. Jimmy reaches for his rifle, which is leaning against the wall.

Suddenly the FBI agent stops. The cop does too. They've heard a sound.

An engine. A vehicle approaching on the road.

Jimmy moves back to the south-facing window, and what he sees sends a flush of heat running up his spine to the back of his neck. He watches as it rolls closer: a white shape glowing in the sunlight.

Sean's pickup truck.

Molly Winter

From the choir loft, Molly can't see a thing.

Khadduri is sitting motionless with his eyes closed. She doesn't know what he's thinking. He showed a spark of courage before, talking back to Kelly. But now he seems afraid.

Molly was afraid before. Now she's hopeful.

Before Jimmy went up into the steeple, he warned her and Khadduri to stay quiet.

"If either of them makes a sound," he said to Nick and Kelly, "kill them both." He pulled the hunting knife from the sheath on his belt and added: "Quietly."

He jammed the blade of the knife into the wooden railing of the loft. There it waits. Ten feet away. Maybe less. Maybe eight. Molly stares at it. She pictures it cutting through the zip ties that bind her ankles.

Kelly sees her staring, and a grin twists his mouth. "You're something," he says, keeping his voice low. "I can see the wheels turning in your head." He looks at the knife and then back at her. "Come get it," he says. "I'd like to see you try."

Nick has his hands stuffed in his pockets. He shifts his weight from one foot to the other, nervous.

"Shut up, Kel," he says.

"Seriously," Kelly says. "That's some ninja shit, if you can get this knife from over there, with your legs tied and your hands behind your back. I want to see it."

Molly doesn't move. She lets out a breath through her nose.

"I can't get the knife," she says. "But I don't need it. You're going to cut me loose."

Kelly's laugh is nothing more than a noise in the back of his throat.

"Why would I do that?" he asks.

"Because it's smart," Molly says. "You know this thing has gone off the rails." She looks up at the ceiling, a gesture toward Jimmy in the steeple. "It's not going to end the way he wants, and that means it won't go well for you. Unless you switch over to the right side. Then I'll make sure everyone knows you did the right thing."

Kelly's grin is wider than before. "You'd do that for me, huh?"

"Absolutely."

"Well, that's nice of you," Kelly says. "That's generous as hell. But I think I'll maybe take my chances."

He stands by the railing and does the laugh again at the back of his throat, but Molly sits still and pays him no mind.

He's not the one she's trying to convince.

Jimmy Harper

Through the scope of the rifle, Jimmy watches the white pickup roll to a stop. Sean steps out of the cab with a backpack. Slings it over his shoulder. He scans around him. Pushes shut the door of the truck.

In the steeple, Jimmy wavers. A conversation plays out in his head.

Take the shot.

No. It's too far.

This is what you wanted.

Too far. I want to look him in the eye.

Liar. You're afraid of what'll happen after.

No.

You are. You goddamn coward. Just like Knoxville. You could have shot him at the lawyer's house.

There were witnesses.

So? It's never gonna be perfect. Do you want to do this, or not?

Sean Tennant

It looks wrong.

It feels wrong.

There's one car parked in the road: a nondescript sedan that looks like a rental. Sean was expecting to see the black SUV.

"Something's been bugging me," Cole's voice says.

Cole has been AWOL since yesterday. Sean drove here from upstate New York, seven hundred fifty miles, without a peep from him. Now he wants to talk.

"About that kid," Cole says. "The cop."

"What about him?" Sean asks.

"Would you have killed him, if it came down to it? If he had decided not to play nice."

"That's not a real question."

"Sure it is."

"I'm not killing any cops. I already told you."

"That's what's bugging me," Cole says. "It makes me question your commitment to this mission."

Sean doesn't respond. Because something really is wrong. There are buildings off to his right. Cabins. And two people just walked out from behind one of them.

A tall man and a short woman. Sean has never seen them before, not in person. But Dalton Webber showed him pictures.

He remembers their names: Rafael Garza. Rachel Massoud.

Sean adds up the details as they come closer. They're wearing Kevlar. They're drawing their guns. They're frowning at him.

"Show me your hands," Garza says.

He's twenty feet away and coming closer.

"There really should be more than two of you," Sean says.

"Your hands," says Garza. "If you please."

Sean holds them up, palms out. "Unless you already arrested them."

"There's no one else here," Massoud says.

Sean gets a hollow feeling in the bottom of his stomach. "You shouldn't be here," he says. "They're here. We need to take cover."

He starts to walk backward, toward the rental car, toward his truck. Garza advances, gun raised, keeping pace with him. Massoud's frown deepens. She turns to face the bunkhouses and the chapel. She has her gun up too. She's sweeping it around in an arc.

Sean sees the shot an instant before he hears it. The bullet grazes Rachel Massoud's chin and opens a gash in the side of her neck.

Jimmy Harper

It's been a while since he practiced with the rifle, and it shows.

The first shot was too low, and the second takes too long. Jimmy has to aim again, and everyone is moving. The FBI agent turns and stumbles, and the cop, Garza, catches her as she falls. She throws an arm around his shoulder, and he pulls her back toward their car. Sean draws his pistol from under his coat and aims it in the direction of the chapel. He's searching for a target, but he doesn't find one. He's being cautious, Jimmy thinks. He doesn't want to fire blind, for fear of hitting Molly.

Jimmy's second shot strikes Garza's right leg, low on his thigh. His third shot misses altogether. By the time he's ready for a fourth, Garza and Massoud have taken cover behind the car. There's an instant when the crosshairs of Jimmy's scope hover over Sean's head. Then Sean lowers his pistol and dives behind the car as well.

Jimmy fires three more times, but it's mostly out of anger. It does no good. All he's hitting is metal and glass.

Molly Winter

When the shooting starts, Molly has her eyes on Nick.

He's leaning against the railing of the choir loft, and the crack of the first shot makes him flinch.

Kelly moves toward the spiral staircase. Maybe he's waiting for orders from Jimmy, or maybe he wants to feel closer to the action.

Five more shots follow. Then silence.

"Have you had enough?" Molly asks.

She's talking to Nick, but Kelly is the one who answers her.

"Sweetheart, we're just getting started."

Nick stands frozen at the railing.

"How much of this are you going to stick around for?" Molly asks him. "How far are you willing to let this go?"

Nick doesn't answer.

"We can all get out of here," Molly says to him. "It's up to you."

His eyes looked blank before, but now something stirs in them.

"Right," he says.

He reaches for the hunting knife, pulls it free of the wooden railing.

Kelly catches on to what's happening. "Don't do anything stupid, Nicky," he says.

Nick ignores him and approaches Adam Khadduri with the knife. He bends down and slices through the zip ties on Khadduri's ankles. Then the ones on his wrists.

Kelly draws a pistol from the pocket of his leather coat. Aims it at Khadduri.

"You stay put," he says.

Nick steps toward Molly and bends again with the knife. She feels the zip ties on her ankles give way to the blade. It's a sweet moment.

"Jimmy has the handcuff key," Nick says. Apologetic.

"No one's leaving," Kelly says.

He's closer now. Agitated. He still has his gun trained on Khadduri.

Khadduri looks up at him and laughs. "Two-bit hoodlum," he says.

Nick stands up straight. He jams the hunting knife into the railing again and turns to face Kelly.

"Put the gun away," Nick says. "What's the point?"

There's a moment when Kelly looks uncertain, and Molly wonders if he might give in. Then Khadduri makes a mistake. He starts to get up from the floor.

Kelly takes a single step forward and shoots him in the head.

"Call me a hoodlum again," he says, as Khadduri's body falls back against the wall and slides down. Molly hears a strangled cry. Realizes it's coming from her own throat.

Kelly aims his gun at her. "I'm sorry," he says. "I didn't catch that."

"Come on, Kel," says Nick. "It's enough."

"No, no. I want to hear what she has to say."

Molly holds still and makes no sound. She's looking at the floor. Khadduri's blood is flowing out of him. It's creeping over the wooden boards. Getting closer to her.

There's a shout from above. Jimmy in the steeple.

"What's going on?"

"Everything's under control," Kelly says. His voice is loud, confident. In a softer tone he adds, "Right, Nicky?"

Molly looks up in time to see Nick shake his head. "No."

Kelly starts to bring his gun around, but Nick is already moving. He plucks the hunting knife from the railing of the loft and buries it in Kelly's stomach. Kelly gets off a shot that slams into the floor.

Nick twists the knife and Kelly screams. Kelly tries to raise his gun, but Nick knocks his hand aside. He lets go of the knife and takes hold of the collar of Kelly's coat. Swings him around and smashes his face into the railing.

Kelly's gun goes off a final time, the bullet traveling across the chapel, shattering a window behind the altar.

Then Nick lifts him up and pushes him over the railing, out into empty space.

39

Sean Tennant

People babble when they get shot. Sean has heard it before.

Rachel Massoud is calmer than most.

"I don't want to die, Ray," she says. "Not like this. This is stupid."

"You're not going to die," Garza says.

They're sitting in the road with their backs against the car for cover. All three of them in a row: Sean and Garza and Massoud.

"It's a lot of blood though," Massoud says. "I can feel it."

Garza has a hand pressed to her neck, trying to stop the bleeding. Sean shrugs his backpack off his shoulder and unzips it. It's full of cylinder seals wrapped in white handkerchiefs. He starts shaking them free and passing the handkerchiefs to Garza, who packs them on the wound.

"Did you get shot, Ray?" Massoud asks.

"Not me," Garza says.

Massoud wipes at her chin and looks at the blood that comes away on her palm.

"I'm bleeding everywhere," she says. "How bad is this one?"

"It's nothing," Garza says. "You'll have a beautiful scar."

Sean takes his cell phone out to call 911 for an ambulance. When the operator answers, he describes the situation as best he can. The operator sounds skeptical but says she's sending help.

At that moment Sean hears a gunshot. It makes him duck down instinctively, but it doesn't sound like the others from before. It's more remote, and there's no impact on the car or the road. It's followed by another shot. And one more.

"What was that?" the operator asks.

"That would be gunfire," Sean says. "You'll want to let the sheriff know. Make sure you tell them there's an active shooter. At least one."

"This is at Grass Lake?" the operator says. "Nobody ever goes out there."

"They're here now."

"What's your name?"

It's a question, but she makes it sound like a warning. Like he's going to get in trouble if this is all a hoax.

"My name is Garza," Sean says. "Rafael Garza."

He kills the call and hears Massoud laughing softly.

"There's two of you, Ray," she says.

Garza shifts around so he's kneeling in front of her. He keeps one hand on the wound on her neck and uses the other to take out his own phone. He places a call to someone named Jansson. Sean is close enough to hear both sides of the conversation. When Garza explains where he is and what happened, Jansson sounds angry, but he's all business. He promises to send sheriff's deputies, local cops, FBI, everyone he can muster.

At the end of the call, Garza puts his phone away and sits again with his back to the car. As he settles in, Sean sees him grimace in pain. Massoud sees it too.

"What's the matter?" she asks.

Garza shakes his head. "It's fine," he says.

But it's not. There's blood on the right leg of his pants. Sean finds the bullet hole in the fabric and tears it wide to get a better look.

It could be worse. There's an entry wound on the back of Garza's thigh, no exit wound. The bleeding seems slow.

"You lied to me, Ray," Massoud says. "No fair."

Sean unwraps some more cylinder seals and presses the handkerchiefs onto the wound. He secures them in place with Garza's belt. Garza keeps his right hand on Massoud's neck all the while.

"Just like old times," a voice says. "Sean saves the day."

Out of the corner of his eye, Sean can see Cole's black boots. Cole is standing by the rear fender of the car. Another shot rings out from the direction of the chapel, and Sean, without thinking, gestures for him to get down.

"You're a trip," Cole says, laughing. "What have I got to worry about?"

Sean lets a few seconds pass, then gets up to a crouch and looks out over the trunk of the car. There's no one in sight. He was worried that someone might approach while they were pinned down. He scans the chapel, sees the south-facing window on the steeple. He decides that's where the very first shots must have come from. Where the shooter might still be.

"Get down," Garza says. "Help is coming."

"Sure," Cole's voice says. "Eventually."

Sean sits on the ground again and reaches for his backpack. He unwraps the rest of the stones and piles the handkerchiefs in Garza's lap.

"What are you doing?" Garza asks.

Sean zips up the backpack. "I have to go in."

"You're not going anywhere," Massoud says. "Tell him, Ray."

Garza is quiet for a moment. His eyes look thoughtful. His gun is holstered on his hip. Sean wonders if he'll reach for it.

"Doesn't matter," Cole says. "It's not like there's a lot at stake. Right?"

Garza leaves his gun where it is. "I think it would be unwise to try to enter that chapel," he says.

"So do I," says Sean. "But I have to go anyway."

Garza nods. It's a neutral gesture. He's not agreeing; he's acknowledging a fact.

"You believe she's inside?" he says. "Molly?"

"Yes."

"Still, you should wait," Garza says. "There's too much open ground to cross, between here and there. It's too risky."

Sean is thinking the same thing. The chapel is too far, but the bunkhouses are closer. If he can reach them, they'll provide him some cover. Then he can approach the chapel from the side.

"I'm taking the long way around," he says to Garza.

Nick Ensen

This is bad, Nick thinks.

He's looking down at Kelly, who's folded at an unnatural angle over one of the wooden pews. The fall must have broken his back. His arms are spread out at his sides. His gun lies on the seat of the pew.

His eyes are open, staring up at nothing.

Nick hears Molly moving behind him and turns to see her struggling to rise with her hands behind her back. She gets onto her knees and then up on her feet. But she's hardly worth noticing. She's a blip on the radar. Something else has all of Nick's attention.

He can hear Jimmy tromping down the spiral stairs from the steeple.

There's a second set of stairs that lead from the loft to the ground floor of the chapel. Nick watches as Molly rushes toward them, but she's too late. Jimmy catches her and shoves her carelessly across the loft. She trips and stumbles to the floor.

Jimmy has his rifle slung over his left shoulder. His right hand holds his Ruger pistol.

He points it at Nick.

Nick has one just like it in the pocket of his coat. He knows better than to reach for it.

Jimmy looks at Adam Khadduri, slumped dead against the wall.

"What happened here?" he asks. "Who did that?"

"Kelly," Nick says.

Jimmy spots the zip ties on the floor. "Did Kelly cut him loose first?"

"No," Nick says. "That was me."

Molly is up on her knees again. She braces one foot to stand.

"You were gonna let her go too?" Jimmy says.

"Yes."

"Why?"

Nick feels a pressure behind his eyes. His mouth tastes sour.

"I had to make a judgment call," he says.

Molly is standing now. Jimmy shifts his pistol suddenly and fires into the floor at her feet. She backs away from him.

"What was your judgment?" Jimmy asks, turning back to Nick.

"I thought with the cops here it didn't make sense to play this out," Nick says. "We couldn't win."

"Huh," Jimmy says. His eyes have that lifeless look they get. Unreadable. "Did Kelly share your opinion?" he asks.

"No." Nick says.

"Where is he?"

Nick nods at the railing of the loft, and Jimmy steps over and glances down.

"You did that?" Jimmy says.

"Yes."

"Killed my cousin?"

"It seemed like the right thing at the time."

"Why?"

Nick shrugs. "He aimed his gun at me. It was a charged situation."

There's a change in Jimmy's eyes. A spark. He smiles.

"I told you he was a hothead," Jimmy says, raising his pistol to aim it at Nick's face. "I warned you."

"That's true," Nick says. "You did." He closes his eyes, but it seems wrong. He opens them and looks at the muzzle of the gun, at Jimmy's finger on the trigger. The finger starts to squeeze, and Nick braces himself.

Off to the side, Molly takes a step toward the stairs.

Jimmy whips the gun around to stop her.

"Don't," he says.

She freezes, then backs up against the wall.

In that moment of distraction, Nick draws his pistol from his pocket, and the draw is smooth as silk. A thing of beauty.

When Jimmy turns around again, Nick trains the gun on his forehead. The look on Jimmy's face is not what he expected. It's not angry. It's impressed. Almost pleased.

Jimmy laughs. "Do you want to shoot me?"

"No," Nick says. "I want to leave."

And, somehow, those are the right words. They do the trick. Jimmy lowers his gun slowly and steps aside.

"Go ahead," he says. "I don't need you anymore."

Sean Tennant

It's fifty yards from the car to the eastern end of closest bunkhouse. Sean covers the distance at a sprint with his head down. The cylinder seals rattle like marbles in his backpack.

No one shoots at him.

He cuts through the space between the first pair of bunkhouses, running through wild grass, and reaches the second pair. He braces himself for a moment against a wall of charred wood. The smell of the burning lingers, like smoke from a long-ago fire.

One more sprint and Sean reaches the last pair of buildings. Call them bunkhouse five and bunkhouse six. He turns the corner of bunkhouse five, and what he sees surprises him, though it shouldn't. It's the black SUV, the one Khadduri's men used to abduct Molly in Knoxville.

There's another car behind bunkhouse six. A gray Cadillac.

Both vehicles are empty.

From here Sean can see the side of the chapel, forty yards away. There are three windows of clear glass, each one divided into a dozen small panes. Half the panes are cracked or shattered.

The windows are high on the building. Probably too high for anyone to be looking out. But to be safe Sean retreats to the cover of bunkhouse five.

Standing with his back against the bunkhouse wall, he hears Cole's voice.

"Someone's nervous," it says.

Sean mutters his reply. "Not now."

"Happens to everybody," Cole says. "Take a minute to gather yourself, and then let's go."

Sean smiles. "What are you gonna do?"

"Moral support. But you won't need me. Look at you, all tricked out like a commando."

Sean is wearing Garza's Kevlar. He touches it, feels the rough texture beneath his fingertips. As he was about to leave, Garza told him to wait. Sean thought there might be trouble, but Garza only wanted to offer him the vest.

"Brothers in arms," Cole says. "We all have to stick together."

Sean has his windbreaker on over the vest, and his shoulder rig under the windbreaker. He draws out his Glock, checks that there's a round in the chamber.

He's got fifteen rounds in the magazine. In his pocket there's another full mag, plus a dozen loose bullets. All the ammo he's had with him since Houston.

"Should have picked up more along the way," Cole says.

It's too late now. Sean readies himself to leave the cover of the bunk-house and cross the last distance to the chapel. But before he takes a single step he hears an unexpected sound.

An electronic double chirp.

The sound of someone unlocking the doors of the SUV.

Nick Ensen

The whole time walking away from the chapel, Nick feels an itch on the back of his neck, as if there are bugs crawling over his skin.

He knows what it is. He doesn't believe Jimmy's really going to let him go. He's waiting to get shot.

He thumbs the key fob of the SUV, walks up to the driver's door, and tugs it open.

A ridiculous feeling of joy washes over him. It makes him tremble. He drops the key.

When he gets down on one knee to retrieve it, he feels a hard touch of metal on the back of his skull.

"If you move," a voice says, "I'll blast your head off."

Sean Tennant

"I'm not part of this," the kid says.

Sean pats him down. Awkwardly, left-handed. He finds a gun and slips it into the pocket of his windbreaker.

"Do you have any other weapons?" he asks.

"No," the kid says. "I swear."

Sean hauls him up by the collar. Turns him so he can see his face. Pushes him against the SUV.

"What's your name?"

"Nick."

"Well, Nick, I know you're part of this. The stitches on your cheek give you away. You were at the ranch in Montana."

"That was a mistake."

"You're right. It was."

"I tried to help her."

"Molly?" Sean says. "You attacked her."

"I mean today. I tried to help her today."

Sean nods in the direction of the chapel. "Is she in there?" he asks. "Is she still alive?"

"Yes."

"Who else is in there? Khadduri?"

The kid looks away. "Khadduri's dead."

It's a simple declaration, but it catches Sean off guard.

"What about his men?"

"They're dead too."

Sean shakes the kid by the collar. "You're telling me the guys who were in Knoxville, the ones who were driving this car—"

"Clinton and Reed," Nick says. "They're dead."

Sean's eyes narrow. "Then who's in the chapel?"

"Just Jimmy."

The name doesn't register at first. Sean can't make sense of it. When he does, it throws him. It's an unnerving sensation, like falling in a dream. Everything around him is the same as it was before, but he feels unsteady. He leans into Nick to regain his equilibrium. He pushes the muzzle of the Glock into the kid's chest.

"Don't screw with me," he says. "Jimmy's dead."

Nick spreads his arms like he's sorry. "Not yet."

Sean bears down on the Glock. "I killed him."

"You're hurting me," Nick says. "Ease up. I don't have a vest. If you shoot me, I won't get back up again."

Sean blinks. The air he's breathing feels suddenly cold. The night at the high school in Tennessee comes rushing through his mind. Firing three shots and seeing Jimmy fall to the ground. Standing at a distance while he died. Not wanting to look.

Sean moves back from Nick and withdraws the Glock. He lets go of the kid's collar.

Nick looks at him warily. "They're in the chapel. Her and him and nobody else. I'm done with this. I want to go."

Sean fades back another step. Pulls things together.

"There's a cop named Garza and an FBI agent named Massoud," he says. "You'll see them on your way out. If you're smart, you'll surrender to them."

Nick runs a palm over his injured cheek. He climbs in behind the wheel of the SUV.

"Nobody ever said I was smart," he says.

Sean decides not to argue with him. "How far do you think you can get?"

Nick shrugs and turns the key in the ignition. "I guess I'll find out."

He closes the door and puts the SUV into drive. Heads toward the chapel, then past it and away. He goes slowly at first, and Sean jogs along beside him, taking advantage of the cover. When the right moment comes, Sean breaks away and runs for the front steps of the chapel.

40

Jimmy Harper

He's standing near the ruined altar with Molly. The Ruger pistol in his right hand. He left the rifle up in the loft.

They're waiting together in silence. It's not exactly a comfortable silence, but it's not a hostile one either. To Jimmy it seems peaceful.

Molly struggled when he brought her down here. Cursed him. But he put the gun to her head and said he would use it and now she's calm. She's staring along the length of what used to be the center aisle. Watching the two carved wooden doors at the chapel's entrance. Waiting for them to open.

Jimmy has his left arm around her throat, holding her close against him. He can feel her breathing gently. He wonders if she might be resigned to what's coming.

Sunlight glows in the high windows on either side of them. It falls on chunks of white marble that lie scattered on the floor, remnants of the altar.

Above them, a small brown bird flutters in the rafters.

There's a squeal of rusted hinges as the doors open at the back of the nave.

Sean is silhouetted in a rectangle of light while he passes through. The doors swing shut behind him.

He walks along the aisle until the three pews block his way and he has to skirt around them. He glances at Kelly's body and keeps moving.

Jimmy lays the muzzle of the Ruger against a spot just below Molly's ear.

Sean's gun is pointed at the floor. He has a backpack in his left hand.

He calls out to Molly: "Are you all right?"

"I'm all right," she says. "Better now."

Sean stops when he's twelve feet away. "This is over, Jimmy," he says. "The police are coming. FBI. This place is going to be overrun."

"There's time enough," Jimmy says, "for what I need to do."

Sean holds up the backpack. "I've got the stones here," he says. "They're all I have to offer you. If you take them now, you might get away before anybody comes."

Jimmy shakes his head. "I told you before: those stones don't mean anything to me."

"Then tell me what you want."

"You know what I want," Jimmy says. "Drop the backpack on the floor."

Sean lowers it, then tosses it aside.

Molly tries to pull free, but Jimmy tightens his grip on her.

"There's a loft behind you," he says to Sean. "I want you to throw your gun up there."

"Don't," Molly says.

After a moment's hesitation, Sean turns around and lobs his Glock underhand. It clears the railing and clatters when it lands.

He turns back and shows Jimmy his palms.

"Let her walk out of here," he says. "I'm begging you."

There's a flutter of wings up in the rafters, but Jimmy ignores it. He brushes the muzzle of his Ruger lightly over Molly's skin.

"When I asked you to stop Cole from joining the army," he says, "what did you do?"

Sean lowers his eyes. "I'm sorry, Jimmy."

"And when I told you not to involve him in stealing those stones—"

"I'm sorry."

"Say it again."

"I'm sorry."

Jimmy feels the warmth of the sun coming through the windows, the stillness of the air all around him. He weighs things one last time.

"I believe you," he says. "But I don't care."

He shifts Molly out of the way, turns the Ruger on Sean, and fires four times.

Rafael Garza

The shots sound hollow and far away.

Garza is layering the last of the handkerchiefs on Rachel's wound when he hears them.

"That's him," Rachel says.

"Probably," says Garza.

"Shooting. Or getting shot."

"One or the other."

Her breathing is rougher than he would like, and her eyes look tired and glassy. He leans in and kisses her cheek.

"Are you leaving?" she asks him.

"Of course not," he says.

"You can, if you have to. He might need you."

Garza touches his forehead to hers. "He's on his own. Whatever happens, I won't leave you."

Jimmy Harper

Three out of four.

Molly struggled against him, and it threw off his aim. His fourth shot went wide. But he scored three hits, center mass.

Molly is still struggling, pushing at him with her shoulder, trying to slam her head into his chin. Jimmy shoves her away, but she comes back at him. He brings a knee up into her stomach, throws an elbow across her jaw. When she comes at him again, he slams the butt of the Ruger pistol into her temple.

It spins her around and she goes down headfirst to the floor among the broken pieces of the altar. She doesn't get up.

When Jimmy looks at Sean again, he's on his knees, drawing a gun from the left-hand pocket of his windbreaker. Another Ruger. Nick's gun.

Jimmy throws three more shots at him. He aims at Sean's torso like before, even though he can see the Kevlar underneath Sean's jacket. Jimmy knows what it's like to be shot while wearing Kevlar.

Sean's body jerks three times. He slumps forward onto his hands and knees, gasping.

Sean Tennant

The kid's pistol is right there under his left hand. But his hand isn't working the way he wants.

Nothing is. Everything seems blown apart. It hurts to breathe. His ribs are moving in ways they shouldn't.

Jimmy comes down from the altar, and there's a lightness in his steps. He moves like someone happy. Sean gets his fingers to go where they should be on the pistol, but before he can lift it, Jimmy's there. Kicking it away.

Jimmy's wearing black boots. Like Cole's. One of them stomps down on Sean's left hand.

Sean hears a groan that's got to be his. Jimmy's not groaning. Jimmy's happy. He steps around and kicks Sean in the stomach. The kick lifts Sean up, and when he comes down he's lying on his right side. Another kick turns him over onto his back.

There's Jimmy, smiling, with the rafters in the background.

There's Jimmy's gun hand, complete with gun.

Jimmy shoots him again. In the heart. But the Kevlar stops it.

"Hurts," Jimmy says. "Doesn't it?"

Sean agrees, but he can't say it. He can't catch his breath.

"Like a son of a bitch," Jimmy says.

His gun is still there, aiming at Sean's heart. Jimmy shifts it up and to the left and shoots him in the shoulder.

The little brown bird squawks up in the rafters, and the same sort of noise comes out of Sean's mouth.

"That's better," Jimmy says. "I don't know if it hurt more, but it drew blood. Makes the damage seem more real. I'm gonna do the other shoulder."

The gun moves slow. Sean works on his breathing. It's panic as much as it is pain. He manages a single word.

"No."

Muzzle flash. The bullet slices into him.

Jimmy sniffs, standing over him. "You don't really have a say in this."

He alters his aim and shoots Sean's right leg, midthigh. Then his ankle.

Sean cries out again, but it's less like an animal noise, more like something human. A cry of frustration.

He gets out another word. A syllable anyway: "Nuff."

He tries to sit up, but bending at the waist is agony. Jimmy points the gun at his face.

"You really want to stay down. I'll let you know when it's enough."

The gun moves. Sean tracks it with his eyes. Jimmy shoots his ankle a second time, and pauses. Maybe so he can watch it bleed.

Cole's voice is right next to Sean's ear. As if he's lying on the floor with him.

"I'm not real impressed by your plan of attack," Cole says.

Breathe in and talk, Sean thinks. Talk on the exhale.

"I know," he says.

Jimmy shoots his ankle yet again.

"This keeps up," Cole says, "I'm afraid you might lose your foot."

Sean laughs, but it's lost in the mess of his breathing.

He wants to say: "I think that's what he's going for." But it's too long. He settles for: "You and me both."

"Time to rally," Cole says. "Turn this thing around."

"You bet," Sean says.

The gun hovers in the air. Jimmy is looking at him curiously.

"Who are you talking to?" Jimmy asks.

"Why don't you leave me alone and go fuck yourself," Sean wants to say, but it comes out garbled. Jimmy can't understand it. He's been standing near Sean's feet, but now he steps around to Sean's right and squats down to hear better.

Keep it simple, Sean thinks. Two words.

"Cole's here," he says.

Bad idea.

Jimmy's eyes go dark and his voice turns icy cold. "He's not. Not anymore."

The gun shifts here and there, and when it settles Sean can see straight into the black circle of the muzzle. He looks at Jimmy's finger on the trigger, the white edge of the nail like a crescent moon. The moon goes blurry.

Sean's gaze moves past the gun, up along Jimmy's arm, to a spot above his shoulder.

"Wild about you," Sean says.

Jimmy's dark eyes show confusion.

Molly is behind him, lifting up a chunk of white marble with two hands.

Molly Winter

She doesn't know how long she was out. Maybe only a few seconds.

When she came back, the world felt woozy. Blood trickling along her cheek.

Everything soft and hazy, until the gunshots snapped her out of it.

Moving her cuffed hands from back to front took longer than it should have. Helpless on the floor on her back, she felt sure Jimmy would see her.

She got the cuffs behind her knees, no problem. Stepping her legs through was harder. Torturous. There's a pain in her lower back like someone drove a blade into her spine. Her shoulders ache as if they're in danger of tearing from their sockets.

No time to think about it. She's on her feet. She picks up a piece of white marble. Part of the altar.

There's a tinny echo in her ears from the gunfire, but that's good. It must be worse for Jimmy. He doesn't hear her coming up behind him.

She swings the marble at the side of his head. It's glorious, the connection. Solid.

Maybe the best thing she's ever felt.

The impact knocks Jimmy over sideways. His gun goes off, but the bullet misses Sean. It punches a black hole in the floor.

The slide stays open. The gun is empty.

Molly lifts the chunk of marble again. Jimmy is half-sitting, half-lying on the floor, trying to push himself up with his left hand. She takes a second swing with the marble, at the same spot on the side of his head. Then a third.

The third blow tears off a hunk of his scalp and lays him out. She stands over him, waiting for him to move.

Off to her right, Sean moans. She turns to see him sitting up.

She drops the marble and goes to him. He's bleeding in four places, but the ankle is the worst. Molly can see bone.

She tugs his belt free to make a tourniquet, but Sean grabs her arm.

"Get his gun," he tells her.

"He's out," she says.

He shakes his head. "Spare clip."

Which makes sense. Jimmy could have a spare clip. But it's not what Sean means.

"My pocket," he says.

She steps over to Jimmy and takes the gun from his hand. There's no resistance. When she returns, Sean has his spare clip out. Molly ejects the one from Jimmy's gun, replaces it, and works the slide to load a round.

The handcuffs clink and rattle with every movement.

Sean holds the gun while she makes a loop of his belt and applies it as a tourniquet. She places it up close to his knee and cinches it. She needs a lever to twist it, but there's nothing around. She tightens it as best she can with her hands.

"I know," Sean says suddenly.

His voice sounds a little airy, but it's stronger than it ought to be.

"What do you know?" Molly asks.

He laughs quietly. It seems to be directed at himself.

"Talking to Cole," he tells her. "He says it's not the worst thing, losing a foot. He says I'm lucky."

"You're not gonna lose it," Molly says.

Sean looks to his left. Seems to listen.

"Cole says you're an optimist, but he likes that about you."

"Maybe you should lie down," Molly says. "Elevate the leg. Does that make sense?"

"I would," Sean says. "But I don't know if I'd get back up."

Right then, as she's worried that he's fading, she hears the tone of distant sirens. When they're closer, he picks up on them too.

"See?" he says. "Lucky."

The brown bird sings in the rafters, making a pretty counterpoint to the sirens. It flies down and alights on the back of a pew. From there it descends to the floor and hops toward Jimmy.

He raises his head to look at it.

Sean has the gun in his lap. He brings it up. Aims it.

Jimmy starts to crawl away.

Sean's grip on the gun seems secure, but his arm is far from steady.

"I'll do it," Molly says.

"You don't have to."

"I don't mind."

She takes the gun and moves Sean's hands to the tourniquet.

"Tight," she says.

"I've got it," he tells her.

When she rises to her feet, the bird flies back to the rafters.

Jimmy is moving slow, dragging himself along on knees and elbows.

Molly walks behind him. She wonders where he's going—until she sees it. There's another gun, on the eastern side of the chapel, near the wall.

It's a twin of the one she's holding.

Jimmy crawls through dust and fragments of glass and splinters of marble to reach it.

Molly lets him get close enough to touch it, then puts a bullet in his brain.

Epilogue

TWO AND A HALF YEARS LATER

Rose Dillon

The road that leads to the site of Camp Antioch might have had a name once, but there's no name on the map and no sign at the place where it joins up with the main road.

There are only two wooden posts with a chain hanging between them. The chain isn't serious about keeping anyone out. It's not even secured with a padlock. There's just a hook that fits into an eyebolt on one of the posts.

Rose Dillon gets out of her car to unhook the chain so she can drive through. The sun is out and it's springtime. She can hear birdsong from the trees nearby. There's a caterpillar crawling on the ground.

It makes her think of Henry Keen.

To be fair, Henry Keen is seldom far from her thoughts.

When the police searched Keen's apartment after the shootings at the Galleria mall, they found pages of notes that he'd written, sort of a rambling manifesto. The *Houston Chronicle* printed parts of it. There were several references to caterpillars squirming in his head. It made him sound suitably insane.

Rose needed no proof of Keen's insanity. She had seen it up close.

In retrospect it's hard to believe, but there was a time when he seemed harmless. She went on two dates with him, and they were okay but nothing special. She decided against going on a third. She stopped returning his calls; it seemed like the easiest way to break things off.

What happened after will never leave her. It's a memory she can't get rid of: the moment when she saw him again that day in Brooks Brothers where she was working. He didn't seem angry, even when he raised his gun and shot the customer she was helping, a man who only wanted to buy a suit.

Rose remembers the look on Keen's face, the excitement. Like he wanted to show her something. And he did. He took hold of her and dragged her along with him on his shooting spree. She looked into the faces of his victims.

She believed she would be one of them, that he would kill her. But it didn't happen. She lived, and Keen died. Sean Tennant killed him.

It's over. It's in the past. But Rose is still dealing with it.

She dealt with it poorly at first. In those early days, she was pursued by reporters who wanted to talk to her about Keen. She left Houston and hid out at her parents' house in Fort Worth, but they found her there and parked their vans on the street. She remained inside for days, for weeks, and the reporters got bored and left. But even when it was safe to come out, Rose stayed in.

There was no place she wanted to go, no one she wanted to see.

She stayed with her parents for more than a year.

They took care of her for all that time. Rose slept late and watched television, and as long as she showered every day and ate regular meals, they left her alone. But in the end they began to show signs of impatience. They wanted her to talk to someone. Someone professional. They said she needed to move on.

She agreed. She told them she was going on a trip.

She had some money in the bank, and her car was in her parents' garage. Her father had been starting it and running the engine every week, religiously.

Rose left on a Saturday morning. Told her parents she was going to visit friends. She drove for an hour before she admitted to herself that it was a lie. She'd lost touch with her friends. She'd lost everything she used to be. All she had left was the thing that had happened to her.

It took her another hour of driving to remember that it had happened to other people too. Oscar Lindauer, for one. He was the first of Henry Keen's victims. He'd been shot through the eye. Rose pulled her car over and found his obituary online. He was buried in Lone Grove, Oklahoma, the town where he grew up.

She made it her first destination.

From there, it was only a matter of deciding to go on. She gathered the names of all of Keen's victims, and over the course of a year she visited each of them, the wounded and the dead. She stood over five graves and spoke with eight survivors. All the survivors had taken their leave of Houston. Seven of the eight had left Texas altogether.

In between her visits, Rose has done a fair amount of wandering. She lives cheap, stays in hostels and no-name motels. Sometimes she sleeps in her car.

Three months ago, when she came to the end of her list of names, she realized she needed a new purpose, and she found one.

Sean and Molly.

Their story is bound together with hers, and she intends to find them. But she's in no hurry. She's working up to it. She's been to Long Meadow Ranch in Montana. She stayed there for six weeks, helping tend the horses in exchange for room and board.

She's been to Rusty's All-American in Knoxville. She picked up some work there, waiting tables.

Now she's made her way to Michigan, to Camp Antioch on Grass Lake. There used to be a chapel here where Sean almost died. There's nothing now, no buildings left. Everything torn down and hauled away. As Rose drives closer to the lake, all she sees is a beat-up truck parked at the roadside, with a travel trailer hitched to the back.

She leaves her car in the road and walks down to the water. There's a dock on the shore, long and narrow. Out at the end, there's a guy with a fishing pole.

Rose is as leery of strangers as anyone, but she knows that the worst trouble in her life has come from people she was acquainted with. She's not going to let herself be afraid of a guy on a dock.

She walks out halfway and says, "What are you fishing for?"

The guy turns to her briefly, gives her a friendly nod.

"Lunch," he says.

She moves closer. "Beautiful day."

He looks up at the sky as if he hadn't noticed it before.

"Yup," he says.

She ventures closer still and takes him in. His clothes are worn, but they seem clean. He's around five ten and slender, midtwenties. He's got a ball cap on and shaggy brown hair spilling out from under it. He's got a beard that covers a lot of his face, but not the crooked scar on his left cheek.

"Do you come here a lot?" Rose asks him.

He shakes his head without looking at her.

"Do you know what happened here?"

He's quiet for a beat, staring into the distance.

"Did something happen here?" he says.

She lets it go. Stays out there with him for ten or fifteen minutes, feeling the breeze that blows over the water.

He doesn't ask her name, and she doesn't ask his.

*   *   *

Two days later, Rose is in Detroit. She drives through Corktown and looks for Harper Auto Repair, but in the place where it's supposed to be there's a Midas muffler shop.

She tracks down a phone number for Rafael Garza. She's done some research on him, and she knows he left Houston two years ago. These days he works homicide for the Detroit police.

She arranges to meet him in the evening downtown, by the fountain in Hart Plaza. She gets there early and waits, and when she sees him he's with a woman. It's a cool day and they're both wearing black wool coats.

An image flashes through Rose's mind: Henry Keen walking toward her in his black coat. It's there, and it's gone.

The woman with Garza has sleek black hair and wears a silk scarf around her neck. She kisses Garza and parts from him, heading for the path that runs along the Detroit River.

When Garza reaches the fountain, he's smiling.

"You look well," he says to Rose. "Better than the last time we spoke."

He interviewed her once at her parents' house—one of many detectives who questioned her about Keen.

"I feel better," she says.

They walk in circles around the plaza, and Rose tells him what she's been doing for the last fifteen months and what she wants. She followed Sean and Molly's story in the news, and she knows Sean was never charged for the burglary that led to his friend's death. But she doesn't know what became of him. The information she's been able to find is sketchy.

"You want to talk to him," Garza says.

"That's right."

"Why?"

Rose hesitates. "Honestly?"

"Honestly."

"Because it's either that, or I stop. And if I stop, I don't know what I'll do."

Garza walks along with his head bowed, as if he's considering her answer.

"The truth is I'm not sure where Sean and Molly are," he says. "The one thing I know is they want to be left alone. I could make a guess, but if you want guesses, all you have to do is go on the internet. You can find any number of people who'd be happy to tell you where to look for them. I've read some of that stuff. People say they moved to Canada. Or Mexico. Or Australia."

Rose has seen the same rumors. And more. "I heard they went back to Houston," she says. "Or maybe they're living on the beach. In California, near Coronado."

"I heard that one too," says Garza. "Only it was North Carolina. The Outer Banks."

You could go round and round this way, Rose thinks. It's a game of speculation. But she doesn't mind playing.

"Someone on Twitter said Sean rejoined the army," she says. "He's running missions in Afghanistan with the Special Forces. Someone else said that was bullshit. They said he was making furniture in Elkwood, Indiana."

Garza slows and comes to a stop. The two of them stand on the edge of the plaza.

"There you are," he says with a shrug. "Plenty of options to explore. But if you like, I can give you some advice."

"Please," Rose says.

"First, if you find them, keep your hands in plain sight. They spent years looking over their shoulders, worried about who might be coming after them. Those habits die hard."

She nods. "And second?"

Garza offers her a gentle smile. "I believe you'll find there's no such place as Elkwood, Indiana."

*　*　*

Rose lingers another day in Detroit. Spends most of it looking at paintings in the halls of the DIA. The following morning, she drives to Indiana.

She went back to Twitter for the name of the city and discovered she had misremembered it. It's Elkhart, not Elkwood.

She arrives in the early afternoon, crossing a bridge over the Saint Joseph River. She parks on Main Street and has a look around. The people seem reserved but friendly. The kind who would surely hold a door for you and depending on their mood might stop and pet your dog.

There's one small furniture store downtown. Rose goes in and chats with the owner. Says she'd like to have some custom pieces made. The owner tells her he knows a guy. Works with him all the time.

She leaves with a business card: SEAN MORGAN DESIGNS. The address is on County Road 7.

It's farm country: barns and silos and open fields. The houses are set far apart from each other. Sean and Molly's house is two stories, white clapboard, a foundation made of fieldstones. SEAN MORGAN DESIGNS painted on a plank above the door of the garage.

Sean is working in the driveway, applying wood stain to a trestle table. Molly is walking in the yard, pulling a toddler behind her in a red wagon.

Rose passes the house and drives half a mile before she finds a place to turn around. When she comes back, she parks in the grass beside the road.

Sean finishes his work and joins Molly and their son in the yard. He lifts the boy from the wagon and holds him up high in the air.

Rose rolls down her window and watches. There's an oak tree growing near the house, with a swing suspended from one of its limbs. Molly keeps the swing steady while Sean places the boy in the seat.

They take turns pushing. They're cautious at first, but then they push him higher.

The boy squeals.

The sound comes to Rose clearly across the distance. It's a happy sound, a normal sound. It tells her she shouldn't be here. She should leave these people alone.

On the drive from Detroit, and long before, she thought about what she would say to them. One obvious thing: she would thank Sean for saving her life. But there are other things she needs to say, things she's kept from everyone:

That she sees Henry Keen's face almost every day, at random moments, in the faces of strangers.

That when she dreams, she dreams about his victims. She sees the fear in their eyes, and the fear is directed at her, as if she's the one who's trying to kill them.

That on that day in Houston, she felt terror every time Keen pulled the trigger. But she also felt relief. She felt hope, every time, because as long as Keen was aiming his gun at someone else, he wasn't aiming it at her.

That's the worst of it. That's the thing Rose doesn't dare tell anyone else.

It was foolish of her to think she might tell it to these people.

But she needs to say it. If she doesn't say it, she doesn't know what she'll do. She doesn't know where she'll go from here.

Rose steps out of her car, closes the door, and leans against it. The road is empty. There's nothing coming. But she's stuck. She can't bring herself to go any farther.

On the other side, they see her. Molly spots her first and points her out to Sean.

Sean stops the swing and lifts the boy from the seat. Hands him to Molly, who holds him on her hip.

The sun shines on the boy's dark hair. The wind ruffles it.

Sean walks to the road and pauses before making his way across. He moves with a limp, favoring his right leg.

His expression is neutral, until he gets close. Then Rose sees it warm. He recognizes her. There's a kindness in his eyes she never saw that day at the mall.

"This is unexpected," he says.

She can't think of a reply.

He reaches for her hand.

"Come on," he says.

Acknowledgments

I'm profoundly grateful to Victoria Skurnick and Otto Penzler for everything they've done to help send this book out into the world. Thanks also to Lucy Stille, Sara Vitale, Deb Seager, Samantha Trovillion, Erica Nuñez, Julia Berner-Tobin, Paula Cooper Hughes, Matthew Huff, Kirsten Wolf, Melissa Rowland, Elizabeth Fisher, and Miek Coccia.